Work Me Out

Andrew Grey

An Anthology of Andrew Grey Novellas

Dreamspinner Press

Published by
Dreamspinner Press
4760 Preston Road
Suite 244-149
Frisco, TX 75034
http://www.dreamspinnerpress.com/

Work Me Out

Cover Design by Mara McKennan

ISBN: 978-1-61581-928-7

Printed in the United States of America
First Edition
September 2011

eBooks previously published individually by Dreamspinner Press:
Spot Me (8/13/09), Pump Me Up (6/9/10), Core Training (10/20/10), Crunch Time (3/16/11), Positive Resistance (6/8/11), Personal Training (8/3/11)

This story is dedicated to all the guys at my gym.
Know it or not, you've been a source of inspiration.

Spot Me

Andrew Grey

I

HIS phone vibrated on the desk next to his keyboard. "Chest @ 4." Dan hit reply and texted back, "K." This was a normal exchange that happened almost every day, and Dan smiled to himself. The familiar message meant that in an hour he'd be leaving work and heading to the gym.

"You were vibrating again," Dan's co-worker Michelle called out from over the cubicle wall.

"I know, but at least I remembered to turn off the ringer." He snickered, glad she couldn't see his face. Michelle was the phone Nazi, picking on co-workers who forgot to silence their cell phones. "Just an hour and I get to leave."

He heard a snide, "Yeah, yeah." float over the wall as he got back to work on the report he was finishing for the director.

At quitting time, Dan made sure everything was saved, shut off his computer, and grabbed his stuff before stopping on his way out of the building to fill his water bottle with ice from the machine. Like many things in Dan's life, this was part of his daily ritual.

Leaving the building, he walked to his car and dumped his bag in the back seat. He slid the water bottle into his gym bag before climbing into the driver's seat and starting the engine. The drive to the gym was the usual quick and painless five minutes, though it seemed like a world away. The daily pressure of work slipped away as he pushed open the glass doors and walked into the huge, new, gleaming temple of exercise. This was one of the few things Dan did for himself, and he relished it.

"Hey, Dan." The woman behind the counter greeted him as she scanned his card.

"Hi, Denise." He didn't stop to talk; it wasn't expected. Instead, he hefted his bag and walked to the locker room, choosing one of the polished wood lockers and pulling off his clothes to change.

"Big Pimpin'!"

Dan grinned and shook his head, not bothering to look up. "Hi, Lon." Lon pulled off his shirt and toed off his shoes before slipping his pants down his legs. *Smack.* "Geez, Lon." Dan rubbed his butt where Lonnie'd smacked him. "You wait!" Dan pulled on his shorts and slid on a string tank, and then he sat down to put on his shoes.

"Nice panties."

Dan ignored the old and familiar comment. Dan hated the baggie shorts most guys wore; they felt funny on his legs. "Big ass." Dan reached out and swatted Lonnie's butt as he teased, "Do these pants make my butt look big?"

Lonnie twisted around, trying to get a look at his own butt. "Do they?"

Dan rolled his eyes as he got up and locked the locker before grabbing his gloves and water bottle. "No, your ass makes your pants look big." Dan ducked under Lonnie's swipe and laughed as they left the locker room together. "You are the most ass-obsessed straight man I've ever met," Dan chided as they walked to the weight area. "Am I fat? Does my ass look big? God, Lon, sometimes I think you're the gay one—either that or a woman."

"Would that make Corey a lesbian?" Lonnie said it with such a straight face that Dan couldn't keep himself from laughing.

"Come on, let's get started. Bench press or dumbbells?"

"We've been using barbells for a while; let's use dumbbells."

Dan nodded in agreement and grabbed a bench. After setting down his things, he grabbed the sixty pounders for a warm-up set, with Lonnie completing his own set when Dan was done.

They'd just completed their third set and Dan was grabbing the eighty-five pounders when he looked up into the mirror and faltered for a second before picking up the weights. "Lon, who's the guy on the incline press?" Lonnie knew everyone, either because they were his clients or because he was the most outgoing person on Earth. Dan picked up the weights for his set while Lonnie turned around. As Dan lifted the weights and checked his form in the mirror, Lonnie wandered away, returning just as Dan was finishing up his last reps before dropping the weights.

Lonnie scoffed, "That's Gene Harper."

The name meant nothing to Dan, and he shrugged slowly, looking in the mirror again as the man finished his set, watching those muscles work as they pushed up almost three hundred pounds.

"He's a professional," Lonnie added.

"Do you know him?"

Lonnie shook his head. "Not personally, but he's been on the cover of just about every muscle and bodybuilding magazine at some point."

"Oh."

Lonnie took his place on the bench, and Dan helped him hoist the hundred pounders onto his legs before he began his set. Lonnie was more than capable of handling the weight, so Dan found his attention and his eyes shifting to the mirror and the absolute vision working out at the bench behind them. He watched as the bodybuilder finished his set and clanked the weight into the bench rack. Dan returned his attention to Lonnie and then glanced back in the mirror and right into the bodybuilder's reflected eyes.

The intensity of his gaze made Dan shiver slightly, and he quickly turned his eyes away as Lonnie's weights thudded onto the floor. Dan took a sip from his bottle and got the weights for his own set, doing his best not to check in the mirror again, but he couldn't help it.

"Quit making goo-goo eyes and do your set," Lonnie scolded.

"Look who's talking." Dan watched as Lonnie's fiancée approached and his expression went all mushy.

"Hey, Chicken." Dan couldn't help snorting softly. Lonnie was the only man on Earth who'd nickname his vegan fiancée "Chicken." Pulling his eyes jealously away from their cooing and light kisses, he reclined on the bench, and pushed his weights into position. He got five reps with the ninety-fives and then dropped the weights and sat back up, his eyes checking the mirror again, but the bench behind them was empty.

Dan's attention turned back to Lonnie and Chicken—Corey—and smiled as he watched them. "Lonnie, don't you two do enough of that at home?"

Corey walked over and gave Dan a brief kiss on the cheek. "How are you?"

"I'm good, gorgeous, how are you?"

Corey swiped at Dan's arm and looked away. "Stop it." Lonnie's fiancée was a beautiful, fit, bright woman who refused to believe how attractive she was. Lonnie gave her another quick kiss.

Lonnie waved toward the benches as he took a swig from Dan's water bottle. "Let's grab an incline bench."

Dan nodded and picked up his things, moving to the only free bench and grabbing the weights. He'd just gotten them in place when he saw the bodybuilder walk alongside him and pick up one of the weights from the rack. Dan almost dropped the weights on his chest when he saw the man bend over, his pants drawing tight over a butt to die for. *Jesus, Dan, pay attention*! He returned his focus to his repetitions and completed the set, just barely, before dropping the weight. He and Lonnie continued with their sets, with Dan peeking in the mirror and watching the bodybuilder as he went about his routine while they finished theirs.

"Sauna?" Lonnie picked up his weight belt and took another swig of water.

"Yeah, I need it." Dan's muscles were tight, and the heat would help loosen them up so they wouldn't be sore the next day. He filled the water bottle from the drinking fountain and headed into the locker room. Lon pulled off his shirt and headed into the shower and sauna area while Dan changed into a bathing suit and followed behind him.

When he got in the sauna, Lonnie was already regaling the others with some of his stories of past debauchery. "Nice suit, Princess," he teased.

Dan turned around and wiggled his butt at him. "Thanks, Tinkerbell." Most of the guys had heard this type of exchange before, and it didn't faze them at all; they knew Lonnie. The conversation turned to workout routines, as it usually did.

"I need to lose weight." This was another of Lonnie's refrains.

Dan couldn't restrain himself. "It won't do you any good, and you know it. Dieting is not going to shrink your J. Lo ass." Lonnie was indeed unfortunate in the butt department. "You just have to face it: you're seven percent body fat with your middle-aged mother's ass." They guys all laughed, mainly because it was true.

In response, Lonnie grabbed Dan's water bottle and blew a fountain of water at him.

"I owe you two, Lonnie," Dan quipped as he snatched back the bottle.

After relaxing nicely, Dan left the sauna to get cleaned up. Walking into the shower area, he took one of the stalls and started the water. Dan heard Lonnie wander in a few minutes later. Now was the time. Reaching outside the shower, Dan grabbed the water bottle and filled it, the ice still clinking. Slowly he opened his curtain and saw Lonnie's head of black hair. With a quick move, he dumped the water into the other shower.

A scream of surprise from the shower made Dan smile. The shower curtain opened, and Dan found himself face-to-face, naked body to naked body, with… the bodybuilder.

"What the hell do you think you're doing?"

Dan didn't know what to say, and he stammered an apology as peals of laughter echoed from one of the other stalls. Dan turned toward the laughter. "You bastard!" Then he turned back to a still fuming and still very naked man. "I'm sorry, I thought you were him." Dan did his very best to keep his eyes above the equator, and even tried to look at the man's face, but he couldn't help peeking at his bodybuilder's chest. There was just so much to look at, after all.

The angry look faded, to Dan's relief. "It's okay." Then the bodybuilder turned around and stepped back into the shower, giving Dan a look at the naked version of the butt he'd seen earlier through the man's gym shorts. Dan had to bite his lip to restrain the small whine that tried its best to escape. Forcing himself to turn away, Dan retreated to his shower and pulled the curtain tight, letting the hot water beat down on him.

There was no way in hell he could step out of the shower, not after the eyeful he'd just gotten. Using the soap, he took himself in hand, stroking a few times as visions of the wet, tanned, muscled Adonis showering a few steps away took hold of his mind's eye. He wondered what it would feel like to stroke those muscles, feel that skin against his, run his hands over that ass of death. Dan found himself clamping his eyes closed as his climax approached, biting his lip to stifle any sound that might escape.

Once Dan was breathing normally again, he finished his cleanup and turned off the water. Grabbing his towel, he dried himself, noticing that the other stalls were empty. *Thank God.* At least he wouldn't have to face the man right away. Dan wrapped the towel around his waist, grabbed his suit, and walked out toward the locker room, making a point to keep his eyes straight ahead. But as soon as he got there, he got another eyeful. There was Mr. Bodybuilder standing on the scale in a pair of skin-tight boxer briefs, and this time, Dan got to look. Briefly. To his credit, Dan maintained his control and made it to his locker. Unlocking and opening the door, he dropped his towel and stepped into his briefs before pulling on his pants.

"Excuse me." A deep voice wrapped around Dan's ears as his locker door moved slightly.

Dan did himself a favor and finished dressing quickly before making his escape from the locker room. Lonnie was waiting outside, and Dan walked up to him and socked him in the arm. "Thank you very much. I thought he was going to punch me."

Lonnie started laughing again. Corey came out of the women's locker room, and Lonnie managed to tell her what he'd done through his laughter.

"Lonnie, it wasn't that funny," Dan said. It really was, but Dan couldn't let him think so, not right now.

"Aww, come on," Lonnie said. They grabbed their stuff and walked toward the front door. "Why don't you follow us back to the house? I need to get something, and we can go to dinner."

Dan acquiesced and followed Lonnie and Corey out to the parking lot. Getting in his car, Dan followed Lonnie's royal blue Porsche out of the parking lot and onto the highway. Ten minutes later, Dan pulled into Lonnie's driveway and got out of the car. Lonnie came out of the house and tossed something at him.

"We're leaving for the Dominican Republic in a few days, so take the Boxster while I'm gone." Lonnie opened the garage door, and Dan got in the sleek silver convertible and pulled it onto the driveway. "Empty out your stuff and pull your car in the garage," Lonnie instructed. Dan smiled as he moved the stuff he'd need from his car to the storage compartment under the Porsche's hood before pulling his car into the garage. The overhead door came down, and Dan went inside the house through the garage entrance.

"Where's Corey?" Dan called out as he walked into the massive living room.

"She's upstairs." Lonnie turned on the television and sank onto the leather sofa. "So what's with you making eyes at Mr. Muscles the entire time we were working out? I take it you like him, or at least would like to do him." Lonnie was never subtle or tactful about anything.

"What's not to like? But let's be real here. He's what, about twenty-eight? And way out of my league. Even if he is gay, a guy like that is not going to go for a skinny old guy like me." Dan couldn't suppress his smile. "Especially after I threw cold water on him." Dan couldn't resist taking another swipe at Lonnie's arm.

"I'm not so sure he isn't interested. He was looking at us the entire time we were working out, and I don't think he was looking at me." Lonnie swiped back at Dan, catching him lightly on the shoulder. "Besides, you have to admit, he did notice you."

"Only after I threw ice water on him. God, Lon, I'm forty."

"Fuck, would you stop whining about that already? You turned forty six months ago; it's getting old; and you know you could pass for thirty any time you wanted. If I were gay, I'd do you any time."

"Thanks, I think."

Lonnie got up from the sofa and rummaged through a pile of magazines before tossing one into Dan's lap. He turned it over and saw a picture of Gene Harper on the cover. Dan leafed through the magazine until Corey came down the stairs. Then he set it on the table.

"Take it with you if you want," Lonnie said. He got up and met Corey with a kiss at the bottom of the stairs, and Dan followed them out to the cars.

Dan started the powerful Porsche engine and followed Lonnie and Corey to the restaurant. Their dinner was great, and in the parking lot afterward they said good night, with Lonnie hugging the stuffing out of Dan. "Man, don't sell yourself short. I know Mike did a number on you, but you deserve all the happiness in the world," Lonnie said.

Dan found himself hugged again as Lonnie added, "I've got appointments for the next two days and then we leave for vacation. Be good, Bro, and I'll see you when we get back." Lonnie thumped Dan on the back and released him. After final goodbyes and hugs, they left and Dan walked to the Boxster and drove home.

Pulling up to his house, Dan parked the car and put up the top before unlocking the front door and walking inside. He dropped his work bag near the door then put his dirty clothes in the laundry. As he rifled through his bag, he found the magazine and headed to the living room to watch TV, taking it along with him.

The television droned on as Dan opened the magazine, turning directly to the cover article, which, to his surprise, wasn't the usual crap about what workout routines the guy used. Instead, it was an interview. Dan skimmed it, half expecting the usual fluffy crap, but his eyes stopped when one word jumped out of the page at him: GAY. Dan stopped and read closer.

"Well, I'll be damned." The gorgeous hunk from the gym was gay, and out, no less. And if the article was any indication, the guy seemed articulate. Dan read the rest of the interview before closing the magazine and dropping it on the table with a sigh. Just because he was gay didn't mean that Gene Harper would ever be interested in him, but Dan could dream. At least he'd gotten to see the muscled Adonis naked in all his glory. Turning off the light, he headed to bed, telling himself that he wasn't going to whack off to thoughts of Gene Harper. Well… at least not again.

II

THE three o'clock text message didn't come, and even though Dan knew Lonnie had appointments, he missed his afternoon touchstone with his friend. Glancing at the clock, he realized it was time to leave. Gathering his things, Dan followed his routine and left the office.

The gym was the same, but Dan felt out of sorts. It wasn't often that he worked out alone. He and Lonnie met every day after work and even on Saturday and Sunday mornings. Walking to the locker room, he changed clothes, grabbed his gear, and headed to the weight floor.

The place was packed, but Dan was able to secure the last squat rack in the place. "Excuse me, are you just starting?" Dan turned around and found himself staring into the eyes of his fantasy bodybuilder.

"Yeah, I was just getting started. You can work in if you want." After all, it was only proper gym etiquette, and it would give him an excuse to watch.

"Thanks."

Dan loaded up the weight and added his squat pad before positioning the bar on his upper back and lifting. He did ten smooth squats and put the bar back on the rack.

"If you don't mind my saying, you aren't going down quite far enough. Your legs aren't quite parallel." His voice held no malice, and from his tone, he was trying to be helpful.

"Yeah, I know. I had hip problems as a kid and don't have the full range of motion." Dan stepped from under the bar and extended his hand. "I'm Dan, by the way, and I'm really sorry about yesterday."

"I'm Gene, and don't worry about it." He shook Dan's hand and then added additional weight to the bar. "Do you mind if I use your pad?"

"Go ahead." Gene positioned the bar and did his set while Dan watched every movement of that body. Every time he squatted, those thick, smooth legs flexed and bulged, and that butt… Dan had to tear his eyes away to keep from staring. He tried not to be too obvious, but it was hard—and frankly, so was he. Thank God his jockstrap kept it hidden reasonably well.

When he heard the bar clink back onto the rack, Dan pulled off some of the weight and began his set. "Go down a little further; I'll spot you."

Dan squatted and made a point to go a little deeper. He felt his balance faltering a little, but then Gene steadied the bar.

"Good, you can do it!"

Dan heard the words, but his body registered the heat from Gene's body, the lightest touch of Gene's breath on his neck, and the gentle brush of Gene's fingers against his. He almost faltered again when he looked in the mirror and saw Gene right behind him—so near and yet so far. Somehow Dan managed to get his thoughts back where they belonged and finish the set, placing the bar on the rack.

"Great job! Your legs were parallel, and you got a real good stretch."

Did that mean Gene had been looking at his legs? Dan was almost embarrassed. He'd been working out for years, and while he was lean, he was never going to be particularly muscular. He always thought his legs looked like pencils. "Thanks." Dan smiled and tried to wipe away his doubts.

Gene loaded up the weight, heavier this time, and cinched a belt around his waist. "Would you mind spotting?"

God, yes! Any excuse to get near you! "Sure."

Gene positioned himself under the bar, his strong, wide back flexing as he lifted it. He stepped back, and Dan moved and steadied the bar as he lowered himself in time to Gene's squats. Up and down, he kept his attention focused on what Gene was doing, even though this was as close to real sex as he'd come since Mike left eight months earlier. In spite of standing in front of more mirrors than at a beauty contest, he was hard and throbbing in his pants, the fabric gently rubbing against him as they moved.

Gene finished his set, and Dan reached for his water bottle, desperate for something normal to do. He'd spotted Lonnie many times—he just needed to pull himself together. This wasn't the place, not when he was spotting someone squatting three-hundred-plus pounds.

"It's your turn. You willing to try a little more weight?"

Dan nodded as he finished his drink. "Two hundred oughta be good."

Gene helped him load the bar, and then Dan got into position again with Gene right behind him. This time he felt Gene's hands on his hips, and he did his best not to tense or jump. As he started his set, Dan felt the heat from those palms through his shirt. Concentrating, he did his set, keeping his mind focused, but it was difficult. As he did the lifts, his tank top rode up his sides, and by the end, Gene's hands were resting on his bare skin.

"You can do it, Dan! One more!" He'd squat until he died if it meant Gene's hands staying where they were. Dan straightened from the last squat and stood there. He could feel the heat from those hands on his hips, and he didn't want to move. That simple touch felt so sexy. He flushed as the direct contact slipped away, Gene's fingers lightly gliding over his skin.

Switching places again, they adjusted weight and got into position, Dan placing his hands where Gene had placed his. Fuck, the man was hot. And as Gene squatted, Dan could feel the muscles flexing beneath Gene's skin as he encouraged Gene to push harder.

They continued this unusual dance, and Dan tried not to think too much of it. They were working out together, making sure neither man got hurt, particularly as the weight increased with each set. For his final set, Dan attempted a weight he'd never done before, and with Gene's guidance he squatted the weight four times with Gene's encouragement in his ear and his hand and fingers steadying his hip.

"Now that's a workout!" Gene plunked the bar into the rack and stepped back. "Six heavy sets is plenty." Dan had to agree; his legs already felt a little squishy. "You up for extensions and curls?"

"Sure, lead the way." Gene looked surprised, and Dan smiled inwardly as they walked to the leg extension machine.

This was one of Dan's strongest exercises, so he set the weight high and pushed through the set. "Just one more. You can do it!" Gene's encouragement got the last rep out of him before Dan let the weight collapse and got off the machine. "Your legs are a lot stronger than they look." So Gene *was* looking at his legs.

Dan walked for a few seconds and stretched while Gene took the machine.

"What do you do for work?" Gene asked.

"I'm a computer programmer." Dan decided to play dumb to keep the conversation going. "What do you do?"

"I do recruitment for technology positions." Gene started his set, grunting as he hoisted the same weight as Dan. "As a hobby, I'm a competitive bodybuilder." *Holy fuck.* According to the magazine article, Gene was one of the top bodybuilders in the country, and to him it was only a hobby.

"Nine, ten. Come on, Gene, two more!" Dan called as Gene's face contorted, and he pumped out one more, with Dan helping slightly on the twelfth rep. "Super! That was twelve."

Gene got off the machine, and Dan took his place, increasing the weight. "Do you like what you do?" Dan started his set.

"Yeah, it's rewarding, and my schedule's flexible." Gene began counting as Dan finished the set. "That's ten; give me two more." Dan breathed deeply and powered out two more reps. "Damn, you did good."

"I've always had strong legs, even if they are skinny." Dan got off the machine, stretching as he walked.

"Your legs aren't skinny; they just fit your body type. And I bet you can eat whatever you want without gaining an ounce because of a jackrabbit metabolism." Gene got himself situated on the machine and ready for his set.

Dan scoffed lightly. "I used to, yeah, but not anymore. As I get older, I have to be more careful." He took a gulp from his water bottle. "Not that I ever ate terribly badly." Gene began his set, grunting as he extended his legs. "Come on, seven, eight...." Dan encouraged.

Gene let the weights fall with a clunk. "You did twelve at that weight?" Dan nodded, and Gene whistled. "Bet you can't do the whole stack for eight reps."

"How much?"

"Protein shake."

"You're on." This could be good. Dan sat at the machine and put the pin below the lowest weight, positioned his legs, and began his set. "Six... seven... eight... nine...." Dan let the weights clunk as his legs gave out. Slowly, he got up from the machine and walked around to get the blood flowing.

"Damn! I give." Gene took the seat and lowered the weight to finish his last set. "Let's finish up with leg curls, and I'm done."

"You're done?" Dan said with a touch of sarcasm. Dan hadn't done this intense a leg workout in a while. He knew he'd pay for it, but it felt good to push what he could do.

They walked to the leg curl machine and challenged each other to weights and reps. To his surprise, Dan was able to come close to Gene in both categories.

Gene thunked the weight as he completed his last set. "That's it." He breathed heavily and took a gulp of water. "I'm heading in."

"Me too. The whirlpool has my name on it." They walked back to the locker room. "That was a great workout, but I'll be feeling it tomorrow."

Gene shrugged. "My legs feel worked, but it's rare for me to feel soreness anymore." They entered the locker room and went their separate ways as they headed to their lockers. Dan opened his lock and stripped off his sweaty clothes, changing into his bathing suit. Slipping on shower shoes and grabbing his towel, he walked to the pool area.

To Dan's surprise, Gene was already in the swirling, hot water, his massive chest with nubby, quarter-sized nipples hovering invitingly just above the water. Too bad the invitation wasn't for him. Slipping off his shoes, Dan lowered himself into the water, sighing softly, trying not to be too obvious but not able to turn his eyes away from Gene. There was just so much to look at. "This'll really help the legs relax."

Gene nodded slowly. "Usually works for me too." Dan watched as Gene's head reclined against the tile. "When we're done, I'll meet you out front so you can collect that protein shake you won."

"You don't have to," Dan dismissed.

Gene's head snapped up again. "Hell, you earned it."

Dan felt Gene's smile rush through him, and he had to tell his dick not to get interested—Gene was just being nice.

"Can I ask something without being too forward?" Gene said.

Dan replied with a hesitant, "Sure."

Gene's hand slipped from the water and pointed at Dan's chest. "Did that hurt?"

He smiled and looked down at the silver hoop through his right nipple. "It was sore for a few days, but I didn't feel much when they did it."

"How long have you had it?" Dan followed Gene's eyes, and he could almost feel them raking over him.

Dan blushed, which was thankfully covered by the heat from the water. "Eight months."

"I bet there's a story there," Gene said. Dan nodded without thinking. "Good, you can tell it to me over protein shakes."

Gene stood up, sitting on the edge of the whirlpool to cool off, and Dan tried to keep his eyes in his head, swallowing hard before shrinking involuntarily a little further under the water. The man was intimidatingly gorgeous. It wasn't fair that one person could be smart and interesting *and* that fucking breathtaking... Dan glanced at Gene's bathing suit... fuck.

"I'm going to head in; I'll meet you out front," Gene said.

"Cool." Dan heard his voice crack a little, and he hid his embarrassment by taking a drink of water. "I'll meet you there." There was no way he could get out now; it would be way too embarrassing.

Gene got out and walked to the locker room, with Dan sneaking a peek at his bathing-suit-covered butt. Dan spent the next few minutes thinking unsexy thoughts to get himself under control before getting out and walking to the showers.

Dan took the first empty shower and pulled the curtain closed, stripping off his suit and washing up. When he was done, he grabbed his towel and dried himself before wrapping it around his waist and heading to the locker room. Just like the day before, Gene was standing on the scale, but this time he was naked. Dan practically ran into him, he was so distracted.

He managed to get himself to his locker, chastising himself under his breath as he opened his lock and began getting dressed. *Eyes front and center, eyes front and center.* Dropping the towel, he pulled on his underwear and then slipped on his pants and shirt. Now safely covered and free from embarrassment, he sat down on the bench and finished dressing before putting his things in his bag. Checking the locker one more time for anything else, he left the locker room and walked through the gym to the front door, sitting in one of the chairs to wait.

Gene came out a few minutes later, and Dan stood up, following him out the door. "Groovy Smoothie is just down the road," Gene commented as they walked.

"Sounds fine. I'll meet you there." It was a warm day, so Dan put his bag in the car and climbed into the little silver sports car, pulling the lever to release the top. After starting the car, he pressed the button and the top folded back, letting in the sun and warmth. Dan pulled out of the parking space and drove to the juice bar.

THE Groovy Smoothie parking lot was nearly full, but Dan was lucky and got a space right in front. He left the top down and went inside, looking around for Gene. Not seeing him yet, he got a table and waited, trying to figure out why he was even here.

He found himself constantly looking around the room and staring at the door. A few minutes later, he saw Gene get out of a truck and walk toward the door.

The man looked really good in his designer jeans and tight T-shirt. Suddenly Dan's own pants felt a little tight. *Down boy, don't get yourself too interested. I'm sure he's just being nice.*

"Sorry it took so long; I got caught behind a slow-moving semi." Gene walked to the table, but didn't sit down.

"One of the central PA hazards." Dan got up as well.

"Have a seat and hold the table. Do you know what you'd like?"

Dan sat back down and looked at the menu board. "Something without dairy and fruity." He wished he could take the words back. That sounded so gay, even to him.

Thankfully, Gene didn't seem to notice. "I'll be right back, and you can tell me that story you promised." He didn't remember promising, but he did feel a tingle from the way Gene looked where his nipple ring was pushing against his shirt.

Dan watched as Gene got in line, fantasizing about what that butt would feel like in his hands. His phone buzzing knocked him back to reality.

"Big Pimpin'!"

"Hey, Lonnie." Dan smiled.

"Corey and I are leaving tomorrow morning for Philly, and I just wanted to call and say goodbye."

"Thanks. You two have a good time, and I'll see you when you get home. Bring me back something."

Lonnie's laugh sounded devious. "Maybe something tall, dark, and hot." The leer in his voice came through loud and clear.

"Thanks, but I don't drink coffee."

"I'll see you when we get back, you little shit." They disconnected, and Dan returned the phone to his pocket as Gene walked back to the table.

"I got you a soy protein with berry." He placed the cup on the table as he sat down.

"Perfect." Dan sipped the smoothie as he got comfortable.

"So you going to tell me the story, or do I have to wheedle it out of you?"

Dan took another drink of the smoothie and set it on the table. "It was sort of a midlife crisis thing."

Gene let his straw slip from between his lips. "Come on, you're not old enough for a midlife crisis."

Dan looked at Gene in surprise. "How old do you think I am?"

"I'm twenty-eight, and I'd guess you're about thirty-two."

"First, let me say that you're really sweet to say that, but I'm almost forty-one." The surprised look on Gene's face was something he'd expected. "About nine months ago, I turned forty, and my partner of almost ten years announced that he was leaving me for some twink he met—" Dan flipped his hand involuntarily, "—somewhere." He couldn't keep a touch of bitterness out of his voice.

"Sounds like your ex was a stupid ass."

Dan didn't try to hold back a smile. "So I kicked him out of the house, and a month later I found myself at a tattoo parlor asking to have my right nipple pierced."

"Is it sensitive?" Gene had lowered his voice and moved a little closer.

"You mean during sex?"

Gene nodded knowingly as his eyebrows raised.

"I don't really know," Dan answered honestly. He gave Gene credit for not acting all shocked or laughing that he hadn't had intimate relations with anyone since Mike left. "I haven't been interested." Truth was, he now found himself interested in someone for the first time since Mike's out-of-the-blue announcement. A slurp from Gene's cup brought the pity-party in his head to a stop. "How about you?" Dan asked.

"What about me? I'm twenty-eight. I work, sleep, eat, and train for competitions."

Dan didn't know how to take his reaction. "You must do things for fun?"

"Not really. I spend most evenings at home when I'm not traveling."

"Do you travel a lot?"

"Sometimes. Mainly depends on the time of year. A lot of the competitions are in Florida, Nevada, or California."

"What do you do for fun?" Dan noticed that Gene had changed the subject.

"Garden, take care of the house, read." Dan finished his smoothie, and Gene threw their cups in the trash can near the table. Dan noticed that Gene checked his watch and figured he was boring the poor man to death.

"I should let you go," Dan said as he stood up and pushed in his chair. Gene did the same and followed Dan out to the parking lot. "Thank you for the shake," Dan said.

He opened the car door and slid down into the leather seat, shutting the door with a soft click. He was about to start the engine when he saw Gene lean over the driver's door.

"Look, I was wondering if you'd like to have dinner with me?" Dan turned and Gene's face was so close he had to look away. "Dan—"

Dan turned again, and their lips brushed together. "Will you go out with me?" Gene asked.

Dan nodded, unable to speak. Then Gene pressed another light kiss to his lips. "Can I have your number?"

Dan fumbled in his wallet and gave Gene a business card with his home number on it.

"I'll call you later, and we can set a date," Gene said.

"Okay." Dan returned Gene's smile and started the car, waiting until Gene was in his truck before pulling out of the parking space.

III

DAN sat on his sofa, a finger going to his mouth as he bit his fingernail. Realizing what he was doing, he forced his hand away and turned to look out the window once again. A weight landing on the cushion next to him followed by purring and soft fur rubbing against his hand helped calm his nervousness.

"Thanks, Oliver." The big, white cat rolled onto his side. Dan ran his hand over the soft fur and the purring intensified to just shy of jet engine. "You be good while Daddy's on his date." The big white head cocked to one side, nudging his hand when he stopped stroking. "Yeah, you're a big attention slut, aren't you?"

The doorbell rang, and Dan gave Oliver one last stroke and then stood up and walked to the door, opening it with a smile that quickly faded.

"Hi, Mike." His ex didn't look so good, which made Dan perversely happy.

"Can I come in?"

Dan didn't answer immediately but stepped back so he could come inside. He shut the door behind him. "Why are you here and not with your twink?" A white streak flew past them and up the stairs.

"He left me about a month ago. Said I was too old and couldn't keep up with him." That sounded familiar. Looked like Mike got a taste of his own medicine. "Can we talk?"

"There isn't much to talk about." Before Dan knew what was happening, he felt himself being pressed back against the wall, strong arms holding him still as a hand fumbled with his pants.

"You know no one can give you what you need like I can." Mike's voice deepened, low and sort of growly, the exact tone that always made Dan melt. The words were whispered into his ear, just like always. For months, this was what he'd dreamed of, what he'd wanted—Mike coming back to say he'd been wrong, that he was sorry, and that he still wanted him.

"No, Mike." That was before he'd spent those same months getting over him and learning how to do without him, even learning a few things about himself. Dan squirmed against the force. Mike now had his pants open and was sliding his fingers inside. Then he felt Mike's fingers on him, but nothing was happening. No arousal, no pleasure, nothing.

"Come on, Danny, give it up for me." That talk always used to work him up, but now it sounded pathetic and false.

Dan huffed a sigh of boredom, rolling his eyes. "No, Mike." The fingers slipped out of his pants, and Dan refastened them before checking himself in the hall mirror.

"I've had nine months to get over you, and I am." He stood back, making sure he looked okay.

"I was really stupid—" The doorbell rang, interrupting him. "You expecting someone?"

"As a matter of fact, I have a date." Dan opened the front door to a smiling Gene carrying a bouquet of flowers. Gene leaned forward and gave Dan a soft kiss. "Come inside."

Gene stepped into the entryway and saw Mike, turning to Dan with a confused look on his face. "Gene, this is my ex, Mike. He was just leaving." Dan stood by the door and waited for Mike to move. "Good night, Mike."

But Mike didn't move; instead, he turned to Gene, "You're dating Danny?"

"Good night, Mike!" The annoyance in Dan's voice came through loud and clear. Dan may not have been able to figure out why Gene had asked him out, but he'd be damned if he was going to let his ex cast aspersions. Mike slowly walked to the doorway, stepping outside without another word, and Dan closed the door behind him. "I'm sorry. He stopped by wanting to talk."

"Did you?" Gene's eyes wandered, looking everywhere but at Dan.

"Nothing to talk about." Then Dan smiled. "Are these for me?" Gene handed him the flowers. "No one's ever brought me flowers before." Dan practically bounced as he walked into the kitchen to put them in water. "They're beautiful." Filling a vase with water, he put them in the center of the table. "Thank you."

"You're welcome." Gene looked expectant, and Dan smiled, moving closer so Gene could kiss him. "Now that's a proper thank-you," he said.

Gene looked down at the floor. "Who's this?" The cat rubbed against Gene's leg.

"Oliver." Dan bent and picked him up. "He likes you." Dan turned the cat in his hands to look into his eyes. "You have good taste, yes, you do." With a final rub, he put the cat back on the floor.

"I made reservations for seven, so we should get going."

Dan turned off the kitchen light, and they left the house.

"It's a great night. Why don't you drive?" Gene suggested.

Dan popped the locks on the car and got in. Opening the latch, he started the car and lowered the convertible top. He sighed to himself. "I'd love one of these."

"This isn't yours?"

Dan laughed. "No. A friend let me borrow it while he's on vacation."

"Must be a good friend." Gene's hand rested on Dan's thigh.

"He is. The very best I've ever had, and it has nothing to do with the car. He's one of those people who'd do anything for you—including listen to me cry for a week solid when Mike left." Dan put the car in gear and pulled away from the curb.

The night was gorgeous, and Dan reveled in the feel of the wind making his hair flutter, tickling his neck. After Mike left, he'd let it grow, and thick waves of blond hair reached almost to his shoulders. Between the wind, his blowing hair, and Gene's hand, which was still resting on his leg, his senses were on a very happy hyperdrive.

Gene pointed. "The restaurant's just up on the left."

Dan glanced to Gene and smiled as he pulled into the parking lot, the car bouncing slightly. He turned off the engine, and Gene got out, closing his door and stepping around to the back of the car. Dan checked that everything was okay and then got out himself to find Gene waiting for him. As they walked to the restaurant, Dan felt Gene's light touch on his lower back.

Gene opened the door and held it for Dan, entering right behind him as they approached the hostess. "I have a reservation for Harper."

The hostess checked her book and flashed Gene her most dazzling smile. "Of course. Please follow me, and I'll show you to your table." She stepped out from behind the podium, looking like a goddess in silk, and glided through the dining room, the soft material shimmering as she walked. Dan took his seat, and the hostess leaned a little closer to Gene. "If you need anything—" she actually paused, "—just ask."

Dan reddened as Gene's gaze rested on him and didn't waver. "Thank you." The hostess glided away.

"Have you been here before?" Dan looked around the room but found himself returning to Gene's gaze.

"Quite a bit. I know the chef, so when I come here, he makes sure the food meets my training diet."

Dan picked up his menu and looked it over. There were so many wonderful things to choose from.

"Would you like something from the bar?" Dan closed his menu to look at their waiter. Gene motioned for Dan to order. "I'd like an iced tea, please."

"I'll have an iced tea as well, unsweetened with just a splash of cranberry juice," Gene said.

The waiter nodded. "Would you like to hear the specials?" Dan nodded, and the waiter described them before leaving to get their drinks.

"What type of music do you like?" Dan figured that if this was a date, then he should ask date-type questions.

Gene colored slightly, and Dan wondered why. "When I'm working out, I use really heavy, pumping music, but otherwise I listen to classical, mainly symphonic music."

Dan smiled. "Me too, uh, I mean the classical part. Have you ever gone to the symphony? I went a few years ago when they did both Beethoven and Mozart. It was great."

"Beethoven's Fifth?"

"Yeah."

Gene grinned. "I heard that performance as well."

A little of the nervousness ebbed from Dan. "That was the first time I'd ever been to the Forum. The music was great, but I really loved the building. The constellations on the ceiling were amazing. Then the lights dimmed, and the stars seemed to twinkle." Gene smiled as he kept looking at him, and Dan felt some of his nervousness return. "Is something wrong?"

"No." Gene leaned forward slightly, lowering his voice, "You sparkle when you smile. The nervousness drains away, and you look so—" he searched for a word, "—radiant. Your eyes shine, and you have this energy."

"Oh." Dan didn't know how to respond, and they were interrupted by the waiter bringing their drinks.

"Are you ready to order?" the waiter asked.

Again Gene motioned for Dan to go first. "I'd like the pear salad to start and then the duck," Dan said.

"Very good." The waiter turned to Gene. "Would you like your special?"

"Yes, thank you."

"Have you ever been to the opera?" Dan inquired once the waiter left.

"No."

Dan found himself retreating again, not sure what to talk about.

"Have you?" Gene asked.

"Yes, I've been to quite a few, mostly in New York." Dan saw a scowl form on Gene's face, and he stopped talking, taking a drink of his tea, wondering what he'd done wrong.

"Can I ask you something? And if it's none of my business, just tell me, but what were you doing with a guy like Mike? He hardly seems like the opera type."

Dan scoffed lightly. "You're right there. He definitely wasn't the opera type, but he goes to New York on business, and I'd go along. Some evenings he had business dinners, and I'd go to the opera."

"The man was a fool."

"Mike just liked things on his terms." Dan didn't really feel like explaining his relationship with Mike, but he tried. "Mike tended to be very dominant and liked things his way. That didn't mean that I didn't get to do what I wanted. But sometimes it meant that I had to go to the opera alone." Dan was relieved when Gene seemed content with his answer.

"The man left you for some twink kid? He was a fool."

Dan smiled both outside and inside at Gene's remark. It had been a long time since anyone stood up for him unconditionally.

"What's the smile for?" Gene asked.

"Lonnie's the only person who stood by me when Mike left. Most of our friends turned out to be Mike's friends and took his side. Even my family couldn't understand why I didn't try to patch things up with him."

"Your family?" Dan noticed Gene's shocked look.

Dan nodded slowly. "They loved Mike, thought the sun rose and set on his ass. But when he told me there was someone else, it was over. I could forgive a lot, and did, but I couldn't forgive that—at least not enough to let him back into the house or my life. All trust was gone and...." Dan let his voice trail off and took a drink of iced tea. He really didn't want to go there.

"The more you tell me, the more I stand by my comment," Gene said.

Gene looked so hot, and Dan felt himself rising in his pants. There was no pity in his face, no "I'm so sorry for you" look that friends had given him once they'd found out about Mike leaving. Just a fierce, determined look that told Dan he was sincere in his assessment.

The waiter brought their salads, and they began eating.

"Your home is very nice. How long have you lived there?" Gene asked.

"Twelve years. I bought it two years before I met Mike." Dan ate a bite of the poached pear from his salad. "It was one of the things that made it easier during the breakup. The house was mine."

"It looked very comfortable."

"When we get back, I'll give you the grand tour. It takes a whole five minutes."

They finished their salads, and their dinners appeared as if by magic. Dan's roast duck with raspberry sauce looked and smelled divine. The plate the waiter put in front of Gene surprised Dan a little. "What are you having?"

"Chicken breast with herbs, steamed vegetables, and wild rice." Gene began eating slowly, but Dan could tell the man was hungry. "Here, try a bite." He cut a piece of the chicken and placed the fork near Dan's lips.

"That is so tasty and moist." Dan cut off a bite of his duck, dipped it in the sauce, and returned the favor, placing the morsel between Gene's lips.

"It's been a long time since I had duck. Usually it's too fatty, and I need to be careful."

"I bet." Dan had seen that body at the gym, and it looked to him like Gene hadn't eaten anything fatty since he was in diapers. "Can I ask you something? And I don't mean to be insulting, but have you ever used any chemical enhancers?"

"You mean steroids? No. I'm a natural bodybuilder and very proud of it. My dream is to win Mr. Universe as one-hundred-percent natural. When I was in college, I played a lot of team sports and needed to build up my strength. As soon as I hit the weight room, I began to grow. My coach said they'd never seen anyone respond so quickly to weight training. Within a year I'd added twenty pounds and a year later another fifteen."

Dan took a bite of his duck, watching Gene as he did. "What do you weigh now?"

"I'm 197 pounds, which is exactly where I need to be. My weight class goes to 198 pounds." Gene continued eating, finishing his chicken and starting on his vegetables. "You look like you've kept yourself in good shape."

"I was never heavy, but I decided a few years ago that I needed to work harder as I got older, so I joined the gym. That's where I met Lonnie. He and Mike got along like oil and water. Looking back, that probably should have been a tip-off. Lonnie gets along with almost everyone. After the crap with Mike, Lonnie invited me to work out with him, and since then I've slimmed down a little and put on ten pounds of muscle, which is a real accomplishment." It was one of the things Dan was proud of. He'd worked hard and actually managed to add some mass. He was never going to look like Gene, but he was happy with his progress.

They finished their dinners, and when the waiter took their plates, Dan excused himself and went to the restroom. At the sink, washing his hands, he checked his watch and was surprised to realize that they'd been talking and eating for two hours. Even more of a surprise, he'd forgotten to be nervous and was really enjoying himself.

Returning to the table, he noticed that the bill had arrived, and he saw their waiter scoop it up.

"We're all set, shall we go?" Gene asked.

"Sure."

Gene followed him out of the restaurant and to the car. The night was still warm, so they left the top down and rode back to Dan's.

"Would you like to come in? I have a special treat for you." As soon as the words were out of his mouth, Dan cringed, but he didn't try to explain, fearing he'd only make things worse. Instead, he raised the top and led them up the front walk.

Opening the front door, he turned on the light and ushered Gene into the living room. Gene sat on the sofa, and Dan wasn't sure if he should as well, but Gene patted the seat next to him.

Gene said nothing. Instead, he slipped an arm around Dan's waist to steady him as he leaned closer, touching their lips together tentatively. Gene deepened the kiss, and Dan felt himself tensing. To his surprise, Gene immediately backed off, gentling the touch and letting Dan set the pace.

Dan thought his head was going to explode. Gene tasted so good. The herb flavors from dinner were mixing with what Dan could only describe as Gene's own natural, heady taste. Their lips moved together, and Dan parted his slightly. Mike would have taken that as an invitation and surged forward, but Gene didn't. He seemed to be willing to let Dan set the pace, which was refreshingly different for him. Then he felt the pressure on his lips diminish and fade away.

"Was that your treat? Because if it was, can I have seconds?"

"It wasn't, and yes, you can have seconds," Dan answered.

No sooner were the words out of his mouth than Gene's lips were back, and this time his fingers threaded their way through Dan's long hair. Dan could feel them moving, and his first reflex was to tense, but he pushed it aside when he realized that Gene was reclining on the sofa, guiding him so he was on top of Gene as a hand stroked his back, soothing him.

Dan could feel Gene's warmth through their clothes, feel himself rising and falling slightly with Gene's breathing. *Man, that was nice.* He wanted to slip his hands beneath Gene's shirt and feel the hot skin, the ridges he knew ran across Gene's stomach, pluck the nipples that graced those powerful pecs, but he held back. Years of conditioning still controlled his behavior. Dan felt Gene gentle the kiss again, and he sat back up, breathing heavily as Gene sat up next to him. He wanted to say something about how wonderful that felt, but words failed him. However, he knew Gene understood when he felt Gene's lips at the base of his neck.

Dan shivered with desire and leaned back against the sofa. This time, Gene took him in his arms and pulled him close. The kiss was harder and full of passion. Dan had no misgivings about what Gene was asking, but he wasn't ready. Gene got the message and back away.

"I'm sorry, but I'm just not ready for more right now. I can't rush." Dan braced himself for rejection but instead felt a hand caress his cheek.

"No, you're right. We should take this slow. I want to get to know you before we do anything." Gene leaned close. "That way it'll be special." He got up from the sofa and waited for Dan to walk him to the door. "Good night." He kissed Dan again and then opened the door.

Dan watched as Gene walked back to his car. He didn't close the door until the red tail lights turned the corner. As soon as the door closed, the doubts that had been nagging at Dan began to creep in.

"Hi, Oliver." He reached down and picked up the cat. "He wanted me, and I let him go." Dan wanted to bang his head against the wall. "It's not as though nice, considerate, built Greek gods are beating down my door."

The cat cocked his head, and Dan put him down, the feline ambling off toward his food dish.

"You're a big help, you know that?" Dan walked to the kitchen, muttering, "Jesus Christ, I'm talking to the cat." Then he looked and saw the plate of low-fat cookies he'd baked still sitting on the counter. Dan sighed. So much for the special treat he'd made for Gene. Not that it would matter now anyway.

Finding his phone, he dialed a number he knew by heart and waited, hoping for an answer, but all he got was voice mail. "Lonnie, it's Dan. I know you're probably having fun, but I need to talk to you. Please call me." *Now I'm leaving whiny voice mails.* He hung up the phone and sat at the kitchen table while Oliver rubbed himself against his legs. "I should just go to bed." Dan got up and turned off the lights. Just as he reached the bottom of the stairs, his phone rang.

"Dan, what's wrong, bud? You sound awful," Lonnie said.

"I think I fucked up really bad. I had a date, and he was really interested."

He knew what was coming: Lonnie's "kid in a candy store" voice. "Did you get lucky?" Yup, he wasn't disappointed.

"Can I talk to Corey?"

"Man, that hurts." This time he got Lonnie's fake wounded voice.

Dan was fast approaching a meltdown. "Then quit being a jerk and help me, Lonnie. I had a date tonight, and he was incredible and fun and interested, but I couldn't. Not on the first date. He was so nice, and we talked for hours."

"Do I know this guy? It was a guy, right?" *Smartass.*

"Yes, it was a guy. And he's so out of my league, but he was interested, and I told him I didn't want to rush." Dan was beginning to pace throughout the house. He was so nervous.

"What'd he say to that?"

"He said he wanted to get to know me. But Lonnie, what if I drove him away?" Dan was starting to sound whiny even to himself, so he took a few deep breaths. "He's smart, funny, considerate, and he can have any guy he wants. I just can't figure out why he'd want me."

"He'd want you because you're smart, funny, and the most caring person I know." Dan scoffed, but Lonnie just continued. "When my dad was sick a few months ago, you were the one who got me through. You patiently listened to me go on and on. So no one is out of your league, and if he doesn't want you, then it's his loss." A pause. "By the way, do I know this guy?"

"Sort of, it's Gene Harper," Dan admitted.

"Gene Harper! You turned down Gene Harper! God, *I'd* let him fuck me."

"Lonnie, you're not helping." Dan had stopped pacing, Lonnie's familiar banter calming him down.

"Sorry." He heard whispering, and Dan knew Lonnie was relating the highlights of the conversation to Corey. "Look, what I said goes. So go to bed and don't OCD over it."

That was rich coming from Mr. Obsessive-Compulsive himself. "Let me guess, you've waited a year to use that line on me, haven't you?" Dan said drolly.

"Sure. You use it on me often enough. It may surprise you to know that I do listen," Lonnie said.

"Only when you want to."

Dan heard Lonnie laughing. "Go to bed. I bet he calls you tomorrow." There was more movement on the other end of the phone. "Look, I gotta go. Corey's ready for her bing-bing." In his mind Dan could see the fist-pump that went along with that comment.

"Thanks for returning my call. Have a good time, and I'll see you in a week."

Dan disconnected the call and went upstairs, definitely feeling a lot better. He undressed and cleaned up and was about to get into bed when his phone rang again. Picking it up, he didn't recognize the number. "Hello?"

"Dan, it's Gene. I know it's late, but I wanted to call and thank you for a terrific evening. Can we meet at the gym tomorrow? I could use a workout partner."

"Sure." Tomorrow was Saturday. "Ten o'clock?"

"Cool. I'll see you at the gym. Good night."

IV

DAN got to the gym a little before ten to find Gene in the locker room, changed and ready to go. "I'll just be a minute." Dan grabbed a locker and got out his workout clothes.

"Take your time. I'm a little early."

Dan expected Gene to leave the locker room and start warming up, but he sat on the edge of the bench, looking at him. Suddenly Dan was extremely self-conscious. Taking off his shirt, he put on his T-shirt and then dropped his pants before slipping on his workout shorts. Normally he wasn't such a shrinking violet, but even though his back was turned, he could feel Gene's gaze on him.

Sitting down on the bench, he pulled on his shoes and got his workout gloves before shutting and locking the locker. "What are we working today?"

He felt Gene lean closer. "You're so cute when you're shy." Dan glared back at him. "Aww, come on," Gene said as he bumped Dan's shoulder. "I need to work chest today. Does that work for you?" Gene asked.

"Sure." Dan got up and followed Gene out to the weight floor.

"Good. Will you spot me? I need to lift heavy this week, and I don't like to do that alone."

"Of course." There were two benches free. "Why don't we each take one; that way you won't have to strip off the weights after every set."

Gene started loading the weights onto one of the benches, and Dan loaded the other one before reclining and doing a light warm-up set. When he was done, he looked over at Gene, who was stretching his chest before performing his warm-up set. Gene was wearing a very clingy tank top, and Dan could see every ridge and cut of his muscles, and he had to force himself to stop staring.

Adding some weight, Dan waited for Gene to finish and get into position behind him. Then Dan reclined and lifted the bar off the rack before slowly lowering the weight. It wasn't too heavy, but he was having trouble concentrating. He could see Gene's smooth legs flexing as he followed Dan's movements.

"Come on, Dan, you've got two more." Dan pumped out the two and then clanged the bar back on the rack. "Really good," Gene praised.

"Thanks. How much weight do you want?"

"Two twenty-five should be good." Dan loaded one side of the bar while Gene loaded the other, and then they got into position. Gene lifted the weight and powered through his set with very little effort.

"Was that as easy as it looked or were you showing off?" Dan asked as he turned back to his bench and loaded up the bar with the same two hundred and twenty-five pounds.

Gene looked skeptical but got into position to spot. Dan had to concentrate as the pronounced bulge in Gene's shorts skirted his field of vision.

Dan lifted the weight and lowered the bar, pushing it back up before lowering it again as Gene counted slowly. "Six, seven, come on, Dan... eight."

Gene helped him put the bar on the rack. "That was sweet!" Gene tapped his hip before moving back to his bench. "You're a lot stronger than you look."

"That's not hard when you look like a weakling," Dan joked.

Gene added another plate to each side the bar. "You do not. You're lean and strong." Suddenly they were very close. "And very attractive." Gene moved away and finished loading the bar before getting ready for his set.

Gene's comment took Dan completely by surprise, and he couldn't help looking in the mirror to see if something had changed. The same face and body reflected back to him.

"All set?" Gene asked.

"Yes." Dan got into position, and Gene hammered through the set, working to get the eighth rep, with Dan giving him encouragement.

"That was great," Dan said. "You got eight at three hundred and fifteen pounds."

Gene looked pleased. "The most I ever got at that weight was six." Gene sat up, and they each got some water before continuing. "I think it's you."

"Me? How could it be me?" Dan asked.

"I don't know. It just is."

Damn, his lips were so close, and Dan remembered how they'd felt last night and how he wanted to feel them again.

"Are you ready?" Gene prompted.

They alternated sets, each increasing weight. For Gene's last set, just as he and Dan were both ready, a voice called out, "Hey, let me do that!"

Dan found himself edged away, and Gene lifted the weight while this huge guy spotted for him. Shrugging his shoulders and feeling a little disappointed at the interruption of his time with Gene, Dan walked to the drinking fountain to get some water. When he returned, Gene had finished his set and was talking to the guy.

"Dan, this is Kabe. We used to train together."

"We used to do a lot of things together." The guy leered unmistakably at Gene and then turned to Dan. "I've got him from here on out."

Dan didn't know why he felt so dejected, but he did. He'd been expecting something like this to happen. The kiss, the attention from Gene—it was just too good to be true. He'd allowed himself that first glimmer of hope that Gene really liked him, and now he felt like a fool.

"Kabe, Dan and I are working out together."

"Then you mind if I join you?"

"Actually, we do. We're working well together, and besides, it's over, Kabe." Gene's tone was curt and clearly dismissive.

"Does that mean we can't be friends?" Kabe whined. Dan wondered if the pout usually got Kabe what he wanted.

"With you, yes. I can't trust you, not even with a spot." Gene turned his back to Kabe and gave Dan his full attention, "I think we're done here. You ready for incline?"

Dan was so surprised that he just nodded in response and followed Gene to an incline bench. Dan looked over his shoulder and saw Kabe shooting daggers at him. "I take it Kabe is an ex?"

"Yes, he is." Jesus, the anger rolled off Gene like water. "But I really don't want to talk about it."

"Maybe you should." Dan forced himself to meet Gene's gaze, "Maybe we both should."

"What are you saying?"

Dan took a deep breath and then released it. "I guess I'm saying that after we're done here, we could go back to my place, and I'll tell you mine, if you'll tell me yours."

Gene thought a minute while he loaded the bar for his set. "Okay, but let's talk about happier things until then."

"Like what?" Dan stood in the spotter's place as Gene got into position for his lift.

"We could talk about how cute you'll look in your bathing suit when we're in the hot tub." Gene lifted the weight, and Dan blushed, trying to keep his mind on helping Gene as opposed to the vision of Gene in his own bathing suit, slipping into the hot, swirling water, smooth, taut skin stretching over hard muscle.

"Dan, you with me?" Gene was sitting up, already done with his set.

"Sorry, I was, uh, someplace else for a second."

Gene smiled, and they switched places. Before he started his set, Dan looked in the mirror and saw Gene standing over him. Gene must have caught him looking because he smiled into the mirror.

"Would you give me a lift?" Dan asked. Gene helped Dan lift the bar, and Dan started his set.

"Eight, nine, ten." Gene helped him set the bar in the rack. "That was too easy. You can do more," Gene said.

They alternated throughout the entire exercise. Often, between sets, guys would approach and talk to Gene. He'd be polite, but Dan noticed that his attention always returned to him.

"That's enough incline, you up for decline?" Gene asked.

"Lead on, Gene."

"We don't need to do as many of these."

They got lucky and managed to scarf the only decline bench in the gym and began their sets, but Dan noticed something very different. This time, when Gene spotted him, he had to get much closer. And with every rep, the heady scent of sweat, skin, and man assaulted his nose. A few times he felt himself becoming lightheaded from the aroma. By the time they were done, Dan's chest was smoked with a pleasant, dull ache thudding deep in his muscles.

"Let's finish off with pushups," Gene suggested. Dan thought he was going to die, but nodded in agreement. "Just one set to failure."

"Okay, but I need a drink before we start." Dan went to the drinking fountain and got a large gulp of water, using the interruption to stretch before returning and dropping on the mat. "What's the goal?" he asked.

Gene looked across at Dan. "Whoever does the least buys protein shakes."

Dan did his best to look skeptical.

"I need a chance to get even," Gene justified.

Dan stretched out and began doing pushups, counting softly as he did. After ten, he was good; after twenty, he was beginning to tire. At thirty, his chest was starting to protest. What Dan hadn't told Gene was that pushups were a regular part of his routine. Counting forty, Dan watched as Gene collapsed onto the mat. Dan did a few more and then his arms gave out. "Looks like you're buying again."

"How'd you do that?"

Dan winked. "I do pushups all the time. My record is fifty-four." They stood up, and Dan gathered his things, following Gene into the locker room. As soon as they stepped inside, Dan's nerves started again, but this time, he did his best to calm them. Gene seemed to like him, and he was going to see him in his bathing suit, so he might as well man up.

Opening his locker, Dan pulled out his bag and began stripping off his sweaty clothes. He was down to his underwear before he noticed Gene two lockers down. *Screw it.* Dan slipped the underwear off, pulled on a bathing suit, and then grabbed his towel and scuffed into his shower shoes. Turning around, he saw Gene turned toward him, pulling on his suit. And what a sight that was. Dan felt his mouth go dry and the muscles in his legs tense. That the man was truly stunning and interested in him seemed almost unfathomable.

"You ready?" Gene asked as he grabbed his towel and waited.

Dan closed his locker and followed Gene to the showers, watching that Lycra-encased derrière flex in front of him. Dragging his eyes away from Gene's butt, Dan stepped into a shower to rinse off. He turned the shower on cold and let it cool him off before stepping out.

The whirlpool was in the far corner of the pool area, and as Dan approached he saw it was empty. Hanging his towel on a hook, he slipped off his shoes and sank into the water, resting his head against the edge.

Dan sensed someone approaching and perked up, expecting to see Gene—wanting to see as much of him as he could. Instead, he saw Kabe in a micro bikini that left nothing to the imagination. Dan turned to look to the side so Kabe wouldn't see him smirk. Lonnie had told him once that some men worked out to get huge bodies as compensation. It looked like Kabe proved that rule, because it was obvious that Gene didn't.

Kabe settled on the far side of the whirlpool, and they spent the next few minutes with Dan ignoring his glares. He was about to get out when he saw Gene walk around the corner, his broad shoulders and narrow waist accentuated by a blue square-cut bathing suit. Dan swallowed the small whimper that threatened to escape as Gene stepped into the water and settled next to him, completely ignoring Kabe. "Do your muscles feel tight?"

"Yeah, the hot water helps, though."

"I know something else that'll help." Gene leaned closer. "When we're back at your house, maybe I can show you."

"Jesus Christ!" Kabe stood up, the water swirling around his tree-trunk legs. "If you wanted to make me jealous, you could have picked someone better than him. I mean, this is barely believable."

Dan looked from Gene to Kabe and then back to Gene.

"Sit down, Kabe." Dan felt Gene's hand on his leg, stroking his skin. "There's nothing for you to be jealous about. We worked out together and dated for a few months, but that's over. You're no longer my friend, and you're certainly not my lover, and you never will be again."

"Okay, but why him?" Kabe asked.

Dan wanted to slink under the water and disappear, but Gene's hand kept gently stroking his leg, and he could feel himself hardening in his suit.

"He's smart, funny, and he doesn't need help with the big words when he reads. He's an adult, Kabe, not an overgrown child. And I like him." Gene turned to Dan. "I *really* like him."

Gene had never raised his voice above his normal tone, but now his voice sounded so sexy, Dan felt a tingle zing right up his spine. Gene liked him, and it wasn't just the words, but that hand resting on his leg, reassuring him that what Gene said was the truth. "Are you about done in here, Dan?"

Dan stood up, hoping his excitement wasn't too evident. "Yeah, I think I've had enough." Getting out, he slipped his shower shoes back on and grabbed his towel.

This time, Gene followed him into the locker room. Dan couldn't help peeking over his shoulder. "Are you looking at my butt?"

"Yeah," Gene said as he reached out, and Dan squeaked as Gene lightly squeezed the butt in question. "Do you have a problem with that?"

"No." Dan really didn't. "Just so we're clear."

"Okay, then."

Dan walked to the showers and slipped off his suit, standing beneath the hot spray. He noticed Gene. Hell, his body seemed to know where he was on its own. God knows his now-throbbing dick has been pointing in Gene's direction like a compass needle. Dan washed, his hands gliding over his skin, fingers automatically wrapping around his length.

Gene's rich voice drifted over the partition. "Dan, do you have any shampoo?"

"Sure, just a second." Dan flipped the shower to cold, shivering under the frigid water. Then he grabbed his shampoo and stepped out of the stall. "Here you go."

The curtain to Gene's stall parted, and Gene turned to him, taking the shampoo with a smile. "Thanks."

Dan tried not to look, he really did, but he just couldn't help it as he stood there gaping at the naked Greek god in front of him. Realizing he was standing naked in the shower room openly gawking at Gene, he croaked, "Uh... you're welcome?" His mind had suddenly switched off, short circuiting completely.

Dan finally noticed that Gene wasn't moving either. Gene was looking his fill in return. Finally, pulling himself together, Dan stepped back into his shower, pulling the curtain closed before readjusting the water temperature and resting his hands against the tiles as the water poured over him.

Part of him wanted Gene so badly, it was pushing him to join Gene right here, right now. The other part of him—the scared, fearful part—held him back. If Lonnie were here, he'd tell him that not everyone was like Mike and that he had to take a chance. Granted, from Lonnie, it'd come out like "Fuck, what are you waiting for?", complete with a rude hand gesture and sound effects, but the meaning was the same, and he'd be right. What was he waiting for? He was no virgin, and it certainly wasn't as though there was much Gene could do to shock him.

Dan rinsed himself off for the last time and turned off the water. Grabbing his towel, he dried himself and wrapped it around his waist. Sliding the curtain open, he got the rest of his things and shuffled to the locker room, keeping his gaze to himself. Gene was already at his locker when Dan approached. Dropping the towel, Dan dressed quickly, trying to keep from feeling nervous. Gene had already seen everything Dan had, so there was no sense in being modest now.

He could feel Gene's eyes on him, watching, his gaze making Dan's skin color and get warm despite the air conditioning. Gene's attention began to make him nervous, and he fumbled as he pulled on his clothes, missing a button on his shirt and needing to fix it. When he was done, he packed up his things and followed Gene to the front door.

"I'll meet you at Groovy Smoothie," Dan said.

Gene was waiting, protein shakes already on the table, when he arrived. "I got you the same as before."

"Thanks." Dan sat and sipped the shake. "So, what happened with Kabe?"

Gene set his shake on the table. "We dated for a few months, but he was just using me. He wanted a way into the pros, and he used me as his ticket, and he lied about it." He took another drink of his shake. "I've always had the worst taste in men."

Dan waited for him to continue.

"I always went for guys who looked like me: nice houses, but unfortunately nobody was home," Gene said.

"So why me? You can have any guy you want, why me?" That was the big question—the million dollar question, the one Dan had wanted to ask but had been afraid of the answer. Hell, he still was.

"It was your hair."

"What?" Dan nearly spilled his shake. "My hair?"

Gene nodded. "I saw you looking at me, and I started to wonder how your hair would feel. What it would be like to run my fingers through it. Then I saw the way you looked at me, and I felt a jolt shoot through me. Most guys look at me like piece of meat, but you looked at me differently, like I was a person. Then you threw cold water on me, and you looked so adorably embarrassed. So I made sure I came back to the gym at the same time the next day." Gene drank some more of his shake. "So, I told you about Kabe."

"You did." Dan finished his shake and threw away the cup. "I was with Mike for ten years, and for most of that time, Mike was the dominant force in the relationship."

Gene finished his shake. "Do you mean that Mike's a Dom?"

"Yeah. Our relationship didn't start out that way, but we sort of grew into it. He became more dominant, and I became more submissive."

"Is that what you like?"

Dan shrugged. "I really don't know anymore. If he hadn't cheated, I probably would have spent the rest of my life with him. But he found some twink kid, and I'm starting to think that maybe it was for the best after all."

"That night, did he want you back?"

"Maybe; we never really got that far. But if he does, then he wants me back the way we were, and I could never trust him again. Besides, I don't think I want the type of relationship we had."

Gene's brow furrowed. "I don't understand."

"I wish I understood it all, but—" Dan searched for the right words to explain, "—if you're told something often enough, you start to believe it. Mike told me for ten years how great we were together, and I bought into it, even when things weren't what I wanted or needed. He'd always say how no one could make me feel as good as he could, and I think I believed him."

"But now you want something different?" Gene coaxed.

Dan found himself nodding. "Yeah, I want something different." He took a deep, heaving breath to clear his head. "I think that's enough of that." Dan found himself smiling, and Gene smiled back, his face radiant and warm. "Would you like to come back to the house?"

"Yeah, that'd be nice," Gene said.

Dan felt his jeans getting tight again, and he adjusted things before getting up.

"I'll follow you," Gene said.

They left together, and Dan sank into the Porsche, driving back to his house.

DAN came into the living room with glasses of iced tea and handed one to Gene before sitting next to him on the sofa. "Do you need anything to eat?"

"I want a taste of something, but it isn't food."

Dan found himself being drawn closer, and then soft, warm lips tingled against his. Fingers wove their way into his hair, and he heard a deep guttural moan as Gene's tongue slid past his lips. As Gene kissed him, Dan found himself doing something he could never remember doing before: taking charge. He shifted on the sofa and began pushing Gene back against the cushions. Dan sensed himself letting go for the first time in a very long time. He could feel the heat from Gene's body beneath him, a strong arm cradling him around the waist.

Dan lifted his head slightly. "God, you taste good." Without giving Gene a chance to respond, he took the man's lips again and slipped a hand beneath his shirt, firm, hot skin passing beneath his palms. "Gene," Dan pulled away and looked down at the man beneath him, clothes disheveled, lips red from kissing, "would you like to go upstairs?"

"No."

Dan froze, not sure how he should react. Slowly, he backed away and started getting to his feet.

Gene tugged him forward. "I meant that I want to stay right here. We don't need to rush." Then Gene was tugging him back down, lips on his, as hands slid beneath his shirt, rubbing his skin, gently plucking his nipples. "Are you busy next weekend?"

Dan could barely think but managed to eke out a "No."

"You are now, okay?"

Dan nodded as Gene stopped talking and put his lips to better use.

V

DAN could barely sleep wondering what Gene had in store for them. He'd told Dan that he'd be over first thing Saturday morning and that he should have an overnight bag packed, but nothing more. The bag was already packed, sitting on his bedroom floor. The room was still dark, and Dan rolled over again and finally fell asleep.

A ringing pulled Dan out of his sleep. He reached over and silenced the alarm, but the ringing continued. Then Dan recognized it as the doorbell. Throwing back the covers, he pulled on a pair of sweats and walked through the house to the front door.

"Aren't you ready yet?" Gene teased lightly as he leaned in for a kiss and stepped through the open door.

Dan yawned and tried to cover it with his hand. "Sorry, I didn't sleep very well." Gene cocked his head waiting for Dan to elaborate. "I was too excited to sleep and finally dropped off early this morning." Dan stifled another yawn and met Gene's lips. Suddenly parts of him were very awake and ready to go.

Gene made no move to let him go. "You should get dressed." They stood together, a hand slipping into the back of Dan's sweats. "You really should get dressed or I'm not going to be able to stop, and I have something very special planned." Slowly, Gene's hand retreated, and after another kiss, Gene stepped back and closed the front door.

Dan gulped for air just like he did whenever Gene kissed him. Those kisses just seemed to pull all the air right out of his lungs. Through the week, they'd seen each other at the gym and had gone out a few more times, and they'd kissed, hard, and let their hands roam, but they hadn't done anything else. The amazing thing was that the fearful, doubtful part of Dan's mind had been silent—amazingly silent.

"I'll be right back." Dan went upstairs and quickly cleaned up. Putting a few last things in his bag, he dressed and met Gene downstairs. Setting his bag near the door, he walked to the living room and found Gene sprawled on the sofa.

"All set?" Gene asked.

Dan nodded. "Are you going to tell me where we're going now?"

"I'd better—you're driving." Gene got up and followed Dan through the house, picking up his bag from the hall. "I made a reservation at a wonderful hotel in downtown Philadelphia. We're on one of the top floors with a great view of the city, a beautiful room, and a huge bed." Gene bent and tickled the back of Dan's ear with his tongue. "Tonight I get to sleep with you in my arms."

Dan shivered and nodded slowly as Gene's tongue gave way to lips, nuzzling his neck.

"We should get our things in the car," Gene murmured.

Dan's nodding continued, but there was no way he could move, not with the things Gene's lips were doing to his skin. "I could move if you'd stop teasing."

The lips didn't stop. "Not teasing, just giving you a preview of what's to come," Gene assured him. Then the feel of Gene's lips faded away and Dan found he could move again. "Shall we go?"

"Uh-huh." Dan followed Gene outside, closing and locking the door behind him. Popping the hood of the Porsche, they loaded their bags and sank into the leather seats.

Gene's hand grazed along Dan's leg as the top slid back, and they pulled away from the curb. "Let's go."

The car zoomed down the road heading toward the turnpike, and as they picked up speed, the wind blew through Dan's long hair. He loved the free feeling of the wind through his hair, and as he drove, he felt Gene's fingers on his head.

"I love your hair, you know that?" Gene said.

Dan turned and smiled at Gene as he drove.

"This is so great!" Gene enthused.

"It is. I wish I could afford one of these, but Lonnie's been very generous," Dan said.

God, this was incredible, zipping down the highway, top down, sun shining, with Gene sitting next to him, a hand resting on his leg. They talked, they laughed, and Gene maintained physical contact throughout the trip—a touch on his leg or fingers sliding into Dan's. Those simple touches had disappeared from his relationship with Mike long ago, and Dan suddenly realized how much he'd missed them and how important they were.

As they neared Philly, they transferred from the turnpike to the Schuylkill Expressway—or as the locals called it, the "Sure kill." Traffic slowed, and they inched their way closer and closer to the city, winding around the river and passing beneath the neoclassic monolith that is the Philadelphia Art Museum perched on its hill, the *Rocky* steps hidden from view.

As they exited the freeway, Gene fed Dan the directions he'd printed from the Internet. "The hotel is right downtown on Market Street." They wound around City Hall and turned onto Market, saw the hotel on the right, and followed the signs to the parking garage.

Dan popped the hood, and Gene got their bags as Dan handed the keys to the valet.

"Come on," Gene said as he indicated the door to the hotel. "From here on out, you're in my hands."

Dan waited while Gene checked in. "Our room isn't quite ready, but they gave us a pass so we can use the hotel facilities until the room's ready."

"What did you have in mind?" Dan asked.

"We could use the gym and get our workout done so we can do other things later," Gene suggested.

The way the words wrapped around him left no doubt as to what those other things were, and Dan felt a tingle and a stirring of excitement.

Gene led the way to the elevators, carrying their bags, and pressed the call button. When the car arrived, they stepped inside, and a few minutes later, they stepped off and through the doors to another world. Quiet music and muted colors greeted them as they moved to the desk and went through the sign-in process. Then the attendant handed each of them a locker key, and Gene guided Dan to the men's locker room.

The soft music also played in the locker room, and Dan opened his locker, finding a robe and a pair of shower slippers. Pulling off his clothes, he changed into his workout gear. He'd just finished getting dressed when a pair of hands slid around his waist, and he felt a warm body press against him. Dan groaned softly. "What are you doing?"

A soft chuckle rumbled in his ear. "I like touching you."

Dan leaned back against Gene. It was nice being touched in a way that didn't involve sex. "What are we doing for a workout?" Dan asked. Not that he was in a hurry to move. If Gene was going to hold him, he'd stay where he was for the rest of the day.

"How about an intense circuit training to work our muscles and get our heart rate up at the same time?"

Dan nodded as he felt the hands slip away.

"Then let's do it, and when we're done, I have a great surprise for you," Gene said.

Dan followed Gene out to the exercise floor, and they put themselves through a body-pounding workout. By the time they were done, Dan was exhausted and worn out.

"We're done here," Gene said.

"You promised me a surprise," Dan reminded.

"That I did." Gene led him back to the locker room, where he grabbed two towels from the rack and threw one to Dan. "Strip down and meet me in the sauna."

Dan went to his locker and complied with Gene's request, stripping off his clothes, slipping on the shower shoes, and wrapping the towel around his waist before walking to the sauna near the showers. Dan pulled open the door and walked inside. Lying on one of the benches was a naked Gene sprawled out, soaking up the heat. Acres of skin called to his hands, and all Dan wanted to do was explore every inch of that body now glistening with sweat.

"Gene, that's just not fair."

His head rolled to face him. "What?"

"How am I supposed to keep my hands to myself? You're just so incredible."

Gene smiled. "Just spread your towel on the bench and relax. I promise that you'll be able to touch all you want when we get in the room, and I intend to caress every inch of you too."

Gene's deep, rich voice got Dan going, but he dropped his towel and spread it on the bench before lying down. He made sure he could see Gene and did his best to relax, but it wasn't working very well. The more Dan looked at Gene, the less certain parts of his anatomy refused to relax.

"Looks like someone's ready to go," Gene said, a smirk in his voice.

Dan chortled softly. "What do you expect? You're lying there all sexy and naked. It's like being in the sauna with Hercules or something."

"Look who's talking." Gene's head rolled to face Dan. "Your blond hair and long, trim body make me want to take you right here."

"Come on, Gene. You're the hot one. I'm just...." Dan couldn't say it. If he said it, then Gene might agree, and he didn't want to feel old. He liked how Gene made him feel.

"I'm serious, Dan." Gene sat up and looked Dan square in the eyes. "You just don't see what I see, do you?"

"I see myself just fine. I just don't know what you find interesting."

"Then let me show you how I see you." Gene got up and walked to Dan, standing right next to him, leaning close. "I can't do what I want to here, but as soon as we're in the room, I intend to show you just what I mean." Gene's voice wrapped around him, settling at the base of his spine and shooting to his balls.

Dan nodded slowly, as his mouth went dry. He tried to reply, but Gene's lips cut off his words. Whatever he'd been thinking was gone, and his worries took a back seat to the plundering Gene was giving his mouth.

"Can we go now?" Dan panted breathlessly, as Gene pulled back from the kiss.

"If you want."

Dan nodded as he tried to catch his breath. "I want, I want." Besides, he was going to make a spectacle of both of them very soon.

Gene stepped away and wrapped his towel around his waist while Dan did the same, both of them displaying very indiscreet bulges.

Dan went to one of the showers and stepped inside, pulling the curtain closed. He half expected Gene to join him, but to his relief he didn't. There was no way he was going to be able to resist any advance Gene made, and he didn't want their first time to be an illicit fumble in the shower. And that appeared to be what Gene wanted as well—to make it special. Turning on the water, he cleaned up quickly, paying special attention to certain areas before rinsing off and stepping from under the water. He dried himself with a fresh towel and walked back to the locker area.

There were other men changing, so he finished dressing quickly, glad that Gene was taking a long shower, and left the room, waiting in one of the lounge chairs. Gene joined him a few minutes later.

In the lobby, Gene finished checking in and got their keys before leading the way to the elevator. Dan watched as Gene inserted a key into the elevator panel and pressed the button for the top floor of the hotel. "We're on the concierge level," Gene explained. The car zoomed them to the top. They stepped off the elevator and walked down the hall to their room. Gene inserted the key and opened the door, letting Dan go inside first.

"Gene...." The room was beautiful, and as Dan looked around, Gene pulled open the curtains. "This is wonderful." Dan walked to the windows. "City Hall looks amazing." Dan moved to look out other windows. "Look, I think you can see Independence Hall from here." Dan heard the sound of fabric rustling.

"I can see something even better," Gene murmured. Arms worked their way around Dan's waist, and he felt lips tugging gently on his ear. "Do you like it?" Dan turned around and nodded softly as he found himself lips to lips with Gene. "Good." Fingers entwined in his hair, and Gene kissed him.

Dan closed his eyes and let the feeling wash over him.

"Imagine how beautiful it will be tonight with all the city lights laid out beneath us," Gene said as he guided Dan toward the bed, and Dan grunted when the back of his legs met the mattress.

Neither tried to speak, and Dan felt fingers on the hem of his shirt. Then it was pulled up, and the lips backed away. Lifting his arms, Dan allowed his shirt to glide off his body.

Dan opened his eyes just in time to see Gene leaning forward, and then a pair of hot lips latched onto the pierced nipple, tugging gently.

"Gene!" Dan arched into the sensation as the lips tugged gently at the piercing, a zing of painful pleasure shooting straight from his chest to his cock. Dan found himself rocking against Gene but stopped himself, unsure of how that would be received.

Fingers worked at the buckle of his belt, opening it before popping the fastener on his jeans and sliding down the zipper. The lips rejoined his as his jeans slid down his legs, and Dan did a little dance to get them off his feet. A palm slid down his stomach and glided beneath the band of his briefs, sliding further, cupping him before sliding the fabric down to join his jeans.

There was something very naughty about being completely naked in front of a fully clothed partner, and Dan vibrated with the excitement of it all. Then, slowly, he was guided back onto the cool sheets covering the bed, his body lifted and positioned in the middle. Dan scooted up so his head was on a pillow, looked into Gene's eyes, and waited.

"Dan, what's wrong?" Gene's concerned tone took Dan completely by surprise.

"Nothing." What had he done wrong? Did Gene want something he hadn't anticipated?

Gene sat up looking at him, and Dan felt himself wither under Gene's perplexed expression. "You're not doing anything. Is something wrong?"

Oh God, Dan wanted to die. Reaching for the sheet, Dan pulled it over himself and looked for a way to escape.

"Talk to me, Dan."

"I don't know what you want." Dan burrowed deeper beneath the covers and tried to figure out how he could get to his clothes. "Mike always told me what he wanted me to do, and I, um...."

Gene's eyes widened and softened at the same time. "I'm not Mike, and I don't want to tell you what to do. So why don't you do whatever you want? Why don't you tell me what *you* want?" Gene stood beside the bed. "I'm all yours, Dan. Tell me what you want. But first, let go of the sheet. I want to see you."

Dan relaxed beneath the covers and tried to hide his embarrassment as he pushed the covers aside.

"That's much better. Now, what do you want?" Gene asked.

"I want to see you," Dan said.

"Then tell me what to do."

"Take off your shirt," Dan tried. Gene complied, slipping the polo over his head, the muscles elongating as he stretched his arms. The shirt dropped, and Gene lowered his arms. Dan moved closer, stopping nervously.

"Whatever you want, Dan. It's all okay."

"I want to feel you against me, want to taste you, want to run my hands all over you. I want it all, and I don't know where to start."

"Then why don't we start with this?" Gene unbuckled his belt and pulled it through the loops before dropping it on the floor. Then he popped the buttons on his jeans, letting them fall open.

"Turn around," Dan ordered. Gene smiled as he faced the wall. Dan had waited for this for so long. Reaching out, he took hold of the waistband of Gene's pants and pulled them down, exposing Gene's firm butt cheeks. Dan reached out and ran his fingers over them, soft, almost invisible hair tickling his palms. "Mike would never let me touch him like this; it was too submissive."

"There's only one rule: no mentioning him, okay?" Gene said softly.

Dan smiled as he leaned to Gene and brought his lips to the skin behind his ear. "Yeah." Dan continued caressing the warm, hot skin, almost unable to believe his freedom to explore. "Whatever I want?"

"Yes, do whatever will make you happy," Gene assured him.

Dan stood up and plastered his body to Gene's back, maneuvering him onto the bed, his stomach on the mattress, legs hanging off the edge. "I think you'd better help." Dan heard Gene chuckle as he positioned himself in the center of the bed. Dan then straddled him and started at his shoulders, kissing and tasting the skin. "I've wondered what your skin would taste like since I first saw you."

"Tell me," Gene said.

Dan licked a path down Gene's spine. "Salt, a little sweat, a tinge of soap, and something that's all you." Dan worked his tongue lower, over the divot at the base of Gene's spine and across his cheeks before working back toward his shoulders. When he reached Gene's ears, he heard a laugh, and then he was captured. Gene whirled beneath him, taking him in his arms and rolling them over, pinning him beneath the larger man.

Gene began laughing as he leaned forward, capturing a nipple once again. "You know what I taste?" Dan shook his head as Gene continued working his tongue over his chest. "Hot, sexy man. That's what you are, Dan. One very hot, very sexy man." Each word was punctuated by a lick or a tug at his skin.

Dan was going wild, clinging to Gene, letting his hands roam over that powerful back as that tongue worked magic on his skin. "Gene…." He was whining; he knew he was whining, but he couldn't help it. Fingers wrapped around his length, tugging gently, a thumb doing something that just drove him wild. "I can't hold on."

"Then don't, baby."

The hands, the endearment, and the kisses all mixed in Dan's mind, throwing him into a mind-numbing, light-flashing climax. He tried his best to be quiet, but as the orgasm built, he cried out Gene's name as he came.

Dan collapsed back on the bed, breathing like he'd just run a marathon, his eyes unfocused as he gasped for air. "What did you do to me?"

Gene chuckled and rolled to the side. Dan rolled toward him, still breathing hard. "Whatever I want?" Dan asked. Gene nodded, and Dan pushed him back on the bed, fingers gripping the long, thick erection. "I want this," Dan said. He was talented, and he displayed that talent, taking Gene deep in his throat in one fluid movement.

"Jesus!" Gene gasped as Dan sucked, let him slide out, and then pulled him back in again. Dan's hair had fallen around his face, and he shook his head, letting it slide along Gene's skin. He felt Gene start to buck, but he held him still. This was all for Gene, and he was going to give him his best.

Small whimpers and moans combined with curses and groans, which intensified as Gene got closer and closer to the brink. A desperate cry signaled Gene was right there, and Dan sucked hard, pulling Gene's orgasm from him as he took him deep, swallowing and savoring as Gene thrashed through his climax. Then he felt Gene relax, and Dan let him slip from his lips, the look of bliss on Gene's face making him smile. There was definitely something to be said for experience.

"Dan." Gene moved to the side and patted the bed next to him. Dan lay down and found a large body cuddling next to him as lips nibbled on his ear. "You were terrific. So unselfish, so giving," Gene murmured.

Dan didn't know what to say, so he accepted the praise and kisses as they rested in the afternoon glow.

"I MADE reservations at a bistro for dinner." The sound of Gene's voice roused Dan from his nap. Dan yawned and stretched as the warm body next to him curled closer. "We'll need to leave in about half an hour."

Dan let his hands wander slowly over Gene's bulging chest before his fingers glided lower. "I just have to ask; do you ever lose your keys in these?" Dan asked as he trailed his fingers over Gene's deeply cut abs. "I swear you could hide things in them." He smiled as he looked up into Gene's eyes.

"You're silly, you know that?" Gene asked. Arms tugged him closer, and a leg slid in between his, sliding along Dan's calf and thigh. "I'm just a guy like you."

"You are so not. You're so far out of my league it isn't funny." Dan still couldn't figure out why Gene was here.

"Remember I said I liked you because you saw me as a person? Well, why can't you accept the same thing from me? I see you for who you are, and I like you for who you are."

Wow, that was some declaration.

"Do you know what it's like to have guys be nice to you simply for the way you look?" Gene asked as he pulled Dan's chin around so he could look in Dan's eyes. "Did you ever see *Torch Song Trilogy?* 'Guys take one look at me, and all they want is sex'."

Dan smiled and finished the quote. "'They look at me, and all they want is conversation'."

Gene chuckled softly. "I definitely want more than conversation."

Dan found himself pinned to the bed with the weight of a huge man pressing him into the mattress. Lips skidded over the skin of his neck. Dan arched slightly, rubbing against Gene, getting just a bit of delicious friction.

"But not right now. We need time," Gene continued. His lips slid lightly over Dan's, slowing the pace and cooling him down.

Dan was falling, right there; he could feel it. Just the way Gene's hands felt on his skin set his heart on fire. He knew what he was feeling, but he was scared to admit it to himself, and there was no way he could say anything to Gene. He'd barely known him a week—the man would think him nuts.

Gene slid off him and got up, and then turned and extended a hand to Dan. "I think we need to clean up." Gene led him to the bathroom and closed the door before starting the water. "You look confused."

"It's just that I've never…." Dan let his voice trail off. He was starting to sound stupid, even to himself.

"You mean you and Mike never showered together?" Gene tested the water and then stepped beneath the spray, waiting for Dan to decide to join him.

"Mike was a little finicky about certain things." Dan finally stepped into the tub, and Gene closed the curtain behind him.

"Well, I repeat, Mike was an ass on so many levels." Gene's hands slid through Dan's hair, soaping the golden locks and letting them run through his appreciative fingers. "For one thing, he let you go. And for another, he allowed both of you to miss something very special." Gene finished washing Dan's hair. While he rinsed, Gene lathered his hands. "Turn around and I'll show you."

Dan complied, waiting expectantly as Gene glided his soapy fingers over his back. "Sex is wonderful, but this is intimacy," Gene said as his fingers slid lower, caressing Dan's butt and slowly gliding between his cheeks.

Dan started when he felt Gene's fingers glide across his opening. "Gene, what are you doing?" The fingers repeated the motion, gently caressing, but no more.

"When we wash like this, your entire body is open to me." Gene lathered his hand again and slid it down Dan's butt and between his legs, gliding over the skin and cupping his balls with his fingers before retreating. Then his hands slid down Dan's legs. Thighs and calves were stroked and washed. "Turn around, baby."

There was that endearment again, and the way Gene said it, that rough edge to his voice, told him that it wasn't an affectation. It held meaning. At least he sure hoped and prayed it did.

Gene slicked his hands again and slid them over Dan's shoulders. "Lift your arms." Gene's fingers glided along his sides, against ticklish skin, and up his arms. Then lathered hands stroked his chest as Dan lowered his arms and rested them on Gene's shoulders. A nipple slid between slicked fingers. A soapy hand stroked his pecs and then slid down his stomach to slide along his length.

Dan's legs vibrated as Gene washed him, hands gliding over him in turn. "Gene, I thought we didn't have time."

Lips pulled on one of his ears. "This isn't about sex. It's about intimacy, so just relax and rinse off."

Dan turned around and let the water sluice over him, washing away all the soap, but not the tingles from Gene's touch.

Then Dan lathered his hands and began exploring Gene's body. He washed Gene's hair and then slid over that powerful back, the winged muscles rippling under his touch. Gliding lower, he washed that hard butt, fingers teasing along the crease and sneaking between his legs, just like Gene had done to him. God, he hoped he was doing this right, because he was loving every second of it.

"Dan, what are you doing?"

"Something I've always wanted to." He spread Gene's cheeks and, kneeling down, ran his tongue between them, zeroing in on the small, twitching opening.

"Dan!" Gene cried, as his legs shook. Dan ran his hands along the powerful thighs as he speared the opening while Gene cried out softly against the onslaught.

"Turn around," Dan urged. Gene moaned softly as Dan backed away. "This is a beautiful sight," Dan said.

Gene's ramrod manhood was just an inch from his mouth. Dan quickly lathered his hands and began washing Gene's thighs while his tongue lapped at the underside. Gene's cock bounced, and Dan caught it on his tongue again. "Does that feel good?"

Gene nodded desperately, and Dan saw him swallow hard.

"Let's try this." Dan raised his hands along Gene's stomach and chest until the nipples passed under his palms. Dan rubbed small circles against them.

"Dan, that's so good."

You ain't seen nothin' yet. With a smile, he sucked Gene into his mouth, drawing him deep as his hands worked those hard points. Gene's hips started rocking, his eyes closed, hot water flowing over both of them. Soft moans and cries filled the shower as Dan worked him. He could feel when Gene was close, and he stayed with him until Gene's flavor burst into his mouth.

When Gene's eyes opened again, Dan let him slip from his lips. "I'm sorry," he said.

"What on Earth for?" Gene asked.

"You said we were going to wait, but I didn't."

Gene put his hands beneath Dan's arms and lifted him onto his feet as anger flashed on his face for a split second. Then Dan found himself pressed back against the tile with Gene kneeling in front of him.

"Take what you want, Dan."

Suddenly, Dan was engulfed in hot wetness, pressure building around him. He began to rock just like Gene had. Pleasure zipped through him. He felt a hand glide along his leg, and a finger pressed against his opening, making small circles and then entering him, sliding past his muscle. Small lights flashed behind his eyes as Gene's finger found his magic spot, and he could hold back no longer. With a cry, he spilled into Gene, calling out his passion until his legs gave out, and he slumped to the floor of the shower.

"Gene," Dan panted as he tried to get to his feet, "that was incredible." Gene helped him up and pulled him close.

"Don't tell me your ass of an ex never did that for you." Gene turned off the water and grabbed towels, wrapping one around Dan. "You're not saying anything."

"You told me not to tell you," Dan said. A wry smile curled on his lips as he heard a low growl from Gene.

Stepping out of the shower, Gene began drying off as he said, "You deserve to be treated like the wonderful man you are. Not like someone's sex toy!"

Dan stepped out of the shower, and Gene began rubbing the towel over his skin, the nubby fabric heightening his already-tingling skin.

"We need to get ready," Gene said regretfully.

"I know, but this feels too good to stop." Dan leaned against Gene as the towel continued skipping over his skin.

"We can always do this again after dinner."

Dan reluctantly left the bathroom and began getting dressed.

THEY were already late by the time they left their room to ride the elevator to the lobby.

"I had planned to walk, but a cab will be quicker, and we can walk back," Gene said.

Dan nodded his agreement, and one of the doormen hailed a cab. They rode the few minutes to the restaurant and paid the driver.

Luckily, the restaurant still had a table for them, and the hostess led them to a spot at the very front. The restaurant was unique in that it had huge glass panels that shifted to one side, opening the entire front to the street. Their table, while inside, was almost like they were seated on the sidewalk.

"I like this place. It's just outside the Gayborhood," Gene reached across the table and put his hand on Dan's, "so we can be affectionate without feeling self-conscious."

Gene didn't even look at the menu, and when the waitress came by, he ordered water and the steak frites. Dan ordered the same, not wanting to break contact with Gene, even to look at the menu. It was funny, but Gene was touching him a lot, and Dan realized how much he liked it, how much he'd missed being touched and caressed.

"I love this place," he told Gene.

Their salads arrived, and they started eating, watching people as they strolled in front of the restaurant. "On a warm day like this, the fresh air is nice," Gene said as he touched the back of Dan's hand. "I always wanted to come here with someone special."

Dan stopped eating for a second and smiled. *He was someone special.* Slowly he turned his hand over, lacing his fingers with Gene's. He didn't really know what to say, so he just smiled and held Gene's hand, eating more slowly with the other, but very happy all the same.

Their main courses arrived, and Dan stared at the plate. It was a large steak covered in a fragrant mustard sauce accompanied by an obscene portion of French fries. Dan popped one in his mouth and grinned as he chewed, sticking another in his mouth immediately. "We're going to have to go back to the gym after this meal."

"I think we can find something to do to work off the calories," Gene said, the naughty leer leaving no doubt about what he was thinking, and Dan felt himself blush as he continued eating.

The rest of the meal was a gorge fest. They laughed, they talked, and they ate until they thought they were going to burst. The waitress tried her best to interest them in dessert, but they weren't buying.

The waitress brought the check, and Gene snatched it away from Dan and paid. Leaving the restaurant, Dan started walking back to the hotel, but Gene guided him in the other direction. "Rittenhouse Square is just up the street, and I thought we could stroll through."

Gene took his hand, and they walked through the flower-filled square before strolling back toward the hotel and beyond to Independence Hall, the city parks, and down to Penn's Landing. On their way back, the city lights were coming on when they approached the hotel. Their entire stroll, Gene had held Dan's hand, at times even putting an arm around his waist.

In the elevator, they rode quietly to the room, Gene holding Dan close. When the elevator doors opened, they walked to their room, and Gene slipped in the key card, opening the door. In the room was a cart with a champagne bucket and a large bowl of strawberries.

"Would you open the bottle?" Gene asked. He turned off the lights and opened all of the curtains, revealing the entire city laid out below them.

Dan popped the cork on the bottle and poured two glasses, handing one to Gene. "The view is incredible," Dan said as he looked out the window. Then he felt Gene's lips against his neck. Turning his head, he got a champagne-flavored kiss as Gene's tongue stroked along his lips.

"Yes, it is." Dan shivered slightly as Gene's heated gaze met his eyes. Then Gene took his glass, setting it on the bedside table. Their lips came together, and Dan found himself pressed onto the bed. Their clothes ended up in a heap on the floor, their mouths and hands feasting on hot skin and moist lips. Their banquet went on for much of the night, Gene driving Dan to passionate heights as they moved together, the room dark, the lights from the city shining and twinkling beneath them as their spirits soared and flew on their own wings of passion.

VI

MONDAY, it was back to the real world, but the warm glow from the weekend hadn't dissipated completely. At three o'clock, Dan's phone vibrated with the usual Monday afternoon "Chest @ 4" message. Ah, Lonnie was back from vacation. Dan responded with his usual "K" and got back to work. Life was back to normal—well, partially, anyway. Dan returned to finishing up his tasks for the day.

As he was getting ready to leave for the day, his phone vibrated again.

"Dan, it's Gene."

He couldn't keep a smile from slipping onto his face. "Hi."

"I just wanted to call and thank you for a special weekend and see if you were free for dinner on Wednesday. I'd like to see you earlier, but I've got to work late today and tomorrow."

"Wednesday sounds great."

"I'll see you then, baby."

Dan disconnected, smiling again at the endearment. He continued smiling until the doubt and worry began to creep in again. He hated it, hated feeling like this, but he just couldn't help it. Finishing up his work, he said his good-nights and left the office, going right to the gym.

He walked into the locker room, practically running into Lonnie as he was changing. "So, did you miss me while I was gone?"

"Do you want the truth or what you want to hear?"

"Ha, ha." Lonnie smacked his ass, and Dan jumped, rubbing his butt. "So, how'd things go? Did you get some?"

"You are the gayest straight man I've ever met, you know that?"

"Yeah, yeah, now spill." Lonnie finished changing and sat on the bench, waiting for Dan. He must have been interested; Lonnie usually left right away to get the equipment he wanted.

Dan finished changing, trying his best to ignore Lonnie's stares, but found himself caving. "He took me to Philly over the weekend." Dan closed his locker and sat down to put on his shoes. "It was incredible."

"So what's the problem?"

Dan looked around the busy locker room and finished putting on his shoes. Grabbing his things, Dan followed Lonnie out, not really wanting to talk about his love life in front of everyone. "Lonnie, look at me. He's twenty-eight, and I'm forty."

"So, what's the problem?" They made their way to one of the dumbbell benches.

"Lon, I'm serious."

"So am I." Lonnie picked up his weights and pounded through a light warm-up set. "Let me ask you something. Does he pay attention to you?"

"Yes." Gene had paid very careful attention to every part of him over the weekend, but he wasn't going to tell Lonnie that. Or, maybe he should—that was one of the few ways he'd found to get Lon to stop talking. "We have a lot in common."

"That's not what I meant. Has he done anything special?"

"Besides surprising me with a trip to Philly?" Dan did his warm-up set, stretching his muscles to their fullest.

"Yeah."

"He brought flowers to our first date." Dan crinkled his forehead while Lonnie picked up the weights for his set before pumping out ten reps. "What I can't get over is that he's incredible and he could have any guy he wants."

"Maybe he wants you." Lonnie sat up and wiped his face with a towel before stealing a drink from Dan's water bottle. "He's brought you flowers." Dan nodded as he picked up the weights. "Let me guess, he's turned down offers from other men."

"Yeah." Dan hoisted the weights and grunted his way through his set before dropping the weights with a thud. "I saw him turn down a couple of guys when we were in Philly, but that was just because I was with him." Lonnie smacked him lightly on the side of the head. "What was that for?" Dan rubbed the side of his head.

"For a smart guy, you're pretty dumb. The man brought you flowers, he listens to you and pays careful attention to you, and to top it off, he turned down other guys flat. Am I right?"

"Yeah, so?"

"And I bet he smiles this goofy smile whenever he sees you."

"Yeah, so…?" Dan exaggerated the words, hoping Lonnie would get to the point, but his friend picked up the weights and did a set instead, making Dan wait for whatever point he was going to make. Lonnie powered through the set and then sat up. "So…?" Dan prompted.

"So, ya dumb fuck, he's in love." Lonnie rolled his eyes. "Guys are simple. We don't sit around and analyze our feelings; we act on them. So if he's turning down easy sex, paying special attention to you, and looking at you with a goofy smile, then he's interested."

Dan sat down and started doing his set. Lonnie started talking again as soon as the weights hit the floor, his OCD kicking in big time. "Here's a novel idea. Why don't you just ask him?"

He was just about to swat Lonnie on the head when he felt a hand on his shoulder. Turning around, he found himself looking at Kabe.

"I hope you're happy," the big man growled in Dan's face.

The man was a Neanderthal. "About what?" Dan felt Lonnie stand up behind him.

"Gene threw away his chances at Mr. Universe because of you. Regional competition was this weekend, and Gene was with you instead of at the competition."

Dan knew nothing about it and looked to Lonnie for help, but he just shrugged as well. Kabe stormed away, looking over his shoulder to give Dan a final glare before picking up a bar for bicep curls.

He turned around to see Lonnie smiling, a "See, I told you he likes you" and "I told you so" look on his face. But Dan's stomach twisted, and he wished it were that easy.

DAN kept hoping he'd see Gene at the gym later on Monday or even on Tuesday, but he didn't. Wednesday evening he was cleaning up for dinner; he'd just stepped out of the shower when he heard a knock on the front door. Drying off quickly, he tugged on a pair of jeans and checked the clock. It was too early for Gene.

Opening the front door he saw Mike standing on his doorstep. *What is this, a romance novel?* "Dan, can we talk?"

Dan checked the clock in the living room. "I'm getting ready to go out."

"Five minutes, please." Mike never said please—it was too "submissive."

Dan huffed slightly. "Fine, but I need to get dressed." Mike stepped inside, and Dan closed the door. Dan went back upstairs with Mike following.

"What is it you want?" Dan asked.

"I want you back, Dan."

Yes, this is a romance novel. "Mike...." Dan went to his closet and pulled out a dress shirt, slipping it over his arms.

"I've missed you." This time Mike's voice was right behind him, the words breathed into his ear. There it was again: that ingrained, almost Pavlovian response. Then he felt Mike's body against him, maneuvering him, pinning him up against the wall, a hand running down his chest.

"No, Mike." He felt a hand at the button on his jeans. "I said no!" Dan pushed against Mike, and he found himself pressed harder against the wall. He was starting to feel trapped, and when Mike eased his grip on one of his hands, he was able to get it free. He slapped Mike as hard as he could, his hand leaving a red print on his face. "I said no, Mike!"

Mike rubbed his face and backed away, having the decency to look contrite. "I thought you were playing." He peeked in the mirror. "Geez, you pack a wallop."

Dan continued gulping air, his heart rate beginning to return to normal.

"I'm sorry, Danny. I didn't mean to scare you." Mike's expression softened. "I really do miss you, every day." He stepped closer, but kept his hands to himself.

Dan whirled away. "I missed you for months." He pushed Mike out of his way. "And it took me six months before I could stop sleeping just on my side of the bed." Dan heaved a breath, trying to keep his whirling emotions under control. "We were together for ten years, and you threw it away for some cute kid. I would have spent the rest of my life with you, and I would have been happy, but not now."

"Is it him? That guy you were with the last time I was here?"

Dan thought for a split second. "Partly, but mostly it's me."

He pulled a pair of dress pants out of the closet, setting them on the bed and stepped to his dresser. "Turn around," he told Mike. Mike did as he asked, and Dan slipped off his jeans and pulled on a pair of boxers before stepping into his pants.

"I want more, Mike. What we had was good, but I want and deserve more." Dan's momentary anger slipped away. "You did me a favor. I now know that I can have better than you, that there's someone who makes me feel like I'm the most important thing in the world to them."

Mike turned around, a sad, almost pathetic look on his face. "He'll leave you, you know." It was funny, but Mike's tone wasn't mean or cruel. In fact, Dan heard a touch of sadness in Mike's voice, like he was still trying to protect Dan the way he always had—by being the big, dominant protector.

"Maybe, but he couldn't hurt me as badly as you did. And right now, I'm willing to take the chance. I like him, and he treats me well, Mike, very well." Dan saw him swallow hard. "I'm not comparing Gene to you. What we had was special, but it's over, and we can't go back." Dan could hardly believe he was saying these words. Going back to what they'd had was something he'd dreamed of for months after Mike left.

"I do love you." Mike's voice was soft and rough.

Dan lifted his hand and trailed it over Mike's cheek. "I know you do. I love you too, but it's time I moved on—" Dan corrected himself, "—we moved on." *Damn, that felt good.* Just saying the words out loud gave him confidence. The fluttery, unsettled feeling in his stomach that had been there since Mike left fell away. He was doing the right thing for both of them.

"I need to finish getting ready." Dan sat in the corner chair and tied his shoes. "I'll walk you out."

Dan led Mike to the front door. "'Night, Mike." Dan opened the door, and Mike left quietly, passing Gene as he came up the walk. Dan watched as Gene's head craned so he could look at Mike as he left.

Dan had to give him credit; he didn't ask the obvious questions as he climbed the steps. "Hey, baby." His eyes scanned over Dan, "You look really nice."

"Thanks." Dan leaned forward for a kiss, which he got. "Come on inside." Dan closed the door behind them and ushered Gene into the living room.

"Why do I get the feeling I'm about to get bad news?" Dan sat on the sofa, and Gene sat in one of the chairs. "He wants you back, doesn't he?" Gene sighed softly. "I knew it."

"How'd you know?"

"You're too great a guy to let go." Gene got to his feet.

"Where are you going?"

Gene looked at Dan, saying nothing.

"I told him it was too late," Dan explained.

Gene broke into a grin. "You told him no?"

"I told him no." Dan nodded as he answered.

Gene shifted, sitting next to him on the sofa. "Was it because of me?"

"A little, but mostly it was because of *me*. It's taken me a long time to get over him, and I'm not going to do that again. I figured if I was with him, I'd always wonder, and that's no way to live. Besides, I'm starting to realize that I can have more."

Dan found himself pressed against the sofa cushions, a tongue sliding along the edge of his lips. Dan forced himself to think through the haze that gripped his brain. "Gene, we still need to talk."

He felt the weight pressing against him lessen. "Oh."

"It's not bad; I just have some questions." Dan got up and began pacing, trying to figure out how to phrase his questions. He was about to blurt them out when he felt himself being tugged back on the sofa.

"Would you relax and just ask me what you want to ask?"

"Gene, there's so many things. I could fall for you, but I'm afraid of getting hurt again. I'm just now really getting over things with Mike." Dan's thoughts drifted away as he realized he wasn't sure where he was going with this. The questions would just all come tumbling out.

"Is it the age difference?" Gene looked so earnest.

"Partly, yeah." He felt Gene's fingers slide along his arm, sending a tingle through him.

Gene huffed softly, "And part of it is the way I look."

"Jesus, Gene. You could have almost any guy you wanted at any time." Dan knew he wasn't communicating his thoughts very well.

"Yes, I probably can. But the one person I want is you." That stopped Dan's babbling in its tracks. "And if you don't know how attractive and sexy you are, then I'll just have to show you." Gene's lips were back, and this time the kiss was much more insistent, but again, Dan stopped him.

"Gene."

"What?" He lightly mocked Dan's tone.

"Kabe told me Monday that you gave up your chance at Mr. Universe because you took me to Philly. He said that you missed a regional competition. I don't want you to give up your dreams."

Gene laughed, rich and warm from deep in his chest. "Kabe doesn't know squat; never did. First, I was with you because that was where I wanted to be. And second, I don't need to qualify like he does; I've been invited. Besides, when I told you my dream was to be Mr. Universe, I wasn't being completely accurate." Dan crooked his eyebrows. "Oh, I want to win Mr. Universe, but I always hoped there'd be someone I loved to see me do it." Gene waited for a moment. "Is there anything else?"

Dan shook his head, Gene's lips so close he could barely think.

"Good."

This time, Dan didn't try to stop Gene, except to mumble something about dinner, and he got a mumbled "later" in return as he was kissed within an inch of his life.

"Take this upstairs?" Dan nodded in response, and Gene stood up. Taking him by the hand, Dan was led upstairs to his own bedroom where the kissing began again.

Gene's hands cradled Dan's head as he felt Gene's lips explore his own. Softly and tenderly, they slid across his, tongue exploring the soft skin, slowing down the pace, letting the urgency slip away. Dan felt fingers working open his shirt buttons, and then the fabric parted and slid down his arms and off his body, rustling as it landed on the floor.

Gene's thumb circled a nipple, and Dan threw his head back, hissing softly as Gene's lips joined it, sucking and nibbling at his chest. "So soft." Gene's hands slid over Dan's skin. "I love how smooth and soft your skin is." They moved around to his back before sliding into his pants, cupping his butt as Gene sucked on the base of his neck.

Dan's belt opened, and his pants parted, sliding down his legs. Dan stepped out of them, standing naked in front of Gene. "Can we take this to the bed?"

"Whatever you want, baby."

Dan smirked as he stepped closer. "Whatever I want?" Gene nodded and grunted as Dan slammed into him, maneuvering him onto the bed. "Did you really mean that?"

"Yeah."

Dan opened Gene's shirt, his lips zeroing in on a tawny nipple, "Can I... fuck you?"

Gene brought Dan's lips to him. "I want you to, baby. Want you inside me."

"Oh God."

Gene lifted his head and looked in Dan's eyes. He didn't ask the question; he didn't need to. The look of ecstatic disbelief on Dan's face told him all he needed to know. "But you need to get my clothes off first."

Dan's eyes twinkled with delight. "Oh, I will."

Dan slid down Gene's body, his tongue sliding between Gene's pecs before tracing the deep grooves on his stomach. "I'm on a treasure hunt." He licked the tender skin just above the waist of Gene's pants. "And I'm getting close." Dan smiled as he opened Gene's belt and popped the button on his pants, parting the soft fabric. Gene's erection was already straining to get free.

"Dan." He smiled at the slight quiver in Gene's voice. Sliding the pants down Gene's legs, Dan dropped them on the floor and stood at the foot of the bed, looking down at this magnificent man. Gene was vibrating, his excitement overwhelming his body, and Dan could hardly believe what he was doing to this incredible man.

"Please," Gene murmured.

Dan crawled back up the bed, his legs straddling Gene. When he reached his face, he kissed Gene and whispered into his ear, "Roll over and spread your arms out."

Gene complied, and Dan settled with his butt on Gene's legs, hands roaming over the wide, powerful back. "You're incredible, you know that?" Starting at his shoulder, Dan nibbled and licked his way down Gene's back: over the powerful shoulders, along the muscles that flared like wings down his sides, to the narrow waist just above the waistband of his black briefs.

Gene squirmed beneath Dan's touch. "So are you, baby. So are you."

Dan lowered Gene's briefs, slipping the fabric over that incredible butt and down his legs. Dan let his hands glide over the smooth calves and up the soft skin of Gene's thighs as his legs parted. Leaning forward, Dan slid his tongue along Gene's crease. "Need to get you ready." Gene raised his hips, kneeling slightly, his butt in the air as Dan swirled his tongue around the small, tight opening.

"Baby!" Gene arched his back, leaning toward the sensation as Dan thrust his tongue deep, feeling the muscle tighten and then relax. "Please. Just do it!"

Gene rolled on the bed while Dan got a condom and slicked himself and then Gene. Slowly, he pressed into Gene, the strong man's muscles stretching to welcome him. "Gene." He could barely believe how good this felt, Gene's passage gripping him so tightly. "You're so hot!"

Gene pulled him into a kiss as he sank deep. "So are you. baby. Give it to me. Want to feel you for days."

Dan began to move, thrusting slowly at first, but then picked up the tempo. Gene met each movement. Adjusting the angle slightly, Gene began crying out as Dan hit his sweet spot, further fueling their desire. "You're so hot," Dan rasped.

"Harder, baby. Give me what you got." Dan began driving into him, his head swirling as his brain, overwhelmed by the sensation, threw his body into overdrive. He felt Gene's muscles contract hard around him and heard him cry out. His own release rolled through him in waves as he spilled himself deep in his lover, his body giving out, and he collapsed into Gene's strong arms.

Gasping for breath, Dan didn't move as he felt himself slip from Gene's body. "We should take care of things," Gene murmured.

Dan looked into Gene's eyes, nodding slightly. "But that would require moving."

Soon Dan got up and cleaned them up a bit before snuggling back into Gene's embrace, quickly dozing off against the warmth of his lover's body.

A HAND smoothed its way over Dan's head. "Wake up, baby." Lips ghosted over his.

Dan cracked his eyes open, peering into Gene's. "Sorry." A yawn escaped before he could stop it. "I guess we missed dinner." Hands stroked along his back. "I have a few things in the house I can make." Gene nodded slowly. "Is something wrong?" Dan asked as he felt tension creep into his body.

"No, nothing's wrong."

Dan searched Gene's eyes for something but came up empty. Then he realized what he was seeing: joy. Happiness.

"I don't want to scare you, but I have to tell you. I love you, Dan." Big hands brought their lips together, kissing hard and long and deep. "I'd like very much to see if we can make this work."

"Me too."

"Will you help me train for Mr. Universe?"

Dan chuckled as he snuggled against Gene's warmth. "I always wondered what it would be like to sleep with Mr. Universe." A pillow bonked him on the head, and Dan tried to squirm away, but Gene pulled him closer.

"You're a nut," Gene insisted. Dan felt fingers slide through his hair. "So you'll help me then?"

Dan grinned as he looked in Gene's eyes. "Love, I'll *spot you* every step of the way."

Pump Me Up

Andrew Grey

I

HE TURNED the key in the lock. "No—not again," Maddoc groaned to himself as he looked at the stems sitting next to his front door. Bending down, he picked them up. Being careful of the thorns, he gingerly dumped the headless flowers in the trash, the note that came along with them slipping between the porch floorboards. "Why does this keep happening?" Maddoc looked around but saw no one in the early morning darkness. He never did, but the damn stems kept showing up anyway. Turning around, he walked down the steps, stumbling on the last one as his knee nearly gave out under him. "What did I ever do?"

Still shaking, he made it to his car without falling on his face. After looking at each of the tires, he opened the car door and got inside. Starting the engine, he put the vehicle in gear and inched forward before hitting the brakes. Everything seemed to work. Turning on his headlights, he sped in the direction of his office, but he couldn't help looking back to check his house before turning the corner.

The office was bright with plenty of people around, and Maddoc allowed himself to relax as he got to work, a day like any other day, at least for him lately. People said good morning, and Maddoc felt the tension begin to slip away. This was his routine, and while it was often hectic, it was known and comforting.

His work day went normally enough, and by late afternoon Maddoc was shutting down his computer. He looked down at the bag near his desk. "I really should do this." Picking up the bag, he carried it with him to his car and drove the half mile or so to a large, bright fitness center. Entering nervously, he approached the desk.

"Um, I got a two-week pass from work." He couldn't meet the receptionist's gaze and found himself talking more to the counter than to her. "I thought I'd give it a try." He fished out the pass and set it on the counter.

"We're glad you did," she responded in a high, perky voice, and Maddoc raised his gaze to see her huge, genuine smile. "Take a seat at the first desk, and Mark will be right with you." Maddoc did as he was asked, and a big man in a tight shirt sat down across from him and went through his sales pitch.

Maddoc listened, fidgeting nervously. "I'd really just like to see how I like it first."

"No problem." Mark smiled. "I'll give you a quick tour. I see you brought workout gear. Excellent! Bring it with you, and I'll show you around."

Relief flooded through Maddoc as he got up from the chair. He hated disappointing people, but he needed to know he was going to like this. "I've never worked out before," he confessed as they started the tour.

"You're not alone. A lot of people who come in are just trying to get in shape. That's why we have all kinds of equipment. Machines are great for starting out." He pointed to the rows of what looked like new equipment. "Free weights are also available." Mark pointed to the back of the gym where huge guys were lifting and grunting loudly.

Bang! A sharp sound echoed through the building. Maddoc jumped and looked around for cover.

"Sorry. When they're working with the heavy weights, they drop them to prevent getting hurt," Mark explained as he continued the tour, thankfully ignoring Maddoc's jitters. "You get used to it. A lot of gyms don't allow it, but we have a number of high-powered lifters...."

Maddoc looked at the men getting up from the bench. "I wouldn't want to tell them no, either."

Mark laughed, "Actually, they're great guys." He led the way toward the back of the building. "Here's the men's locker room. There's a sauna near the showers and the entrance to the pool and whirlpool area." Maddoc slowly nodded and thanked him for the tour before finding a locker and pulling off his shirt.

"Maddoc?" a vaguely familiar voice said from behind him. Turning around, he saw one of the guys from his office. "I thought that was you." The man smiled brightly and stepped around the bench, extending his hand.

"Hey, Dan." Maddoc returned the smile and shook the offered hand.

"I haven't seen you here before, are you a member?" Dan inquired as he started looking for an empty locker.

"Not yet. I got a pass at the office and thought I'd give it a try." Maddoc hung up his polo shirt and pulled a T-shirt out of his bag, slipping it over his head. "I'm a real newbie." He lowered his pants and hung them in the locker before pulling on a pair of shorts.

"You're welcome to join us." Dan opened his shirt and slipped it off his shoulders. Maddoc found himself staring and had to turn his eyes away. He knew Dan was about his age, but he'd never have guessed, and he found himself stealing looks at the man's flat stomach, wide shoulders, and pierced nipple. Maddoc turned away suddenly, afraid he'd pop wood right there in the locker room... in front of a coworker no less.

"H-have you been working out long?" He needed to get himself together, but he couldn't help asking. Maybe there was hope that he could get strong like that.

"Years. But you'll be surprised how much you can change once you work out regularly." Dan dropped his pants, and Maddoc forcibly turned his attention to putting his things in his locker. "Join us," he repeated, as he pulled on a pair of tight shorts and a tank top.

"If it's okay." Maddoc didn't want to impose, but he needed some help and wasn't really sure who he should ask.

"Of course." Dan closed the door and locked his locker. "Do you have a water bottle?" Maddoc shook his head, closing his own locker. Turning around, Maddoc saw Dan open his locker again, handing him a plastic water bottle before relocking it. "You'll need it." Maddoc thanked Dan and took the bottle before following him like a puppy out of the locker room.

"Big Pimpin', you ready?" a guy called as he slapped Dan on the butt. "I haven't seen your other half yet, is he joining us?"

"Probably not. He's on a competition regime, so it's just us." Dan turned to him and said, "This is Maddoc. We work together, and he's thinking about joining."

The man immediately extended his hand. "I'm Lonnie. You gonna join us?" The man seemed genuine, and Maddoc found himself nodding. "Don't worry, we'll take it easy on you." Lonnie turned and began striding toward the equipment before turning around. "You homos coming?" Maddoc looked to Dan, shocked, not sure how to react. "No offense," the loud man added automatically.

"That's just Lonnie," Dan explained. "He's got the biggest mouth of anyone I've ever met." Dan began trailing behind Lonnie. "You really are an ass sometimes—you know that, Rosen?" Not sure what to do, Maddoc found himself following slowly. "Don't let him bother you. The man's a complete pig," Dan continued to explain. "He's living proof that there is such a thing as Jewish pork." Maddoc couldn't help laughing. "Just give it back to him. Comments about his big ass are surefire winners, particularly if they're original."

Maddoc found himself relaxing as Dan led the way to a flat bench. Lonnie was already doing his set, and Maddoc watched. When Lonnie was done, Dan took his turn and then stripped off the weights and indicated for Maddoc to go. Dan explained the exercise and helped him perform it right, even standing behind him to help in case he needed it. When Maddoc was done, Dan put the bar in the rack. "That was really good."

"I could probably do more," Maddoc said, pleased with himself, even though Dan had said it was only ninety pounds.

"Don't push it right away or you'll be really sore tomorrow. Let your body get used to it."

Maddoc nodded and watched as they each took their turns, doing the exercise three more times before switching to an incline bench. "Who's that?" Maddoc saw a huge man approach, his chest and shoulders bulging out of a string tank.

"That's Gene, Dan's partner." Maddoc looked at Lonnie in disbelief. "He's training for Mr. Olympia." Lonnie gave him a surprised look. "Don't you guys work together?"

"We work in the same office, and we've worked on projects together and stuff," Maddoc stammered, unsure why Dan had invited him to work out with them in the first place. Hell, he hadn't even known the man was gay.

"Come on, you two. Play hide the sausage later." Maddoc saw Gene glare at Lonnie for a second before the man actually gave Dan a kiss right there in the gym. "Geez, you two." Lonnie started making gagging sounds, and Maddoc didn't know how to react, but Dan and Gene began to laugh, and he figured this was normal for them. The two hunky men separated, and Dan rejoined them, watching Gene walk across the gym. "Can we get back to work?" Lonnie groused good-naturedly.

"Look who's talking," Dan retorted. "The man who turned gabbing into an Olympic sport."

Maddoc laughed and added tentatively, "You mean he'd be as big as Gene if talking counted as exercise?"

"Exactly," Dan responded with a grin.

"If you're done Lonnie-bashing, can we get jacked already?" Lonnie walked over to a large, gray machine and began putting weights on it as Dan explained it was a decline press machine. They took their turns, the talk diminishing as they got to work again.

"Hey, Lonnie." A man approached as Maddoc was finishing what he hoped was the last set. He let the arms fall back against the stops, then got up and watched as the guys all talked.

"You joining us for dinner?" The man didn't answer right away. "Don't be a pussy all your life come eat with us."

"Okay," the man answered. "Since you asked so nicely. What time?"

Maddoc listened to the exchange as details were finalized, watching the man really closely. He had to be about Maddoc's age, with close-cropped graying hair and broad shoulders. Maddoc couldn't tell anything else from the baggy clothes he was wearing, but his imagination quickly took over.

"You gonna join us, too, Docky?" Lonnie's question pulled him out of his daydream, and he nodded. *Docky?* "Good." Lonnie finished up his last set, clanking the arms against the stops. They finished the routine, and Maddoc thought he'd need someone to carry him into the locker room, but somehow he made it under his own power.

Pulling off his sweaty clothes, Maddoc found himself naked just as the man who'd been talking to Lonnie entered the locker room. Maddoc felt himself color as he reached for his bathing suit, pulling it on quickly and grabbing a towel, figuring he'd try to find the whirlpool. He'd never gotten used to being naked in public, and he felt especially shy around all these super-hot men. The whirlpool was easy to find, and Maddoc lowered himself into the hot, swirling water, thankful he was alone. Relaxing his head back, Maddoc felt his muscles turn to JELL-O, and didn't look up when he heard someone else enter the tub.

"Hi."

Maddoc looked up toward the voice coming from next to him. "Hi." He saw the man from earlier settling into the water next to him. Maddoc wished he'd been paying attention, because what he could see above the water looked... really nice. He even liked the graying hair... sexy.

"I'm Ivan." The man lifted a hand out of the water.

"Maddoc." He shook the offered hand and found that Ivan held it a little longer than necessary. He didn't know what to say and resettled in the water, watching the man through half-closed eyes. God, he was handsome. He had to keep his imagination in check or he'd completely embarrass himself. Maddoc kept watching until he began to feel slightly cooked, and then got out of the water, doing his best not to turn for one last look before he left. But it happened anyway—he just couldn't help it.

In the shower area, Maddoc saw Dan and Gene coming out of the sauna as he headed to the showers to clean up. Turning on the water, he washed quickly, feeling self-conscious the entire time. Turning off the water, he sneaked his hand outside the curtain, snatching his towel inside with him. Drying off, he wrapped the towel around his waist and pushed the curtain aside. In his hurry to step out, he bumped into a naked and very hot Ivan, hand brushing against his.... "S-s-sorry," Maddoc gulped and stammered before grabbing his bathing suit and rushing into the locker area. Maddoc figured he'd get changed as fast as he could and leave, when he saw Dan come in wearing only a towel.

"See you at dinner?"

Maddoc felt like a trapped rat. How could he go to dinner with Ivan when he'd just had his hand against the man's balls? But Dan and his friends had been so nice, Maddoc couldn't let him down or embarrass him. "Yes," he answered against his better judgment, and turned toward his locker and began dressing. Maddoc had never been so mortified in his life. Not only had he felt the man up, but he'd liked it. God, he'd practically molested the man right there in the showers. After pulling on his underwear and pants, he slipped on his shirt before sitting down to put on his shoes.

Looking up, he saw Ivan walk in with only a towel around his waist, sitting low on the hips. The man looked like some sort of god: tall, fit, with wide shoulders tapering to a small waist. How in hell could a man his age have a waist that small? And those abs! There was no mere six-pack—the man had at least a ten-pack glistening above that low-slung towel. "See you at dinner?"

Maddoc blushed as his eyes took in the sight before him, hoping he wasn't too obvious. "Sure, I'll see you there." Maddoc lowered his eyes again and finished dressing. Packing his bag, he fled the locker room with a small sigh of relief. He needed to get himself under control. He nearly tripped over an uneven spot in the pavement while heading to his car but kept his balance. Unlocking the car, he climbed in and shut the door.

Sitting in the driver's seat, he felt himself heaving for breath. It didn't matter what Ivan looked like or how stunning he was. Maddoc would never be able to talk to him anyway. Getting himself under control, he started the car and backed up, immediately stepping on the brake. He put the car in park, got out, and walked around to the back. There was a rose stem affixed to the base of the back window. Maddoc looked around and found himself shaking again. Was no place safe? As he threw it away, he did his best to try to convince himself that it was there from that morning and that he wasn't being followed, but he wasn't so sure. Getting back into the car, he locked the door, his hands shaking.

It took him a few minutes of deep breathing, but he got himself together and began pulling out. A horn stopped him, and he let the other car pass before finishing backing out of the parking space and driving the short distance to the restaurant.

Maddoc parked near the entrance and got out, looking around to see if he was being watched, but saw no one. Finding himself still shaking a little, he walked into the restaurant and looked around. He didn't see anyone he knew, so he grabbed a handful of peanuts from the barrel, took a seat in the log-lined waiting area, tossing the peanut shells on the floor with the rest, and waited.

The guys began to arrive a few minutes later, and Maddoc followed them to the table. Taking a seat, he was relieved when Dan and Gene sat next to him. To Maddoc's nervous excitement, Ivan sat right across from him. Lonnie arrived a few minutes later, and the stories began. Between drink and dinner orders, Lonnie regaled the table with story upon story of lurid conquests, which Maddoc thought strange since Lonnie's fiancée Cory was seated at the table, but no one else seemed to think anything of it.

"I've never seen you at the gym before." Ivan seemed to be talking to him.

"Today was my first day."

"Did you like it?"

"Dan and Lonnie let me join their workout." He found himself rubbing his shoulder a little without thinking about it. "It was more fun than I thought it would be."

"So you're going to join?" Ivan asked with a smile.

"I think so."

"That's good. You'll be surprised at the changes you'll see in yourself." That got Maddoc's attention, and he waited for Ivan to continue. "You'll look younger, feel better, and have more energy." Ivan seemed to wink at him, and Maddoc felt his cheeks heat a little.

"I just don't want to feel weak anymore." Maddoc looked down at the table.

"Working out will make you stronger and feel better about yourself, but strength has to come from inside." There was that wink again, and thankfully their drinks arrived to give Maddoc something to do with his hands.

Maddoc wasn't sure, but Ivan seemed sincere and really smart. "I just want to be able to defend myself."

"From what?" Ivan's tone became serious.

Maddoc made light of his fears, not really wanting to discuss them. "Just in general." The arrival of their dinners interrupted the conversation, and Maddoc began eating. The conversation continued, most of it driven by Lonnie.

After they'd eaten, the server took the dishes, and after the group had talked awhile, the check arrived. Maddoc pulled out his wallet, but Lonnie grabbed the check and paid the bill, insisting that it was his treat and he wouldn't hear any argument. Then they all got up and headed toward the exit. Maddoc walked to his car and looked it over. No flowers or anything attached. Unlocking the door, Maddoc got in and turned the key. The starter ground for a second, and then the car was silent.

A tap on his window had Maddoc jumping out of his skin. Clutching his chest dramatically, he looked and saw Ivan looking back at him. Catching his breath, he pushed the button to lower the window, but nothing happened, so he opened the door. "Do you know anything about cars?"

Ivan shrugged. "A little. Pop the hood." Maddoc pulled the lever and Ivan lifted the hood, peering inside. "I think the battery's shot." Maddoc looked to where he was pointing and saw all kinds of corrosion and stuff around it. Stepping back, he let Ivan close the hood. "We could try giving it a jump. You might make it home."

He didn't like the sound of that. The last thing he needed was to be stuck on the side of the highway. "I'll call a cab or something." He began reaching into his pocket for his phone.

"You don't need to do that. I'll drive you home." Maddoc looked up and saw Ivan's deep brown eyes looking at him so intently that he forgot what he was going to say and merely nodded before remembering his manners.

"Thank you." For a second his fear kicked in again, but Ivan's eyes told him he wouldn't hurt him. After locking his car, Maddoc followed Ivan to a little sports car and climbed into the passenger seat, buckling himself in. "I appreciate this." He told Ivan where he lived.

"It's not a problem." Ivan started the car and pulled out of the lot, zipping down the road.

"Have you known Lonnie long?" Maddoc needed something to talk about, and after that dinner, he figured Lonnie was a safe topic.

"Don't let him get to you. Lonnie's just one of those loud guys, but I've known him for years, and he'll help anybody." Ivan drove up the freeway on-ramp. "There was a guy like him in my unit when I was in the Corps. Bigger mouth than Lon. He was also the guy I most wanted watching my back. Lonnie's sort of like that. Big, filthy mouth, needs to be the center of attention, but loyal and a great friend when you need one."

"Seems like a weird combination."

"That's Lonnie."

"Are you a Marine?" Maddoc asked quietly.

"Yeah." Ivan turned to him, squinting slightly.

"My dad was in the Corps, and he always said, 'Once a Marine, always a Marine'," Maddoc explained. "His biggest disappointment was that I didn't enlist too. But by the time I was seventeen, I'd had enough of his version of military discipline." He turned away and looked out the window. "Dad was a good guy and a good father, but being a Marine was the most important thing in his life." He turned back to Ivan. "Besides, I knew I was gay and just didn't want to lead the kind of double life I'd have to. Not that I ever told him that." Why he was telling Ivan all of this, he had no idea. Maybe it was because although he'd never gotten along with or understood his dad, Maddoc always knew he could trust him. He'd have liked to think he was talking because he just wanted to fill the empty space in the car, but the Marine thing had thrown him just a bit, and he found that he kind of trusted Ivan. "Dad used to tell me stories about the guys who got drummed out for being 'queer', and I decided I didn't want that to happen to me. So I went to college instead. To his eternal disappointment." Maddoc turned back to the window and stopped talking. Ivan didn't need to hear all about his troubles. "Did you like the Marines?"

"Loved it. I never had much of a family growing up, so the guys in my unit became a sort of substitute family. The only member of my real family who's still around is my mom." Ivan's voice remained strong, but Maddoc could hear a slight longing anyway.

"What happened?"

"Don't ask, don't tell.... I told." Maddoc found himself nodding. "I couldn't live a lie any more. I stayed away from anyone I was attracted to for years. I didn't date and didn't socialize. I just wanted to be the best soldier and Marine I could."

"But something changed," Maddoc supplied softly. He knew this was difficult for the strong Marine, and he was surprised Ivan was even telling him any of this. Maybe the Marine family thing ran both ways.

"I met Gerald. He was bright and smiled at the slightest provocation. I didn't want to admit it, but I fell for him and fell hard." Ivan's voice remained level. "After Gerald was killed in action, I decided it was time to go."

"I'm sorry," Maddoc said sincerely.

"That was some time ago." Ivan took the freeway exit and turned onto the main street. Maddoc provided directions to his house.

"It's the one on the left," Maddoc supplied, and Ivan pulled up in front, stopping the car. Maddoc got out and walked toward the front door, seeing a bunch of what looked like flowers leaning against the front door. "Not again." He stopped and felt his legs start to shake again. For a few hours he'd been able to forget this crap, but here it was again.

"What is it?" He jumped slightly when the car door closed behind him but relaxed a bit when he remembered it was Ivan's voice.

"Someone keeps sending me flowers." He took a few steps toward the house. "At first they were nice bouquets with sweet, secret admirer type notes. But lately the notes have gotten disturbing. For the last few mornings the flowers have been wilted and then dead." Maddoc looked at the flowers, or what was left of them. There were only stems. "Damn it." This was really starting to scare him. "I'm sorry." He began to fumble for his keys and unlocked the door, then picked up the mess gingerly and threw it under the thick shrubbery, the card falling to the porch floor. He scooped it into his hand and crumpled it, getting ready to throw it with the stems.

"Can I look at it?" Ivan asked, and Maddoc handed it to him, pushing the door open and stepping inside, letting Ivan follow him.

"This is twisted." Ivan read the note. "There's nothing here directly threatening, but the tone seems menacing."

"I know." Maddoc shuddered as he stood in his living room, shaking like he usually did when these appeared. "I've been frightened to go out of the house."

"Have you called the police?"

"Yeah, but they didn't do much and just thought it was my imagination. Maybe it is." He slumped into a chair, pulling his feet under him, doing his best to curl into a ball.

"Is there anything I can do?" Ivan stepped closer, and Maddoc found himself curling further into the chair.

"No. I'll be all right." He forced his feet out from under him. He had to get a grip on himself. "Thank you," he added with more conviction than he felt.

"Oh." Ivan looked skeptical, but to Maddoc's relief didn't push it. "Here's my card with all my numbers on it. Please use it if anything happens."

Maddoc took the card, wondering if this was for real or not. "Marine to the rescue?"

"A friend, if you need help." Ivan turned, and Maddoc heard the front door close.

"Wow." His eyes followed Ivan's exit. He knew the guy was only being nice, but there was something inside that told him Ivan could be trusted to help him. Getting up from the chair, he locked the door and went through the house turning on lights, spending the evening before going to bed jumping at every noise in the house. Whoever this was might or might not be out to hurt him, but they already had him scared of his own shadow. "This has to stop somehow," Maddoc told himself.

II

IVAN looked back at the house and watched lights appear in the windows. He hated leaving but hadn't been given much choice. Maddoc was one scared man, and he wished he could help him, but he knew from that look on Maddoc's face that he wasn't about to trust him or anyone. Opening his car door, Ivan slid into the driver's seat and slowly pulled away, looking back at the house.

He kept seeing the look in the redhead's eyes when he'd seen those flowers on his steps—the fear and worry. He'd seen that look before on the face of civilians in Baghdad after neighborhood shootouts, and now, as then, he wanted to help. Besides, he couldn't get that smile he'd seen a few times at dinner out of his mind. The man was adorable. Tight, red curls with just a touch of gray, those big blue eyes, and he'd definitely noticed that small, tight butt when Maddoc had bent over on the porch.

He couldn't believe he'd actually told him about Gerald. He hadn't told anyone about Gerald ever, including his mother, but somehow he'd felt like he could tell Maddoc. That was really strange, although he got the feeling Maddoc didn't open up about himself to many people, either. So maybe they were even. His phone rang, and he peered at the screen, not recognizing the number. "Hello."

"Ivan? It's Maddoc, I just wanted to call and say thanks for the ride… and everything else." The man's voice sounded so small.

"I was wondering if you'd like to meet me at the gym tomorrow? We can work out together, and I'll show you some of the Marine workout we used to get into shape fast." If getting Maddoc in shape would help give him some confidence, he'd try to help him.

"You would?" He heard the first hint of hope in Maddoc's voice.

"Sure." Ivan smiled into the phone.

"I'll try. I don't have a car. Can I call you tomorrow?" Damn, the defeat crept in fast.

"Please do, and if you need it, I'll pick you up at your office."

"You're sure?" There was that slight bit of hope again.

"Of course. Just give me a call."

"Okay. Thanks." He could almost hear Maddoc's smile as he hung up, and Ivan closed his phone, finding himself smiling as well at the slight flutter he felt in his stomach. Turning on the radio, he got on the highway toward home.

It took about half an hour for Ivan to reach his condo. Parking in his spot, he walked toward his unit, unlocking the door and going inside. Throwing his keys on the table, he sat in the chair and turned on the television as his phone buzzed.

"Hi, Mom." He picked up the phone, knowing her ring.

"Ivanovich, you're alive." It was her usual taunt when he hadn't called her recently.

"Sorry, I've been a little busy lately." He hated excuses, but she deserved an explanation.

"Too busy to call your mother? What, it takes forever?" The familiar nag was perversely comforting.

"I'm sorry. I was out with some friends for dinner."

"On a date?" She sounded excited and hopeful.

"No, Mom. Just some friends."

"I could fix you up." Just what he needed—his mother fixing him up with all the gay sons of the women in her neighborhood, good Lord! He felt lucky his mother had been so supportive, and he knew she wanted him to be happy, but letting her find men for him was just too much.

"No thanks, Mom. I can find my own dates." He kept his voice light. He knew she was only trying to help. "I should be able to come by this weekend to see you. Is that okay?"

"I'll be here." They said their good nights and hung up. Ivan spent the rest of the evening watching television before shutting off the lights and walking to his bedroom.

IVAN'S phone rang a little after three the next afternoon. "Maddoc, is everything okay?"

"Yep. Is that offer of a ride still good?" Just the sound of his voice made Ivan smile.

"Of course. I know where your office is. I'll pick you up out front at about four."

"That'd be great, thank you."

"It's no problem." In fact, Ivan was more than a little pleased that Maddoc had actually asked him for help, even for something as small as this. Ivan knew that the kind of unwanted attention Maddoc had been receiving made it hard to trust or even ask for help of any kind. "Were there any more presents?" He hated to ask, but he'd been wondering all day if Maddoc was okay. He wasn't sure if it was his protective nature asserting itself or something else, but he'd been concerned and preoccupied for most of the day.

"No, thank goodness." Ivan's mind flashed on Maddoc's expression from the night before, and he silently berated himself for even bringing it up.

"Did they tow your car?"

"Yeah." An exasperated sigh came through the line. "But the mechanics won't be able to get to it for a few days. I should be able to get a loaner tomorrow."

"Good." Ivan's desk phone began to ring. "I've got to go, but I'll see you at four."

"Okay… and thanks."

Ivan hung up and answered the other phone before getting busy and completing his tasks for the day. But he couldn't get the redhead's scared expression from the night before out of his mind. Completing his last item of the day, he grabbed his bag, said good night to his coworkers, and hurriedly left the office.

A few minutes later, Ivan pulled up in front of the large office building and saw Maddoc step out the door, walk toward his car, and open the door. "I shouldn't have bothered you. I probably could have gotten a ride with Dan."

"It's not a problem, honest. I work just up the road in the industrial park." He didn't want to say that he'd have driven across town to pick him up. The last thing he wanted was to spook the man even more than he already was. "Besides, I promised you a Marine workout." Ivan smiled over at his passenger and saw a slight smile in return. "Are you sore from yesterday?" He put the car in gear and moved through the parking lot to the exit.

"Yeah." He watched Maddoc rub his chest. "It feels kind of good but a little tight. I didn't do anything very heavy, not like Dan and Lonnie."

"Don't worry, I won't work you too hard, but I can show you some basics that'll stick with you."

Maddoc rested in the plush seat as Ivan guided the car through traffic and into the gym parking lot. Getting out, they retrieved their bags and walked together into the club.

The locker room was crowded, and Ivan grabbed a locker, beginning to change. He could almost feel Maddoc's gaze on him, and he smiled to himself, pleased he was drawing the man's attention. He knew he turned heads, even at his age and with his gray hair, but until now, very few had turned *his* head, not in the way Maddoc had. But with everything going on in Maddoc's life, he couldn't act on it like he might have otherwise. The last thing he wanted Maddoc to think was that he was taking advantage of his vulnerability. That didn't stop him from sneaking a few furtive looks at the smaller man, with his light skin and that little butt that stretched those black briefs invitingly. God, he was cute.

Ivan pulled on his tank top and sat down to tie his shoes. "I'll meet you out there."

"Okay." Maddoc smiled up at him as he pulled on his shorts.

Ivan walked out into the workout area and saw Dan and Lonnie walking in together. He said hello as they passed and glanced up at the televisions as he waited. "Anything interesting?" Maddoc asked, joining him.

"No." He pulled his attention from the silent, flashing images. "Just waiting for you." Ivan led them to the padded floor mats. "We'll start with some stretching and then a brief warm-up to get our heart rates up."

"Okay. What do I do?"

"Stand near the pole and hold it with your hand." He watched as Maddoc did as he asked. "Now twist your upper body. Feel that in your chest?"

"Uh-huh. That feels really good."

"It should, after the workout you had yesterday. Now do the same thing with the other arm." He stretched as Maddoc finished up. "Now let's do your back." Ivan helped him through all the stretches, steadying him as he moved, and asked him to return the favor. "Would you hold my wrists?" He stretched his chest back, having Maddoc hold his wrists steady. He could feel the heat from Maddoc's smooth hands when they touched him, and he wanted to keep stretching just so he could keep Maddoc touching him. "Let's walk on a treadmill for five minutes to warm up."

They took two matching treadmills side by side, and Ivan made sure Maddoc's was set correctly. When they were done, he led them to a low bar. "What we're going to do are exercises that use your body weight. Normally I'd start with push-ups, but you did chest yesterday, so we'll start with rows for your back." He showed Maddoc how to do the exercise and then stood back, watching him perform the movements. "It's okay if you don't do many, as long as next time you do one more." When Maddoc was done, he took his turn, easily doing a set of twenty. "We'll do three of these and then move on."

"Hey, Dances with Dick." Lonnie strode over, grinning at his own witticism, and Ivan saw Maddoc smile, which was good.

"Lonnie, your mother just called," he heard Maddoc respond as he picked up Lonnie's cell phone from next to the machine Lonnie had been using. "She wants her butt back."

Dan joined them, laughing. "Man, that was a good one," Dan crooned as he patted Maddoc on the shoulder. "Damn, Lon, he got you bad." Ivan joined Dan and Maddoc as Lon tried to look at his own butt in the mirror, sending them all into renewed fits of laughter.

Damn, he never would have guessed that Maddoc had such a wickedly quick sense of humor. It was surprisingly nice. "You ready?" he asked. Maddoc nodded, and they started their next exercise. "Pull-ups are great for your overall upper body." Ivan demonstrated the movement.

Maddoc stood under the bar, looking up, eyes wide. "You've got to be kidding."

"Try it. If you only get a few, that's okay."

Maddoc nodded and reached up to the bar, giving it a try. "Well, that was pathetic." He groaned as he let go of the bar after four, and Ivan took his turn, pumping out twenty easily.

"Next time, bend your knees and I'll hold your feet. You should be able to get a few more." Maddoc looked at him skeptically, but did as he asked. Ivan held his ankles, the warmth of Maddoc's skin making his hands tingle. When he was done, Ivan felt his hand glance lightly along Maddoc's calf before pulling away. "You got six that time." He took his turn and then helped Maddoc again, finishing up the exercise before showing him a few more.

By the time they were done with their workout plus ten minutes of cardio, Ivan was tired. But Maddoc was flushed, eyes wide, breathing hard, and Ivan couldn't help wondering what he'd look like if he was doing those same things for a very different reason. "Are you doing—"

"Hey, homos—you going to dinner tonight?" Lonnie's voice carried across the gym, riding over Ivan's question.

Ivan looked at Lonnie, cursing the man's timing under his breath. "I think I'm busy tonight, but maybe later in the week." At least he hoped he was busy tonight, and he hoped that he'd be busy with Maddoc, but he wasn't sure how to ask him and he certainly didn't want to do it with Lonnie watching.

"You aren't going to dinner?" Maddoc asked, looking a little disappointed.

"Not with Lonnie." Ivan watched as Lonnie went into the locker room, leaving them alone temporarily. "But I was wondering if I could take you to dinner?"

"You mean just the two of us?" Maddoc looked around like he was making sure Ivan was talking to him. "Like a date?"

Ivan had never felt so nervous and unsure of himself in his life. He'd gone into battle with guns blasting, shells exploding, bombs falling, and sometimes his friends dying, but he'd never been as shaky as he was now. "Yes." Even with Gerald, they'd never really dated. Things were different. They'd just clicked and sort of fell into bed and then into each other's lives. "I'd like to take you on a date."

"Why don't you two just go somewhere and…." Lonnie stepped between them and began making obscene gestures that involved a lot of hip thrusts.

"Maybe later, but he needs to feed me first," Maddoc deadpanned, and Ivan watched Lonnie's energy deflate a little. Damn, the man was really quick. It took a few seconds for Maddoc's words to sink in. He must have been kidding.

Before Lonnie could retort, Maddoc smiled and stepped into the locker room. "Looks like you've met your match, bud," Ivan said with a smile and headed into the locker room as well, stopping when he saw Maddoc's naked butt as he stepped into a blue bathing suit. Trying not to leer, he went to his own locker and began stripping off his sweaty clothes before pulling on his own suit, grabbing his towel, and walking through to the whirlpool.

He'd hoped to see Maddoc, and he wasn't disappointed. "Is it hot?"

Maddoc sat in the bubbles, lounging like he had the day before. "Uh-huh." But this time, he saw Maddoc checking him out, and it made him smile as he lowered himself into the swirling water. "Would you go back in the Marines if you could?"

The question took him by surprise. He'd spent years wishing he'd stayed, wishing he could have stayed. "Not now. If things had been different, I'd like to have stayed in the Corps, but you can't go back. I wouldn't change it, but I wouldn't go back, either, if they changed the rules. How about you—if you had it to do over again, would you change anything?"

Maddoc's answer was fast. "No. I like my life." Ivan watched as Maddoc's expression changed. "I used to like my life, anyway, before…." Ivan watched Maddoc swallow around what must have been a huge lump in his throat, and he could almost visibly see the fun and confidence he'd shown earlier backing away. Maddoc became quiet, and Ivan wasn't sure what to do. His first instinct was to get angry, but that wouldn't help; the person responsible wasn't there.

"Instead of going out to dinner, would you like me to cook?"

That seemed to draw Maddoc out of himself, at least for a while. "You cook? Because I sure as hell can't."

"You better believe it."

He saw Maddoc smile and knew he'd made the right decision. "Then we'd better get moving if we want to eat before midnight."

"Would it be okay if we went to my house?" Maddoc asked.

"Sure. We'll stop at the store on the way," Ivan answered. Whatever allowed Maddoc to feel more comfortable was fine with him.

Maddoc stood up and climbed out of the tub. "I'll meet you out front in a few minutes?" Ivan nodded and watched Maddoc pad toward the locker room.

"You like him, don't you?" Ivan looked up and saw Dan and Gene slipping into the water.

"Yeah, I do. Is it too early to feel all weird about him?" Ivan asked as the newcomers settled in the water.

"How so?" Dan queried.

"I wish I knew."

Dan chuckled softly. "Don't question it; just go with it."

Ivan looked over at Gene and saw both of them go all gooey-eyed. He knew it was time to leave. Not that they'd do anything, but he suddenly felt like an intruder.

Ivan walked through the club, still a little warm, and saw Maddoc sitting in one of the chairs near the door, leg bouncing with what Ivan hoped was excitement that matched his own. His face was bright, eyes wide and cheeks slightly flushed, for a second he looked… like one of the newbies fresh out of college. "Are you ready?"

Maddoc stood up and grabbed his bag, following him to the car. "What's that?" He pointed toward the back window, and Ivan walked closer and saw it was a flower caught in the edge of the trunk lid. He snatched at it and threw it on the pavement as they both looked around the parking lot.

"I'm getting so tired of this," Maddoc said, sighing softly. "They're following me."

Ivan saw Maddoc start to shake and dropped his bag, pulling the smaller man into a hug. All the doubts he'd felt earlier had been overwhelmed by the helpless look on Maddoc's face.

"It's okay." The man felt good in his arms, too good. This wasn't how he was supposed to react right now, but he could feel Maddoc's heat against his skin and he felt his body start to respond. Pushing those thoughts away as best he could, he concentrated his attention on comfort and support. "Look." He backed away and pointed to another car a few parking spaces down, "There's one on that car too." Maddoc lifted his head and looked to where Ivan was pointing. Multiple cars in the lot had flowers on either their back windows or their windshields.

He felt Maddoc relax and pull away. "I'm sorry," he said softly as he wiped his eyes, "I don't…."

"It's all right. I thought the same thing you did." Unlocking the door, he put his bag in the tiny back seat before sliding down the soft leather of his driver's seat. Maddoc closed his door and stared quietly out the window. "You don't have anything to be ashamed of, you know," Ivan said. "Someone's doing this to you. It's not your fault."

"My head knows that, but I keep wondering what I did." He didn't turn away, and Ivan was thankful for that. "Maybe I led someone on without knowing it…. I…."

Ivan turned in his seat, facing his passenger. "You didn't do anything. Someone's harassing you, and it's not your fault."

"But how do I make it stop?" The helplessness in Maddoc's plea tore at Ivan's heart like nothing before. He'd seen things that he never wanted to remember, but this man's pain shot right to his gut. He'd only known him two days, but he could keenly feel Maddoc's confusion and sorrow as though it was his own. He'd spent years insulating himself from these feelings, and this adorable redhead shot right through all the defenses he'd built up after Gerald died.

"We'll figure something out." The offer of help was out before he could even think about it. Someone had to help, and if Maddoc would accept it, Ivan would try to help him. "Let's get to the store. You'll feel better on a full stomach." Starting the car, he drove to the market, and they got what he needed for dinner before putting the top down and speeding toward Maddoc's house with the air rushing around them. The exuberant fun lasted until they pulled up in front of Maddoc's house, and he heard his passenger gasp.

Multiple bouquets of pink roses rested all over the porch floor and around the door. The display would have been stunningly beautiful if the whole situation hadn't been so creepy. "What the hell?"

Maddoc opened the door and slowly walked toward the porch. "They… they…." Ivan followed him as he walked around to the side of the house. "They cut down my roses." Maddoc pointed to naked branches that had been what looked like tall, flowing rose bushes. "Goddamn them!" Maddoc raced back to the porch, ripping down the blooms, throwing them on the sidewalk before stomping on them. "If you can hear me, I've had enough, you sick bastard!" he yelled into the quiet night.

Ivan didn't know what to do but thought it best to let Maddoc get it out of his system. The man had been through a lot and had most likely kept it all bottled up. He'd seen it before on the battlefield and knew the best thing to do was to let him get it all out. Maddoc disappeared around the corner of the house, returning with a large trash barrel, and ripped down more of the flowers, throwing each one in the trash.

"Feeling better?" Ivan asked as he watched Maddoc throw the last bloom in the now-full can.

"Yes… no… fuck. I don't know what I feel. I raised those plants from cuttings I took from the house after my dad died."

"They'll come back." Ivan bent down and examined the stalks. "There are still some leaves. They may look funny for a while, but they're not dead."

"You know plants?" Maddoc knelt down to look where he'd indicated.

"After I was discharged, I decided to spend my time making things grow." He left out the part where he'd seen enough destruction to last a lifetime. He didn't think Maddoc needed to hear that right now. Standing up, he touched Maddoc on the shoulder. "Let's get you inside." He could tell Maddoc's adrenaline was wearing off and figured the fear would start to rear its head again. "I promised you a nice dinner, and I intend to deliver."

Silently, Maddoc nodded and walked back around to the front, opening the door and leading them inside. "I guess I should be grateful they haven't tried to get inside." He set his keys on the hall table. "The kitchen's in back." He pointed to the door at the rear of the hall.

"I'll bring in the things." Ivan left the house and retrieved the bag of groceries. Moving through the house to the kitchen, Ivan was glad he'd planned comfort food. Maddoc wandered in behind him, showing him where things were located. "I got pasta and thought I'd make pesto with chicken."

Ivan knew he'd chosen correctly when he heard the small happy humming sound Maddoc made. "Can I help?"

"Sure. Put a large pan of water on the stove and get it heating." It took him a few minutes, but he figured out where things were and got the chicken cooking. "I should have gotten some wine."

"I have a few bottles." Maddoc opened a door that appeared to go to the basement, returning with a bottle in each hand. "I wasn't sure which would work." Maddoc set them on the counter and got the corkscrew. "Which one do you think?"

"This one should go nicely."

Maddoc opened the indicated bottle with a pop and got a pair of glasses, pouring them each one before pulling up a stool, watching as Ivan cooked, sipping his wine. "I hate this." Ivan stopped moving until Maddoc explained. "Feeling scared all the time, and it's getting worse. I just don't know what to do." Maddoc rested his forehead on the counter. "God," he moaned as he lifted his head again. "Here I am with a nice guy, and all I can talk about"—he bobbed his head toward the front door—"is that crap."

"Dinner's almost ready," Ivan said lightly, letting a hand slide along Maddoc's arm.

"I'll set the table." Maddoc slid off the stool, and Ivan watched that tight backside as it moved around the room.

A popping sound pulled his attention back to his cooking, and he turned off the heat. Cutting up the chicken, he added it to the pesto pasta and began filling the plates and bringing them to the table. "I guess the thing we need to do is try to figure out who could be doing this." He placed a plate at each of their places. "Have you gotten flowers anywhere else?"

"I thought I found one on my car at the gym yesterday, but I'm not sure." Ivan watched as Maddoc took his first bite and smiled at his blissful expression. "This is heavenly."

"Thanks." Ivan took his own bite and had to agree, for store-bought pesto, it wasn't bad. "My fresh pesto's better." Even if he did say so himself.

"Then it must be amazing, because this is fantastic." Ivan smiled as Maddoc shoveled in the food like he hadn't eaten in days. They'd worked up an appetite at the gym, but good God, could this guy eat.

Returning to the earlier topic, Ivan said, "Let's not rule out anything, and assume whoever's stalking you is either following you or knows your schedule." Ivan saw Maddoc's reluctant nod. "Are there people you see both at home and at the gym?"

He tried to think but nothing came to mind. "Not really."

"Is there anyone new in the neighborhood?" Maddoc shook his head as he chewed. "Did something change about the time you started receiving the flowers?"

"I got a promotion at work. But I doubt that has anything to do with it." Maddoc kept eating, and Ivan grinned as the smaller man cleaned his plate and got up to get some more. "This is really good," Maddoc commented as he heaped more on his plate and returned to the table.

"Is there someone else who wanted the promotion you got?" Ivan asked between bites, watching as Maddoc continued eating.

"I don't think so. It really seems to me like it's someone from town. Things often show up early in the morning, like they either bring them late at night, or just before I leave for work." Maddoc swallowed and yawned. "Sorry. I haven't been sleeping really well. I hear noises and worry that it's them."

"I understand." Ivan got up and put the dirty dishes in the sink. "Where are your plastic containers?" Maddoc pointed to a cupboard, and Ivan put the leftovers away in the refrigerator. "I should let you get some sleep." He stepped to where Maddoc was leaning against the counter.

Moving slowly, giving Maddoc time to react, he leaned forward and lightly touched their lips together. "I'll call you tomorrow."

"Okay." Maddoc followed him to the door, and Ivan saw the same fearful look he'd seen the night before.

"Do you trust me?" Ivan asked, to his own surprise, and smiled when Maddoc nodded slowly. "Then you go up to bed, and I'll stay here." He indicated the large chair in the living room. "Is there a place out of sight I can move my car?"

"Yeah, but you can't sleep in the chair." The look on Maddoc's face was priceless.

"I've slept in holes in the ground and even sitting up in a moving tank. I can sleep in a living room chair. Besides, if you have a visitor, I'm hoping to catch him."

"You don't have to do that." Maddoc's face was a study in slightly masked confusion.

"I know I don't. But somebody has to get this guy, maybe even scare some sense into him."

Ivan watched Maddoc's eyes as his emotions warred behind them. "If you're sure." He still seemed so tentative.

"I'll move the car and be right back." Ivan opened the door and tugged Maddoc close. "If you're being watched, let's give them a show." Leaning forward, he took Maddoc's mouth, his lips tasting the soft sweetness of Maddoc's for a few seconds before letting the man go. "I'll be right back."

Ivan stepped outside and sneaked a final glimpse at Maddoc's flushed face before the door closed softly behind him. Striding down the walk, he got into the car and drove away, parking in the next block and walking through dark yards before knocking on the back door.

He saw a shock of red hair in the window, and then the door opened. "You scared me."

"Sorry, but if you were being watched, I didn't want to be seen coming back." Maddoc shut and locked the door behind him. "Go on up to bed. You look like you're about to fall over."

Maddoc nodded and said good night, walking up the stairs. "Thank you." The man was so tired he could barely keep his eyes open. Ivan went to the living room and saw a couple blankets and a pillow on the chair. Smiling to himself, he settled into the plush chair after turning off the lights.

In the darkness, his senses came alive just like they had years earlier. Footsteps upstairs sounded as clear as if Maddoc were in the room with him. Water running, a squirrel chattering outside, the sound of a car passing, even the squeak as Maddoc got into bed. He couldn't help picturing what Maddoc looked like. Did he sleep naked? The thought was distracting, and he brought his thoughts back to the present. He had a job to do, and maybe if he took care of this guy, he'd have a chance to find out if his imagination was right. Resting back in the chair, he willed his mind to settle as he half-dozed in the chair.

III

MADDOC tossed and turned for a while, thinking about Ivan and listening to the house, but everything sounded normal. His eyes eventually got heavy, and he drifted off to sleep.

He woke to the sound of the front door slamming shut, and he was out of bed and on his way down the stairs before he could think of anything. Downstairs, he rushed to the door and peeked out into the night, but saw nothing. Checking the living room, he saw a pillow by the chair and a blanket pooled on the floor. Flipping on the front lights, he watched out the windows until he saw movement along the front walk. As the figure stepped into the light, he raced to the door and opened it. "Are you okay?"

Ivan stepped into the house, and he shut the door. "I'm fine. Bastard got away." He was barely breathing hard, and Maddoc followed him into the living room. "I heard footsteps on the porch and snuck to the door. But it was dark, and as soon as I opened the door, he took off. I chased him through the yard and down the street, but he disappeared in the empty lot, probably hiding, and I didn't want to leave you alone."

"Did you see whoever it was?"

"A little bit. It was definitely a man, medium height and weight, probably younger than us and rather fit. The guy took off like a shot, and I couldn't match his speed." He looked embarrassed. "I must be getting older."

"We all are." Maddoc sighed softly. "And right now, every muscle in my body is telling me just how old I am." He saw Ivan's eyes sweep over him, and he peered down, remembering he was wearing nothing but his underwear.

"Looks pretty good from where I'm standing."

"What do you say we put the old guys to bed?" Maddoc locked the door and held out his hand. Ivan took it, and Maddoc led his protector up the stairs. Without saying anything, Maddoc walked toward his bedroom and slid beneath the covers, watching Ivan as shoes thunked on the floor, a shirt was pulled overhead, and pants slid down powerful legs. Maddoc couldn't take his eyes off the figure moving in the dark room. He couldn't see details, but what he saw was pretty amazing.

Ivan walked to the other side of the bed, and Maddoc felt the covers lift, and then the bed dipped and warm skin slid against him. Rolling over, Maddoc nestled against Ivan's shoulder, and strong arms pulled him close. Lips touched his forehead, and a hand stroked along his back. He wanted to stay awake and get to know the body next to him, but for the first time in weeks, he fell into a deep sleep, the sound of Ivan's breathing like a lullaby.

He woke to a bright room, an arm around him, a hand against his stomach, and hips pressed to his butt. Maddoc's alarm sounded, and he jumped slightly before reaching to the nightstand and silencing the electronic intruder.

Maddoc knew he had to get up, but he didn't want to move. Ivan felt so good next to him. "Just relax a few minutes." Ivan's voice was deep and raspy with sleep. "This feels too nice to rush." Maddoc could echo that as Ivan pulled him closer, and he felt a sizable length press against him, and a warm hand rubbed small circles over his chest and belly.

It had been quite some time since he'd woken with anyone in his bed, and Maddoc suddenly realized how much he'd missed it. The quiet moments together, the closeness—that was what he missed most of all. Ivan moved behind him, his hand slipping away, and then the warmth dissipated as Ivan got out of bed and began moving through the room. Rolling over, Maddoc watched as Ivan pulled on his pants. Slipping from under the covers, he walked to him, doing nothing to hide his excitement. He wanted Ivan to know the effect he had on him just like he'd known the effect he was having on the handsome man. "Thank you." He slipped his arms around Ivan's waist and rested his head against the strong man's shoulder.

"You're welcome." He felt a warm hand slide over his back as Ivan's musky scent filled his nose, making him almost painfully hard. "I hate to bring this up, but if we don't get moving, you're not going to make it to work." The hand on his back slipped lower, ghosting lightly over his butt. Then Ivan pulled back, pushing him lightly toward the bathroom. "You need to get cleaned up."

Maddoc glanced at Ivan's face, making sure this wasn't a rejection, but saw what looked like a struggle for control. Doing as requested, he disappeared into the bathroom, going through his morning ritual before emerging to dress. Alone in the room, Maddoc pulled on his clothes and walked downstairs to the kitchen, hoping to see Ivan, but it was dark and empty. Moving through the house, he saw the blankets folded on the chair with the pillow stacked on top. His heart fell to the floor when he realized that Ivan was no longer in the house. "Couldn't wait to get away I guess." Turning around, he wandered back to the kitchen to get ready for work.

The front door opening made him jump slightly before stilling.

"It's just me. I moved my car around front."

"I'm such a girl," Maddoc muttered to himself as he poured two cups of coffee.

"What?" Ivan asked as he walked into the room.

"Nothing," Maddoc responded as he handed him a mug, noticing the "how'd you know" look and hoping the coffee, which he knew was the Marines' nectar of the gods, would distract him. "Dad always said the Marine Corps ran on black coffee, guts, and sweat." He sipped his coffee and set the mug on the counter. "Would you like something to eat?"

Ivan shook his head as he drank, eyes closed, much to Maddoc's amusement. "I need to go home to change after I drop you off."

"I'll be ready in a minute, then." He set his mug on the counter and made sure he had everything all set before finishing his coffee. "Ready when you are."

"Not quite." To his surprise, Ivan backed him against the counter and kissed him. Where last night's had been soft, this one was harder, more forceful, and definitely hotter. "Now I think we're ready."

"Uh-huh." Maddoc waited until the weakness in his knees subsided before getting his things and following Ivan out the front door, locking it behind him. "No gifts," he said with a smile as he bounced down the steps.

"I think I put a pretty good scare into him." Ivan unlocked the car, and Maddoc put his things in back before sliding into the seat.

"Do you think he's gone?" Maddoc asked hopefully.

"Maybe, but I wouldn't count on it." Ivan shut his door and started the car. "I may have scared him away or just made him mad. I'm sorry, but I may have made things worse."

Maddoc smiled. "Are you kidding? I actually slept last night for the first time in weeks." The car began moving into traffic. "And I don't feel so scared now." He was still nervous about what else they'd do, but Ivan's actions last night had given him a real shot in the arm. This guy, whoever he was, wasn't infallible, and Ivan had almost caught him. That alone made him feel better.

They sped down the freeway, the sun peeking above the mountains. "Are you coming to the gym?"

"Yeah." He smiled at his companion.

"Will you need a ride?" There was a hopeful look in Ivan's eyes, and Maddoc wondered for a second if he was hoping his car wouldn't be ready.

"I don't think so. They should be able to get to it today, and they said they could provide a loaner if they were still backed up."

Ivan pulled into the parking lot of Maddoc's office. "If you need a ride, call me. Otherwise I'll see you at the gym." The leather creaked as Ivan leaned over and gave him a soft kiss. "Have a good day." After that kiss, how could he have anything but?

Maddoc unbuckled his seat belt and grabbed his bags from the back. Walking into the building, he watched Ivan speed away and touched his lip as the door closed behind him.

"MADDOC." A hand waved in front of his face. "You okay?" Maddoc snapped out of his daydream, swiveling his chair as Kyle smiled back at him. "You seem a million miles away."

"Sorry." He half smiled as he again thought of what had him so distracted.

"I was wondering if you needed a ride home?" Kyle lived near him and had been nice enough to drive him in to work before.

"No, thanks. I'm good. The dealership agreed to deliver my car since they took so long to get to it."

"Did they say what was wrong?"

"Just the battery, but they're so backed up, it took them a few days." Maddoc was just happy he'd have his car and his mobility back.

"Okay. I'll let you get back to work and whatever it was you were thinking about." The smirk on his friend's face spoke volumes.

The rest of the workday was quiet for a Friday, and he left on time, climbing into his car. It felt good to have it back, but his sedate sedan was nowhere near as much fun as Ivan's convertible. Starting the engine, he pulled out and drove to the gym with an excitement he never thought he'd have felt going to a health club. Pulling out his bag, he shut the door and whistled as he walked to the club and reached for the door.

"I see you made it."

He knew that voice. Turning around, he looked into Ivan's eyes. "I was looking forward to it all day," he said truthfully, although if it was the gym or the chance to see Ivan, he really couldn't say, and he didn't really care. "What are we doing today?"

"We're taking it easy today. You've had a heavy workout for the last few days, and I don't want you overdoing it." They scanned their cards and went to the locker room to change, and as soon as he stepped out of the locker room, Maddoc found himself engulfed in a hug.

"I thought that was you." The slip of a girl stepped back.

"Lisa." He grinned as he recognized the radiant black hair, bright smile, and deep, almost black eyes. "I didn't know you were a member." He stood back. "Jesus, you're amazing. You must live here." He grinned at her and got one of her radiant smiles in return.

"I don't look like that at all." She slapped Maddoc's arm lightly. He knew her well enough to know that she didn't see herself as pretty, even though she was stunning. "What brings you here?" At that moment Ivan walked out of the locker room, and Maddoc couldn't help following with his eyes. "I see." She winked at him. "You have good taste." Lisa leaned closer and said, "But I didn't know he was gay."

"He is." Maddoc gave her another hug and waved as he followed Ivan through the gym.

"Have fun," she called after him before hopping on a treadmill.

Just watching Ivan move sent a warmth through him like he'd never experienced before. Maddoc had had other men in his life, but none had made him feel this way. It scared him and thrilled him at the same time. Ivan did something to him that he couldn't quite understand. "So what are we doing today?" He had to get his head on straight.

"I thought we'd try something different, if you're up to it." Ivan opened the door to the gymnasium portion of the club. "Usually this is full of kids playing basketball, but it seems to be empty, so I thought I'd show you some self-defense moves."

"Oh." Maddoc wasn't sure he could fight anyone, not really.

"You don't have to fight." Ivan chuckled as if he could read his mind. "But if something happens, you should know what to do to give yourself time to get away."

"Okay." He looked around. "Don't we need mats or something?"

"I'm not going to throw you around." Ivan moved closer. "Unless you want me to." Ivan leered at him playfully, and Maddoc began laughing.

"Maybe later."

"Okay." The leer was back. "We can get some mats from the aerobics studio and get started." Working together, they dragged four padded mats into the gym and laid them out on the floor. "Take off your shoes."

Maddoc slipped off his sneakers and stood in the center of the pads. "What do you want me to do?"

"Nothing for the moment." Ivan joined him on the mat, facing him and smiling. "Don't look so nervous. I'm not going to hurt you at all. This isn't *The Karate Kid*— no punches or kicks, and you won't be throwing me to the mat, either. That's a bunch of Hollywood crap."

"How about you throwing me to the mat?" Maddoc teased.

"Nope." Ivan looked around as if contemplating something. "Well, maybe." He turned into a whirl of movement, and Maddoc found himself flat on his back, looking up at the ceiling with Ivan looming over him. "You looked too good to resist."

"I did, huh?" His head was spinning a little as he made sure nothing hurt. It didn't. Ivan reached out his hand and pulled him to his feet. "I'm not going to teach you that, but there are things I can show you that'll allow you to protect yourself."

"Okay."

"First thing is that you need to know the tender spots." Maddoc nodded, listening intently. "Did you ever see the movie *Miss Congeniality*?"

Maddoc nodded, smiling. "You mean when she beats the guy up during the pageant? Yeah, I love that part."

"What she said was accurate. S. I. N. G." Ivan reached toward him. "Solar plexus, instep, nose, groin. If you can punch or elbow someone in the solar plexus, right here"—Ivan demonstrated, making Maddoc squirm and try to get away—"you'll knock the wind out of them and they won't be able to breathe for a few seconds. The instep works great as well. Someone hopping around because you mashed their foot isn't going to be able to chase you very well. The nose will break if you hit it hard enough, and the body's reflex is to grab the nose when it's hit, so they'll release you if they've got their arms around you." Maddoc nodded, trying to take everything in. "I want to talk about the groin." Maddoc raised his eyebrows questioningly. "Not yours, although it's very nice, from what I felt last night." Maddoc colored. "Behave. When you're attacked, you use everything at your disposal. There's no such thing as fighting like a gentleman. You go for anything that's available." Ivan moved in front of him. "If he has you from behind, use your fist." He demonstrated with just the lightest touch that made Maddoc's dick stand up despite the material being covered. "If he's got you from the front, like this"—he demonstrated on Maddoc—"move your hand slightly and squeeze, twist, and yank with everything you've got. I can guarantee they'll let you go and reach immediately for their balls."

Ivan stood back, letting Maddoc go. "It's important that as soon as they do, you take off as fast as you can, yelling at the top of your lungs, 'Call 911'." Maddoc began to laugh. "I know it sounds cliché, but people will react to that even if they don't know what's going on."

"What are you fudge packers doing?" The door banged closed and Lonnie strode over, followed by Dan and Gene, both of them shaking their heads. "No offense."

Ivan showed great restraint and ignored the comment, but Maddoc didn't. "None taken, you limp-dicked breeder." Both Dan and Gene howled with laughter as Lonnie shook his head.

"I'm showing Maddoc some ways to protect himself," Ivan explained.

"Looked more like buttsex foreplay to me." Lonnie grinned and stepped back off the mat.

"In your dreams," Maddoc crooned as he turned his attention back to Ivan.

"Gene, would you help us?" Ivan asked the huge man, and he stepped forward. "Grab him from behind." Gene put his arms around him, holding him firmly. "Don't hurt him, but touch the areas we talked about," Ivan instructed.

Maddoc thought it a little silly, but even in Gene's strong grip, he could move enough to elbow his side, and since his legs were free, stomp his foot. He didn't go for the nose or groin, but he could do it.

"See, it's not a matter of size or strength, but of surprise." Ivan stepped forward, and Gene let him go. "Thanks, Gene."

"No problem." He stepped off the mat. "I'll see you guys later." He and Dan wandered away with Lonnie following behind.

"You ladies coming to dinner?" Lonnie called from the door. Before they could answer, the door banged closed behind him, and they both shook their heads in wonder.

"The element of surprise can't be underestimated. You may only get a few seconds, so don't look, just run. Knee the guy in the nuts"—he lifted his knee slowly—"and then run like hell." Maddoc nodded, his concentration returning to the lesson.

Ivan spent the better part of an hour showing him basic moves and then helping him practice. A few times, Maddoc found his hand full of Ivan's substantial package, and each time he could feel himself blush. "What are you so shy about? You've already felt me up in the showers."

"That was an accident," Maddoc replied indignantly, the flush returning to his cheeks.

"There are no accidents," Ivan replied as he winked at him. "I think we're done here. Let's put the mats away and go clean up."

"Thank God. I wasn't sure I could make it through another workout like yesterday."

"Not today, but I'm not letting you off so easily tomorrow." Ivan's smile faded slightly. "I have an appointment tonight, but I was wondering if you'd like to meet me at the gym tomorrow morning at about ten. We could work out and then go for lunch." Ivan trailed off. "Shit! I forgot. I promised my mom I'd see her tomorrow. We can still have lunch together, unless you'd like to go with me."

"To meet your mother? You want me to meet your mother?" Maddoc didn't know if he should be scared or exceedingly honored. "Does she know about...?"

Ivan burst into rich laughter. "God yes. My mother actually tried to fix me up. Before we immigrated, the women in my family were matchmakers, and my mother's got the bug bad." Ivan became serious. "You don't have to, but I'd sort of like you to meet her."

"Okay." He was game for just about anything, as long as it involved spending more time with Ivan. "I'd like to meet your mother."

"Then how about if I pick you up at your house in the morning. We can go to the gym and then I can take both you and my mom to lunch." Ivan picked up half the mats and began stacking them where they belonged.

"That'd be great." Because Ivan would need to drop him off afterward, and his mind flashed on all the possibilities.

"Then I'll see you tomorrow?" Ivan walked closer to him with a sort of feral look on his face. Maddoc found himself backing away until he bumped into the wall with a thud, a pair of strong arms pinning him there.

Maddoc couldn't hold back a small gasp as Ivan leaned closer and kissed him. "Just so you know, I would rather spend the rest of the evening with you." The way Ivan took his lips left little doubt as to his veracity. Maddoc's knees began to buckle as Ivan plundered his mouth with lips and tongue before pulling away. "I just wanted to be clear."

Maddoc blinked a few times in utter amazement. "Oh, you were."

"Good. I'll see you in the morning." Maddoc could only nod feebly as his lips were taken a final time. "And please call me if something happens, okay?"

"I will. I promise." Just knowing that Ivan wanted to help him gave him a strength he hadn't felt a few days earlier. "You'll be the first."

Ivan seemed happy with that response and let Maddoc go. They both walked into the locker room to clean up. Once he'd changed clothes, Maddoc talked awhile with Dan and Gene before leaving the club and heading home.

Pulling up to the house, he released a breath when he saw that his porch seemed untouched: no flowers and no notes. Wandering through his yard, he looked at his naked rose bushes and silently agreed with Ivan that they would probably survive but would look weird until they grew in. Finishing his walk through the yard, he admired his gardens before walking back around to the front.

"Maddoc."

"Hey, Jerry." Turning around, he saw one of his neighbors.

"I heard you had some excitement last night." Jerry walked up to the base of the steps. "Was someone trying to break in?" He stepped closer, and Maddoc found himself backing away, feeling a little uncomfortable.

"Word gets around fast." Maddoc backed up further, putting his bag in front of him to provide some distance.

"It's not often that someone gets chased through the neighborhood in the middle of the night."

Maddoc crinkled his brow. "How did you know that?" He suddenly got this jittery feeling in his stomach and wanted to get out of there.

"I saw them running when I was getting home last night." Now that he could believe. Jerry was a notorious drinker, and neighborhood gossip had it that he spent a lot more time in the bars than he should. "A guy ran in front of my truck, and I nearly hit him as I was rounding the corner." Jerry pointed as he continued his story.

Maddoc wasn't completely convinced and made a note to himself to find out if there was someone on the road when Ivan had chased the guy away. He really didn't think it was Jerry, they'd been near-neighbors for years, but it wouldn't hurt to ask. "I have to take care of a few things." Maddoc suddenly had an overriding urge to get away. Maybe he was just seeing things, but he wasn't feeling comfortable right now. "I'll see you later." He turned around and caught his foot on the step, stumbling up the stairs and against the door. Jerry rushed up and helped him to his feet, taking his arm. Maddoc nearly wrenched his arm away but restrained himself, muttering a thank-you as he got himself inside and shut the door, dropping his bag on the floor.

A knock a few minutes later had him jumping. Looking out the window, he saw his neighbor Corky peeking back at him. Calming his racing heart, he opened the door.

"Are you okay?" Maddoc stepped back and she walked inside, using her cane. "I saw Jerry leaving and heard about your excitement last night."

"I'm fine." Remembering his manners, he offered her a chair in the living room. "Would you like a cup of coffee or tea?" He could certainly use something.

"Coffee would be nice." Her eyes twinkled. "Irish would be better."

Maddoc went to the kitchen to put on a cup of coffee, grinning the entire time. Corky was an absolute gem. Getting the coffee maker going, he pulled out mugs and put a splash of whiskey in Corky's cup before pouring the coffee and rejoining her in the living room. "Here you go." He set her mug on the coffee table and settled on the sofa. "So what's the rumor?" he asked as he sipped from his mug.

She lifted her mug and then set it back down. "I've been worried about you," she confided. "Henry from across the street said that someone was chased across your yard last night, and I saw your rose bushes and knew you'd never do that to them. What's been happening?" She sipped her coffee and made a face.

"Is something wrong?" Maddoc asked, surprised.

"There's whiskey in here." She set the mug down.

He was totally confused and got up to take her mug. "It's what you asked for."

"Dear, that was for you." She picked up the mug and handed it to him. "I figured you could use it." She settled back in the chair. "So what's been happening?"

He figured *what the hell,* and told her everything. "At first, I was getting flowers from someone, and secret admirer type notes. I think whoever sent them figures I should know who they are."

"And you don't." It wasn't a question.

"Heavens, no. Then they started sending dead flowers, and then just the stems, and the notes kept coming." He tried to keep himself from reliving the fear he'd experienced each time he'd come home to another threat. "Then yesterday, someone cut down my roses and put them all over the porch." He couldn't keep the loss out of his voice. "A friend stayed at the house last night and heard him trying to leave another message and chased him through the neighborhood."

"A friend, huh? Is this a really good friend?" She leaned forward, expecting more.

Maddoc wasn't ready to tell anyone about Ivan. He wasn't even sure there was anything to tell. "He's a friend from the gym. He used to be a Marine." He tried, but he couldn't keep the happiness out of his voice. Just thinking of Ivan was enough to put a smile on his face. "He was the one who chased the guy."

"I'm glad he did," she replied, and Maddoc used the opportunity to change the subject. He and Corky talked for a while about general neighborhood gossip, thankfully avoiding the subject of Maddoc's stalker.

After a while, she used her cane to help stand up. "I'll keep an eye on things while you're at work." She walked toward the door, her cane barely touching the floor. Maddoc had thought for years that the cane was a prop, either that or a weapon. "I hope your friend chasing him was enough to scare this guy off for good." She said goodbye and kissed him on the cheek before leaving the house. As Maddoc waited on the porch, he hoped she was right, but something told him this wasn't over. As she crossed his yard, he looked over at the Henry's. The curtains were drawn, light peeking around the edges. Corky had said that Henry had told her about the excitement the night before. *The man was a little quiet....* "Jesus Christ.... This has got to stop. I'm starting to suspect everyone." Stopping himself from going down that path, he walked to his front door.

IV

IVAN grinned like an idiot as he drove toward Maddoc's house on Saturday morning, checking to make sure he had his phone in his pocket. Ever since he'd left Maddoc the night before, he'd kept his phone next to him. When his mother had called to confirm that he was coming, he'd jumped out of his skin, afraid that something had happened to Maddoc. Pulling up to the house, he parked and walked up the walk: no flowers on the porch, and the yard looked the same.

Ringing the bell, Ivan smiled when the door opened and Maddoc stood looking back at him. Without thinking, Ivan found himself stepping forward, hands on Maddoc's neck, kissing the man for all he was worth. Maddoc's firm lips stood up to the onslaught, and Ivan found himself gasping as Maddoc's tongue slid into his mouth. Kicking the door closed, he began moving both of them toward the stairs, but Maddoc broke the kiss, gasping, "Please, I can't," and stepped back slightly.

Ivan didn't know what he'd done. "Is something wrong?" Confusion and doubt invaded his lust-clouded mind. Maddoc looked embarrassed and turned away. Ivan reached toward him and touched his shoulder. "Tell me what's wrong."

"Can we go in the living room?" The tension and fear in Maddoc's voice made Ivan swallow around the lump in his throat as he followed behind and sat in the chair he'd slept in a few nights earlier. "It's not that I don't want to be intimate with you, but I can't. Not yet." Maddoc took a deep breath and blew it out. "I've had boyfriends, some of them lasting a while, but...." It looked like Maddoc was shaking. "I like you, I really do, but I always got physical with the guys I liked, and they never stayed around for long. So I promised myself that if I ever met someone I really liked again, I'd wait the next time. I know I sort of led you on the other night, and I'm sorry, but I just need to take it a little slower." Maddoc looked over at him, and Ivan knew he was expecting him to run for the door.

Standing up, he walked to the sofa and sat down next to him. "We'll take things as slow as you like." He saw Maddoc relax a little. "I like you, too, and I'm willing to wait." He moved closer. "We'll limit our activities to the kissing and touching variety if that's what you're comfortable with." He watched Maddoc's eyes as he moved closer until he picked up where they'd left off, with a kiss that short-circuited his brain. The little moans and gasps that Maddoc made went right to his dick, and he slowly pulled back, breathing heavily as he kept himself under control.

Ivan's dick throbbed in his pants at the first touch of Maddoc's lips. He knew he should stop this torture, but he couldn't. His instinct-driven brain drew him closer. Fingers wound through Maddoc's red curls as he deepened the kiss. Small mewling noises from deep in Maddoc's throat told him he was enjoying this just as much as Ivan was. Ignoring practicality and reason, he slipped a knee between Maddoc's and got a sharp gasp when he felt a hard length slide along his hip. This was what his body called out for, what he really wanted. Ivan's tongue thrust deep and his cock throbbed with each movement, desperately wanting to get in on the action.

Something deep inside, probably his Marine training kicking in, he wasn't sure what, pulled him back from his passion-induced haze, breaking their kiss. Ivan looked at Maddoc's lust-hazed eyes, tousled hair, and kissed-red mouth. His body urged him forward to claim the man. It was funny to Ivan. In the Corps, he'd never understood how his buddies could become so possessive of wives and girlfriends. He hadn't felt that way with Gerald, but that's exactly how he felt with Maddoc. "We need to go to the gym, or I'm not going to be able to keep my promise." His breathing ragged, he forced himself to look away from Maddoc, but he couldn't for long.

Maddoc moved around him, giving him a wide berth, and bent over to pick up his bag. The jeans Maddoc was wearing tightened around that firm, small butt, and it took all Ivan's resolve not to move toward him as his dick did its best to try and split his pants open.

Jesus, when did I turn into such a caveman? Walking was slightly painful, and Ivan adjusted himself before following Maddoc out the front door and down the walk to his car.

Starting the engine, he pulled away and turned onto the main street and then entered the freeway. Ivan's thoughts kept racing to the man sitting next to him and he had to force his attention onto the road, letting his training from long ago center himself and his attention.

"You don't have to do this. I'll understand." Maddoc's voice cut through Ivan's thoughts, and he turned to glance at his passenger. Maddoc nervously chewed on a fingernail, shifting in his seat.

"You'll understand what?"

"If you don't want to date any more. I know I'm asking a lot." The hand pulled away from his mouth, but joined the other one fidgeting in his lap. *Where had this come from?* Putting on his blinker, Ivan pulled off to the side of the freeway, putting on his hazard lights.

Popping off his seatbelt, Ivan twisted in his seat. "There's nothing to understand. You're worth waiting for." His heart was drawn to Maddoc, and a little time was a small price to pay. Reaching out, his fingers carded through red curls, slowly pulling him closer. "Don't get me wrong, Maddoc. I want you... bad." Ivan brought their lips within inches of each other. "I want to feel you from head to toe, run my tongue over every inch of you, and I want to mark you so everyone will know you're mine." *God, where was this coming from?* He'd only known Maddoc a few days, and yet the words were out before he could stop them. "I want to bury myself so deep inside you we can feel each other's heartbeats." He ran a thumb over Maddoc's quivering lower lip.

"You got so quiet before," Maddoc explained nervously.

"Only because I was thinking." Ivan smiled. "And trying to keep the car from running off the road." Taking Maddoc's hand, he placed it on his lap. "That's what you do to me." He saw the redhead smile. "No one can fake that, not even a Marine." He let their mouths get closer, Maddoc's warm breath tingling his lips. "So you take your time. It's important that you feel comfortable and ready when we express our feelings physically." Ivan moved a fraction of an inch closer, letting their lips touch before pulling back. "Now, for the rest of the ride, you need to keep your cuteness to yourself, or otherwise when I change clothes, my dick will still be pointing in your direction, and that could be embarrassing." He could feel his cheeks heating, and that never happened.

Maddoc snorted. "Well, you'd have one hell of an audience." He put his hand over his mouth and began to laugh. "They'll probably give you a standing ovation." Ivan joined in Maddoc's mirth and put the car in gear, speeding them down the freeway toward the gym.

Inside the club, they scanned their cards and walked toward the locker room. Ivan chose a locker and began changing his clothes.

"Hey, Maddoc."

Ivan looked around and saw someone approaching. Turning to look, he saw Maddoc pale slightly.

"Hey, Jerry." Maddoc's words sounded guarded. "I didn't know you were a member."

"I'm thinking of joining." The guy seemed genuine, but Maddoc's continued reticence had him wondering. "My pass is almost up, and I need to make a decision soon." He saw Maddoc nod and back away slightly.

"I'll see you around." Maddoc plastered on a smile that looked totally fake and went back to dressing.

"Is something wrong?" Ivan asked in a whisper. "Who was that?"

"A neighbor." Maddoc's eyes darted around the locker room.

"Could he be the one?"

Maddoc shrugged and pulled on his shorts and sat down to tie his shoes. "I'll tell you later." Ivan had to be content with that and finished dressing, following Maddoc out of the locker room. "What's on for today?"

Ivan pulled him into the deserted gym. "Nothing until you tell me what's up with Mr. No Personal Boundaries?"

"You noticed, huh?" Ivan nodded his head. "He was asking me about you chasing someone away the other night."

Ivan felt his eyebrows furrow. "How did he know? It was after two in the morning." For a second, Ivan hoped they'd found their guy. He wasn't sure Jerry could outrun anybody, but he wasn't ruling anyone out.

"He said he was coming home from the bar and almost hit the guy you were chasing."

Ivan nodded, "That's possible. The guy did dart in front of a car as he was running, so that could have been this Jerry guy. But then it could also have been the guy I was chasing." Ivan watched as Maddoc's nervousness returned. "It doesn't mean it was Jerry. I just don't want to rule him out."

"So what do we do now?" He knew Maddoc was talking about his stalker, but he purposely misunderstood.

"We get to work."

"That's not what I meant." Man, he was cute when he got indignant.

"I know, but there's nothing we can do about your unwanted visitor, but we can get to work so you can defend yourself. So let's get the mats, and we'll start." Maddoc nodded, and the two of them dragged mats into the gym and spent time going over what they'd covered before, practicing together for the better part of an hour. "I know this is repetitive, but it only works when you don't have to think about it." Maddoc's hand stopped just short of his groin. "Okay, you're getting too good at that one."

Maddoc chuckled. "But I like that one." The chuckling lasted until Ivan wrestled him to the mat. "Hey!"

Now it was Ivan's turn to chuckle. "One thing you have to do is stay on your feet." He helped Maddoc to his feet. "Once you're on the ground, you're at their mercy."

"Like this." Ivan saw Maddoc coming a mile away, but played along and let him take him down. "That's not fair, you let me do it." Maddoc playfully slapped him on the arm.

"I know. You were moving slowly, but you did it right. I just saw it coming." Maddoc tried again, but Ivan stayed on his feet. "That's probably enough for today. Why don't we spend some time on a treadmill before cleaning up."

They put away the mats and spent the next half hour walking at a steep incline before cleaning up and leaving the club. "So what's your mother like?" Maddoc asked as they walked across the parking lot.

"She and my father migrated from the Ukraine forty-five years ago, just before I was born. They both came over alone and met here at a church function. They married six months later." Ivan unlocked the car and they got inside. "When I was growing up, we spoke only Ukrainian in the home. My father's English was never very good, but Mom picked it up really fast. She has a heavy accent that she's ashamed of, so don't be surprised if she tries to speak Ukrainian when I'm around." He started the engine, lowered the top, and sped through the parking lot.

"Do you think she'll like me?"

Ivan found himself laughing, "She'll probably try to pin a medal on you. Remember I told you her people were matchmakers? Well, I'm one of her notable failures. For years she tried to fix me up with girls, and when I finally told her I was interested in men, once she went to church to talk to the priest, she came home and tried fixing me up with every gay man she could find."

To Maddoc's credit, he didn't laugh for about three seconds. "Oh my God. I know you told me she'd tried, but I figured maybe once or twice."

Ivan began to laugh as well, a deep belly laugh that he couldn't stop. "Try thirty-two times, and that was just the guys."

"Jesus." Maddoc calmed himself down.

"I turned her down enough that she eventually stopped. She'll be happy I'm bringing someone home to meet her, but don't be offended if she grumbles a little. She figures the only way to make a good match is through a matchmaker."

"But she met your father," Maddoc replied, and Ivan looked at him and waited. "You mean they...."

"Yup, they had a matchmaker." The two of them continued talking as the car sped through quiet residential streets, pulling up in front of a small ranch house.

"Is this where you grew up?" Maddoc asked excitedly as he got out of the car, looking around. "This must have been a great place to be a kid."

"It was. There were lots of other kids to play with." Ivan looked up the road—he could almost hear the laughter from his friends playing baseball or tag. "Come on." Leading Maddoc toward the door, he placed a hand on the small of his back.

The front door opened. "This must be the young man you were telling me about."

Ivan couldn't keep the smile of his face. "Mom, this is Maddoc."

She extended her hand, and Maddoc took it. "It's nice to meet you, Mrs. Bradoff." A shiver went up Ivan's spine. He loved the lyrical way his last name fell off Maddoc's tongue. He'd always thought it sounded rough when most people said it, but Maddoc made it sound sensual somehow.

"Please, call me Maria." She opened the door further and motioned them inside. Ivan nearly tripped on the step. Maria? His mother never let anyone call her by the American version of her name. It was always Marinova.

The living room was spotless as usual. "Please make yourself comfortable. Lunch should be ready soon." Something wasn't quite right. His mother was smiling from ear to ear, and Maddoc looked nervous as hell. She'd insisted on cooking, and Ivan couldn't talk her out of it.

When his mother left the room, he touched Maddoc's hand lightly and saw him relax a little in the chair. "It's fine. She likes you."

"Oh." He heard Maddoc's stomach growl along with his own. "What is it she's cooking? It smells wonderful."

"Probably cabbage rolls. They're her specialty and one of my favorites."

"So, Maddoc," his mother said as she returned to the room, "how did you meet my son?" Ivan opened his mouth to answer, and she gave him a don't-you-dare look.

"At the gym. Ivan's been teaching me self-defense." Maddoc looked over at him warmly, and Ivan had to adjust his legs a little to keep his pants from getting too tight. "I've been having trouble with someone bothering me."

"What are they doing?" Her words were a little halted, but Ivan noticed how much better her English had gotten lately.

"Someone keeps sending me flowers."

"And it's not Ivan?" There was a protectiveness in her voice, like she didn't want her son to have competition. That was his mom: defensive as a mother cougar.

"No. Lately, they've sent dead flowers, and then just the stems."

"Someone's been stalking him," Ivan supplied for his mother. "A few nights ago, they cut down the roses in his yard."

She nodded and seemed lost in thought, just looking at Maddoc. Turning his head, he saw Maddoc start to squirm under his mother's intense gaze. "Flowers are love. Sending flowers is a good thing. Using flowers to hurt is bad, only a very bad person do this." Her pronouncement over, she settled back in her chair. A ding sounded in the kitchen. "Lunch is ready." She got up from her chair.

"Where can I wash up?" Maddoc asked as he stood.

"Down the hall, first door on the left." Maddoc walked from the room, and Ivan went into the kitchen to help his mom, but everything was already on the table.

"He's very nice, but scared." She put the casserole dish in the center of the table. "It's good you're helping him."

"I really like him, Mom." Ivan met her eyes.

"I know, and he likes you. He's very smart, and you're very strong—you need each other. He'll show you wonderful things, and you'll help protect him. I could not have done better." Before she could say more, Maddoc entered the room and they sat down to eat. But Ivan knew that from his mom that was very high praise indeed, and he felt his heart warm as he watched Maddoc settle into the chair next to him. They might need to wait, but he knew Maddoc would be his lover. Sooner or later, the stunning redhead next to him would be his to love; he could feel it with every beat of his heart.

Lunch was served with his mother constantly trying to get both of them to eat more. "You're both so skinny," she kept saying as she'd put another stuffed cabbage roll on each of their plates. At one point, Maddoc had whispered to him that they'd both need to go back to the gym after this meal. They spent much of the afternoon with his mom, and Ivan was pleased to see Maddoc becoming more comfortable as the day progressed.

"Mom, we've got to go," Ivan finally said as his mother tried yet again to get him to eat. This time it was a plate of cookies. He stood up, and she gave him a hug.

"Thank you for the wonderful lunch, Maria." Maddoc offered his hand, but to Ivan's complete shock, she pulled him into a hug before disappearing into the kitchen, returning and handing each of them a container of food.

"I'll see you soon, Mom." Ivan made for the door, knowing she'd keep him talking for an hour if he didn't. She did her best to keep them talking anyway, and finally Ivan was able to get them outside.

"Your mom's great," Maddoc babbled as they walked toward the car. "I don't think I'll need to eat for a week."

"I know what you mean." He placed the food in the back seat.

"Oh fuck!" Ivan looked at Maddoc and followed his gaze to the passenger seat. Three mangled roses sat on the seat. Reaching over, he picked up the flowers and threw them into the street. Taking Maddoc's container, he set it next to his and waited for him to get in. "I hate this!"

"I know." He didn't know what else to say. He could almost feel Maddoc's pain and fear as though they were his own.

"I want this to end. I need to make this stop!" Maddoc pounded his thighs with his fists.

"*We* need to make this end," Ivan corrected and saw Maddoc's anger begin to slip away. "Let's get you home, and we can try to figure out how to catch this fucker."

"We?" Maddoc looked over at him, hope in his eyes.

"Yes, we." Ivan leaned over the seat.

"Your mother. She'll see us." Maddoc cautioned, backing away.

"So. She knows we kiss, and if she doesn't want to see, she can get away from the window." Ivan captured Maddoc's lips and quickly deepened the kiss before pulling back and looking deep into those sea-blue eyes. "Okay?"

"Uh-huh." That was all he said as his head nodded slowly, and Ivan started the car before pulling away from the curb. He drove fast, imagining the things that might be going through Maddoc's mind.

As they pulled up in front of the house, everything looked the same. No flowers on the porch, but Ivan couldn't help looking around anyway. Someone had been following them to the gym, to his mother's, and God knew where else. Putting up the top, he shut off the engine and walked Maddoc to his front door.

Maddoc unlocked the door. "I'll be fine."

Ivan wasn't buying it. The fear, the jitters, it was all back, and Maddoc looked just as small and scared as he had that first night. He wasn't sure he'd be welcome, but he knew he couldn't just leave. "Let's get you some tea, and we can talk."

Maddoc went inside, and Ivan took his silence for assent and followed him, closing and locking the door behind him. Maddoc walked blankly through the house toward the kitchen. This was hurting Ivan as much as it was Maddoc. As he reached the door, Ivan took his arm, pulling them together. "Look at me." Maddoc raised his head, and Ivan looked deep into those rich blue eyes. "We'll figure this out."

"How?" Maddoc's confusion was swirling in his eyes.

"I don't know yet, but we will."

Maddoc began to squirm in his arms. "I need to make tea." Ivan knew that was just an excuse.

"Not yet." Running his fingers through those curls he loved so much, Ivan captured Maddoc's lips and kissed him, hard. At first Maddoc didn't respond, but soon those lips parted, and Ivan deepened the kiss, exploring the mouth of the man he was determined to make his lover. He wasn't sure what Maddoc was thinking until he heard that first small, throaty moan. Wrapping his other hand around the smaller man's back, he rubbed along Maddoc's spine as he pressed them closer together, their body heat melding. Maddoc began returning Ivan's kisses, and his moans got louder and more insistent.

Maddoc pulled away. "We shouldn't." Then his lips crashed against Ivan's, pulling and tugging on his lips while alternately sucking on his tongue. Ivan's dick wanted in on the action so bad, he thought he'd come just from the kissing.

Not giving any quarter, Ivan swung Maddoc off his feet, Maddoc's legs wrapping around his hips, Ivan's hands gripping that tight, firm butt. Fuck, Maddoc felt good in his hands—if only he could figure a way to get those pants off without breaking their kiss or letting Maddoc go. The slim man's hips began grinding against him as Maddoc tried to wrap himself around him like a vine. "I'll take care of you, Tiger."

"Make me forget everything."

"You won't remember your name by the time I'm through with you." Maddoc's lips were on his again, and Ivan began climbing the stairs to Maddoc's bedroom.

Approaching the bed, he set Maddoc on the edge, pressing him back onto the mattress.

"Is this what you really want?" Maddoc nodded in response. "No, you have to say it." If Maddoc said to slow down, he would, but his dick would probably explode.

"Yes, I want you to fuck me."

Ivan pulled back, looking into Maddoc's clouded, half-closed eyes. "I'll make love to you," he corrected.

Maddoc stilled. "You'll... yes." Maddoc pulled him back down, and Ivan resumed their kisses, using his hands to open Maddoc's shirt before moving to suck lightly on his neck.

"I know I'm not handsome like you." His voice trailed off as Ivan found a spot at the base of Maddoc's neck that had him vibrating beneath Ivan.

Ivan lifted his head. "I think you're beautiful." With a smile, he parted the fabric of Maddoc's shirt and ran his tongue over a pink nipple before sucking on the firm bud. Maddoc's hot skin tasted better than he'd imagined. The man must spend a lot of time outdoors, because his skin smelled like sunshine with a hint of pine, clean and earthy. Maddoc let his legs fall away as he moaned with pleasure.

Letting his lips roam, Ivan kissed his way across Maddoc's chest before latching onto the other bud, his hands sliding down to Maddoc's hips and across his belly. The redhead began to laugh and squirm, but Ivan stilled his hand and brought their lips back together, kissing the laughter away and replacing it with whimpers. Breaking the kiss and stepping back, he unbuckled Maddoc's belt and popped the button on his pants before grabbing the waist of his pants and tugging them down and off. Moving between Maddoc's legs, he murmured, "I told you—beautiful," as he ran his palms down Maddoc's chest and stomach, stopping just before touching his length.

"Please, Ivan," his radiant redhead begged softly.

"What do you want, Tiger?" He knew his eyes were as filled with desire as Maddoc's; he only hoped the other man saw it.

"I want to see you."

Ivan shivered slightly. Those few words were the hottest thing anyone had ever said to him. Stepping back, he slipped off his shirt, draping it over the foot of the bed before toeing off his shoes and stepping out of his pants, standing naked in front of his lover. Maddoc sat up, his arms slipping around Ivan's waist, mouth and tongue sliding over his skin.

When Maddoc sucked on one of his nipples, Ivan threw his head back and hissed as Maddoc bit lightly and scraped the skin with his teeth. "Fuck, you're hot." Maddoc's hands slid down his stomach, fingers tracing his abs. "I've never seen a ten-pack before," Maddoc purred, sliding his tongue over Ivan's skin, lightly tickling.

Ivan chuckled and nudged Maddoc back, pressing him against the mattress. This time, he let his hands glide all over his lover's smooth, pink skin. Legs wrapped around his waist, and Ivan let his fingers graze over that soft, firm butt. Ivan ran his fingers along the smooth crease. The man's body was nearly hairless, and Ivan smiled when he realized that extended to other, more intimate places.

"Ivan," Maddoc whimpered breathily as Ivan's fingers teased the flesh around his opening.

"You like that, Tiger?" Ivan did it again, and Maddoc cried out this time, pressing back against his fingers, trying for more. Looking around, Ivan saw a bottle on the nightstand—the little minx.

Slicking his fingers, he pressed one to Maddoc's opening. The hot body beneath him gripped his finger tightly. "How long has it been?" Ivan pressed his finger deeper.

"T-too long." Maddoc arched beneath him, throwing his head back. "Ivan!"

Smiling, knowing that he'd found that special spot, Ivan used the pleasure point to direct his lover back on the bed. Maddoc's head landed on the pillow, and he lifted his legs, exposing himself to Ivan's gaze. "You're stunning, you know that?" Ivan added another finger, daring his lover to contradict him.

"Whatever you say." Ivan rubbed the spot again as he leaned forward, sucking Maddoc's length into his mouth. Jesus, the man tasted good, and from the sounds he was making, it wouldn't be long and he'd get the full Maddoc banquet. "I'm—" was the only warning he got as the man bucked up into him, and Maddoc's intense flavor filled his mouth and kept coming until his lover collapsed back onto the bed with a deep sigh. "What'd you do to me?"

"Made you feel better." Ivan grinned down at his resplendent lover before opening the drawer in the nightstand and fishing around for... there had to be some... ah, his fingers latched onto a square packet. It was hard to look for condoms when he didn't want to look away.

Preparing himself, he pressed his cock to Maddoc's opening and leaned forward, close enough that he could feel Maddoc's breath against his lips. "Okay?"

"Yes." Maddoc arched. "Fuck."

Ivan stopped just inside his lover, unsure if his cry was pain or pleasure. Looking deep into Maddoc's eyes, he waited until Maddoc's body began taking him deeper on its own. As he pressed further, a low, rumbling moan vibrated through his lover's body as his hips melded to Maddoc's butt. He could feel his cock throb and jump deep in his lover.

"Make love to me, Ivan," Maddoc rasped as he pulled Ivan forward into a forceful kiss that curled his toes.

Lips and tongues battled, ramping up the intensity, and Ivan moved deep inside. He only hoped Maddoc liked it fast and a little rough, because that was all he had left. Snapping his hips back and forth, he plunged deep and withdrew again. "Feel so good!" His cognitive processes began shutting down, reducing him to instinct and animal passion.

"Ivan."

Plunging deep, he lifted Maddoc off the mattress and slid him lower on the bed before resuming his relentless, pounding passion. Maddoc was his and only his. Leaning forward again, he sucked at the base of Maddoc's neck, raising a mark as his lover bucked against him. Maddoc cried out loud and fierce as he came between them, and still Ivan couldn't get enough. Driving deep, he felt his balls threaten to disappear inside him as he came with a brain-stopping climax, howling his release. "Mine!"

All his energy gone, Ivan collapsed onto Maddoc, huffing for breath. His lover's arms cradled him as his head stopped spinning, and he regained awareness of his surroundings and the fact that he was probably crushing Maddoc.

Slipping from Maddoc's body, Ivan tried to shift off him, but was held in place as lips kissed the base of his neck. "That was quite a declaration."

"Maybe it's the Marine in me, Tiger, but something took over." He wasn't going to apologize for how he felt. The declaration had been honest, if maybe a little premature. But he felt what he felt, and he knew he'd fight for Maddoc.

Feeling a tap on his hip, Ivan slid to the mattress, and before he could blink, found himself on his back with a naked Tiger straddling him. "You may be a big, hunky Marine"—Maddoc's eyes shone down at him—"and for the record, you're *my* big, hunky Marine, but that doesn't mean that I'm the little woman." Ivan cocked his head, waiting to see where Maddoc was going with this.

Leaning forward, Maddoc sucked on one of Ivan's ears, pulling slightly with his lips. "Just so you know, I can't wait to fuck you until you can't see straight." Maddoc yawned and rested his head against his shoulder. "Maybe later."

"I look forward to it, Tiger," Ivan replied in a whisper as Maddoc burrowed next to him, using his bicep as a pillow.

As the light faded, Ivan tried to rest with his now-napping lover but couldn't. So many things ran through his mind, and then there were the soft noises Maddoc made and the sweet way he'd hug him tighter every few minutes, like he was afraid he'd somehow get away. His Marine instincts were screaming at him, telling him that this guy stalking Maddoc wasn't going to give up and that his behavior would escalate. He had to figure out a way to catch this guy that wouldn't put Maddoc in danger.

"You can't solve the world's problems by yourself." Maddoc's eyes didn't even open, and he stroked his hand along his lover's skin. "I know what you're thinking about," the sleepy redhead clarified.

"You do, huh?" He hugged Maddoc closer, and those blue eyes slid open.

"The same thing I lie in bed most nights thinking about." Maddoc lifted his head slightly, "The only time I sleep well is when I'm with you." Maddoc rolled over, spooning himself against Ivan.

Jesus, what an admission! Thinking to himself, he realized how little he really knew about Maddoc's life. He didn't know many of his friends or any of his neighbors and had no idea who could be doing this to him. They hadn't known each other long enough. A few days earlier, he'd never have believed he was capable of falling for someone so fast—wouldn't have believed it was possible—but he knew better now. Without thinking, he found his fingers stroking through Maddoc's hair. "Don't look too close. I'm getting gray."

Ivan snickered. "It's a sign of virility."

"On you, maybe…." Ivan's laugh turned to a soft groan, and Maddoc ground his butt against him. "Let's test out that theory."

V

MADDOC closed his front door, looking around like he always did, but saw no one and breathed a silent sigh of relief. No flowers, no notes, and while he'd checked, he hadn't seen or felt like anyone was following him. Locking the door, he picked up his bag.

Jumping back at what he thought were footsteps, Maddoc had his keys in hand already turning to unlock the door when he saw pair of squirrels dash through the bushes, skittering across the mulch before chasing each other up a tree, chattering between them. "Calm down," Maddoc mumbled to himself as he checked the door and walked to his car. He knew he was still jumpy, and just because nothing had happened for a few days didn't mean it was over, but it gave him hope. Releasing a sigh, he unlocked his car, checking the back seat before getting in and starting the engine. Pulling away from the curb, he thought he saw movement out of the corner of his eye. Stopping the car, he watched, but saw nothing as the breeze rustled the leaves of the flowering quince. Pulling away, he forced himself to relax.

His phone rang and he jerked again. "Morning, Ivan."

"Is something wrong? You sound nervous."

"I'm just jittery this morning." Maddoc tried to concentrate on his driving as he entered the freeway. "Give me a minute." Setting down the phone, he merged into traffic. "Sorry."

"Did something happen?"

"Other than my overactive imagination, no. I got startled by a pair of squirrels this morning," he groused into the phone. "This is ridiculous. I'm jumpy all the time, and I hate it." There were times he just wanted to scream.

"I know you do." He could hear the concern in his lover's voice.

"Will I see you at the gym? I've missed seeing you." With Ivan out of town, he'd felt even more alone, and he realized how he'd come to rely on the big man after just a few days. There was something about Ivan that made him feel safe.

"Me, too, but I had to go on this trip. I should be back in town, and I'll meet you there at four."

"I'm looking forward to it." Lonnie and Dan were great workout partners, but he missed working out with Ivan. "By the way, I officially joined the club yesterday, and I've lost four pounds." He heard a soft chuckle come through the phone. He loved the sound of that deep laugh and squirmed on the seat.

"That's really good—not that you had much to lose."

"But I want to look all ripped like you." He squirmed again as images of a naked Ivan flashed through his mind. The man was stunning, and he wanted to look good for him.

"I think you're sexy right now." Ivan used his bedroom voice, and Maddoc's dick throbbed. "I thought I'd stay over tonight, if that's okay."

"It's more than okay." *It's bloody fucking fantastic.* The last few days when he'd gotten home, he'd spent most of the time holed up in the house. A few times he'd heard neighbors outside, and he'd ventured out, but only if other people were around. It felt pathetic—he kept seeing threats everywhere and found himself running scared all the fucking time.

Saying goodbye and closing the phone, he finished his drive to the office, some of his trepidation slipping away just knowing that Ivan would be back and that they were going to get together that evening. He parked in the lot and walked into the office, going right to his desk and checking his calendar. Thank God, he had a very busy day ahead. Turning on his computer, Maddoc sat at his desk.

A knock on the door drew his attention. "Morning." His supervisor smiled as he walked in and sat down. "I know it's early, but I got a call from the San Francisco office, and they have an opening for a program manager." Maddoc was about to interrupt, but Dennis stopped him, "I know it's not a promotion, but it's a larger location, and the position comes with a huge raise. I have to tell you that you were specifically requested."

Wow, what an ego boost. He'd only been in his current position for six months.

"Think about it and let me know at the end of the week." Dennis got up from the chair. "Just for the record, I want you to stay. You're the best program manager we've ever had, but I won't stand in your way, and the San Francisco office is much higher profile."

Maddoc smiled. "Thanks. That means a lot." Dennis left the office, and Maddoc sat dazed in his chair. His first instinct was to turn down the job. He knew it was a great opportunity but it meant moving clear across the country to a state he didn't know and to a city where the cost of living was astronomical. But it would be a chance to start over without his friendly neighborhood stalker. But Ivan.... His thoughts stopped momentarily. Going to San Francisco would mean leaving Ivan. Maddoc sighed loudly. He really didn't want to leave; he liked it here. He had his own house and a garden he'd spent years cultivating. He had friends and a life, one that was quickly expanding to include someone who could mean a great deal to him. Forcing his mind back on the task at hand, he signed on to his computer and tried to get to work.

He spent much of the day in meetings and completing paperwork. Most people complained about it, but he seemed to thrive on it. Part of the reason he was so successful was because he knew what the rules were and was able to navigate them efficiently in order to get his job done.

"Are you leaving soon?"

He looked up and saw Kyle standing in his doorway before checking his watch. "In a few minutes."

"I was wondering if I could ask you something?" Kyle moved into the office, standing right next to his desk. Maddoc immediately began to feel trapped and started looking outside, but no one was nearby. Trying to keep his cool, he looked around his desk for something he could use as a weapon if he needed to. "Are you dating the guy from the gym?"

"You mean Ivan?"

"Big, tall man with short gray hair."

Maddoc nodded slowly, wondering where Kyle was going.

"Yes, we're dating. Why?" Maddoc watched Kyle's eyes and saw them fill with sadness.

"Nothing." He slowly turned away.

Maddoc wondered what was going on. Did Kyle have feelings for him? "Did you send me flowers?" he asked, slightly less confused.

Kyle shook his head. "Is that what he did to get your attention?" The words sounded snide, but there was no heat in them, only what sounded to Maddoc like regret. Kyle left the office, and Maddoc leapt from his seat to talk to him, but by the time he reached the hall, all he saw was Kyle's retreating back hurrying away. Turning around, he went back to work, shaking his head, wondering why everything happened at once and feeling a little stupid. It looked like the man might have been interested in him. Why hadn't he said something? Not that he was interested in Kyle that way, but he didn't want to hurt him.

"This crap has to end," he muttered to himself as he turned back to his PC. Whoever was doing this had not only stripped away his peace of mind and made him jumpy as hell, he'd made Maddoc become suspicious of everyone and everything. "I can't live this way."

"Did you say something?" One of the ladies poked her head in his office, obviously hearing his mutterings. He smiled at her and shook his head, embarrassed. She returned his smile and moved away. But he'd had enough. Opening the file he needed to finish before leaving, he got back to work.

Thankfully Maddoc's day had truly been extraordinarily busy. Back-to-back meetings and a pressing deadline kept his day short and his mind occupied. But that ended as he walked to his car and headed to the gym.

Ivan was walking in as he pulled in the parking lot. Maddoc smiled to himself when he saw Ivan waiting for him on the sidewalk. Grabbing his bag, he hurried to catch up. "How was your day?" Ivan asked as they walked toward the doors.

"Very busy but productive. I was able to eliminate Kyle from my office as my stalker." He told him about their conversation. "I think he liked me."

"You sound sad." Ivan stopped. "Are you regretting your decisions?"

Maddoc stopped as well, "No. But I feel for him, you know. He liked me and knows we're dating." They continued walking, and as they reached the door, Maddoc put a hand on Ivan's arm. "I don't regret anything."

Ivan smiled. "For a second there, I was afraid you'd started to regret what we did before I left." Ivan's smile brightened, and he moved closer. "You're blushing."

Maddoc felt the heat in his cheeks as he returned the smile. "Just thinking about what we did before you left."

"Come on, Hot Stuff, we've got a workout to finish. Then maybe, if you're good, we can arrange an encore." Ivan opened and held the door.

"What if I'm bad?" Maddoc winked at him and saw Ivan's cheeks start to pinken. He scanned his card and continued through the gym to the locker room. After changing clothes, Maddoc followed Ivan to the workout floor.

"I thought we'd go through the body weight exercises again," Ivan explained as he walked toward the mats. "We can start with push-ups." Maddoc followed Ivan down onto the mat and waited to find out what he had in mind. "Start and do as many as you can. Be sure to go all the way down and come all the way up."

Maddoc mimicked Ivan's position and began the push-ups. At ten, he started having trouble, and by twenty, he was flat on the mat, breathing like he'd run a marathon. Looking over at Ivan, he watched him continue as though it was nothing. "Show-off."

"Fifty-one, fifty-two...."

Maddoc grinned as he watched Ivan's tight butt rise and lower.

Maddoc moved close to Ivan's ear. "Do you think you could do that and fuck me at the same time?"

Thump. Ivan's hands slipped on the mat. "That was mean and just plain wicked."

"But effective," Maddoc countered.

"Just for that, we need to do another set." Ivan got in position. "Come on," he prodded, and Maddoc huffed and started doing more push-ups. When he collapsed again, he watched Ivan's tight body raise and lower, butt tightening with every rep, chest bulging, arms pumping, legs rigid. "One hundred."

"That was hot," Maddoc whispered, and Ivan chuckled as he gulped water from his bottle. "And so is that." He watched the man's throat work and had to stop himself from running his tongue along the taut, undulating skin. Ivan must have seen the look on his face because he said nothing as he lowered the bottle and led the way to the next exercise. Maddoc followed behind like Ivan was the Pied Piper.

"CAN you do one more?" Ivan asked as Maddoc pulled himself up to the bar for what he was sure was the last time. Reaching the top, he lowered himself and let go.

"Are you kidding? I can barely lift my arms." Maddoc rubbed his shoulder as he groused lightheartedly.

"Then let's clean up."

After spending time in the whirlpool, letting his taut muscles loosen, Maddoc led Ivan to the showers, where he slipped off his bathing suit and stepped into the stall, glancing over at Ivan and all that tight musculature. Starting the shower, he pulled the curtain closed and let his imagination wander as he soaped his skin. His body definitely had ideas of its own, and he had to stop himself. When he got home he could have the real thing as opposed to just the visions in his mind. Finishing his shower, Maddoc dried himself and wrapped the towel around his waist before heading back to his locker to dress.

Slipping into his clothes, he spent much of his time watching Ivan pull on his pants, the powerful legs disappearing into denim cut to accentuate a narrow waist and broad chest. The last time they were together, Ivan had been the one in control. He hoped that this time he'd have a chance to take his time exploring his lover's athletic, sexy body.

A breath against his ear pulled him out of his daydream. "Are you thinking of something good?" Maddoc colored slightly as he looked up at Ivan and nodded with a small smile. "Then we should get back to your house so you can do more than think." Maddoc finished tying his shoes and packed his bag, grabbing it before following a jeans-clad butt out of the locker room and through the gym, watching as each step made those tight globes flex and bob.

Outside, Maddoc hurried to his car. Unlocking the door, he put his bag in the back and pulled open the driver's door, stopping in his tracks. A pink rose, or more accurately, what was left of a pink rose, sat on the driver's seat. Maddoc stared in near horror, his legs nearly giving out beneath him. They'd been in his car, and if they could do that, they'd be able to get into his house. Brushing the remains of the flower onto the concrete, he climbed in and started the car. Pulling out of the lot, he rushed toward home, hoping that Ivan was close behind him.

Pulling up to the house, he shoved the car into park and rushed up the walk, bounding up the steps to the front door. Unlocking it, he rushed inside. Everything looked the same. Walking through the living room, he noticed nothing out of place. The kitchen looked the same, as did the dining room. Climbing the stairs, he walked through the rooms. Walking normally, getting control of his breath, he walked in his bedroom to use the bathroom and saw a single, pink rose on his pillow.

"Maddoc?" Ivan's voice carried through the house. "Are you okay?"

"Up...." His mouth suddenly dry, the words died on his lips. He swallowed and tried again. "Up here," he said as levelly as he could, even though he could feel panic rising from his very toes.

Heavy footsteps pounded on the stairs, and seconds later Ivan burst into the room and stopped when he, too, saw the flower. "He's been in here."

"And in my car." Maddoc started to shake. Was there no place he was safe?

"We should call the police." Ivan's footsteps sounded around him. Maddoc nodded, unable to move. Then strong arms encircled him and a gentle hand cradled his head as he was pulled into a warm, reassuringly tight hug. "It's okay."

Ivan's scent filled his nose, Ivan's warmth reaching through his clothes to calm his ragged breathing. Tears threatened, but Maddoc pushed them back. He wasn't going to do that, wasn't going to give the bastard doing this the satisfaction. Even in private, he wasn't going to let it happen. "Thank you," Maddoc whispered as he sniffled lightly.

"It's okay." A big hand softly stroked the back of his head and neck. Ivan just held him, making no move to back away, and Maddoc found himself clinging to the man, feeling that without him he'd crumple to the floor. "It's going to be all right."

Maddoc stepped away and reached for the flower, wanting it off his bed, but Ivan stopped him with a touch. "We should leave it for the police." Nodding, Maddoc lowered his hand and let Ivan guide him out of the room, down the stairs, and into the kitchen.

Seated in a chair, Maddoc finally reached for the phone and placed a call to the police. The operator asked all sorts of questions, and he answered each of them mechanically before hanging up the phone. "They said they'd send someone."

Ivan set a mug in front of him, and the scent of mint tea filled his senses. Lifting the mug, he sipped, the familiar taste soothing his rattled nerves. "Can you tell me what happened with the car?"

"There was a mangled version of the rose upstairs on the driver's seat when I got out of the gym." Maddoc took another sip of the tea. "I brushed it out and hurried home."

"Was the car locked?" Ivan asked gently, and Maddoc nodded in response, not trusting his voice right now.

"So how did they get in?" Ivan mused, and Maddoc had a terrifying thought.

Jumping up from his chair, he raced to the cupboard next to the refrigerator, pulling it open. "The extra set of keys is gone." Maddoc pointed to the hook. "I always keep them right here."

"We have to tell that to the police, and we need to get someone to change the locks on the house because we have to assume they have a key to it as well."

Maddoc felt a crushing weight descend on him. They could get into anything they wanted. Turning away, he leaned against the counter, feeling the frustration and fear really start to take hold, and suddenly San Francisco didn't seem like such a bad idea. Maddoc knew he had to get himself under control, but that was precisely what was eluding him right now. "I'll be okay. We'll figure this out." Arms wound around his waist, and he felt a comforting weight against his back, and he leaned against it, taking the strength Ivan offered.

Maddoc jumped at a sharp knock on the front door. Feeling Ivan's arms slip away, he walked through the house, looking out one of the windows before opened the door.

"I'm Officer Aaron Cloud," he said as he showed his badge. "We got a call of a break-in."

Maddoc stood back and held the door so he could enter. "I made the call."

The officer looked around him. "Was there any damage? What was taken?"

Maddoc started to feel embarrassed and a little stupid. Looking around he saw Ivan, who thankfully joined him. "Well... um." The policeman looked confused. "Let me show you." Maddoc turned and led the way upstairs. "I came home from the gym and found this." He led them to the bedroom and pointed toward the bed. "I also found one, or what was left of one on the driver's seat of my car. It appears that whoever broke in also took the extra set of keys to my car, and they probably have keys to the house now too." Maddoc began to shake again.

"Okay, sir." The police officer looked around. "Would you like me to call a locksmith, and we can get the house secured?"

"Could you?" Everything felt out of control. "I don't want them in my house again!" Ivan put his hand on his shoulder, letting him know he was there.

"Certainly." Officer Cloud began talking into his radio, and they waited. "One will be here within the hour."

"Thank you," Maddoc replied, feeling relieved and a little less helpless now that something was being done.

"Would you be more comfortable downstairs? I've got a number of questions I need to ask." Maddoc nodded his response and led them to the living room. Maddoc sat down and told him everything he could think of. "I have a few of the notes." He gave them to the officer. "It didn't seem like anything at first, but it's been getting scarier over the last week or so. I reported the problem before, but I think the previous officer thought it was my imagination and didn't do much."

The police officer wrote down everything Maddoc said and then asked some more questions for clarification. "I'd like to take the flower from upstairs and look at the car as well as the rose bushes."

"Of course."

The officer got up, and Maddoc stayed where he was. He wanted to block the doors from the inside and curl into a ball, away from everyone and everything. Ivan, who'd been sitting next to him, pulled him into a hug, rubbing his back. "It's going to be fine. The locksmith will be here soon, and we'll call the dealership in the morning to see if we can't get the locks changed on the car as well."

Thank God for Ivan's strength, because right now, Maddoc didn't feel like he had any left. The front door opened and closed, and Maddoc saw the police officer glance in before heading upstairs. He returned a few minutes later with the rose in a plastic bag. "I didn't see any signs of forced entry on the car and I found a few pieces from the flower on the floor." Maddoc pulled slightly away from Ivan, but not enough to completely lose contact as he was offered a card. "Here's the case number for the insurance company. Please call if you have any issues. I've already put in a request for extra patrols on the street, and if this guy is watching like you think, he'll have seen that you've called the police."

Maddoc nodded slowly and took the card as the doorbell rang. "Thank you." Maddoc got up and opened the door to the locksmith. Thankfully, Officer Cloud explained what needed to be done and then said good night and left.

"This is good hardware. I can rekey it for you if you'd like."

"Thank you," Maddoc replied, and the man got to work.

"I'm going to get some food—we both need to eat. Will you be okay?" Ivan fished his keys out of his pocket.

Maddoc nodded and smiled the best smile he could muster. "I'll be fine." He needed a few minutes to think, and the locksmith was going to be here for a while anyway. Sinking into one of the living room chairs, he couldn't stop himself from thinking about the job offer he'd received. San Francisco—the city of hills and water that was an entire country away from the man who was making his life a living hell.

He loved his house. Seven years ago, he'd bought this place and fixed it up. Lifting his head, Maddoc looked around the room. He saw the crown molding that he'd spent days cutting just right. The walls he'd stripped layers of wallpaper off of only to find the original impressions of picture frame moldings that he'd restored. He'd put part of himself in every room and every flowerbed in his garden.

Shaking himself back to reality, he began wandering through the house, thinking, ruminating. He wasn't a coward, and he'd never run from things in his life. When he'd realized he was gay, he told his parents. There were plenty of tears and lots of yelling, but he'd done it anyway. "God damn it, I'm not going to let someone scare me out of my own house." He'd faced heartache and loss when his parents died and when his relationships had ended.

The front door closed, and the locksmith came through to the back door and started working, interrupting his thoughts. "I'll be out of your hair soon." He settled on the floor and started talking the lock apart. "This is a great house."

"Thanks."

"Did you do the work yourself? I don't mean to be nosy, but we looked at this house about"—he paused, thinking—"six or seven years ago, and it didn't look anything like this."

"Yeah." Maddoc smiled. "I did most of the work myself." It had been a labor of love. Every room had been cleaned up and redone, from the kitchen and baths to the bedrooms.

"It really shows." He put the lock back in the door and tested it. "If I'd have known it would look like this, I'd have bought it." He closed the door and stood back up, handing Maddoc two keys. "I can make more if you want." He wrote up a bill and handed it to Maddoc. Maddoc wrote him a check and handed it to him before walking him to the door.

"Thank you."

"You're welcome."

Maddoc closed the door behind him and locked it before making sure the back door was locked tight as well. Then he settled in the living room to wait for Ivan.

He didn't have to wait long before he heard a soft knock on the front door. Getting up, he looked out and unlocked the door. "Sorry."

"Don't be." Ivan leaned close, a kiss ghosting lightly over his lips. Maddoc closed the door. Ivan walked to the kitchen, and Maddoc heard cupboard doors opening and closing as he joined him. "I got burgers and salad. No fries." Ivan placed the food on plates while Maddoc got out forks and sat at the table.

"I'm sorry for all this." The adrenaline that had been carrying him for the last hour had drained from his system, and Maddoc felt wrung out, empty, and definitely a little maudlin.

"There's nothing to feel sorry about." Ivan put a plate in front of him. "Eat a little and you'll feel better." Maddoc wasn't sure anything would make him any better, but he took a bite of the burger. "Tell me about work today."

Maddoc looked at Ivan like he was crazy. "What?"

"I just thought talking about something normal would help."

"You're right, I'm sorry." Maddoc took another small bite of burger.

"Stop apologizing and tell me about your day."

"Okay." Maddoc swallowed and took a sip of the wine that Ivan had poured for him. "I told you about what happened with Kyle, but I didn't tell you the best news. My boss stopped in and told me that there's an opening in the San Francisco office for a program manager, and they want me for the job." Maddoc couldn't help smiling a little. That they wanted him for the job was enough to make him smile. It said a great deal about the job he was doing.

Maddoc saw Ivan stop chewing, his eyes going wide for a second. "You're leaving?" Ivan put his food down on the plate.

"I'd be lying if I said I wasn't thinking about it. After all this crap"—he waved his arms toward the door—"it would be hard not to."

"Oh." Ivan swallowed and gulped his wine. "I understand."

Maddoc reached across the table. "I don't think you do."

"Oh, I understand perfectly." Ivan glared at him from across the table. "Things get a little tough, and you're going to run away." Ivan dropped his fork, and it clattered on the plate. "I thought I might have finally found someone I wanted to be with, but you're going to up and leave."

"I didn't say that." Maddoc could feel his own temper starting to rise. "I said they asked me. I didn't say I'd told them yes."

"You told them no?" Ivan crossed his arms in front of his chest.

"I haven't given them an answer yet." That was obviously the wrong thing to say, because Ivan's eyes blazed. It was really quite hot, actually. "Sometimes it's just nice to be asked."

"You're going to tell them no?" Ivan's expression softened just a little, but Maddoc could tell he was still wary.

"I love my house and my job. I like it here. It's quiet with nice people." He stopped himself. "Well, they're nice except for the guy who's stalking me." Ivan even cracked a slight smile. "And I really don't want to pick up and move across the country. My life is here." Now it was Maddoc's turn to fume just a little. "But could you blame me if I decided to take the job after everything that's happened?"

Ivan's arms slid to the table. "I guess not."

Maddoc smiled slightly, "Okay, then. Like I said, sometimes it's just nice to be asked. I mean, I've only been in this position for six months, and they're already offering me the same position in the largest office in the country. That means they think a lot of me, and they'll offer me another promotion if I continue." Maddoc found himself smiling.

"So you're staying?"

"Yes, I'm staying." Maddoc grinned mischievously.

Ivan started eating again, and Maddoc's appetite finally kicked in as well. "Are you staying for me?" he asked sheepishly.

"I'm staying for me." Maddoc returned Ivan's sheepish grin. "You're an added prize."

Ivan smiled, and Maddoc felt himself relax for the first time since he'd seen the flower in his car. "So I'm a prize, huh?"

"I'm still trying to figure out if you're the first prize or the booby prize, but you're definitely a prize," Maddoc replied with a smile and squirmed away when Ivan reached under the small table and began tickling his ribs. "That's not fair."

"I'll give you booby prize," Ivan said through his chuckles as he continued tickling. Maddoc nearly fell off the chair, he was squirming so much.

Maddoc finally squirmed out of reach. "I give."

"That's better." Ivan took a bite of his burger with a satisfied grin.

"I'll let you audition for the kind of prize you are later." Maddoc waggled his eyebrows as he returned to his chair and began eating again.

"Then you'd better eat everything on your plate, because you're going to need your energy." Ivan leered across the table, and Maddoc broke into giggles as he made sure to finish every bite.

"I don't have to lick the plate, do I?"

"No." Ivan's eyes crinkled a little as he smiled broadly. "I have other things in mind for that tongue." Ivan knelt close and kissed him, sucking lightly and drawing Maddoc's tongue between his lips, and Maddoc found himself whimpering softly.

Ivan's lips were firm and moist, and his tongue did things Maddoc had never felt before. "Let's go upstairs, Tiger." Maddoc nodded a little, and Ivan took his hand, leading him out of the kitchen. At the base of the stairs, Ivan turned quickly and pulled him tight, kissing him hard.

Maddoc's mind shut down, and everything that had happened over the last few hours slipped away as everything but the feel of Ivan's lips against his and Ivan's hands as they slipped beneath his shirt were driven away. His knees shook as hot fingers plucked first one nipple and then the other. "Ivan," he murmured against his lips, and a hand stroked the skin just above his belt, a finger sliding under, teasing his oversensitive skin.

A soft tune sounded in his ears, and it took him a while before he realized a phone was ringing somewhere in the house. Ivan's hand slid away, and his lips pulled back. Maddoc groaned audibly as Ivan stroked his cheek. "I have to answer that." Maddoc leaned against the wall and nodded absently as his chest heaved for breath. Ivan's flushed face and unsteady walk told Maddoc that he wasn't unaffected by the kiss, and he smiled.

Maddoc heard the tune stop and Ivan talking softly before returning. "I'm sorry, but I have to go in to the office. There's a problem that I have to fix." Maddoc couldn't keep the disappointment off his face, but he understood. There were times when he'd had to say the same thing. It came with the territory. "Don't worry, Tiger. I'll be back, and we'll pick up where we left off."

"You promise?"

"Oh, yes." Ivan kissed him against the wall. "I'll be back as soon as I can." Ivan gave him another kiss and then walked toward the door, turning around just before he left and giving Maddoc a final smile.

The front door closed, and Maddoc let the tingles of their last kiss fade before pushing away from the wall and locking the front door.

The quiet of the house and the sudden loneliness brought back the earlier fear, and Maddoc went through the house turning on lights. His phone ringing started him, and he clutched his heart dramatically before picking up the receiver.

"Maddoc, it's Corky. Do you have a minute? I can't get my VCR to work, and I want to tape my shows. I'm supposed to go to George's tonight, and I don't want to miss them, but I can't figure out how to program the thing." She always called for help with anything electronic.

"Of course." There was no way he could tell his neighbor no. She'd done so much for him over the years, and she was such a great friend. "I'll be over in a few minutes." Hanging up, he picked up his keys. At the front door, he looked out before unlocking the door and opening it slowly. He turned on the porch light but could see no one in the twilight. Closing the door, he relocked it and hurried down the steps and across the lawn to the neighbor's, where he knocked on Corky's door.

Maddoc heard the locks turn, and then the inside and screen doors opened. "Thank you." She stepped back and walked inside.

"It's not a problem." He walked to where she had her television and VCR. "What time would you like it to start?"

"Have it record from nine to eleven on channel four." Maddoc took the remote she handed him and programmed the device for her, making sure there was a tape in it. The thing was as old as the hills. He'd tried to get her to upgrade it, but she liked it and generally understood it, so the huge relic stayed where it was on top of the old console television. "Would you like something to drink?" She poured a cup of coffee and handed it to him without waiting for an answer, and Maddoc sat at one of the stools. He and Corky had spent a number of afternoons talking at her kitchen counter. "So is this man I've seen coming and going a new boyfriend?"

Maddoc nodded, hiding his smile behind the mug. "Yes, I think so." Maddoc sipped more coffee, letting the smooth roasted warmth slide down his throat.

"Well, it's about time. You've been alone for a while."

Maddoc shrugged. "Sometimes it's what happens." He continued sipping his coffee. "I don't really want to talk about it too much; I might jinx it." Maddoc chuckled at the notion and changed the subject. They talked until it was time for her to leave for her son's. After saying good night, she let him out the back door.

The lock on Corky's door clicked, and Maddoc realized the twilight had turned to near darkness. The shadows of his familiar side garden had lengthened, looking ominous. The porch light at the front of the house cast a weak beam across the front yard but didn't extend around the house. Screwing up his courage, he walked across his own yard toward the anemic light, which flashed and went out.

"Great, I'm in a cheesy horror movie." His own words girded him in a bizarre way, and he stepped toward the front door, moving faster. Walking up the front stairs to the porch, he fumbled in his pocket for his keys, looking around and jumping slightly at the creaks of the porch boards under his own footfalls.

Fishing in his pocket for his keys, Maddoc cursed softly that he hadn't gotten them out earlier. His fingers had just found the metal when a pair of arms grabbed him by the waist and he smelled what he was sure was alcohol.

"Hi, lovely, did you like my flowers?" Maddoc jumped, and the arms tightened, a hardness pressing against his behind as the alcohol-fortified voice behind him continued. "I thought we could have some fun."

Maddoc could feel the stronger man pulling him away from the door. *Stay on your feet.* Ivan's words at the gym rang in his mind.

"You never gave me the time of day, but you will now that your boyfriend's gone." A car pulled along the street, casting just enough light so he could see where he was being led for a few seconds. "You don't even know who I am. Do you?" His attacker yanked Maddoc's hair, and Maddoc let loose a yell from the depths of his frightened soul.

Stomping hard, he caught the top of the man's foot, earning a yell of pain and a loosening of the grip around him, but not enough for him to get away. Using his weight and his arms, just like Ivan taught him, he slammed his attacker in the groin. The wail was gratifying as the attacker grabbed his balls and fell to the decking.

Maddoc ran, leaping down the steps at a bound and running across the yard. Footsteps behind him sent his adrenaline soaring, and he took off like the hounds of hell were after him.

VI

"MADDOC," Ivan called and watched as his lover slowed and finally stopped. Ivan walked up to him and silently folded him into his arms. "You okay?"

Maddoc shook his head against his chest, and Ivan felt his shoulders begin to shake. "I'm sorry," Maddoc said into his chest, and Ivan felt himself smile.

"Come on, Tiger, we need to see if he's still writhing on the ground." Maddoc nodded in response and held onto him as they walked back toward the house.

Ivan saw a bent-over figure trying to descend the stairs. "If you don't sit down right now, a lot more than your balls are gonna hurt! I'll break your fucking neck!" Maddoc let go, and Ivan continued walked closer, standing a short distance away, waiting. "I mean it!" He used the same voice he had with rookies in the Corps. Ivan could see the moment Maddoc's attacker decided to listen—his shoulders slumped further, and slowly he lowered himself to the step, hands still clutching his groin.

Ivan felt Maddoc come up behind him. "Go inside and turn on the light. Let's see who this asshole is, then call the police." He touched Maddoc's arm. "He won't try anything." Ivan looked at the seated figure. "Or he won't have any balls left to hurt!" All Ivan heard was a soft moan and shallow breathing as Maddoc slowly walked up the far edge of the stairs before unlocking the door and disappearing inside.

"I think my balls are swelling."

"Who gives a fuck? If I'd have been here, you wouldn't have any left, so consider yourself lucky." The yard light snapped on, and the door cracked open. "The porch light won't come on, and the police are on their way." The door opened a little further. "Do you want me to come out with you?"

"No, stay inside, I'll watch over blue balls here." Ivan folded his arms over his chest. The man stared at the pavement, occasionally raising his eyes before lowering them again. A few minutes later, Ivan saw flashing lights and a police cruiser pulled up in front of the house. The man started to stand up, but Ivan growled at him and he sat back down.

"Someone called in an attack." The officer approached, followed by another.

The front door opened, and Maddoc stepped outside. "I did. He attacked me." Maddoc pointed at the seated man, his voice becoming agitated.

"It's all right, sir." The first officer turned to the other. "Why don't you take his statement. I'll talk to this one." The second officer followed Maddoc inside, and Ivan watched as his lover closed the door and locked it behind him.

"Do you want to tell me what happened?" The officer addressed the still-moaning attacker.

"He hit me in the balls." He moaned softly, obviously trying to get sympathy.

"Do you need an ambulance?" The man nodded, and the officer made the call and spoke to Ivan, taking his statement as he waited for the ambulance. "We'll get his at the hospital." Ivan nodded and waited as more flashing lights appeared.

The ambulance arrived a few minutes before Maddoc and the officer emerged from the house. The attacker just sat on the step moaning, and Ivan was certain he was going for sympathy, but by the looks the police officers kept shooting his way, it wasn't working. Maddoc stood next to him, and Ivan slipped an arm around his waist. "Do you know this guy?"

Maddoc nodded slowly, his eyes wide as saucers. "He's my neighbor. Henry Hudgins." Maddoc began shifting uncomfortably next to him. "I never saw him much." At hearing his name, Henry moaned again, but Maddoc glared at him. "Shut up, Henry. You're lucky you have any balls left after what you did to me." Maddoc shook with rage next to him, and Ivan rubbed his arm gently before tightening his grip. After everything he'd been through, it was good to still see the fight in him. That more than anything told Ivan that Maddoc was going to be okay.

The EMTs finished with their preparations and bundled Henry onto a gurney, tying him down before placing him inside the ambulance. One of the police officers rode along while the other asked a few additional questions before asking them to come to the station in the morning to sign their statements.

Once everyone had left, Ivan led Maddoc inside. As soon as the door was closed and locked, Maddoc squeezed him tight and began to shake. "It's okay."

"I can't stop thinking about what he wanted, what he was going to do to me," Maddoc replied, voice muffled against Ivan's neck.

"Don't." Ivan lifted Maddoc's chin before stroking his cheek. "He didn't get a chance to do anything because you defended yourself." Ivan looked into those water-blue eyes. "That was all you. You're stronger than you realize, and it's time you give yourself credit for that."

Maddoc's expression didn't change. "I almost wet myself when he grabbed me. I was so scared." Maddoc shifted his eyes to the floor.

"Do you think I wasn't scared when I was in combat?" Maddoc's eyes lifted to meet his. "I was terrified, but I had a job to do, people depending on me. But my training kicked in, and that gave me strength. The same goes for you." Ivan ran a hand through Maddoc's hair. "You may have been scared, but you did what you had to, to defend yourself." He lifted Maddoc's head slightly. "And you did that perfectly. I have no doubt you could do it again." Ivan brought his lips to Maddoc's, tasting the unique sweetness that was his lover. "I don't call you Tiger for nothing."

"I always thought you were teasing."

"Nope. I learned pretty early to be able to read people, and I could tell there was a tiger in you. You're strong; you just needed to realize it for yourself." Maddoc's now-smoldering eyes met his. "Come on, let's go upstairs. I want to wash him off you."

Maddoc's nose crinkled. "Good. I can smell him on me." Maddoc put out the lights, and then Ivan led him upstairs and right to the master bathroom. Slipping off his clothes, Ivan stood naked before a still-dressed Maddoc. Pulling him close, Ivan kissed his lover hard, possessively. "Ivan." Maddoc moaned softly into the kiss, and he felt warm hands slide down his back before cupping his butt.

Stepping back slightly, Ivan grabbed the tail of Maddoc's shirt, lifting it over his head. Their hands in the air, Maddoc clamped his lips onto a nipple, the bud hardening instantly. Ivan arched as he tugged the shirt away. Maddoc's arms encircled him, and he felt warm, sensuous lips and tongue slide over his chest. A slight nip at the hard bud had his head spinning. The lips pulled away, and Ivan watched with rapt fascination as Maddoc turned around and slid his pants down his legs, that white butt bobbing in front of him. "Fuck, Tiger, are you trying to drive me crazy?"

Maddoc stepped out of his pants and slowly turned around. "That's the idea." Ivan watched as Maddoc stretched to turn on the water, and his hands slid along the stretched skin, his own lips and tongue taking the opportunity to taste. As the water warmed, he continued lavishing kisses all over Maddoc's body.

Stepping under the water, he pulled Maddoc to him, letting the spray sluice over both of them before reaching for the shampoo and running his slippery hands through Maddoc's hair. Turning around, Maddoc lolled against him as he washed the red curls before running soapy hands over his lover's chest. Maddoc's moans became a soft cry when Ivan ran his hand along Maddoc's throbbing length. "Ivan." He felt Maddoc shift more weight against him, leaning on him for support. Letting his hand slip away, Ivan washed every inch of Maddoc's skin, making sure anything that remained from earlier washed down the drain with the soap. Ivan knew it wasn't that simple in reality, but it was what he could do. The rest was up to his lover.

Slowly, he let his hands fall away from the smooth skin, and Maddoc turned. Soaping his hands, Ivan stiffened slightly as Maddoc's hands stroked along his neck. "It's like a brush," Maddoc said with a smile as he washed Ivan's hair. "It feels really sexy."

"It does?"

Maddoc nodded, his eyes darkening. "All of you is sexy." Maddoc hands slid down his chest, soaping and stroking. Ivan grabbed the towel bar as Maddoc's hands glided over his stomach, continuing lower until he was stroking him. "Especially this." Maddoc twisted his hand as he stroked, driving Ivan out of his mind. Ivan's hips began thrusting lightly on their own, instinct taking over, his mind narrowing all its attention to Maddoc's hand on his cock. The warm water washed away the soap, and Maddoc's fingers played him like a flute as he again latched onto a nipple, tongue sliding roughly over his skin. Ivan found himself filling the shower with his sounds of need as Maddoc's hand and mouth made every nerve stand up and shout for unabashed joy.

"Tiger!" Ivan gasped in frustration as the hand slipped away. Breathing like he'd just run a marathon, he tried to get control of himself as he looked at Maddoc smiling back at him ferally. "Why'd you stop?"

Maddoc began stroking his skin, washing off the last of the soap before turning off the water. "I want you in bed." Maddoc stepped out and handed him a towel.

"You're a sadist," Ivan grumbled through a smile.

"Maybe, but think how great it'll feel soon." Maddoc leaned close to him, nipping at Ivan's ear.

"It will," Ivan agreed in a deep whisper. "It'll feel incredible when you take me." Maddoc's eyes went wide with excited disbelief. Reaching out, Ivan took Maddoc's towel and dropped it on the floor, adding his own to the small pile. Turning off the light, Ivan led his lover to the bed, turning down the covers before tugging him down on top. Maddoc's weight felt wonderful on top of him, and his lover put his lips and hands to good use. For a while it seemed as though Maddoc didn't know what he wanted to do first. Ivan arched beneath every touch, his skin on overdrive.

Then Maddoc's lips took his and everything fell away: the room, the wind, the sound of the cars outside; everything receded until it was just him and his Tiger. Hands gently lifted his legs, and Maddoc writhed down his body, kissing and nuzzling until a tongue slid along his length.

Ivan gasped as Maddoc took him deep. "Tiger, so good!" He felt Maddoc smile around his cock and suck him harder, deeper. All he could do was rock his head on the pillow, fists clutching at the sheets as his lover drove him toward heaven. But there was more. Ivan felt a finger glide around his opening before working its way inside, then retreating before going deeper. He felt a slight curl and the world went white in a blaze of unimagined pleasure. "Tiger!" His hand pulled, and he heard the sheet rip a little as Maddoc took him deep, and he shot with a force he'd never felt before in his life, like Maddoc had yanked his release from him as he thrashed on the bed.

Collapsing into a ragged heap, he gasped for breath amid the wreckage of Maddoc's sheets. Opening he eyes, he saw his Tiger beaming back at him. Then he was kissing him, the smaller man devouring him, taking everything he had and returning it twofold.

Wrapping his legs around Maddoc's hips, he felt a finger slide into him, then another. The stretch burned for a second, replaced quickly by an inner warmth, knowing that it was his Tiger that was filling him. Then the fingers slipped away, and Maddoc locked their gazes. "Are you sure?"

Ivan's mouth went dry and he rasped, "God, yes, Tiger, make me yours."

Maddoc shook his head. "I'll join us together." Ivan nodded and Maddoc pressed forward, entering him slowly. After what had happened, he'd expected Maddoc to be more forceful, but instead he got a quiet strength as he steadily slid deeper. Muscles stretched, and Ivan threw his head back as he was filled in a way he'd never imagined. "Look at me." Ivan met Maddoc's eyes as his lover began to move.

The thrusts started slow and deep, hitting that white lightning spot every few strokes. Ivan felt himself getting hard again, and he began stroking himself, only to have his hand batted away, replaced with Maddoc's. Every time Maddoc went deep, Ivan thrust into those fingers, torn between the two sensations. Maddoc's thrusts became more erratic, faster, and Ivan felt his own climax approaching again. Maddoc moaned, and he felt Ivan's grip around him tighten, pushing him over the edge.

Maddoc cried out, and he throbbed deep, Ivan following right behind him, crying out his release to his lover.

Maddoc collapsed onto him, arms winding around his neck. His Tiger kissed him softly, fingers rubbing his short hair. Ivan returned the kiss and gasped softly as Maddoc slipped from his body. Maddoc pulled away, their eyes locking. Ivan expected to see contentment, but those blue eyes were as turbulent as a rough sea. "What is it?" Maddoc began to shift, and Ivan rubbed his hand languidly up and down the smooth back.

Maddoc bit his lower lip. "Why me?"

Ivan cocked his head against the pillow. "Why you, what?"

Propping himself on his arms, Maddoc studied his eyes before sitting up, straddling Ivan's body, his gaze drilling into him. "Why'd you pick me?"

"I thought we sort of picked each other." Ivan had no idea where this was coming from, and he felt himself squirm under Maddoc's gaze. He'd stared down enemy fighters, even killed men up close and personal, but that look from Maddoc made him flinch.

"Ivan." Maddoc's hand slid down his chest before a finger traced the lines on his stomach. "You could have any man you wanted. Just look at you. You're a gay man's wet dream."

So that was the source of that look he'd seen on and off but could never quite place. "I learned a long time ago that you go into battle with the best man to protect your back; it doesn't matter what he looks like."

"I'm not a battle." Some of the turmoil in Maddoc's face had dissipated, but the insecurity remained.

"No, you're the guy that has my back, for a long time, I hope." Ivan pulled Maddoc back down on top of him, whispering into his ear. "And for the record, you're you, and that makes you beautiful."

"But—"

Ivan cupped Maddoc's cheeks, kissing him hard. "No buts. You're strong, fun, and sexy as hell."

"I'm not strong," Maddoc countered with a smirk.

"Tell that to the guy with swollen balls," Ivan countered, and Maddoc tried to look away, but Ivan stopped him. "You have nothing to be ashamed of. He stalked you for weeks and attacked you on your own front porch. Hell, you defended yourself and nothing more." Ivan could tell Maddoc didn't fully believe him. "After he was down, did you hurt him further?"

"No, I ran away just like you said."

"You used the force you had to and nothing more."

Ivan saw Maddoc's eyes widen. "I did, didn't I?"

Ivan felt his heart warm, seeing the confidence bloom from within his lover. He rolled them on the bed, pinning his lover to the mattress. "You certainly did."

"When you showed me that at the gym, I honestly never thought I would or could use it."

"No one ever does, Tiger." Ivan gently stroked Maddoc's red curls as he settled on the mattress next to him, tugging his lover close after pulling up the covers as Maddoc mumbled something that nearly stopped his heart. "What did you say?"

Maddoc rolled over to face him. "I said I love you."

There was no doubt or hesitation. "I love you too." He wanted to shout it to the world, but Maddoc brought their lips together. No words had ever made him feel happier than this incredible man telling him he loved him. His heart pounded and his blood raced—those three little words had him so unbelievably pumped.

Core Training

Andrew Grey

I

"HAPPY birthday," the little blonde girl said perkily from behind the counter after scanning his membership card.

"Thanks," Hugh responded, with absolutely no enthusiasm whatsoever. He gave her the best smile he could muster and moped his way toward the locker room, the noise, the banging, the grunting, the damn bouncy music that drove them all crazy, all of it adding to his sour mood. "Excuse you!" Hugh growled as a man hurried out of the locker room, nearly bumping into him.

"Sorry," the man replied, looking Hugh over from head to toe like he was deciding if he was going to give him shit. He must have decided that at six-four and big as hell, Hugh wasn't someone the musclehead wanted to mess with. Lumbering into the locker room, Hugh plopped his bag on one of the benches and began tearing open lockers, trying to find an empty one.

"What crawled up your butt?" Dan opened the locker behind him, and of course it was empty.

"Nothing," Hugh huffed, and he willed his mood to lighten. His friends didn't need to pay just because it happened to be his birthday… with him spending it alone yet again. Granted, it was his own fault. He'd spent his entire life going from man to man. "It's fucked getting old."

"Quit your whining," Dan scolded lightly as he pulled off his shirt, "I'm older than you are. And it's all a state of mind, anyway."

Hugh half watched as Dan lowered his pants. "Then I'm eighty."

"Hey, birdgazers!" Lonnie called as he walked in, taking the locker next to Hugh. "You look like shit, man."

"It's his birthday," Dan teased with a little too much glee.

Lonnie smacked Dan's bare ass, the slap resounding through the room. "You were moaning like a cheap whore about your birthday a few months ago."

Dan glared at Lonnie as he rubbed his butt, pulling on his underwear and shorts. "You'll pay for that."

Lonnie shot him an "ooh, I'm so scared" grin and finished changing. "You gonna work out with us or be a pussy all your life?"

Hugh looked at Lonnie, trying to see if he was serious. He was about to respond when a kid walked into their bay of lockers and undid his lock, and Hugh found his gaze pulled to the blond-headed wisp of a man who looked like a stiff breeze would blow him away.

"Hey, you listening to me or looking at dick?" Lonnie would say anything, and Hugh almost retorted, but it would only draw more attention to the fact that he was indeed looking at the young bit of eye candy instead of paying attention to what was being said.

Hugh forced his eyes away from the smooth back that appeared when the little man slipped off his shirt. God, he was young—cute as hell, but way too young for Hugh. "I don't think I'm going to be very good company."

"Okay, we'll see you out there." Lonnie shut his locker and waited for Dan, and the two left.

With the room quiet, Hugh found his attention drawn to the small man, who was tugging on a fresh T-shirt. Pulling his attention to where it should be, Hugh closed his locker and followed out to the weight floor, enjoying the bouncing globes in front of him the entire time.

Hugh walked as far as the stairs to the mezzanine and stopped. He really didn't feel like lifting, and he didn't feel like cardio. After a few seconds, a blur passed in front of him and up the stairs. Focusing his eyes, he saw that tiny, tight butt and followed it upstairs. What the fuck, at least he could enjoy the scenery.

Ascending the stairs, he found an elliptical machine, climbed on, and started moving, his mind going on autopilot, his attention turning inward. Hugh was always like this—he'd start his cardio workout and let his thoughts take over, the noise fade, and the time fly.

"Your friend is a real ass." A soft voice cut through his thoughts, and the sounds of the gym assaulted him again. Looking at the machine next to him, he saw the man from the locker room looking back at him.

"That's just Lonnie; he has a mouth on him like no one else." Hugh got a good look at the man's face for the first time. "Don't I know you?" Then it hit him; he did know him, if he could only remember the kid's name. "Max."

The blond man smiled. "Yes, Max Pierce. You come into The Grill a few nights a week, but I don't know your name." Max looked a little embarrassed, but there was no need to be. It wasn't as though they'd been formally introduced.

"I'm Hugh Douglas." He returned the man's smile. "I haven't seen you here before."

"This is my first day." He indicated the woman working out next to him, and she smiled at Hugh briefly before stopping her machine. "Lila dragged me here."

"I'm going downstairs, Max. I'll see you tomorrow at work." She touched his shoulder before leaving.

"Are you going to join?" Hugh asked, making conversation.

He seemed to be thinking about it. "Will that mean I'll be able to look like you?" Max's smile was huge, and Hugh wasn't sure, but he thought the kid was flirting with him. "Because if it does," Max went on, "I'll join up today."

Yup, the kid was definitely flirting. "I don't know about that, but you already look just fine to me." Hell, the kid looked more than fine, and he imagined how good it would feel to bury himself in that tight little body. And fuck a duck, if the kid could flirt, why couldn't he? Besides if he'd been a girl, the little thing would have been batting his eyelashes and swaying his hips. As it was, Max's smile was enough to get him going, let alone the rest of the small, hot package.

"I am not," Max argued, but Hugh could tell he was being playful. "I'm skinny and small, not all strong and, if you won't punch me out for saying so, freakin' huge like you." Max's eyes went appropriately wide just before those eyes raked over every inch of him. Hugh could almost feel them before they zeroed in on his crotch, which had definitely taken up a now somewhat visible interest. He saw Max lean in a little closer. "And you're big all over." That smile turned wry, and Hugh tugged involuntarily at the collar of his shirt. Was it getting hot in here or what?

It had been a long time since anyone had looked at him like he was laid out on an all-you-can-eat buffet. Well, happy fucking birthday to me. Maybe the day wasn't going to turn out so bad after all. "You could get somewhat bigger if you lifted weights."

"I don't think everything could get bigger." Max looked down again, and Hugh felt his dick jump and throb. "Not that some things need it." Max's voice seemed to wrap right around his dick and grab a good, tight hold. Taking a look at the man again, Hugh took a deep breath and reminded himself that the kid was probably half his age. And while he wouldn't turn down a good old-fashioned fuck, Hugh had to ask himself what this kid could possibly see in him except the size of the bulge in his shorts.

Hugh heard beeps as buttons were pushed. Max's machine came to a stop, and the man stepped off. Thank God—Max had had his fun getting him all riled up, and now that he was done, Hugh could try to get his dick under control and finish his workout. Closing his eyes, he tried to get back in the zone. He had to tell his body that there was no way the sexy little man was really interested in him anyway; Max had probably just been having a bit of fun with the old guy.

"Hugh."

He opened his eyes and saw Max standing right in front of him, leaning on the machine, face just above the display. "You wanna go back to your place so I can ride you into next week?"

Hugh's feet stumbled, and he nearly fell backward before regaining his balance and bringing the machine to a stop. "You serious?"

Max inclined his head once as he stepped off to the side, glaring straight at Hugh's crotch. There was no mistaking what that meant. "You're damn right." Max stepped close enough that Hugh could smell his breath. "So let's shower and get out of here. The sooner we're at your place, the sooner I can ride you like the stallion you are." With that final invitation, Max turned and walked down the stairs, looking over his shoulder, giving Hugh one last smoldering look before disappearing around the bend in the staircase.

He didn't have to be asked twice. Grabbing a paper towel from the dispenser, he wiped down the machine before hurrying down the stairs and into the locker room. Racing to his locker, he carefully stripped down—it wasn't seemly to be seen sporting wood—wrapped a towel tightly around his waist to hold everything in place, and made a beeline for the showers.

After what had to be one of the fastest showers in history, Hugh returned to the locker room, where Max was already dressing. He knew he was being watched, and since no one was around, he dropped the towel, giving Max a bit of a show before pulling on his briefs, adjusting himself properly, and then putting on his pants and shirt. He knew he saw Max swallow as Max watched him, and Hugh smiled to himself as he finished dressing.

In five minutes flat, he was dressed, packed up, and heading out toward the front door, where Max was waiting for him.

"Do you live close?"

"Just a few blocks," Hugh answered as he watched Max lick his lips invitingly.

"I'll follow you, then."

Without any more preamble, Hugh left the club, briskly walking across the lot to his red Mustang convertible. He saw Max get into his car, and after pulling out, led the way home.

Hugh half expected Max to be playing some sort of joke on him, but the young man pulled up right behind him as Hugh parked his car on the street in front of his house. Getting out, he led the way up the walk and unlocked the door. He could feel Max's gaze on him, and Jesus Christ, it made him feel good. He might be twice the man's age, but there was no disguising the naked desire in Max's eyes. It felt damn good to be wanted like that, even if it was just for a quick fuck and maybe a snuggle for a few minutes afterward.

Walking inside, he dropped his bag near the door. Turning around, he found Max right behind him. The door closed with a thunk that vibrated through the floor, and then Max was trying to climb him. Leaning forward, he took the little spitfire's mouth in a kiss and found his tongue sucked hard as Max did his best imitation of a vacuum cleaner. It felt as though the man was trying to suck his brains out through his mouth. And that small body vibrated against him as arms wrapped around his neck. Straightening up, Hugh lifted Max off his feet as Max's short legs wrapped around Hugh's waist, ankles feeling as though they locked together, and Hugh began to walk both of them toward the bedroom.

He could barely see. Thank God he knew his way around the house, because Max's lips never separated from Hugh's, and he could feel Max's arousal against his stomach. The man's body might have been small, but not everything was proportional, that was for fucking sure.

In the bedroom, he laid Max on his back. Max's arms unwound from around his neck, and fingers began tugging at the hem of his shirt. When their lips separated so they could get Hugh's shirt over his head, Max's lips latched onto a nipple, teeth scraping along his skin, just enough to send a zing down his spine. Dropping the shirt on the floor, Hugh palmed Max's head, hissing softly as those lips and tongue worked magic on his skin.

Tugging gently, Hugh pulled Max's shirt over his head and brought their lips together again, holding Max firmly against him, chests pressed together. Hugh felt Max struggle a little, and he pulled away, looking down into the smaller man's eyes. "Maybe I should have you on top," Hugh commented, and Max took that as an invitation. In no time, Hugh found himself on his back on the bed, Max straddling him, and a hot tongue lapping against his skin as warm fingers worked their way into his pants. "Jesus." Hugh's eyes widened as Max's fingers wound around his length, gripping him hard, and he was still in his pants. But not for long—those fingers slipped away, his pants parted, and Max returned, pulling him free, gripping him tightly.

Hugh had to give Max credit. Hell, more than credit—the kid was a master. Max had him writhing on the mattress like a first-time teenager.

Max stepped off the bed, tugging down Hugh's pants before pulling them off. "Fuck, you are big everywhere," Max commented softly, eyes wide, pink tongue licking his lips.

"Get yourself naked too."

Max didn't have to be told twice. Shoes thunked on the floor, and briefs slid down short, slender legs. Naked, Max stared at Hugh for a few seconds and then jumped, landing on top of him, and Hugh found his arms filled with a bouncing, wriggling, live-wire of a man whose lips, hands, and body all combined to get Hugh's motor running in a way he'd never experienced before. Everywhere Max touched came alive. Max's tongue licked a line up his chest, and Hugh could have sworn he felt the skin almost burn, it was so sensitive. And when Max did it again, Hugh thought he was about ready to come right then and there. It was only sheer force of will and an overwhelming desire to bury himself in that intense, tight body that kept him from going over the edge.

"Damn, you even taste good," Max murmured as lips and tongue trailed down Hugh's chest and stomach. Hugh watched that pink tongue dart out, barely touching his crown, and his dick jumped as though it just had to get closer to Max. "Damn good." Max went in for another taste, and this time his lips slipped over the head, and Hugh felt that tongue do something that made his head throb.

"If you keep that up, I'm not gonna last very long, and I want to be inside you," Hugh groaned as Max took him deep down his throat. "Max!"

The lips slipped away, and Max's huge, expressive eyes glowed back up at him. "Fuck yeah!" Max moved over him again, and Hugh reached to the bedside table, retrieving a bottle of lube and a condom.

"I need to get you ready," Hugh cautioned lightly, as Max was already reaching for the condom, tearing it open, and then rolling it down Hugh's length. The bottle of lube snapped open, and Hugh felt the cool liquid lubricating the condom. Watching in delighted fascination, he saw Max's fingers reach around him, and the man's mouth fell open, eyes glazing over as he prepared himself. Then Max moved himself into position. "Don't you need more?"

Max sank onto Hugh in one smooth motion, and Hugh felt the air fly from his lungs and his eyes bulge as he was completely surrounded by the tightest heat he'd ever imagined, let alone actually felt in his life, and that was saying a lot. Max began to move almost immediately, lifting himself and then sliding down Hugh again. Faster, harder, the small body picked up the pace, tight butt grinding against him.

Then without warning, Max slid away, and Hugh's eyes flew open in surprise. Max said nothing; he just lay on his back, legs in the air. Hugh didn't have to be told twice what he wanted. Kneeling on the bed, he pulled Max to him and slid into that body.

"Yes!" Max practically screamed as Hugh nailed his prostate on the first shot. After all the men he'd fucked over the years, Hugh knew his way around, and the surprised look on Max's face was just what he wanted to see. "That's it, God, fuck me!"

"You got it, hot stuff." Hugh began thrusting deep and hard, the bed rocking.

"I won't break, for Christ's sake. Fuck me like you mean it!" Max punctuated his demand by grabbing the back of Hugh's legs with his hands and driving them together with some sort of unintelligible cry.

Hugh began driving into the smaller man. "That what you want?" He thrust as hard as he dared, the bed jumping beneath them.

"Shit yeah! Now that's a fuck!" Max began fisting his cock as Hugh drove hard and deep, Max crying out after each and every thrust. Hugh saw sweat break on Max's chest, making the other man's skin glow as the late afternoon sun shone through the windows.

Leaning forward, Hugh drove as deep as he could, arms pulling Max to him, their lips crashing together in a mashing kiss. Bending Max until he was nearly standing on his head, Hugh thrust deep into that sweet butt, and felt Max go wild beneath him as the younger man shot ropes on his chest, neck, and cheek, screaming his release at the top of his lungs. "Holy Fuck!" The cry triggered Hugh's own climax, and it slammed into Hugh with the force of a space shot.

Hugh could barely breathe as they both stared at each other, unmoving, trying to catch the breath that had been orgasmed out of them. Slowly, feeling and reason returned to Hugh, and he withdrew from Max's body, helping the smaller man settle on the bed before taking care of the condom and retrieving a warm cloth.

Max practically purred as Hugh cleaned him and then himself before returning the cloth to the bathroom and rejoining Max on the bed. Hugh half expected Max to get up and dress, but the younger man curled next to him. "That was amazing," Max purred, a hand gliding over Hugh's chest. "How soon before we can do it again?" Max's eyes caught his, and Hugh saw the expectant look.

There was no way he could do that again soon. Hell, he doubted he'd be up to doing that again before a nice nap, a good dinner, and maybe a few vitamin E pills. The frustration with his birthday that had slipped his mind returned with a vengeance. There was a time when he'd have been as ready to go as Max was now, and his mind was willing, but there was no way his body was going to be up for it. "Not for a while, I'm afraid." Fuck, he hated those words, and he hated realizing that they pertained to him.

"Okay," Max replied, and he shifted on the bed. Hugh figured that was the kiss of death and that Max would leave, but the other man's weight resettled on the bed. "I'll wait."

Max's hot little body snuggled close, and Hugh could already feel the younger man's awakened arousal. Hugh couldn't stifle the groan of frustration. He wanted to be young again, to have his life ahead of him. Instead, the most energetic and thrilling years seemed to be behind him, and what did he have to show for it? A string of men he'd fucked and an empty house he shared with no one—in other words, an empty life. And it was no one's fault but his own.

He felt Max's long erection glide against his hip. "We may not be able to do that again, but there are other things." Hugh slid his hand down Max's side and over his hip before clasping the man's now-throbbing cock in his fingers.

"Yeah? Like what?" Max's eyes glistened with curiosity and wonder as Hugh slid his fingers over the steely hardness covered with soft skin, letting his thumb slide over the head.

"Oh, there's a lot we can do," Hugh hummed softly as he shifted Max onto his back, spreading those legs wide. Opening his mouth, he slid his lips over the head of Max's cock as he used two fingers to tease the skin around his opening.

"Jesus, yes!" Max began pushing toward him, and Hugh let his fingers breach the opening, careful not to hurt him. Hugh was initially reticent about going inside him, but Max seemed insistent.

"Okay, now slowly fuck my mouth." Hugh took Max deeper, and he began to move. Whenever Max slid into his mouth, his fingers withdrew, and when he pulled back, Max fucked himself deeper on Hugh's fingers. From the sounds and steady stream of soft curses, Max wasn't sure what to do.

"Want more." Max began moving like he was trying to figure out how to get his dick sucked and Hugh's fingers deep into him at the same time.

"Just enjoy them both," Hugh soothed, and then he sucked hard on Max's long cock, giving the man what he wanted, and was rewarded with moans and whimpers.

"Gotta... wanna," Max muttered, as he kept moving, head thrown back, body just writhing between the two sensations. Rubbing Max's perineum with his thumb, Hugh heard a loud hiss and then felt Max throb in his mouth before Max's sweet saltiness burst on his tongue. And fuck if the man didn't look absolutely beautiful when he came: mouth hanging open, eyes rolled back, and head tilted slightly like he was unsure of what was going to happen.

Withdrawing his fingers, Hugh hugged Max to him, kissing the man as he lowered him to the bed. This time when they cuddled, Max didn't stir at all. He just curled close, their heat mixing together. With a slight sigh, Hugh watched Max begin to drift off to sleep. This was nice, almost too nice, and Hugh knew he'd better enjoy it, because as soon as Max woke up, he'd realize the man next to him was too old, and he probably wouldn't be able to get dressed fast enough.

"Aren't you going to rest?" Max's brown eyes slid open. "'Cause if you're not, you could always fuck me again."

"God, are you trying to completely wear me out?"

"Come on." Max smiled, resting his head on Hugh's shoulder. "I was only kidding. I think it was you that wore me out."

Hugh chuckled, feeling a little less old. "Thanks for that." He still figured Max would get up and leave at any minute.

"So, would you like to get something to eat? I'm starved." Max got off the bed, waiting for him.

"You're not leaving?"

"You want me to leave?"

"No." Hugh answered quickly, maybe too quickly, but he really didn't want Max to go, which was unusual for him. "It's just that most guys leave once they've gotten their rocks off, you know?"

"Well"—Max put his hands on his hips, glaring down at him around a smile— "I'm not most guys. Besides, I'm no virgin, and no one has ever blown my mind like that." Max leaned closer, kissing him, lips pulling gently. "So can we get dressed and go eat something so we can come back here and fuck again?"

"Don't you have to work or something?"

"Not till tomorrow, so tonight I'm all yours." Max began pulling on his clothes, and Hugh got off the bed and began dressing as well.

"Do you like Middle Eastern food?"

Max nodded and flashed a bright smile as he finished dressing, and Hugh thought that maybe, just maybe, this was turning out to be the best birthday he'd had in a long time.

II

MAX arrived home at almost midnight. Walking up the driveway, he was relieved that there were no lights on in the house. If he was lucky, his dad would already be asleep, but as he reached for the door, lights flashed on. Max huffed softly as he stepped inside, knowing his dad was waiting for him.

"Where in hell have you been?" Max's father barked.

"Out with a friend," Max answered as he avoided where his father was sitting at the kitchen table, a bottle in front of him—in other words, his usual behavior. "I told you I'd be late."

"Which friends were these?" Max's dad stumbled as he tried to get up, making it to his feet after the second try. "The same friends who kept calling to see when you were going to be home? Or were these different friends?" he slurred as he stepped toward Max, grabbing him by the arm.

"Just a friend, okay?" Max wrenched his arm away and stepped back. "I went to dinner and spent the evening with a friend. Geez, Dad, why don't you go to bed?" It was always like this whenever his dad started drinking.

"Some faggoty friend I bet," his dad slurred as he let Max take his arm to lead him down the hall to the bedroom. "I guess I should expect it having a fruit for a son." He stumbled through the door and flopped on the bed. "A big faggoty fag for a son."

Max thought about helping him out of his clothes, but he was soon snoring, and Max decided against it, pulling a blanket over his dad's shoulders and closing the door as he left. Walking to his own room, Max undressed and stepped quietly into the bathroom where he cleaned up before returning to his bedroom and climbing beneath the covers. He could still smell Hugh's scent on his skin, and he thought about showering, but decided instead that he liked the idea of smelling like the big, sexy man.

His phone rang, and Max reached for the table, grabbing for the phone so it wouldn't wake his dad. Even drunk, the man was a light sleeper, and when someone woke him, he was as mean as a grizzly bear fresh from hibernation. Looking at the lighted display, Max answered the call.

"Max, I was starting to get worried. I called you earlier, but you didn't answer. And when I called your house, your dad started acting weird."

"I'm fine, Lila." She knew about his dad and was always telling Max he should leave and find his own place, but he really couldn't afford it. And if he left, who would take care of his dad? "My phone was off, and I just got home a few minutes ago."

"Were you with that old guy from the gym all this time?"

"Yes, and he was really nice." Max rolled his eyes even though she couldn't see. "Besides, he's not that old."

"I heard some guys talking at the gym. Today was his birthday, and he's forty-four, almost twenty years older than you." He heard the scolding in Lila's voice. "I know you like older guys, but isn't that taking things a little far?"

"He was nice and we had fun. It's not as though we're falling in love or anything," Max replied defensively, although he was hoping he'd be able to see Hugh again. The man really flipped his switches.

"If you say so, Maxie." He heard her sigh. "Just be careful. I'll see you tomorrow at work." She disconnected, and Max closed his phone, listening for a second to the sounds of the house and his dad's snoring before turning off his light and going to sleep.

Max woke to the sounds of banging in the house. Throwing back the covers, he padded down the hall and into the kitchen. His dad was trying to make coffee and had dropped the can on the floor. "Morning, Dad." Max tried to be cheerful.

His dad humphed as he finally got the coffeemaker started. "You got any money?" Max shook his head slowly, and his dad held out his hand. "You always got money, kid, hand it over."

"I was off yesterday so I don't have any tip money. All I got is enough for my lunch." Max backed away a few steps and then turned and walked down the hall toward his room.

"How'd you get home last night, anyway?"

"I drove myself home," Max called back, and then he closed the door loudly to cut off any other questions. It wasn't as though he was the one who'd been drinking. Hugh had been nice enough to offer him a ride home in case he didn't feel like driving. He hadn't asked Max to stay, and if Max were honest with himself, he'd been a little disappointed, but he got the idea that Hugh wasn't much for anything other than a good fuck, which was a shame, because they'd talked at dinner and the man was smart and funny. He'd met guys who were great in bed and could barely put two words together, but Hugh wasn't like that at all. Still, Hugh had offered to give him a ride home, which was nice.

Stepping into the bathroom, Max shaved and then got into the tub, turning on the water and starting the shower. Standing under the spray, he let the water sluice over him and thought of Hugh, wondering what it would be like to have Hugh with him. He could still feel the big man's hands running over his skin, and he could almost taste the man on his tongue. Soaping his hands, he curled his fingers over his length and squeezed just like Hugh had done the night before.

God, he was still sore from Hugh's very athletic fucking, not that he was complaining in the least. If he never saw the man again, at least he'd have that little reminder for the next day or so. Letting his hand slide, he gasped softly as a finger ghosted over the head, just like Hugh had done when he was deep inside him that last time. The man might have been older, but he knew his way around a man's body, that was for damn sure. Wetting his other hand, he slid a finger into his opening and began moving his hips, recreating what Hugh had done the evening before. It wasn't quite as good as Hugh's mouth on him, but his body remembered and reacted with almost as much force. Snapping his hips, Max felt his balls tighten, and he quickened the pace as his climax hit him. He wanted to cry out, Hugh's name on the tip of his tongue, but he stifled any sound as he coated his hand with his release.

Finishing his shower with a satisfied smile, he padded to his bedroom and got dressed for work. Leaving the house awhile later, he heard his dad getting dressed for his job at the mill. "I'll see you later, Dad," he called out, but he didn't listen for an answer—probably wouldn't be one, anyway—and left the house.

As he was climbing into his car, he saw the front door open, and his dad strode up to his door, saying, "I need the car today." Max sighed to himself, turned off the engine, and got out. "Don't look at me like that. I never drink and drive." The lie fell off his tongue so easily. Max knew he shouldn't give him the keys, but did it anyway. "Don't look at me like that, kid." His dad scowled as Max grabbed his things from the backseat and started walking. The spring weather was great, trees flowering, the blossoms falling like rain as he walked the few blocks to the restaurant.

OPENING the front door, he found Lila already getting started. He sat next to her and began rolling napkins around the cutlery and then putting on the paper bands. "You okay this morning?" Lila asked, without stopping what she was doing.

"As good as it can be, I guess," Max replied as he, too, kept working. "I stopped hoping that he'd quit drinking a long time ago."

"Do you know what started it?" She stopped what she was doing and looked up. "He used to be so much fun before…." She paused and swallowed.

He completed the sentence for her. "My mom died. He always drank, but when Mom was alive it was at parties and stuff. But once she was gone, he seemed to get worse and worse. Now I don't think he can function at all without alcohol." Max put his completed work in the tub.

"You deserve better than that, Maxie." Lila touched his hand. "You really do."

"But I'm all he has," was the only thing Max could say that might make any sense. "Let's talk about something else."

Max wasn't sure she'd let the subject go, but then her expression burst into an evil grin. "Okay, tell me all about the silver fox from the gym." Her eyes danced with anticipation.

"What about him?" Max couldn't keep the shy smile off his face.

"Come on, tell me. I want to hear everything."

Max folded his arms over his chest in mock indignation. "I am not telling you about my sex life. If you want to know what one feels like, you should get your own."

"You know I promised to save myself for marriage, so spill. Your stories are all I get until I find Mr. Right."

"You're weird. You won't let yourself have sex because of some religious belief that it's wrong, but you want to hear all about my sex life with other men, which according to those same beliefs is also wrong."

She thought for a minute. "Well, yeah. But you'll be the one going to hell and not me, so spill it." She waved a fork at him like it was a sword, and Max burst into laughter. "Your depraved love life is all I get." She was grinning back at him.

Thankfully, before they could say any more, Jackie walked into the dining room. "I'm opening the doors."

Max grabbed the tub and put things away, and Lila made a final check behind the bar as a few of the regulars wandered in, taking their usual places. Max brought them their cups of coffee and offered menus, which most of them waved away, instead placing their usual orders.

About an hour later, the lunch rush began, keeping Max hopping. Lila elbowed him in the ribs and stopped in mid-stride. "Hey, look who just walked in." She tilted her head toward the door before hurrying away to handle her next order, and Max saw Hugh standing just inside the door, looking around the restaurant. When he saw Max, Hugh smiled and walked toward him.

Max felt himself color with excitement, thankful that in the dim light of the room, Hugh probably couldn't see it. "Take any open table you'd like," Max said, trying to keep his cool even as his body hummed with excitement under the gaze of Hugh's blue eyes.

"Which tables are yours?" Hugh asked softly, and Max pointed quickly before rushing away to put in the order he'd just taken.

Returning, he saw Hugh seated at the table with Lila standing next to him. Max approached and bumped her hip. "Trying to take my tip?" he said as he winked at her.

"No, I was trying to get some of the dirt you wouldn't tell me, but he's not talking, either." She giggled and walked back to her tables.

"So what can I get you?"

"How about an iced tea and your phone number?" Hugh set the menu on the table, and Max saw the older man looking up at him, head tilted slightly. He looked adorable, and Max wanted to taste those lips again right then and there. "Eating here was the only way I could think of to be sure I'd see you again."

"Well"—Max made a show of thinking things over—"I'll get your drink and think about the other." He winked and hurried away, wondering why the temperature had suddenly jumped. He got tea and brought it back to Hugh's table, setting it in front of him. "So did you really come in just to see me?"

"Yeah, I did." Hugh smiled, and Max felt his stomach jump in a really good way. "I was disappointed that we couldn't spend more time together last night."

Max felt some of the happy feeling start to fade. Hugh was only back because he was interested in a little more of what had happened last night. He admonished himself silently that Hugh wasn't really interested in him other than as a good lay. His few past lovers had always told him he was a lot of fun in the sack, but then they'd go on to tell him that he was way too serious and needed to lighten up and have a good time. "I had fun last night too." He tried to muster a little extra enthusiasm—after all, Hugh had been great, and he'd had a fantastic time. Hell, if Hugh was interested in a repeat, which it looked like he was, then Max wasn't going to say no. "You were a lot of fun." Max stood at the edge of the table shifting from foot to foot. "I really should take your order."

"Oh, yeah." Hugh picked up his menu and began glancing through it. "What do you recommend?" Hugh glanced up at him, the expression alone hot enough to melt butter. "What I really want, though, is to spend a little more time with you and not just in bed." Hugh picked up his glass and took a gulp of tea. "I know I'm a little old, probably too old for you, and I don't want to come off like some old letch, but you were fun and I liked spending time with you." Hugh was rambling, and Max thought it adorable that he could make this confident, older man babble on like a teenager. "I guess I was wondering if you were going to the gym this afternoon and if you'd like to meet me there. We could work out together, if you'd like." Hugh held up his hands. "And we don't have to do anything afterwards except maybe dinner if you're interested. Honest."

Max found himself smiling. "I suggest the chicken pot pie, it's incredible, and if you manage to eat all of it, then I suppose I'll have to meet you at the gym so I can help you work it off." Max found himself winking like he had the day before, his insides quivering with excitement.

"Hey, Romeo"—Lila bumped into him lightly—"there are other tables, you know."

"I'll have the pot pie then, and I'll see you at four." Hugh set down his menu but didn't stop looking at him.

"Good. I'll be right back." Max hated turning away, but he had to get back to work before he got in trouble. Not that Lila would say anything, but if the owner caught him talking unnecessarily, especially when there might be other customers waiting, there would be trouble. Hurrying to the terminal, he put in the order and then made the rounds of all his tables, checking on customers and taking additional orders.

When Hugh's order was ready, Max carried it to the table, setting it down in front of the handsome man. "It's really hot, so be careful."

"Are you always this busy?"

"Well, today's rather slow, actually. Sometimes it takes four of us, but that's usually at dinner."

"You're very good at what you do." Hugh picked up his fork and tasted his lunch.

"Were you watching me?" Max asked as he waited for the slight nod and smile of a customer who liked the food.

"Of course. The décor is nice, but doesn't compare to you."

Max began to laugh. "Now you're just being corny."

"Actually, I was being serious," Hugh replied, and Max felt like he'd been mean. The man had paid him a compliment, after all. "But I guess it did sound kinda corny."

"No, I'm sorry, it was really nice." Max beamed a little and saw Hugh return his smile. "I'll let you finish your lunch, and I'll definitely see you at four." Hugh touched Max's hand lightly, and then Max had to scurry away or he was going to get seriously behind.

"I got the drink order at table two for you," Lila told him with a smile as she cornered him at the drink station.

"Thanks," Max replied, and she gave him the rundown on the order. After bringing the drinks, he took their order and got it put into the kitchen. Between handling his tables, he found himself constantly looking at Hugh. The man was fucking gorgeous, with muscles that showed through his business suit when he moved just right. Who cared if the man had a hint of gray at the temples? That wasn't what was important. Hugh had actually asked him on a date, a real sort of date, rather than just inviting him to the gym for a workout and then back to his place for a different workout. For all Max knew, this was part of the guy's routine, but he really didn't think so. If it was, then Hugh would have been more confident and wouldn't have gotten all stammery. After making another check of his tables, he took Hugh's plate, placing it into one of the bus tubs, and brought Hugh his check. He thought about putting his phone number on it, but Jean would see that when she tallied the checks, and he certainly didn't want her asking questions.

Hugh glanced at the check and handed Max a twenty. "Keep the change." Hugh smiled at Max again and then checked his watch. "I need to hurry, but I'll see you at four." With a wink, Hugh walked to the door. Max watched those thick legs as the door opened and closed. It was only after Hugh was gone that Max unfolded the twenty and found a card with a phone number on it. Taking the cash to the register, he shoved the card into his pocket with a smile and forced his mind back on his work.

Thankfully, the rest of the lunch service kept him hopping, and the time flew by. He only got a few quick seconds near the end of his shift to talk to Lila. "Are you going to the gym today?"

Lila gave him her best mischievous smirk. "Maybe."

"Come on." Max wasn't in the mood for coy. "Hugh invited me to work out with him, but I don't have a ride. And since you've been preaching to me"—Max rolled his eyes—"like, since the day after we met, about how I should get more exercise, I'd think you'd be supportive." He glared at her for a grand total of two seconds before they both burst into laughter.

"You know I will, Maxie, but I can't stay very long. I have to work the dinner shift as well and need to be back here at six. What happened to your car, anyway?"

"Dad's using it. His is in the shop," he lied. They were sharing Max's car, but only because his dad had crashed his own and had let the insurance lapse, so he couldn't afford to get it fixed right now. Now it was Max's turn to smirk. "I think I can get home from the gym." He certainly hoped Hugh would be willing to give him a ride home after their dinner, but that he could figure out later. Right now he was too excited to worry about details like that.

"Then we're leaving in five minutes." She went in back and got her bag, before grabbing Max by the arm.

The ride to the gym was relatively short. Even so, it was close to four when they walked inside. Max showed his guest pass and hurried to the locker room, turning to check on Lila, who waved him on with an indulgent smile.

Max found a locker and changed as quickly as he could.

"There you are."

Max knew that voice, but turned around anyway.

"Are you ready?"

Max closed and locked the door. "Yup." With a smile, he followed behind Hugh, watching Hugh's butt in those tight shorts.

"Since you haven't lifted before, I thought we'd start with the basics," Hugh said as he led them to a long line of floor mats.

"Aren't we gonna use all that stuff your friends use?" Max looked over to where Lonnie and some of the guys Hugh had been talking to the day before were grunting and pushing up huge barbells.

"Maybe eventually, but you need to start with your core." Hugh stood on the mat and motioned for Max to join him. "This is where you need to start." Hugh motioned on his own body, sweeping from his neck to just above his groin, which made Max smile. "This is your core, where all your strength starts. Your chest, upper and lower back, and your abs, as well as your upper legs. Those muscles keep you straight and tall. The other muscles all take their cues from those." Hugh touched Max's arm. "You can work your biceps and triceps all you want, but they don't mean much if the basic core muscles aren't strong."

"Okay." Max smiled at the intensity in Hugh's eyes. "How'd you learn all this anyway?"

"I was a personal trainer for a while after college." Hugh motioned for him to sit on the mat. "What we're going to do is start with push-ups. Now, I don't want you to overdo it on the first day, so we're just going to do a couple sets of ten."

Max watched as Hugh got himself into position, arms stretched, back straight, and Max began to snicker. "That looks like what you were doing last night."

Hugh began to chuckle lightly as he demonstrated the exercise a few times and then stopped. "You start too, Mr. Dirty Mind." Max mimicked Hugh's position, and then felt Hugh's hands on his back. "Keep your spine straight, your legs taut, and clench your stomach. Good, now lower your body and push yourself back into position."

Max could feel the tension in his arms as he did what Hugh instructed. After two, he could feel a tightness in his chest and back. Hugh kept counting and encouraging each repetition before telling him to stop. Then Hugh got into position, and Max counted out the repetitions, watching Hugh's back muscles flex beneath the tight shirt. Then Max took his turn again before watching Hugh pound out another twenty with relative ease. "You make it look so easy."

"It'll get easier for you too. You just need to build up your strength, and believe me, at your age, it'll happen pretty quickly." Hugh sounded a little nostalgic, and Max waited to see if he would say more, but he motioned them to their feet and led them to a surprisingly large machine. "This is an upright row, and it's for working your back." Hugh put on some weight and then demonstrated the exercise before standing up and letting Max have his turn.

"Can I ask you something?" Max said as he sat at the machine.

"Of course."

"I was sort of wondering why you're doing this." Max gripped the handles, but didn't start. "I mean, you're really handsome and I'm just some kid who flirted with you. We had a good time last night, but…." Max stopped when Hugh began to laugh. "What's so funny?" Max gripped the handles tighter.

"I was going to ask you the same thing, but from the other direction. Yes, last night was a lot of fun, and you were something else, but I can't help wondering what you see in me. Every time you look at me, you get this smile and your face sort of lights up a little. But I can't help wondering if I'm not too old for you."

Max started the exercise, grateful for the momentary distraction and the chance to think a little bit. When he was done, he let the machine fall against the stops and then stood up. "I can't say anything about how I look at you, but I couldn't care less how old you are if you're nice to me and care for me too. My experience has been that guys want one thing." Max pinked and looked at the floor. "Like I'm one to talk after yesterday," he said, chuckling lightly. "But you actually asked me to work out with you and then to dinner, like a real date with a real person, not just some kid you want to boink."

Hugh added some more weight to the machine and sat down. Max watched the muscles work as the big man pulled the handles forward.

"Hey, I see you came back."

Max turned around and saw Dan standing next to him. "Yeah, Hugh invited me to work out with him."

"Are you going to join?" Dan asked, and Max found his attention divided between the handsome man talking to him and Hugh's muscles flexing on the machine next to him.

"I'd like to if I can swing it." That always seemed to be the issue. He didn't have a lot of bills of his own, but his dad tended to bum most of his extra money, and he never seemed to have any for himself, no matter how much he earned.

"I'll let you get back to it, but it was good seeing you again."

Max watched as the man walked back to where his buddies were working out as Hugh finished his set, but Hugh didn't get off the machine right away; instead he leaned against one of the handles.

"Max"—Hugh looked so serious—"I asked you out because you deserve to be treated as something other than a lay. You're fun, and no one's looked at me the way you do in a very long time." Hugh got up and stood close enough that Max could smell the scent of the older man's musky sweat. "I've spent most of my adult life moving from man to man, never staying with anyone for very long. Most of my relationships barely lasted the night."

"Is that what I was?" Max swallowed hard. He didn't like the thought of being used like that, but it was better to find out now rather than later.

"No. That's why I asked you out. I think you could be more than that, but I don't know how to have a relationship with anyone. Fuck, I don't even know if I'm even capable of it, but something told me I should try with you." Hugh let Max take his turn. "Maybe I'm just an old fool to think someone as young and vibrant as you could be interested in me, but that's why I asked you out."

Max didn't know what to say. That was probably one of the nicest things anyone had ever said to him. He took his turn on the machine before standing up again. Hugh looked like he didn't know what to do.

"Would you at least tell me to fuck off if this is too weird for you?" Hugh said softly.

Max stepped closer and said, just above a whisper, "If we weren't in the middle of the gym and surrounded by guys who'd probably kick my ass out of here, I'd kiss you within an inch of your life." The smile he got from Hugh was nearly blinding.

III

HUGH could hardly believe his luck. He'd told Max how he felt, and the younger man hadn't thought he was some sort of old guy perving on him. He had no doubt that Max's sentiments were genuine. The man's face was just too open for him to really lie, especially about something that was important to him, but Hugh could feel his own doubts exerting themselves, and he had to push them away, at least for now.

"Do you think we can finish this torture... I mean workout"—Max grinned at him—"and then go to dinner?"

Hugh chuckled lightly. "Sure. We've got just a few exercises to go." Hugh gazed across the gym and pointed. "We'll use one of the squat racks next." He led the way to the far mirror-covered wall and stood in one of the large steel cages. "What we're going to do is use a light weight to work our legs, butt, and lower back, all at the same time." Hugh saw Max watching him intently as Hugh got into position, bar across his shoulders. Hugh kept an eye on the smaller man in the mirror as he demonstrated. "Keep your back straight and squat until your upper legs are parallel with the floor, then straighten up again." He did the exercise a few more times and then walked the bar back into the rack before lowering it to Max's height. "Since we're just using the bar, try for fifteen."

"Yeah, right, like I can actually do that," Max scoffed, but he got into position anyway.

"You did the other night." As soon as the words were out of Hugh's mouth, he wished he could shove them back in, because Max took that moment to begin the exercise, and as Hugh saw Max's shorts tighten around that small butt, he nearly lost it and actually had to look down to make sure his thoughts weren't showing. And fuck all if he wasn't sporting wood right in the middle of the gym with mirrors on each and every wall. He tried to think of something else, but whenever he looked at Max, his mind kept flashing pictures of last night, and then his dick would start throbbing all over again.

"What's got you all worked up?" Max had finished his set and was standing in front of him, looking down. "Is that for me?" Damn if Max didn't actually lick his lips.

"Maybe," Hugh retorted, and he took his turn at the bar. He normally did this with considerably more weight, so instead he decided to try a set of fifty, and began setting a steady pace. His body just didn't want to cooperate, and he gave up after twenty-five.

"Why'd you stop? You said you were going to do fifty," Max asked, looking like he was trying to be all innocent and crap.

"Because, do you have any idea how hard it is to squat with a hard-on?" Hugh hissed softly through his teeth, and Max just grinned back at him.

"I noticed, and for the record, that's some view."

"Smart ass," Hugh chimed back.

"Not yet, but it could be later." Max turned around and wiggled his backside a few times, reducing them both to fits of laughter.

"What's got you pole-smokers going?" Lonnie quipped as he walked over.

"Nothing," Hugh answered as his laughter died away.

Lonnie glanced down. "Nice bird, you showing it off for everyone?" The smacking sound resounded off the mirrored walls, and Lonnie rubbed the back of his head. "Hey"—Lonnie turned around to glare at Dan—"what was that for?"

"It's not necessary to comment on absolutely everything, you know! Christ!" Dan replied, and he jumped back as Lonnie took a halfhearted swipe at his friend.

"You know you're going to pay for that." Lonnie glared at Dan, and Hugh saw Max put a hand over his mouth to keep from laughing.

"Yeah, right." Dan rolled his eyes like he'd heard all this a million times before. "Let's get back to work." Lonnie wandered back to the bench, with Dan hanging back for a second. "Nice bird, by the way." Dan grinned and dashed away before Hugh could grab him.

"Are they always like that?" Max asked, lowering his hand, eyes still filled with suppressed laughter.

"Yes." Hugh looked to where the two men were working out. "Lonnie's always been like that, but since Dan started hanging around him more, he's picked up on it too. I'm starting to think Lonnie's behavior is contagious."

"You mean like the flu?" Max retorted.

"I was thinking more along the lines of the clap," he said loudly enough that both men could hear him, and Lonnie flipped him off with a smile before giving Dan a spot. "Come on." He turned his attention to more important things, like Max. "Let's do some abs and then we're done." Max nodded, and Hugh led them back to the mats and showed Max how to do a basic crunch. "We'll start with these for now." They did the exercises together, with Hugh continuing until his stomach muscles burned, before resting back on the mat. Refocusing on the area around him, he saw Max staring. "Is something wrong?"

"God, no." Max stood up and extended his hand. "You just look really good doing that, especially when you bring your legs up to meet your arms."

"Geez, Max, and I thought I was bad."

"Oh, please," Max scoffed, "you know the old saying?" Hugh shook his head and waited. "A dirty mind is a terrible thing to waste."

Hugh made a grab for Max, who tried to dodge out of the way, but didn't quite make it. "Let's get cleaned up so we can go to dinner. Then we'll see just what that dirty mind of yours can come up with." Max nodded against his chest, and Hugh could feel Max's silky hair on his arm and smell the deep scent of a man who'd just exercised. Not wanting to get excited again, he released Max, and they walked toward the locker room.

Hugh tried his best not to watch the other man undress, but failed miserably, and when Max's shorts dropped, he had to force himself to look into his locker and only there. Getting undressed himself, Hugh wrapped a towel around his waist and began walking toward the showers. There was no sign of Max, and for now that was a good thing. He had to get cleaned up and out of the gym without embarrassing himself. Opening the door to the shower area, he walked through and found an empty shower. Turning on the water and dropping his towel, he stepped under the hot spray.

He began soaping down. His hands automatically made their way along his length, and Hugh had to stop himself from jerking off right there. He heard Max's voice calling to him from the next stall, and he wanted some relief, badly. But he forced himself to keep his mind on what was important. Turning the dial, he shivered as cold water coursed over him. Turning the water back to warm, he continued his shower. At least the cold water had taken his mind off that small, nimble body standing naked in the next stall soaping himself all up. Damn! Hugh's libido perked right back up, and he groaned softly.

The water in the next shower stopped, and Hugh jumped when his shower curtain slid back. "Are you doing what I think you're doing?" Max asked with a huge smile on his face, and Hugh felt those big blue eyes rake over his skin.

"No." Hugh turned toward the wall, hiding himself in case other people came by. "Close the curtain." He could feel his face heating despite the cool draft.

"You want some help?" Max looked like he was going to step in with him.

"Here?" Hugh looked around and saw no one else, but then he heard the outer door open, and Max walked back to his own shower, slipping his towel around his waist and walking out toward the locker room.

"I'll be waiting for you."

Hugh knew he should be angry, but he just couldn't manage it. The man was playful and fun, and whenever he was around, Hugh felt younger and more alive than he could remember feeling in years. He'd also noticed another thing: when Max was around, he had no interest in looking at other guys. He'd always checked out the other men when he was at the gym, but Max seemed to occupy all his attention. That was new and a little bit scary. How in hell could he meet someone and almost instantly feel them deep inside? Returning to his shower, Hugh rinsed off the soap and turned off the water.

Back in the locker area, Hugh dressed quickly, grabbed his stuff, and walked out through the club toward the front door. Max got up from the chairs and followed him out to his car. "I thought we'd go for Italian."

"Cool, I love pasta." Max made some nearly indecent motions with his mouth, and Hugh wondered how in the hell he was going to make it through dinner.

He unlocked the car doors and climbed into the driver's seat. "I half expected you'd follow me like you did yesterday." Hugh leaned close to his passenger, kissing the man hard, letting some of the pent-up energy flow into the kiss. "I'm glad you're not, though; you look almost as good in my car as you do in my bed."

Max rolled his head against the headrest. "Do you want to go right back to your place?"

God, did he ever, but Max deserved better than that. He wasn't just a lay—Max was someone he wanted to get to know, and Hugh hadn't met anyone like that in quite a while. "Yes. But we're not going to. I asked you to dinner, on a real date, not back to my place for a quickie or something." Hugh saw Max smile and started the engine.

"Does this mean you really like me?" Max's words were very soft, like a scared little boy.

Hugh stilled a minute and glanced over before returning his attention to his driving as they glided through the parking lot. "Of course I like you. Why?"

Hugh heard Max swallow. "You have a bit of a fuck-and-run reputation."

He figured he should probably be angry, but there was no heat in Max's voice, no accusation, just a touch of confusion. "I probably do, and that accounts for the reason I'm forty-four, alone, and dreading each passing year and each gray hair."

"When was the last time you took someone on a 'date'?"

Hugh had to think about that one. "It's been awhile. I guess it would have to be about five years ago. I met this guy"—Hugh smiled to himself—"Rod was his name. He was a great guy, and we seemed to get along well. Turns out a little too well. I thought we had a chance, but I guess that we were just too much alike. I wanted to give things a try, and he wasn't interested. After that, I went back to having a good time." Hugh turned onto the street and they rode toward the restaurant. "It's funny, I can fuck a different guy every night, but the few times I met someone I was really interested in, I had no interest in sharing. Rod said we could still see each other; he just wanted to see other guys too."

"And you couldn't do that?" Hugh answered by shaking his head, and he saw Max nodding. "I couldn't, either." Max shifted in his seat. "I love sex." He had the decency to color, because from their last night together, that was obvious to anybody. "But I have no interest in installing a revolving door in my bedroom. I've been with lots of men, but that was mostly in college, when I was younger and really stupid. Now I'm a little more careful and definitely more selective."

Hugh pulled the car into the parking lot of one of his favorite restaurants. Parking right in front, he got out and waited for Max before guiding him gently toward the door. Inside, they were greeted by one of the servers and ushered to a table. "Your usual martini?" she asked, and Hugh nodded. She took Max's drink order as well and then hurried away, leaving them alone in the quiet dining room.

"I come here about once a week. The food's good, and they make everything themselves, including the pasta." Hugh flipped through the menu and then set it aside. He already knew what he wanted to eat and was having fun just watching Max. "You know, I still can't understand why you're interested in me."

Max put down his menu as he shook his head lightly. "I've been out with lots of guys my age, and mostly I find them boring. They're interested in their clothes or going out to the clubs every weekend. The last time I went out, it was to the symphony in Lancaster." Hugh's eyes widened in surprise. "See, that's just how they look when I tell them." Max's voice became louder. "Like they can hardly believe I'd spend my time doing something other than prowling for dick."

"I think I get it. By the way, what did you hear? I was there with friends last year when they did Beethoven's Ninth. It was quite something." The server brought their drinks and took their food orders before leaving them alone again. "I know this couple—they've been together for years and keep trying to fix me up; we go to the theater and symphony quite a bit."

"So you understand?" Max added with surprise. "I think sharing interests and having fun together is more important than how old someone is."

"But there are a lot of differences between someone your age and someone my age." Hugh was having a difficult time expressing what he wanted to. It wasn't as though he wanted to drive Max away, but it wasn't fair to hold the younger man back. "I'm at the peak of my career. I've worked hard and done very well for myself. I like my job as a financial consultant, and I'm not really hungry for more." He took a sip of his drink and set the glass back on the table. "You've got your whole life ahead of you." There were so many thoughts that raced through his head at this point, so many ways he could finish that statement, but he just left it there.

Max took a gulp of his beer before saying anything. "You're way too hung up on how old you are. It's not as though you're over the hill or something. So you're forty-four and I'm twenty-six. What is it you're really afraid of?"

"I don't know." Hugh had taken the easy way out and he knew it. He liked Max, and he was afraid of getting hurt, really hurt. This man spoke to him deep down. "I don't want to get hurt." He finally said the words.

"Who does?" Max grinned back at him. "But even I know that if you don't take a chance sometimes, then nothing will ever happen." Hugh didn't quite know what to say, and thankfully the server brought their salads. "I won't hurt you, Hugh, at least not on purpose."

"I didn't think you would, but will you outgrow me? Or hell, will I be able to keep up with you?"

Max grinned and winked. "That didn't seem to be a problem last night." Max took another gulp of beer.

Hugh wasn't quite sure what to make of Max. He really seemed interested in Hugh. The eyes don't lie, and Max's eyes got soft and sparkly whenever he looked at Hugh. Maybe he should just relax and go with the flow. Wasn't that what he'd always told the rest of the guys he'd been with? Of course, he'd used that line when he was interested in backing off, and that was the last thing he wanted to do now. They got quiet, and Hugh saw Max looking at him, eyes all warm. How many times had he seen his friend Maddoc look at his new partner Ivan that way and wished someone would look at him like that? Max was, right now, and all he could do was worry about what might be.

"I know this is going to sound really dumb, and probably kind of lame after what we did last time, but I'd like to take things slow, or at least slower." It was the only way Hugh could think of to keep himself from really getting hurt, and at the same time, show Max that he was more than just a quick lay.

"Does that mean I don't get a repeat of last time?"

"It means that I want the chance to treat you right, spend time with you, and get to know you." Jesus Christ, those were words he never thought he'd ever say, and here he'd actually said them... and meant them. "I always jumped into bed with men first and then that was it." The server returned and brought their meals. Hugh waited until she was gone before continuing. "If you don't want that, I'll understand."

Beaming eyes greeted him. "Of course I understand. So we'll take it slow, but not too slow, okay?"

"I'll do my best." Hugh wasn't really sure he was fully capable of going slow, but he was willing to try. Changing the subject, he said, "Would you like to try my pesto?"

"Okay, if you'll try one of these ravioli." Max hummed after he swallowed. "They're unbelievable." Spearing a bite onto his fork, Hugh reached across the table as Max opened his mouth. Max's eyes drifted closed in near ecstasy. "God, that's awesome."

Max returned the favor, spearing a ravioli, feeding it to Hugh, his fingers sliding along his chin as the fork glided between his lips. The rich sauce and cheesiness burst on his tongue as he chewed, and Hugh couldn't hold back a soft sigh of pleasure. "That's one of the few dishes I've never had here—looks like I've been missing something."

They ate and talked, spending the rest of dinner laughing and getting to know one another. Max ordered tiramisu for dessert and fed more of it to Hugh than he ate himself. Eventually, after they'd talked for hours, Hugh paid the bill and they walked to the car. Part of Hugh wanted to take Max home with him and forget what he'd said earlier about taking it slow, but he forced himself to keep his word and had Max give him directions.

"It's the house on the left." Max pointed just after they turned onto a working-class street, surprisingly close to the restaurant where Max worked. Hugh parked the car and opened his door, waiting for Max to get out. A bang caught Hugh's attention, and he turned as the front door to the house Max had indicated slammed closed, and a figure not much taller than Max hurried down the walk. He couldn't have weighed more than 110 pounds soaking wet.

"Where the fuck have you been?" The man's flushed face and slight wobble told Hugh that he was probably drunk. Hugh looked to Max; the smaller man's face was pale as he tried to melt into the car seat. "Is that some fag you're with?" The man's voice got louder, and as he got closer, Hugh could see the curl around his mouth, face pinched in disgust.

Hugh stuck his head in the open doorway. "Who's that?"

"My father," Max replied very softly.

"Is he drunk?" Hugh barely got the words out, and he could already smell the man coming near him; the alcohol stench seemed to ooze from his skin. Hugh saw Max nod softly, and he whirled around, looking into the face of Max's very drunk father. "What's your problem?"

A shaky hand pointed at Max. "That's my fag of a son, and I need to teach him to be a man so he'll stop taking it up the ass."

"What you need to do is go back inside and sleep it off," Hugh replied calmly. It was obvious the man was drunk off his ass and could barely stand; talking made him wobble and bob his head.

"What I need is to defag my son." His lethal breath was enough to knock Hugh off his feet. "You his fag boyfriend or something?" Hugh saw bloodshot eyes try to focus. "Little long in the tooth, aren't you? But I suppose you old guys have to recruit the young ones." The drunk tried to bend down and nearly fell against the car. "That what happened, boy, he turn you into a fag?" His voice grew louder. "I knew it. No son of mine would be a fag unless some queer put him up to it." Max's dad straightened up too quickly and wobbled before taking a swing at Hugh and bouncing on his butt in the grass, looking like something out of a cartoon.

"Can we just go?" Max asked, still belted into his seat, looking miserable.

"Sure." Hugh got back in the car and closed the door, pressing the automatic locks. "Isn't that the car you drove yesterday?" Hugh motioned toward the blue sedan parked with the front wheels up on the curb.

Max peeked over the dashboard. "Yeah, he wrecked his and needed to get to work." Man, he sounded miserable—the quick smile and sparkling eyes were nowhere to be seen now.

"Do you have your keys?" Max nodded again, and Hugh pulled his car up next to Max's, keeping an eye on Max's father in the rearview mirror as the falling-down drunk tried to get back on his feet. "Then get in your car, and I'll follow you back to my place. At least that way, he won't try to follow you and kill himself or someone else."

The seatbelt unsnapped and Max opened his door, fishing out his keys. Hugh waited until Max was behind the wheel and on the road before falling in behind him.

At the stop sign, Max stopped, and Hugh saw him waving for Hugh to take the lead. Realizing Max didn't remember the way, Hugh rolled past and Max fell in behind him.

Hugh continually checked his mirrors to make sure Max was behind him. Pulling up to the house, he turned off the engine and opened his door, waiting for Max.

"I'm sorry," the smaller man said as he approached, "I didn't want you to get involved in all this."

Hugh put his arm around Max's shoulders and guided him up the walk. "Don't you worry about it." He unlocked the door and walked into his living room, settling on the sofa with Max next to him. "Do you want to talk about it?"

Max shook his head and rubbed his eyes with his fingers. "No, but I guess I have to."

"No, you don't, but you'll probably feel better."

Max raised his head, finally looking up at him. "My dad drinks a lot, has for years. When he's sober, he's really great," he said as his gaze traveled to the floor, "but he's rarely sober anymore."

"Does he hit you?" Hugh asked, afraid of the answer.

Max shook his head vigorously. "I've never seen him physically violent before today. He usually just calls me names and laments that his only son is gay." Hugh felt Max's arms slide around his waist, and Max buried his head against Hugh's side. It wasn't until he felt the slight wetness that he knew for sure Max was crying. Hugh could feel the bile and anger rising in his chest. That damned bastard. How could he do that to Max? The man was sunshine and smiles, with bright eyes that danced with mirth, and his fucking father had reduced him to tears with an alcohol-soaked fury.

"Why do you stay?" Hugh let his hands run through Max's short hair.

A sniffle was his initial answer. "I'm all he has."

"Max." Hugh waited until Max lifted his face up. "No, because what's really important to him is at the bottom of a bottle. That's all that matters anymore, isn't it? He goes to work, comes home, starts drinking and wandering through the house talking to people that aren't really there and then falls into bed so he can wake up and do it all over again. The only reason he isn't drunk at work is because then he wouldn't be able to buy his next bottle."

"H… how'd you know?" Max sat back up, still leaning against Hugh's shoulder.

"My dad did the exact same thing—didn't care about anything except his next drink. Friends, family, we all tried to help him, but he wasn't interested, just drank himself to death."

"Do you miss him anyway?"

"I miss the way he was before he turned to alcohol." Hugh got up and walked to the cabinet near the television. Picking up a framed picture, he handed it to Max.

"That's me and my dad when I was about nine. He took me to the shore and we went swimming." Max took the picture, staring at it.

"Where's your mom?" Max handed back the frame.

"Behind the camera. I have tons of pictures of us, but almost none of her. She loved taking pictures. She died just after I graduated high school. I went off to college at Dad's insistence. Didn't want to, but he said it was for the best." Hugh breathed deeply, steadying himself. "I went to college, and Dad crawled into a bottle and never got out again. After a while, I stopped coming home. Dad wasn't pleasant when he drank. He yelled and often lashed out at God knows what. Toward the end, he didn't even know who he was anymore."

Max's hand slid into his. "You couldn't have stopped him. You staying home from college wouldn't have changed anything. I know it's hard to accept, but it's true. I agonized over my dad's drinking and finally, one Saturday afternoon while he was sleeping one off, I had an epiphany." Max stopped and waited a second. "I very suddenly realized that his drinking was his fault and his problem. It was only mine if I let it be. I know it sounds stupid, but I had to let go of the guilt. Yes, my dad hates that I'm gay and tries to make that the reason he drinks, but it's just an excuse. It hurts, but it's still only his excuse." Max wiped his eyes with the back of his hand, looking steadier and stronger by the second. "I figured I could let it define my life, or I could let it go."

"But... what if you could help him?"

"You know from your dad that you can't help someone who doesn't want to be helped." Max stood up and began walking through the room. "I love my dad and I've tried to be there for him, but I can't stop him, and you couldn't have stopped your dad, either." Max sat back down. "I noticed that you had a drink at dinner."

"Only one," they said in unison, and they smiled together as Hugh nodded. "I think it's my way of saying that he's not me."

"Exactly," Max reinforced with a slight smile, "you're not him, and I'm not my dad."

"Is that why you're always so happy?"

"I am?" Max looked surprised.

"Yes, you are. I've seen you smile almost constantly in the last few days."

"Maybe it's the company." Max's eyes began to sparkle, and that bright smile appeared once again.

That took Hugh a little bit by surprise. As far as he knew, he'd never made anyone smile like that. A warmth flowed though him, settling in his chest. "If it's the company, then it's definitely because of you," Hugh replied softly as he leaned closer. Kissing Max seemed like the most natural thing, but he stopped himself.

Max's eyes fluttered open when their lips didn't make contact, before a small head-tilting motion conveyed his silent "what happened?"

"Does it seem strange that I really want to kiss you after the discussion we just had?" There were times when he felt like some sort of old letch, and this was definitely one of them. They'd just had a frank discussion about their alcoholic fathers, and his reaction was to jump into kissing. Yes, he'd said he'd take it slow, but having Max right next to him, touching him, seeing those big eyes full of sad disappointment, made him want to kiss those emotions away forever.

"No." Max moved closer. "It's not strange to want to replace disappointment with hope, or hatred with happiness." Then it was Max who kissed him. Those smooth lips, tasting of the espresso from the tiramisu, touched his, lightly at first and then with more heat. In a split second, the tender kiss went hot and needy, their lips sliding together, and Hugh felt Max's hands against his cheeks as the kiss deepened further. Passion and heat rippled through them, starting in Max and slamming into Hugh with the force of a train. The man might be smaller, but his lips sure packed a wallop.

"Max"—Hugh pulled back, gasping for breath—"are you trying to kill me?" His breathing was ragged as he tried to say more but couldn't when Max pulled him back into another kiss. This time Hugh tugged them down onto the sofa, straddling Max's lithe body, knees against his hips. Max's heady scent filled his nose, his flavor filled Hugh's mouth, and his heat seared Hugh through his clothes as tiny sighs and whimpers reached his ears. The sensory overload threatened to overwhelm his brain, but something deep inside called Hugh back, and he lifted his head away from Max's sweet lips, touching their foreheads together as they both heaved for breath.

"Fuck, that was hot." Max moved his hips slightly, and Hugh could feel Max's hardness against him. "I know... I should probably go." Max wriggled back into a seated position.

"Go where?"

"Home," Max said matter-of-factly.

"But what if he hurts you?" The thought of Max returning there scared the crap out of him. Hugh knew firsthand that people weren't stable when they'd been drinking. Max's dad was capable of just about anything right now.

"He's probably passed out and won't remember a thing in the morning anyway."

"You don't know that. Stay here for the night, and I'll follow you home in the morning. You can take the guest room if you want."

Conflict, doubt, and confusion all flashed across Max's face in an instant. "Guest room? I know you said we should take this slow, but what if I don't want to?" Tears filled Max's eyes. "What if I want you? What if I don't want to feel alone?" Max moved against him, tackling him on the sofa, lips searing, imploring hands wandering everywhere.

"Max, that's the pain and hurt talking. I know, that's what I did for years, what I've always done. You can hide it behind a smile or upbeat attitude, but it's still there." Hugh hugged Max tight, stilling his movements, comforting the hurt. "And it won't go away through sex or anything else."

A frustrated groan echoed off the walls, filling the room, and Max stilled in his arms. "Will you hold me?"

"All night, if that's what you want." Max hugged him back and said nothing, but the message was loud and clear. It might kill Hugh to have Max sleeping next to him, but the man didn't need someone to fuck him, he needed someone to love him. Hugh swallowed at the thought and wondered.

IV

MAX woke slowly, as if from a drunken stupor. At first he wondered what he'd been drinking, but realization slowly bloomed inside. Arms wound around his waist, and as he began to move, they tightened, hugging him closer, a warm hand making small circles on his skin. He knew the arm was Hugh's, and soft, light breath caressed his neck with each breath Hugh took.

"It's not time to get up yet." Hugh's sleep-filled voice smoothed over him.

"I was just thinking," Max murmured, as the memories of last night came back to him. Turning over slowly, he buried his face in Hugh's strong chest as the emotions he'd done his best to keep hidden deep down threatened to surface again, like they had last night. Hugh had seen right through his smile and his laughter to the pain and hurt. Yes, his father was a drunk, one who hated what his son was, and used it as the cause of his drinking.

"Shhh…." Hugh's hand stroked along his head. "It's okay."

Max lifted his head away from Hugh's skin, looking up into those blue eyes with the small crinkles in the corners. Inching upward, eyes locked, Max brought his lips to Hugh's. At the first touch, he felt Hugh's lips respond, moving with his. Then Max was rolled on the bed, Hugh's weight pressing down on top of him, Hugh's lips taking his in a hard, demanding kiss. Arms pulled them together, Max's breath heaving, his chest crushing to Hugh's with every breath he took. Hugh's lips tugged on his, and he opened willingly, hungrily, as Hugh's tongue licked and teased for entrance, which he granted with equal hunger, returning every kiss, meeting every thrust of Hugh's demanding tongue. Max raked his fingers along Hugh's back, feeling the powerful muscles flex and ripple beneath them. Hugh's skin pressed to his, as though he were trying to meld their bodies together, Hugh's chest tight to his, hips bucking together, hairy legs stroking along his, nearly overloading his mind. "Hugh, I want…."

Hugh's kisses stilled, eyes peering deep into his. "What? What is it you want?"

"You. I want you," His thoughts were a jumble of raw emotion, and his body longed for Hugh to be with him, to… love him. The realization hit him that he'd never truly been loved, at least not by anyone since his mother. His father hated him, and all the men he'd been with had only wanted his body. Max stilled and Hugh stopped moving, looking down at him, eyes warm and lips so close to his that Max could feel the heat of Hugh's breath.

"Are you okay, Maxie?" Hugh whispered as he caressed Max's cheek. "What's wrong?"

Max shook his head, no longer able to meet Hugh's gaze. It was just too intense, almost as if Hugh could see deep into his soul. "Is this just sex? I mean, if it is, that's okay. I understand that we've only known each other a few days, but I need to know if this is just sex to you or if you care for me." Max could barely see through the tears that filled his eyes. "I know I sound like a girl." Max began to struggle, suddenly embarrassed and feeling badly that he was ruining the moment. Hugh probably thought he was some sort of freak who couldn't make up his mind about anything.

"It's okay, Max." He felt Hugh stroking along his arm, and then the weight was gone and Max jumped off the bed. He knew he must have looked to Hugh like some startled deer caught in a car's headlights, but he had to get out of there before he completely lost it. "Max." Hugh's voice was so soothing. "There is more to this than sex—a lot more, I think."

Max bent down to pick up his pants. "Then why do you look so scared?" Max held his clothes in front of him, looking down at Hugh, head resting on his hands, worrying his lower lip between his teeth. The man was adorable and smokin' hot, even with the worried look on his face.

"Because this is new to me, and the first time I tell a guy that he means more to me than just sex, he stands on the other side of the room, holding his pants in front of him like an embarrassed virgin, which I know you're not." Hugh patted the mattress next to him, and Max dropped his pants on the floor, moving toward the bed. He climbed back onto the mattress, and Hugh pulled him close. Then those sweet lips were on his again, kissing him hard, and Max was under his spell again. Hugh's scent filled his nose, and his heady taste made him fly. "I am scared, Max. Scared you won't feel the way I do and scared that you'll realize you couldn't care for an old man."

Now it was Max's turn to kiss, and he took Hugh's lips with the energy of a soldier attacking the enemy. "You don't feel like an old man." Max kissed him again before tilting his head down and capturing a nipple. Hugh hissed softly, and Max knew he was doing it just right. Swirling his tongue around the now-hard bud, he sucked hard, feeling Hugh arch his back beneath him. "You don't taste like an old man, either."

"So are you telling me you have experience with that? Tasting old men?" Hugh's gentle laugh rang through the room until Max clamped down on the other nipple, the chuckle turning to a groan, and then a soft, whiny cry. "Maxie."

Lifting his lips, Max licked the abused bud, soothing the skin as Hugh's cries lessened to soft, whimpering moans. That was what he wanted, to reduce the man to soft sounds so he'd forget about all this "old man" business. On some level he knew Hugh was teasing, but Hugh said things like that often enough that Max knew his age was the source of worry. Kissing the skin on Hugh's chest, Max snaked his body lower, sliding down the bigger man's body as he kissed a trail across his belly. Max looked up when Hugh's belly began to flutter against his lips. "Ticklish, huh?"

Hugh propped himself up on his elbows, eyes wide. "Yes, but please don't."

Max returned to his kissing, letting his tongue lap at the salty skin as he inhaled deeply. Hugh had this wonderfully rich scent of musk and something sweet that he could never figure out where it came from. "Wouldn't think of it," Max replied between licking kisses, hands sliding up over Hugh's chest. "Hate being tickled," Max said as he looked into Hugh's eyes, "but I love this...." He gave Hugh what he hoped was his best mischievous smile and then tucked his head lower, sliding his tongue along Hugh's length.

"Shit!" Thunk. "Oww."

As he let Hugh's length slip from his lips, he saw Hugh rubbing his head. Knowing the best way to make Hugh forget his head, Max took him deep, letting the heavy cock slide over his tongue.

"Jesus God!"

Max hummed around Hugh's length, tongue swirling around the head. Fuck, Hugh tasted good, and felt even better.

"Gonna...," Hugh gasped softly. Max slowed his pace and let Hugh slip from his lips, bringing his lips to Hugh's, his kiss met with equal fervor and need. "Why'd you stop?" Hugh asked between kisses, sounding a little disappointed.

"'Cause if you come, you can't fuck me." Max went for another kiss, but heard a deep growl and found himself flipped on the bed, lips kissing the breath out of him. Hugh's knees spread his legs, and he opened himself, wanting Hugh inside him, needing to know that the man felt something for him, that someone cared for him.

Strong fingers brushed over his opening, slick and hot as one of them pressed inside. Max felt his back arch and he cried out, but any sound was swallowed by Hugh's deep kiss. Another finger joined the first, stretching him so full, so very good. The fingers slipped away, sliding back inside, sliding away again. Hugh's kisses stopped, and Max flopped back on the bed, wired from the electric excitement that coursed along his spine. Then Hugh was back, pulling him close, guiding his legs around Hugh's waist. Slowly, exquisitely, their bodies joined, and Hugh filled him. Eyes rolling to the back of his head, Max cried, "Yes!" Hugh stopped moving, and Max's eyes flew open, wondering what was going on. He saw Hugh looking back at him. "Give it to me!"

"No." Hugh continued looking into his eyes, unmoving except for the occasional flex deep inside. "I'm going to take my time, and I'm going to love you." With near agonizing slowness, Hugh withdrew and then re-entered him.

Max arched into the movement, thrusting himself forward, trying to increase Hugh's pace, but Hugh was having none of it. Slowly, steadily, stroke by passionate stroke, everything but thoughts of Hugh were driven from his mind. Wrapping his arms around his lover's neck, Max held on as Hugh tugged him forward, holding him tight against that powerful chest, driving into him, touching him so deeply that for a few seconds he couldn't tell where he ended and Hugh began. Their breathing became synchronized, the cries of each echoed a second later by the other—nothing intelligible, but the understanding was as clear as anything ever said. Sweat broke out, muscles cried out from exertion, and still Hugh continued that pace, replacing thought and reason with a blaze of white-hot passion.

A cry cut through the haze: "Come for me, Maxie!"

"I can't. I can't get...."

"Yes, you can. It's all in your heart—let it loose and come for me."

Max could feel it racing like a fire, welling up from deep inside him. "I can't." He could feel tears running down his cheeks as Hugh drove deep and hard, holding him, a steady stream of soft words washing over him, carrying him along.

"Yes, you can. Show me how you truly feel. Come for me now, Max!"

The pressure inside built to unbelievable heights, and Max felt himself coming, holding on to Hugh to steady himself through the flashes of light and almost epileptic convulsions of his body. Gasping for breath, he fell back against the bed, floating on a wave of endorphins that seemed to go on and on forever.

The next thing Max remembered, he was lying on the bed, feeling warm, with an arm around his waist, and soft words with a definite hint of worry were being whispered in his ear. "Max, you okay?"

Max gasped for breath. "Uh-huh."

"Oh, thank God."

He felt the bed dip and heard footsteps pad away. Water ran, and then the footsteps returned. He knew something was happening around him, but he didn't have the energy to even open his eyes. A warm cloth caressed his skin, followed by a fluffy towel. Then the warmth was back, cuddling him. Sleep tried to claim him, but his mind wasn't quite ready to let go, not yet. Something Hugh had said kept him from sleep. Hugh had used the word love, said he was going to make love to him. Max thought it was probably something said in the heat of the moment, and he told himself not to put too much stock in it. That's what his head told him, but his heart had already grabbed onto it and was holding on for all it was worth.

The next time Max woke, light was streaming through the windows. With a start, he bounded out of the bed, looking around for a clock before relaxing. He hadn't overslept.

"Nervous much?" Hugh teased from the bed. "We've still got a few minutes, I think."

"I have to get home so I can change before I go in to work." He truly did feel nervous, and not just about work. The words were on the tip of his tongue to ask Hugh if he'd meant what he'd said, but he couldn't bring himself to do it. If Hugh said he didn't, Max knew he'd just feel silly and the small hope that had taken root in his heart would be dashed—and he'd had enough of that. No, it was better to say nothing.

Hugh threw back the covers and padded around to where Max was standing. "Then why don't we get cleaned up, and I'll take you home." Hugh's arms snaked around his waist, holding him close to that furnace-like body. "You're incredible, you know that?"

Max shook his head. "No, I'm not."

A hot tongue glided over the skin behind his ear. "Oh yes, you are. Last night was incredible, and you, my little spitfire, are absolutely amazing." Hugh's hand glided over his chest and down his stomach, circling his length, which had awakened long before the rest of him.

He wasn't sure about that, but those hands felt pretty amazing. "Hugh," he cried softly as fingers wrapped tightly around him, stroking briskly along him. "What?"

"You're just beautiful, you know that?" Hugh whispered into his ear, but Max couldn't reply. "You wanna see what I see? Then lift your eyes and look straight ahead."

Max found himself looking into the full-length mirror on the back of the closet door, and he tried to get away. He knew what he looked like—small and scrawny. He didn't need to be reminded of it.

"Don't squirm, look. See what I see." Max stopped and looked. "See how your eyes shine when I stroke you, feel your leg shake." He could, he did.

Max saw and felt a hand slide over his chest, fingers stopping to pluck at one of his nipples, watched as Hugh nibbled on the base of his neck. Hugh's length slid along his butt. Max wanted to look away, but Hugh held him there, not through his will, but by his touch. The last thing Max wanted was for Hugh to stop.

"See how beautiful you are?" Max could only nod once in response. "Love how you respond to me." Max's leg shook harder as Hugh picked up the pace of the stroking, and Max rested his head back against Hugh's shoulder, getting lost in the myriad of sensations Hugh was providing. "That's it, let it all go, just feel."

"Hugh!"

"That's it, let yourself go."

His climax built from his toes, legs shaking, hands clutching, stomach clenching, and he came over Hugh's hand and onto the floor, gasping for breath as Hugh held him tight to his body.

"I've got you, just relax and feel."

Max couldn't respond other than to gasp for breath and let himself fall back against Hugh. Lips smoothed along his neck as he allowed his eyes to drift open. "What did you do to me?"

"I hope I showed you just how beautiful you are."

"If you say so, but I still think you're the one who's beautiful." Max turned in Hugh's arms, kissing his lover deeply. "What about you?"

Hugh looked surprised. "I came when you did." Now that Hugh mentioned it, his butt was a little damp. "You looked so fucking awesome, I couldn't help myself."

"Can we shower now?" Max moved away, taking Hugh by the hand, leading him into the bathroom. Turning on the water, Max stepped in, with Hugh behind him. Hands explored, slowly stroking over warm skin. Soapy fingers slid around nipples; hands caressed muscled limbs. There was no rush, no hurry. Bodies sated, there was just time for two, time for them. Lips found their companions as water cascaded over them.

Finally, only after time re-exerted its influence, Hugh turned off the water. Stepping out first, he was waiting for Max with a huge, fluffy towel and a smile. Max groaned softly as he was wrapped and then lightly buffed within the towel, Hugh's hands providing a vigorous rubdown that invigorated his skin.

Max turned to return the favor, but Hugh had already dried himself and motioned him toward the bedroom. Unfortunately, he didn't have clean clothes and had to put on what he'd been wearing the day before. "Do you have time to eat?" Hugh asked.

Max smiled as he followed Hugh down the stairs. "I wish, but if I don't get home soon, I'll be late for work."

"Okay." Hugh grabbed a cup of coffee, drinking it as quickly as he could. Max followed Hugh out, and Hugh then locked the door behind them. After getting a kiss, Max walked to his own car.

"Do you want me to follow you in case your dad gives you trouble?"

"I'll be fine." Max smiled over at Hugh as he opened his door. "He should be at work and probably won't remember anything anyway. He rarely does."

"You sure?" Hugh's concern made him tingle inside, and the hope he'd been nursing bloomed a little more.

"Yeah, I'll be fine." He got in the car and was about to close the door.

"Promise you'll call me if there's trouble." Hugh gave him his cell number, and Max reached into his pocket, programming the number into his phone.

"I'll call, I promise." Closing his door, Max started the engine and waved as he pulled onto the street.

Pulling up in front of the house, Max watched for a few minutes, but the house appeared quiet. He hoped his dad had gotten a ride into work and wasn't home. Parking the car, he got out, walking briskly up the walk. Inserting his key, Max unlocked the door and pushed it open.

Breathing a sigh of relief, he walked inside the quiet house, closing the door before walking through the messy living room with beer cans on the coffee table and an ashtray filled with cigarette butts. Sighing to himself, he ignored the mess and made his way down the hall toward his bedroom.

Opening the door, Max stopped when he got a good whiff of cigarette smoke. The house always smelled like that, his dad smoked like a chimney, but it shouldn't have been coming from his room. Pushing the door further, he saw his father sitting on the side of his bed as a cloud of smoke billowed out of the doorway. Waving his arms and coughing, he waited for the cloud to clear before stepping inside. "What are you doing in here?"

"Waiting for you." The words were clear, and Max could see by the rare clarity in his dad's eyes that he was unusually sober.

Max hesitated. "Why aren't you at work?"

"You took the car."

"I took my car." Max knew he had to be firm.

His dad snuffed out his cigarette before standing up. "Let's get something straight, boy. As long as you live here, everything is mine." The man may have been shorter than Max, but his personality more than made up for it, especially with Max. This was his dad, his family. No matter what Max thought of the man personally, he was still his dad. "So let's get something straight, right here, right now, I don't want you seeing that old man anymore." His dad shuddered. "How I could raise a fag is beyond me, but it seems I did, and I'm not dumb enough to think I can change you. Lord knows I've tried."

"You didn't do shit!" Max bellowed as his temper threatened to break, and then he did his best to calm himself down before continuing. "Except drink yourself numb and expect me to watch out for you. Well, that's over."

"I may be older, but if you think I'm going to take that crap from you, you've got another think coming."

The smack reverberated around the room, and a flat pain bloomed across Max's face. Fuck, that hurt, but Max did his best not to let it show. "So that makes you a man? Hitting me makes you a man?" Max shook his head, letting his eyes fill with pity, making sure his dad saw it. "You're a pathetic drunk, and I've had enough of you. Cook for yourself, do your own laundry, wallow in your own filth. Hugh was right, all you care about is what's at the bottom of a bottle."

"Maybe if I didn't have a fag for a son...." He left the rest unsaid and glared at Max, undoubtedly knowing that had worked in the past.

"That's enough of that shit, dad! You drink because that's all you want to do. You're an alcoholic, and the only person at fault for it is you. I kept telling myself that the dad I remembered, the one who took me camping and fishing, was still in there somewhere, but he's not. The dad I knew is long gone." Max felt his throat close as a wave of sadness and loss came over him.

"You gonna cry, boy?" his old man sneered as he stepped closer.

"For you, no." Max rubbed his sore cheek with his hand. "You're not worth it. Now get out!"

"This is my house, so you'll be the one doing the leaving!" He folded his arms in front of his chest.

Max had no freakin' clue what to do, but he'd definitely had all he could stand. "Fine, but I don't want you stinking up the place while I pack. So get out!"

For a second, Max saw a touch of fear in the old man's eyes, but then he walked around Max and into the hall. Max slammed the door and leaned against it, breathing heavily, wondering where in the hell he was going to go. One thing he was certain about, there was no way in hell he was going to apologize to his dad. Hugh was so right; he'd allowed himself to take the blame for his dad's problem. Well, with Max gone, his dad would have to find someone else to pin his drinking on.

Snapping himself back to the present, he opened his dresser drawer and pulled out clean clothes for work. "Fuck, everything stinks." Dropping the clothes on the bed, he opened the window, letting in some blessed fresh air, and then stuffed his work clothes into a bag. Leaving the room, he saw his dad leaving his own room, dressed for work. With a glare, Max walked toward the front door.

"Where do you think you're going?"

"To work, if it's any of your business." Max had had enough, and he didn't give a shit what happened to his dad. The days of caring for a drunk were over.

"Not without a car you aren't."

Max stopped and turned, grinning at the man who seemed to be getting smaller by the minute. How could he have stepped around the man all those years? "It's my car and in my name. You try anything and I'll report it stolen." He was done being a doormat and taking the man's crap. "I'll drive you to work, but that's all. You can get your own ride home." Max threw his bag in the back seat and got behind the wheel. He didn't look at his dad, and as soon as the door shut, he put the car in gear and took off as fast as he dared.

Out of the corner of his eye, he saw the man reach into his pocket. "Light up and you'll walk!"

They rode in silence, his dad staring at him and Max ignoring it. He'd ignored plenty over the years, and this was it. Stopping in front of the gritty building, Max heard the door open, but didn't look as his dad got out. Once the door closed again, he peeled away, feeling free, hurrying to the restaurant.

As Max pulled into a parking space, his phone started vibrating in his pocket. Stopping the car, he pulled it out.

"Are you okay?" Hugh's voice rang through the phone, and for a second Max wondered if he could read his mind.

"I will be," he sighed into the phone, as the adrenaline that had been carrying him suddenly vanished.

"What happened? I knew I should have gone with you. Did he hit you?" Hugh's questions flew at him, and Max couldn't help smiling slightly. Hugh wouldn't be upset if he didn't care.

"We had a fight of sorts and decided that we shouldn't live in the same house anymore." Max knew he was being flippant, but so many things were running through his mind that he needed to make light of them or he'd be overwhelmed.

"Max, did he hit you?" Hugh asked firmly.

The soreness in his cheek reasserted itself. "Yeah, he slapped me."

"I'll kill him!"

"No. He's at work, and I just want to forget about it and find another place to live." He knew he sounded whiny, but he figured he was entitled.

"How late do you have to work?" The sweetness in Hugh's voice settled him down.

"Till closing."

"Then I'll meet you there," Hugh added hurriedly.

"You don't have to."

"Max, I want to," Hugh said softly. "I don't want you to be alone. God, I hate saying this over the phone, but you're important to me."

Max held the phone tight, leaning toward Hugh's voice. "I care for you too."

"Then you'll let me help you?"

Max smiled. "I'd appreciate all the help I can get. I'll see you tonight." Max closed the phone, holding it with a smile on his face. Hugh cared for him. That was a good thing, because Max knew he was falling in love.

V

His watch had to be running backward. Every time Hugh looked, it seemed like there was more and more time until he was to meet Max. He'd thought about going for lunch just to see Max, but stayed away, figuring the man needed to work. And Hugh knew he'd start questioning Max about what had happened with his father right there in the restaurant. He checked his watch for the eight-millionth time; he actually tapped the offending timepiece before forcing his attention back to his work. But it wasn't working. He'd read the same information eight times and it wasn't sinking in, anyway. Finally, it was time to leave, and he shut down his computer and hightailed it to the parking lot. He still had hours to burn and figured a workout would take his mind off Max, at least for a while.

Entering the club, he saw Dan right in front of him, and after scanning his card, Hugh followed his friend into the locker room.

"Where's Max?" Dan asked, as he opened and closed the unlocked doors, trying to find an empty locker.

"Working." Hugh got an empty locker on the first try and began pulling off his shirt. He threw it in his bag and then began fishing for his workout clothes. Out of the corner of his eye, he noticed that Dan had stopped moving. Straightening up, he saw Dan staring at him. Hugh stared back, cocking his head a little.

"What's wrong?"

"Who says anything's wrong?" Hugh countered, and he went back to his rummaging, finally pulling out a T-shirt and shorts.

"Come on. You look worried about something."

Hugh set down the clothes and took a step closer to Dan, lowering his voice. "I guess I'm wondering about Max."

"What about him? He seems like a really nice guy." Dan's eyes widened and his face broke into a sly smile.

"He is, but...." Hugh's voice tapered off, and he pulled on his T-shirt, not sure he really wanted to talk about this here, or ever.

"But what?" Dan's knowing smile stayed in place. "You have to say it."

"Say what? That I'm afraid I'm way too old for him?" Hugh felt his voice rise on its own, and he stopped himself from shouting.

"Yeah, because that's a bunch of crap, anyway. There are almost as many years between Gene and me as there are between you and Max. When we first met, I thought the same thing you did, and Gene showed me that it didn't matter." Dan pulled off his shirt and dropped his pants, hanging them in the locker and pulling on his workout shorts. "If you want my opinion, you're worrying about something that's less important than a lot of other things. Like how you get along, and whether you like the same things—basic things that you get to find out as you get to know him."

"But what if he decides he doesn't want to date someone older than him?" Hugh pushed off his own pants and pulled on his shorts, then sat on the bench to put on his shoes.

"You've had relationships before, you know there are no guarantees...." Dan let his words die away, and Hugh saw him searching his face. "You haven't really had a relationship before, have you?"

Hugh concentrated on tying his shoes. "Not really. A few one-night stands who stayed around for a few weeks, but nothing serious."

"But Max is different?" Dan sat next to him, pulling on his own shoes.

"Yeah, he is. I think that's why I'm nervous about all this shit." Lord knows, he'd never worried about this kind of stuff before. "I mean, I've had lots of younger guys before."

"But none of them got under your skin the way Max has." Dan finished tying his shoes and pulled on his lifting gloves before standing up again. "Have you asked Max how he feels?"

Hugh nodded. "He says it doesn't matter to him."

"But you don't believe him." It wasn't a question.

Hugh stood up as well, putting his bag in the locker before closing the door. "It's not that I don't believe him, because I think that's how he feels now, but what about...?"

"Hugh, you can't worry about tomorrow, next week, or next year. If the looks he was giving you are any indication, he's interested. Take things one day at a time and don't worry about the rest." Dan's hand gripped his shoulder. "Come on, join Lonnie and me for our workout. When we're done, you'll be too tired to worry about anything."

Dan let go of his shoulder, and Hugh followed him out of the locker room over to where Lonnie was talking to Gene, gesturing wildly before turning toward Dan, a gleam in his eyes. "Hey, Dances with Dick, you ready?"

Hugh saw Dan roll his eyes. "Lonnie, you need some new material."

Without missing a beat, Lonnie added, "Fine, Captain Cock, let's get to it."

Hugh couldn't stop his laughter and followed the other two men to the bench presses.

Leaving the gym an hour later, Hugh could barely move. That had been one hell of a workout, and had taken his mind off Max, for a while at least. Walking out to his car, he again toyed with the idea of going to the restaurant, but he headed home instead. An idea was forming, and if it was going to work, there were some things he needed to get done.

HOURS later, Hugh left the house to meet Max, locking the door behind him. Finally, he'd get to see the man again and reassure himself that Max was truly okay. Max had said his dad had only slapped him, but Hugh kept getting visions in his mind of Max really hurt. Pulling away from the house, he drove as fast as he dared, arriving at the restaurant just before closing. He parked out front, and through the large front windows, he could see Max moving around inside. He knew when Max realized he was there: that smile shone through the glass. God, the man was adorable, and his heart took a small leap, knowing that the smile was for him.

Getting out of the car, he walked inside. "Sorry, sir, but we're closed," one of the other servers told him politely.

"It's okay, Gerald, he's waiting for me," Max said with a grin before adding to Hugh, "I should be just a few more minutes. They just paid and are finishing up their coffee."

"Take your time." The agitation he'd been feeling all day seemed to drain away as soon as Max was near. Looking closely, Hugh could see what he thought was a lingering redness on Max's face, but he appeared fine otherwise. Max hurried away, visiting the table in question before returning, placing a cup of steaming coffee in front of Hugh, and then hurrying back to work.

Hugh sat and watched the proceedings as the servers cleaned tables, filled shakers, and did other things that were a mystery to Hugh, but kept everyone busy until the couple got up, saying their good-nights as the door closed behind them.

"I should be just a few more minutes," Max said.

Hugh smiled and nodded, taking a sip of his coffee. Max scurried back to work, obviously hurrying, and Hugh glanced over the top of the cup, watching Max move. The man seemed so graceful, almost elegant, as he walked—no, glided—around the room. Hugh's stomach did a flip when those black pants drew tight around that small bottom. Finishing his coffee, Hugh got up and placed the cup in a tray with other dishes and returned to his seat. He'd barely sat down when he felt a tap on his shoulder.

"We can go now."

Hugh turned, and Max's lips were so close to his that Hugh couldn't resist and leaned a slight bit closer, touching their lips together. Whistles echoed around the room, and Hugh took that as encouragement and deepened the kiss, feeling Max respond.

Not wanting to give everyone a show, Hugh backed away, caressing Max's cheek softly before getting up. "I think we better take this somewhere private."

Max nodded slowly, eyes wide, lips still slightly parted.

"Do you want to follow me?"

Max shook his head. "I can leave my car where it is if you'll give me a ride back in the morning."

Taking Max's hand, Hugh led him out of the restaurant to the car. "I have something I want to show you." Hugh started the car, glancing over at Max. "I think you'll like it, but if you don't, you have to promise me you'll say something." Hugh could feel his heart start to race. "I mean, you don't have to say you like it just to be nice." He felt Max's hand on his arm.

"You can stop being nervous, even though it's kind of nice. I promise I'll be honest."

Hugh glanced over at his passenger, chewing slightly on his lower lip. "Me being nervous is nice?" He wasn't quite sure what to think about that comment. He'd always been the nervous, worrying type, and he absolutely hated it, but had never figured out how to stop it.

"'Cute', then?" Max's eyes glowed with mischief, a wry smile curling his lips.

Hugh ignored the cute remark and checked the street again before pulling out into traffic. The short ride was quiet, with Max relaxing back into the seat. Hugh found he liked it. He'd been alone for years, and whenever he'd been with someone, he'd always felt the need to fill the space, but with Max it wasn't necessary; the silence was comforting.

Pulling up to the house, they got out, and Max started up the walk, but Hugh caught his arm. "Come with me." He couldn't keep the smile off his face.

"This must be good. You feel like you're going to jump out of your skin."

Hugh led Max around the side of the house and into the backyard. "When I bought the house, it came with an unexpected bonus." He carefully led Max down the path through the dark backyard. "It seems that the people who built the house had a relative they needed to take care of, so"—he paused outside a door and opened it, turning on the lights—"it's a mother-in-law's cottage." Hugh placed his hand on the small of Max's back. "If you like it, you could move in here. It needs some work, and I did some cleaning today, but it has a kitchen, living room, bedroom, and full bath. They're kind of dated." Hugh let his eyes travel over the shag carpet and seventies-style ranch cabinets in the open kitchen.

"You're giving me a place to live?" Hugh watched as Max's eyes widened in a kind of disbelief. "I just met you a few days ago, and you're giving me a place to live."

"I know what you're going through. I've been there, and…." The words caught in Hugh's throat. "I like you Max. I like you a lot. But the house comes with no strings attached. We'll come up with a reasonable rent, and if you work on the house, we'll deduct it." Hugh stopped, looking at Max, who just stared back at him, face unreadable. Hugh felt his nervousness return and shifted from one foot to another. "Say something."

"You're the kindest, sexiest, most wonderful man I've ever met."

"Then you like it?"

"Duh, of course I like it," Max replied bouncily. "But is this what you really want?"

Hugh narrowed his eyebrows, questioningly.

"I don't want to cramp your style or anything."

Now Hugh understood. "I think you're my style. That is, if you'll have me."

Max took a step closer. "Is this that age thing again?"

"Partly, I think. The other part is that I don't do relationships well." Hugh took Max into his arms, holding him to his body, needing to feel Max next to him.

"Then how about if we learn together?"

Hugh nodded, his chin rubbing lightly against Max's hair. "I think we can do that."

"But only if you give up on this age thing. You're not old and I'm not young. We're just two people doing a little core training." Max must have seen the confusion Hugh had tried to hide. "When we worked out, you told me that the core was the source of all our strength, and what's more core than the heart?"

Hugh had never thought of it that way, but communicated his agreement by way of a kiss that left Max breathlessly panting. "Can we take this to somewhere more comfortable?" Max whispered as their lips parted.

"Yeah." Turning off the light, they walked hand in hand back across the yard to the back door. Inside the house, Hugh led the way through the dark rooms and up the stairs without bothering with a single light. He pushed open his bedroom door and stepped in as Max decided he'd waited long enough. Arms snaked around Hugh's neck, and legs wound around his waist. Hugh found his hands full of tight, warm butt as lips kissed away the thought of everything except the luscious man in his arms.

Tumbling backward, they bounced on the bed, kissing hard, lips pulling, tongues dueling. "Get naked," Hugh panted, and he watched as Max backed away, clothes flying. Before Hugh could get his shirt off, Max was there, tugging on his shirt. Hugh managed to get it off and hissed softly as Max clamped onto a nipple, hot lips sucking hard. "You're going to kill me."

The suction lessened and a hand soothed over his skin. "I thought we were through with the old man talk."

"Old, young, wouldn't matter. You'd kill me anyway."

"Wouldn't want to do that." Max's fingers worked Hugh's belt open. "That naked thing goes both ways, you know," Max teased, as Hugh shimmied out of his pants, and then Hugh's arms were filled with Max, his warm, squirming, live-wire.

"If I live to be a hundred, I swear I'll never get over how you feel in my arms."

Max stopped moving, their eyes locking together. "You know, that goes both ways too."

"What did I ever do to make you look at me twice?" Instead of an answer, Hugh got a kiss, hard and deep. Suddenly, the question, the answer, none of it mattered, because Max was there. Dan was right—tomorrow didn't matter, because right now he had his spitfire, and that was all the core training his heart needed.

Crunch Time

Andrew Grey

I

HURRYING across the parking lot, George pulled open the doors to the health club, rushing inside, breathing heavily. Continuing his near-frenzied pace, he found his drawer, labeled Higgins, near the wall behind the salesmen's desks. He dropped his bag and winter coat inside. Finally breathing a sigh of relief, he walked to the front desk. "You were nearly late," Tiffany said with a slight giggle. "Do you know you walk funny when you rush?"

George almost retorted with something equally insensitive, but figured it wasn't wise to alienate one of his fellow employees on his first day. "Yes, I'm aware that my hip doesn't work quite right, thank you. It's been that way since birth," he replied calmly and evenly, keeping the smile off his face as her embarrassment became evident. "Don't worry about it," George added with a smile to diffuse the situation. "Are you going to show me what to do?"

She shook her head, long blonde hair waving around behind her. George couldn't stop himself from thinking that if she shook her head much harder, that hair could be lethal. "Joshua said he'd be right back." She turned to check in one of the members, scanning his card through the computer while George took a breather. He hated being late. And here he was, late on his first day, but he'd had an unexpected meeting after school and hadn't gotten out at his usual time.

"George." A deep voice from behind him caught his attention. "I'm Joshua— Josh. Harvey asked me to show you around the desk." Josh directed him to the computer systems. "You need to check in each member by scanning their card. The computer has a picture of each person, so all you need to do is make sure they aren't using someone else's card. Tiff, you can head out if you want." Josh smiled at the blonde, and she returned his smile before walking back through the club, while Josh's eyes bounced with every step she took, before returning his attention to George. "The lost and found is in this drawer." He pulled it out, displaying a pile of clothes, weight belts, water bottles, weight gloves, and other items.

The door opened and five guys walked in together. "Hey, George," Dan, one of the members, said as he handed George his card. "When did you start working here?"

Beep, the scanner pinged as the system accepted the card. "Today's my first day," he answered as he smiled, handing back the card. He scanned Gene's card as well, and Ivan's and Maddoc's. The last guy in the group was Lonnie, and he didn't bother with a card; he simply walked around the desk toward the locker room. "Lonnie!" George called out, inadvertently using the voice he used with his fourth-graders. Then he softened his voice. "I need your card." Lonnie walked back, handing

George a single key with the scan card on it. "Thank you." George scanned it and handed it back.

"You're welcome, ya birdgazer," Lonnie chided as he continued on his way.

"Hey, Lon!" George called back. Lonnie stopped midstride. "You need to have something to gaze at first," he added, rolling his eyes.

Lonnie sputtered something, but it was completed drowned out by Dan and the guys hooting as they continued toward the locker room.

"I see you know Lonnie," Josh said with a distasteful look on his face. "The man's just crude."

"He's been my financial adviser for a few years. He's talked like that for as long as I've known him. Giving it back to him seems to be the best thing I've found to shut him up." George turned his attention to the door as other members filed in. Greeting each one, he scanned their cards and thanked them. Josh finished showing him around and then left him with instructions to call if he had any questions. George assured Josh he would and went to work. Half an hour later, he got a request from a member to update a credit card, and Josh showed him how to use the payment portions of the system. It wasn't hard, and soon George found himself exploring the system between scanning in members.

"George." He looked up to find Lonnie standing at the counter. "Why are you working here?"

George moved closer to Lonnie, not wanting to spread his business through the gym, "I need some extra money." George shrugged. "That teachers' strike wiped out a lot of my ready savings."

"Oh." Lonnie became quiet, which George knew usually meant he was cooking up some clever witticism. Instead, he said, "I'll call you tonight."

"Sure," George answered, smiling. As Lonnie left the club, George went back to work.

Finishing his short shift, George clocked out. Retrieving his bag, he ate the small snack he'd packed before heading to the locker room to change for his own workout before leaving the health club.

On his way home, he bought a sandwich, and after carrying in his things, George sat at his kitchen table, grading papers as he ate, until the phone interrupted his concentration.

"Hello." Shit. He should have looked at the display before answering.

"Hey, cockhopper. It's Lonnie. Am I interrupting an all-you-can-eat dick buffet?"

George looked around the neat kitchen, the house so quiet he could hear the refrigerator kick on. "Yeah right, Lon. You're interrupting a four-gy."

"Yeah, your dick and four fingers." Lonnie laughed at his own joke, and George said nothing because it was too true for words. "Say, I got something to ask you, but this has to stay between us." Lonnie sounded very serious, which was highly unusual.

The only time George had ever seen the man serious was when money was involved—usually his own. "You can't tell anybody or I'll lose a client."

"What's so important?" George had a bad feeling about this.

"I have a client who needs help." Lonnie sighed, and George heard shuffling.

"Where are you?" George picked up his sandwich in one hand, taking a small bite before setting it down again.

"In bed. Cory's about ready to polish my love hammer and she's getting impatient." George chose that moment to try to swallow and nearly choked as he started coughing. "Can you come to my office tomorrow afternoon?"

"I can be there at four." Thankfully he didn't have to work at the club.

"Good." More rustling and a groan before the phone went dead. George looked at it for a few minutes, wondering what the hell was up before setting it aside. Whatever it was, he'd find out tomorrow, but right now he had work to do.

THE final school bell rang and the kids rushed out of the room and into the halls, voices raised in excitement. Already the kids were excited about Christmas vacation. As the sound died in the halls, George straightened the room before gathering his things and heading toward the exit. He knew he was leaving a little early, but the pile of papers under his arm was a visual testament to the work he had yet to do.

Hurrying to his car, he stopped himself from rushing. Yes, he hated to be late, but he hated falling on the ice even more, and besides, his hip ached to beat the band anyway. Starting the car, George pulled out of the lot, driving toward Lonnie's office, pleading with the heater in his old car to start working. Of course, it started blowing warm air just as he pulled into the parking lot. Getting out, George pulled his coat tighter around him, walking stiffly into the quiet office where the receptionist directed him to Lonnie's desk.

Lonnie motioned him into a chair while he talked on the phone, obviously trying to soothe a client, skittish because the market had dropped. "Chris, you're an investor, not a trader, remember. The stocks you're in are solid. Do you want to sell your IBM and Coca-Cola?" Lonnie rolled his eyes. "I didn't think so. Look, the market is tough right now, but you're holding your own and doing better than most." Lonnie sounded so patient as he soothed the person on the phone, ending with an invitation to dinner in the next few weeks, before hanging up.

"Thanks for coming, George." Lonnie shook his hand before peering out through the glass walls around his desk. "Hey, Anne. Is Darren here?"

"No, I haven't seen him." The middle-aged woman sitting just outside Lonnie's office answered without even looking up from her computer screen. "Hello, Lonnie Rosen's office." George did a double take when he realized she was answering the phone, barely breaking the rhythm of her typing.

"Hang on." Lonnie raised a finger, dialing the phone. "Darren, where are you?" Lonnie got quiet for a second, but George could see his anger rising by the second. "I don't care how late you were out last night. Get your butt in this office in ten minutes." The volume in Lonnie's voice rose with every word. "I've told you before. You need me a hell of a lot more than I need you. I'm not one of your sycophantic hangers-on, and when you make an appointment, you get your ass in here on fucking time!" Lonnie was yelling by the end, and whoever was on the phone must have capitulated because Lonnie calmed down. "Ten minutes, and you better not look like shit," Lonnie added before hanging up.

"Come on." Lonnie stood up and led the way across the office to what looked like an empty conference room. George followed behind, wondering what the hell was going on. "Anne, when Darren arrives, send him in here."

"Sure thing," she answered, without looking up.

Lonnie shut the door and motioned him to a chair. "I have a problem client," Lonnie started.

"The guy on the phone?"

Lonnie nodded. "As I said, this has to remain quiet. The client is Darren White." Lonnie paused and looked at him expectantly, like George was supposed to know who that was. "He plays for the Philadelphia Eagles," Lonnie prompted, and George shrugged, not knowing anything about sports. "Anyway, Darren got injured and it may be a career-ending injury. He'll tell you it's not a big deal, but he doesn't exactly live in the real world. For all practical purposes, he's done playing football."

"Okay. How does this affect me? I can't make him heal faster." George had no idea what Lonnie expected of him.

"In about a month, Darren has a chance to guest host a sports program on Channel 4. I've heard through the grapevine that if he's good, it could turn into a regular show. Darren's local and he's played very well over the past three years." Lonnie leaned closer. "The thing is that the kid's as dumb as they come."

"Lonnie," George used his teacher voice, "that's not fair and I won't have that kind of talk. Not from you *or* my fourth-graders." George expected Lonnie to bluster the way he usually did, but the man simply smiled.

"Okay, but you need the facts. You have kids in your fourth-grade class who read better than he does, and he can barely write anything other than his name." Lonnie motioned to Anne. "She writes out his checks for him because he's not capable, and he only signs them."

"What do you want from me?" George thought he could see where this was going and he didn't like it—not one bit.

"I wanted to ask you if you'd work with him. The kid needs help and he'll pay you for your time. I don't know if it's possible to help him at all, but I don't want him to fail, and without help, he will." George could see that Lonnie was sincere. He really did want to help the kid, no matter what he'd said earlier.

But George wanted no part of this.

"Lonnie, I...." George had every intention of telling Lonnie "No, thank you" when the door opened and a tall, broad-shouldered man wearing jeans and a T-shirt walked into the room, cutting him off. "Jesus Christ," George muttered under his breath, as a pair of the deepest blue eyes he'd ever seen met his gaze, and the words died on his lips. The other man, obviously Darren, slouched in a chair across the table from him, leaning back in his chair.

"So whatcha want, Lonnie?" He mumbled so badly George barely understood him. "I got stuff to do, ya know."

Lonnie swiveled in the chair. "Do you want that job at Channel 4?"

"I don't need it. I'm gonna be playing ball again soon," Darren said, or something to that effect. George couldn't be sure; the man's speech seemed as slouchy as the rest of him.

"No, you're not." George could hear the raw edge of Lonnie's temper. "You are probably never going to play football again and you need to face that. So, I'm going to ask one more time, do you want that interview at Channel 4 or not? I pulled strings to get it for you and I can un-pull them just as fast."

The feet of Darren's chair hit the floor and he looked at Lonnie as though he was ready to kill him. "I have to play ball. I can't do nothin' else."

Lonnie's face softened. "That's what we're going to help you with. George here is a teacher, a very good teacher, and he's going to work with you so you can do well on the show next month."

George shifted in his chair. "Lonnie." He looked over at Darren. "I haven't agreed to anything yet." He kept looking at Darren, fascinated with the man, even though he had no intention of going through with this scheme of Lonnie's. Darren obviously wasn't interested in learning anything. George suspected he'd gotten everything in life he'd ever wanted by flashing those deep blue eyes.

"I know you haven't." Lonnie looked at Darren. "So what do you want?"

Darren shrugged. "I'll give it a shot."

Lonnie's gaze turned to George. "Well, I won't." George turned away and stood up, walking stiffly toward the door. "He doesn't want to learn anything, Lonnie. All he wants is what he's always gotten: a free ride because of who he is."

"I can learn. I ain't dumb!" Darren stood up, fire blazing in his eyes, chest puffed out.

George took a few steps closer. "Then act like it! You may not be dumb, to use your word, but no one could tell from the way you speak." George stepped closer, telling himself he wasn't going to be intimidated by the much taller wall of muscle glaring down at him. "Or the way you carry yourself." George turned and walked back toward the door, looking at the stunned expression on Lonnie's face. "I'll see you tomorrow at the gym," he said to Lonnie before pushing open the conference room door.

"Wait." George stopped and turned around. Darren looked alternately at Lonnie and then at George. The huge man suddenly seemed young and small, the cockiness he'd displayed earlier evaporated. "I do want to learn. I don't want to be stupid no more."

"Anymore," George corrected. "And you aren't stupid. You just need to apply yourself." George felt the cold inside begin to melt, realizing just how much it had taken for Darren to admit that. "If you're truly interested, then be at my house at five tomorrow. Lonnie can give you the information you need." George left the conference room, walking through the office to the front door. Pulling on his coat, George walked through the twilight to his car and drove home, wondering what in hell he'd been thinking, agreeing to help Darren. *Well,* he thought to himself, *Darren probably won't show up anyway.* No matter what he'd said, Darren's body language spoke volumes.

GEORGE checked the clock again, returning to his grading. It was ten 'til five. George forced his attention on his work, telling himself it wasn't likely Darren would show up anyway. So the ring of the doorbell came as a complete surprise. Getting up, he found Darren standing on his porch, much better dressed than he'd been the day before, carrying what looked like a messenger bag.

"Come on in," George said before leading them through the house to the kitchen, placing his work back in his school bag. "I'm surprised you came," George commented without malice, as he picked up a book from the stack he had on one of the chairs, handing it to Darren. "Set your bag down, take a seat. I want you to read this out loud."

"But I thought—" Darren stopped talking when George cut him off.

"I need to see where you're at, so I'd like you to try that book for me."

"Okay." Darren opened the book and began reading haltingly, stumbling over even simple words. George let him struggle for a few minutes, and though he did improve once he got used to it, after a page, Darren slammed the book closed. "See. I told you I was stupid."

"You're not stupid. You just haven't been taught how to read properly, and it's not all your fault." George hated to say it, but he knew Darren's teachers hadn't done him any favors. "Keep reading." George handed the book back. "The only way you'll improve is to do it, so I want you to read for me, and we'll work together on any of the words you don't know." George touched the man's hand to reassure him and felt a jolt through his fingers that had him pulling back like he'd been burned.

Sitting back, George listened to Darren's deep voice as he read from one of the sixth-grade reading books he'd borrowed from school. "What's this word?" Darren asked, pointing to the page.

"Sedentary. It means sitting a lot, not doing much," George explained. "Something you aren't is sedentary. You tend to keep very active." Boy, did he ever. George pulled his attention away from the way Darren looked in his tight shirt, forcing himself to focus on the task. Besides, any interest in Darren outside of helping him with his reading would be highly improper. There was no doubt in his mind that Darren was gay—George's gaydar had been going off like a fire alarm ever since Darren had walked into the house—but George had no delusions that Darren would be interested in him anyway.

George continued listening as Darren read, and he continued to stumble over words, trying multiple times to read them and fumbling again. Sometimes they were more difficult words, but mostly, they were simple words. "You can stop," George said gently.

Darren signed and closed the book, resting his head on the table. "I told you I was stupid. The only thing I was ever good at was playing football, and now I can't do that either." George heard a small sniffle.

With stunning clarity, George realized he was watching this young man's life seemingly come apart before his eyes. The one thing he loved, that he was truly good at, that he excelled at above everything else, was now closed to him. "Darren, I want to try something, if you'll let me."

Darren lifted his head, looking heartbroken. He said nothing, but nodded slowly before thumping his head back onto the table.

"Okay." George handed him a piece of paper and a pencil. "I want you to write down the words as I say them." Darren took the pencil and paper and George said a few words, some easy and some harder. Darren wrote them down and George took the paper when they were through. Darren's handwriting was definitely pinched and tentative, but for the most part he'd spelled the words right, or at least he'd come pretty close. "Look. You got almost all the words right, and you missed spelling excellent by only one letter. You did pretty well," George said with a smile. "Now I'm going to write down some words." George took a second to write as Darren watched him, expression wary. "This isn't a test and there are no wrong answers. I just have a hunch and I'm hoping I'm right." He handed the paper to Darren upside down. "What I want you to do is write down on your paper exactly what you see. Don't try to figure out what the words are because they aren't necessarily words, okay?"

"Yeah, I'll try," Darren said with no enthusiasm whatsoever.

"Darren, that's yes, not yeah, and try a little more enthusiasm." George could feel the excitement inside building. Helping kids was what he loved most, and the idea that he could actually help Darren had his heart pounding.

"Okay, yes," Darren said a little snappily.

"If you're going to be on television you not only have to be able to read, but speak properly as well," George explained patiently.

"Sorry," Darren answered and George looked at him, waiting. "I'm sorry," Darren corrected on his own, and George smiled and nodded his encouragement.

"Remember, there are no wrong answers; just write down what you see." George turned over the page and Darren started writing, tongue sticking out between his lips, pencil scratching on the paper in the quiet room.

"Here." Darren handed back the sheet. "I know everything's wrong," he added, sounding defeated.

George looked over the work and smiled. Darren had mixed up the groups of letters, getting some right and coming close with others. "Let me ask you something." George touched Darren's arm to get his attention, the warm skin against his hand making him wonder what the rest of Darren would feel like. He forced his mind back to the topic. "Has anyone ever worked with you on your reading? Did anyone ever help you when you were in school?"

Darren shrugged. "No. The coaches just cared if I could play so they helped me with the tests, memorizing answers and stuff like that. Why?" Suddenly Darren seemed interested.

"I think you may be dyslexic. It's a learning barrier and it means that the letters get mixed up between your eyes and your brain."

"You mean I'm stupid," Darren commented softly.

"No. Many smart people, including geniuses, are dyslexic, and it's nothing to be ashamed of." George stood up, walking to the kitchen counter, his temper flaring, and without thinking he banged a fist on the counter, making both him and Darren jump. "Sorry. But things like this make me angry as hell. Someone should have found this years ago, like when you were in third grade." George pounded the counter again before turning to Darren. "I'd like to have you tested properly just to confirm what I'm thinking, but if I'm right, I can help you."

"How?" Darren asked, bewildered. There was a glimmer of hope in his eyes.

"I've been where you are because I'm dyslexic too. I learned how to deal with it and eventually, with practice, I've been able to retrain my brain. If that's what this is, I can help you too."

"Okay," Darren answered. "What do I have to do?"

"Can you meet me at my school at four tomorrow?" George asked, and Darren answered by nodding his head. "Then I'll ask one of my colleagues to help test you. We'll know pretty quickly if I'm right and then we can develop exercises and things to help you."

"You mean I'm not stupid?" Darren's mouth practically hung open.

"No, you're not stupid." George reiterated as softly as he could, "You were the victim of an education system that never looked past the fact that you could play football." Darren looked up at him, confused, and George walked back to his chair, limping slightly. "Your teachers all looked past your grades and boredom because you could run fast and play well. They never did their job, which was to figure out why you were having trouble. Your coaches never helped, because all they wanted was for you to keep playing."

"Now I can't play anymore. I don't have football and I don't have an education either." Darren looked as defeated as George would have in his situation.

"But we can start to change that." George wrote down the directions to his school and his cell phone number. "Call me when you arrive and I'll introduce you to Mark. He's the developmental specialist." George stood up and Darren did the same. "Just don't be late."

"I won't." Darren smiled, big and bright, and George couldn't help returning it, hoping there would be more of those smiles thrown his way. "I can let myself out." George watched Darren's backside as he walked out of the room and it wasn't until he heard the front door close that he realized he'd been holding his breath.

With Darren gone, George made himself some dinner and settled back at the table to spend the rest of the night grading papers and putting together lesson plans. Not very exciting, he knew, but there was never enough time during the day for him to plan and he almost never got a chance to grade papers. Heck, it was only during gym and art when the kids were out of the room that he really got a chance to breathe at all.

It was only after hours of work that George felt caught up. Getting up from the table, he put his dishes away before limping down the hall to the bathroom. He needed a good soak and an even better night's sleep. But all he got every time he tried to relax were visions of Darren's bright eyes and that smile. Slipping beneath the covers, he couldn't stop himself from wondering if he'd ever find someone who would smile at him every day the way Darren had smiled just that once.

II

DARREN hurried through traffic, pushing his sleek Porsche convertible around cars as he followed the directions George had given him toward the school. He'd promised George he wouldn't be late, but it looked as though he was going to be. Pulling out his phone while he was stuck at a light, he dialed the number George had given him.

"George, I'm stuck in traffic, but I'm on my way," he said frantically as traffic started to move again. He really hated to disappoint the man for some reason. Hell, it surprised even him. Darren knew he was usually the center of attention. It had been that way ever since junior high when he'd made quarterback at thirteen. "I know. I'm hurrying as fast as I can."

"It's okay, Darren," George's voice soothed through the phone. "Don't get in an accident trying to get here. Mark's excited about meeting you, so take your time and get here safe."

"Thanks, George. I should be there in five minutes." Darren hung up the phone and turned onto the quiet street, finally seeing the school on his left. Turning in, he pulled into a spot and walked toward the entrance, a feeling of intimidation coming over him. Stopping for a second, he looked around before pulling open the door to find George waiting for him. "Sorry I'm late."

"It's okay. Just don't make a habit of it," George said and winked before leading him down one of the halls. Everything from the lockers to the tables seemed so small.

"Do you like teaching?" Darren asked as he followed George to the end of one of the hallways.

"Very much." George stopped outside one of the doors. "I love working with the kids. The best part is when I see someone struggling and figure out how to help them. There's nothing better than the feeling that you've reached someone, making their life better even if they don't know it yet." George smiled and opened the door. "Darren, this is Mark. He's going to work with you."

"It's a pleasure," Mark stood, smiling. "I've seen you play. You're really something."

Darren saw George pulling the door open. He started to get nervous. "Aren't you staying?"

"I can if you want," George answered, settling into one of what Darren suspected were the few adult-sized chairs in the building.

"George told me that you have trouble reading," said Mark.

"Yeah," Darren answered, looking at George. "Things get all jumbled up sometimes."

"Like I tell all my students, this is one test you can't fail, so relax and we'll get started," Mark instructed, before launching into a number of questions with flashcards and all kinds of things Darren could barely understand. "What we're doing is testing for a number of things, so be patient. We're almost done," Mark told him before pulling out a few more things, checking his eyes as well as his hearing. When he was done, Mark sat back and sighed. "George was right. You're most likely dyslexic." Darren saw Mark look at George. "And I don't know anyone better at working with dyslexics than George."

Darren felt himself exhale. "So what do I do now?" Darren asked, turning to George, feeling like he was his lifeline. He couldn't play football anymore. The doctor had given him the bad news that morning and the team had put him on the permanent injured list. It was hard to think about it, but that part of his life was over—forever.

Mark looked at Darren, then at George, and back to Darren. "I'll let you talk." He got up and left, closing the door behind him.

"Darren, what is it?" asked George.

Darren couldn't move. He just stared at the wall, which was lined with books. "I've been cut by the team, or I will be soon." Darren looked at George. "I don't know what I'm going to do. Football's all I know." He felt George's hand on his shoulder and he tried to hold back the tidal wave of emotion that surged over him. "The team doctor called me today and said I could never play again." Darren lowered his head, feeling the tears threaten. His dad had always told him men didn't cry, and his teammates, *former* teammates, would smack him around if they saw him, but right now Darren didn't give a fuck.

"It's okay to grieve," George said.

"Someone didn't die," Darren said as he stood up and looked at George, who shook his head.

"Maybe not someone, but you lost a part of who you are, something that helped define you, and it's okay to grieve that loss." George's hand on his arm broke the last of his control, and putting his hands over his eyes, he felt himself give in to his hurt. "It's okay." Almost instinctively, Darren reached out and felt George tug him into a hug, holding him as he fell to pieces. Deep down he'd known this was going to happen, but a small part of him had been hoping for a miracle.

"I don't know what I'm going to do without football."

"Who says you have to give it up? Just because you can't play doesn't mean you're through." George said in his ear, and Darren found himself holding tighter to the smaller man, afraid of letting go and falling into the abyss. "You can coach, you can teach." George's words cut through his grief. "Say, isn't there a possible job as a broadcaster? You could do that."

Darren found himself laughing even as the last of the tears ran down his face. "Yeah…. I mean yes, I could, if I knew what I was doing."

Darren saw George hesitate for a few seconds. "I'll help you as best I can, at least until the program."

"So when do we start?" Darren released George, feeling embarrassed as he stepped back. "Sorry," he added swiping his cheeks dry.

"I'll put together a plan and we'll work on it together. Knowing you're dyslexic will help a lot because I can tailor it to what you need." Darren looked into George's brown eyes and saw something he hadn't seen in quite a while: someone who cared about him and seemed to see *him*, not just his ability to play football. George saw him as a human being. But there was definitely something in that gaze that made his stomach clench in fear and his heart race with excitement at the same time, and Darren knew what it was: George was gay.

Darren knew and finally understood his feelings toward the other man. He'd had them as long as he could remember, but he knew there was no way in hell he could ever act on them. "Fags don't play football," his father had said once when he'd caught Darren looking at one of his teammates just a little too long. Granted, it had been innocent, but the message was clear enough and delivered with such scorn that Darren could still remember the fear that gripped his spine. Realizing that your father could hate you for something you were was an eye-opening experience for him and only deepened his determination to keep that portion of himself buried, deep and forever, at least to the rest of the world.

"Darren." George's voice cut through his uncomfortable thoughts. "Are you there?"

"Yes." Darren faltered for a second, wondering what George had been saying. "I zoned for a bit."

"I was asking you if you were ready to go. I need to go to the gym. My leg is feeling stiff and I'm hoping a little exercise and a soak in the whirlpool will help."

"Do you go to the same one Lonnie does?" Darren asked as he saw George open the door.

"That's where I met him. He works out with a bunch of guys, and they're pretty serious." George closed the door behind them and led the way down the hall past the front door of the now nearly empty building. The only people Darren saw were the custodial staff. "The funny thing is that, of the group, Lonnie's the only one that's straight."

Darren found his feet glued to the floor, unable to move as he gaped at George. "Why would you tell me that?"

George turned around, staring back at him, and Darren saw him sigh. "I didn't mean to make you uncomfortable. I…." His voice tapered away as his eyes widened. "This is my classroom. Why don't we step inside?" Darren watched warily as he passed George, keeping his distance, and once inside his arms crossed defensively in front of his chest. A defensive denial formed on the tip of his tongue as George closed the door. "I already know what you're going to say," George said as he glared at him almost like he could see deep into his heart. "And we can only work together if we're honest with each other. I'm gay, Darren, and I don't hide it. I also don't flaunt it, but I spent time in the closet and I don't intend to go back. I lied to myself, my family, and my friends for a long time and I won't do that again. So if working with me is going to make you uncomfortable, I'll recommend someone else who can help you."

Darren felt part of his insides untwist. Maybe George didn't know. What did it matter if George was gay if he could help him? It wasn't as though anything else was going to happen, even if George was cute in a school-teachery sort of way, with his button-down shirts and khaki pants, and eyes deep as chocolate. "No, George, please," he said with a strength that surprised him.

"Hiding who you are takes a lot of effort, Darren," George added very quietly.

Darren stood, looking at George, stunned. Part of his brain yelled at him to get the hell out of there and not look back. Turning toward the door, he reached for the knob.

"You can face men barreling down the football field, intent on crushing you into the ground, but the thought of who you are scares the hell out of you, doesn't it?"

Darren stopped dead, turning to glare at George, but the other man just looked back at him softly, like he really understood. Darren opened his mouth to deny it, but something else entirely came out. "H-how did you know?"

"I just did. And no," George took a step closer. "It wasn't something you said or the way you acted. I just knew. My gaydar has always been pretty good, and when I met you it went off loudly. I also figured you hadn't accepted who you were and were hiding. I won't say anything to anyone, if that's what you're worried about. I just wanted you to know that you could be yourself and that you didn't have to hide around me." George grabbed his case off the desk and walked even more stiffly toward him, opening the door before stepping into the hall. "If you still want to work on your reading, be at my house tomorrow at seven thirty." George motioned him out, and Darren walked in a bit of a daze through the halls, slipping on his coat before stepping outside into the winter air.

Darren walked to his car and opened the door before sliding into the cold seat. He could see George, limping more pronouncedly now as he slowly made his way toward his car. "Courage" came unbidden to his mind. Darren had never considered himself a coward. He'd taken more beatings on the field than he could remember and he'd never backed down from a fight. But George had more courage in his little finger than he could ever dream of because he was brave enough to live his life and be true to who he was. "Fuck," Darren said out loud as he rested his head against the steering wheel. The thought of telling people, never mind his father, that he liked guys was enough to make his stomach flip, and he had to force himself not to be sick. More than anything he wished he could be like everyone else, but he wasn't.

Starting the car, Darren pulled out of the lot, initially heading toward home, but halfway there, he knew the last thing he wanted was to face his father or anyone he knew. He needed time to think. Turning onto the freeway instead, he drove aimlessly, heading north to nowhere in particular.

The purring engine and humming tires the accompaniment to his thinking, barely aware of the world around him, Darren let the sleek car take him where the road led, his mind too occupied to really care. Football and the fact he could no longer play, an upcoming guest host spot on *Talking Sports* that there was no way he could pull off right now, all on top of the fact that George had forced him to face the fact that he was gay. Jesus Christ, he'd only known the man a few days and yet he'd completely turned his world of denial and suppression upside down. And to make matters worse, he kept seeing the man's face and hearing his voice. "You don't have to hide."

Taking the next exit, he turned left and got back on the freeway, starting back to town. He probably should have gone back to the apartment in Philadelphia, but he decided that what he really needed were answers to the questions he'd had for years that now seemed so urgent.

Nearly chickening out, he almost headed home, but found himself parked outside George's small house, staring at the dark windows. As he watched, a light came on and he almost pulled away. In fact, he'd already put the car in gear when he saw the front door open, George's small body outlined in the square of light. Shutting off the engine, Darren pulled the hand brake and opened his door.

The chill wind cut right through his coat, swaying the naked tree branches as he walked toward the still-open door. "What is it?" George asked with genuine concern as he stepped back from the door to let Darren inside.

"I haven't a fucking clue in hell," Darren replied almost like a prayer as he stood in the tiny hallway.

"Come on in," George said, leading him into the small living room, turning on lights as he went. Darren looked around the room. Bookshelves lined many of the walls, a small television on a stand, papers scattered on the coffee table along with a laptop. "What's bothering you, Darren?" George asked as he lowered himself into one of the chairs.

"Nothin'. Everything. Hell, I don't know where to start." Darren felt his mind racing from topic to topic, question to question, without settling on anything at all.

"Okay," George soothed patiently. "Take a deep breath." George's voice was warm and calm. "Let your mind calm. I'll help where I can, so organize your thoughts. I know they're all scrambled. I get that way too when I'm upset, so just concentrate on one thing." George's voice trailed off and the room silenced, with only the ticking of a clock filling the space.

Darren took a deep breath. "Why do I have to be gay?" He expected George to laugh at his stupid question, but Darren watched as George sat back in his chair.

"That's the million-dollar question for all of us, isn't it?" George said softly. "I think every gay person wishes they were like everyone else at some point in their lives. No one really wants to be different from everyone else, especially not when being different holds you up for ridicule and discrimination. As to why, I wish I could answer that, but I can't. I truly believe that we're born gay, not made gay."

"That's not what my dad says," Darren commented softly.

"Let me guess," George quipped with a smile. "He's one of the dumb ones who says gays have to recruit."

Darren smiled at the mocking tone in George's voice. "Yeah, something like that." Darren sighed. "My dad's okay otherwise, I guess. He was never mean, but once he found out I was good at sports that was all that mattered. School wasn't important unless I couldn't play or something. Then it became a big deal, but only until I could play again. Then it didn't matter."

"What about your mom?" George inquired.

"She and my dad divorced when I was young, and she moved to Vegas or something. I haven't seen her since I was about ten. Since then it's just been my dad and me. He was a high school football player, but never made it in college."

"So you were his dream," George finished for him, and Darren nodded his head. "The thing is, now you have to decide what your dream is. I know you can't play, but you're young and you must have made a lot of money playing pro football, so at least you have options."

Darren found himself smiling. "The best thing I ever did was listen to one of the other players who told me about Lonnie." Darren shook his head when he remembered their first conversation. "He said he had this really good money guy. The first time I met Lonnie, he sat me down and told me that if I was going to be a dumb, shit-for-brains, fuckhead jock and spend every cent I earned, then I could get my sorry ass out of his office and not waste his time."

"That sounds like Lonnie," George said with a smile. "I hope you listened."

"I did, sort of. I bought the car and paid off my dad's house, and I did my share of partying, but I didn't buy bottles of Cristal Champagne like the other guys, and I certainly didn't gamble it away. Every time I thought about it, I heard Lonnie's voice in the back of my head."

George began to laugh, and Darren found himself thinking how good he looked when he did that. "I never thought having Lonnie's voice in your head could be a good thing. I always figured that was one of the levels of hell." George continued laughing, his face lighting up. "Have you eaten?"

"No." Darren suddenly felt very hungry, where he hadn't been a second ago. "I'll get something on my way home."

George wrenched himself out of the chair. "Come on. I think I have something in the refrigerator." Darren followed a struggling George as he limped into the other room.

"Did you get to the gym to soak your leg?" Darren asked, wondering to himself just how painful the leg was because it sure looked like it hurt.

"Yes," George answered as he opened the refrigerator door. "But it didn't seem to help. This time of year, when it's cold, there isn't much I can do. It just aches sometimes. In the summer it hardly bothers me at all." George pulled out the fixings for sandwiches, setting them on the counter. "Help yourself, and you can join me at the table, because if I don't get these papers graded, I'll have a class full of disappointed kids." George limped to the table and Darren set about making a sandwich.

"Do your folks know you're gay?" Darren asked as he slathered mustard on a piece of whole wheat bread.

"Oh sure," George answered, and Darren watched as he sat stiff-legged in the chair. "I told them after college, and they were so relieved I'd finally opened up about it. Mom said she already knew, and Dad," George chuckled softly, "Dad said that he didn't care as long as I was happy. Granted, that was after he disappeared into his workshop for the better part of a weekend, but he accepted it. Whenever I talk to them, they always ask me if I have a boyfriend."

"Have you had one?" Darren inquired as he finished making his sandwich, setting it on the plate George had set out before walking to the table.

"Once." George got quiet and while Darren was curious, he didn't want to pry. "At least I thought I had a boyfriend. It was in college and I thought Julian really liked me. But it turned out to be a bet to see if he could take my supposed virginity." Darren stared across the table at George, mouth hanging open, sandwich halfway to his mouth, completely stunned into silence. "It seemed he bet his friends a hundred bucks he could get me into bed with him. They picked me because they thought it would be fun to pick on the cripple, as they called it." George lowered his head and went back to his work.

"That wasn't cool at all," Darren said, and then his voice trailed off. "Who am I to talk? I probably would have been one of the guys placing the bet if I'd have been out. I used to pick on the smart kids something awful. They intimidated me and I took my poor self-esteem out on them." Darren took a huge bite of his sandwich, feeling like a real dope for what he'd done to people like George. "How did you find out?"

"I heard some of the guys talking outside of one of my classes and I put things together. Julian had invited me for dinner, so I got dressed up and we went out. I made sure to order the most expensive things on the menu and I ate every bit. At the end of the meal I ordered a small glass of port and accidentally on purpose spilled it down his front and onto his lap before walking out of the restaurant." George's eyes glowed with mischief and Darren knew that wasn't the end of it. "When I got back to the dorm, I told everyone what Julian had done; making sure all the other jocks knew full well what happened. You should have seen him walking into the dorm with his pants all squishy, stinking to high heaven." George laughed slightly, but Darren thought it was just a cover for his embarrassment.

"So nothing happened?" Darren asked, and George nodded before turning his attention back to the papers he was grading. "I mean, you've never?" Darren swallowed, suddenly uncomfortable.

"I'm not a virgin, if that's what you're asking. Geez, how did we get here?" George chuckled again as he went back to his papers. Darren finished his sandwich and got up to put the plate in the sink. As he sat back down, George handed him the book from the day before. "I want you to read to yourself and I want you to try to see if you can identify when the words scramble. Sometimes just knowing what's happening is enough for dyslexics to begin to compensate."

"Okay, I'll try." Darren picked up the book and began to read. Some of the words did appear scrambled, but when he looked again, he forced himself to concentrate and the words looked right and he could read them. It was slow going, but after a while, he could start to make out the story and sort of forgot what he was doing and just read. Every now and then, he'd look up and see George working on his papers, putting checkmarks where things were wrong and placing stickers on the papers that were correct.

"What are you grinning about?" George asked with a smile, looking up from his work.

"I was just remembering how much I liked stickers when I was your students' age." He could remember peeling them off the papers and placing them around the edge of his desk. Granted, he hadn't gotten many, but some of the smart kids had them all the way around the edge.

"They still do, and I try to be liberal with the stickers. Anything that excites them to learn is a good thing. In fact," George began writing in his planner, "I need to get some Christmas stickers tomorrow."

"Does the school reimburse you?" Darren asked as George went back to his grading.

"No." George snorted softly. He put down his red pencil and turned toward Darren. "There isn't money in the budget for anything other than the basics."

"That ain't right!" Darren blustered on George's behalf before correcting himself when George smirked at him. "Isn't right." It seemed to him that a nice guy like George was being taken advantage of, and it bothered him. Why, he didn't understand, but it did.

"I don't know of a single teacher who doesn't use some of their own money to buy extras for their class," George explained in his usual patient voice, "It's just one of the facts of life when you're a teacher." George shrugged, and Darren found himself getting angry on George's behalf. "And it's been that way for a long time."

"It's still not right," Darren countered, not willing to concede the argument.

"Maybe not, but if I want the kids to have something extra, I need to supply it, and keep it locked up, because around the school, supplies are like gold." George set aside the paper he'd just finished correcting. "Since you're here, I have an assignment for you." Darren felt George's gaze on him like fire in his belly and he nearly jumped, wondering where that was coming from. "Every night, I want you to watch the news at least once, preferably twice, and each week, you must watch *Talking Sports*. Pay attention to the way the announcers and hosts speak. Imitate them if you like, but you need to really listen to them, because when you're on the show, you're one of them and you need to sound and act like it."

"All right. I'll do that." Darren got up from his chair. "I should probably go so you can finish your work." Darren stared down at George, wondering what he should do. When George stood up, Darren stepped forward and hugged him, feeling the other man's heat through his clothes. "Thank you for listening to my dumb questions."

"Darren," George scolded lightly, "you asked good questions, and you aren't dumb, not at all." George handed him the book he'd been reading. "Finish it and write down any words you don't know." Darren made a face and George added, "I know it's hard, but you'll only get better with practice. Learning to play football wasn't easy, but you did it. Apply that same determination you used on the gridiron to your reading and you'll go a long way."

Darren swallowed. "You really think I can do this?" No one had ever had faith that he could do anything other than play football. All through school, his teachers hadn't bothered with him other than to make sure he squeaked by so he could play. Even his dad hadn't believed he could do anything other than play, and here was this man, someone he'd known just a few days, who seemed to believe in him. Darren blinked as he looked at George.

"Of course you can," George answered, as though there wasn't a doubt in the world.

Darren turned and walked toward the front door. "I'll see you tomorrow."

"Here at seven," George reiterated.

"I won't be late," Darren said with a smile before retrieving his coat. Shrugging it on, he looked around the house for a second before opening the door, calling out a goodbye before closing it behind him and walking to his car, still carrying the book. He really didn't want to go to his dad's but he figured he'd better not be out too late. After all, he had assignments to get done.

The drive to his dad's didn't take long, and Darren pulled his car into the garage before walking into the house. The only sound he heard was the television. Walking through the kitchen to the living room, he found his dad asleep in front of the television, his recliner pushed all the way back, the floor creaking slightly as he walked by. "You not going out?" his dad asked sleepily, arms stretching over his head.

"No. I've got some things I need to get done." Darren didn't elaborate, and if he were honest it was shame that kept him from telling his dad what he was doing, shame that he couldn't really read and shame for who he was. Without saying more, he went right to his old bedroom filled with trophies and mementos to the past, to a person he couldn't be anymore. Shrugging off his coat, he absently laid it over the end of the bed. Picking up a photograph, he stared at the face shining back at him from his college football uniform. George was right. It was okay to grieve the loss. What moved him were the opportunities he'd had and let slip through his fingers. Sure, he'd gone to college, but he hadn't graduated. He'd simply taken classes so he could play football, and they hadn't even been real classes; just pottery making and basic computer classes. All he had really had to do was show up. Putting the picture back on the shelf, Darren kicked off his shoes before climbing on the bed. He propped up his knees before opening the book. If that picture represented his past, then the book in his hand represented the future, and he was going to make the most of it.

Turning on the light beside the bed, he continued reading until the clock read eleven. Darren set the book aside, pleased that he'd gotten through a lot of it and even happier that he'd understood and was able to remember what he'd read.

His dad was still in his chair as the news program came on. Darren settled on the sofa, watching as the announcers read the news stories, becoming more and more frustrated with each passing second.

"I'm going to bed," his dad commented groggily, getting up. "Turn it down, will ya?"

Darren nodded, not looking away from the screen as his dad got up and left the room. Lowering the volume, he continued watching and listening as George had asked him. How in hell was he going to be able to pull any of this off? Leaning forward, he reached for the remote to turn it off, but stopped himself. George had asked him to do this and he'd agreed. A commercial came on and Darren squeezed his eyes closed. "Fuck," he groaned softly. He'd always thought that all he needed to do was make the pros and his life would be perfect. He'd played for three years and he thought he had it made. And all it took was one good wrenching injury to his left hip and it was over. No more running, no more leaping, no more fans cheering and calling his name. No more football.

The commercial ended, and thankfully the sports segment started. He watched the announcer, listening to the way he spoke, and caught the enthusiasm in his voice. As the announcer continued on, he realized he knew what the announcer was saying, he understood it, and he—yes, he—could do that. Getting up, he turned off the television and walked through the dark house to his room. Cleaning up and undressing, he climbed beneath the covers.

Tossing and turning, Darren finally fell asleep. Ever since he could remember, he'd dreamed of football, plays he'd made and ones he'd messed up, but tonight he kept seeing the smiling face of a particular fourth-grade teacher.

III

GEORGE stood behind the desk at the health club, checking people in and helping with their questions. Looking up, he saw the doors open and Darren enter the club, all smiles. They'd been working together almost every day for the past two weeks, and Darren's reading and writing were progressing nicely. Once they'd figured out how to work with Darren's dyslexia, it was as if doors had burst wide open. "Are you here to work out?" George asked curiously. He didn't see a bag in Darren's hands.

"No." Darren smiled and George tried to find something—anything—to keep him busy. Maybe it was just the fact that they'd been spending so much time together, but George found himself developing feelings for Darren, and he knew that was a recipe for emotional disaster. Darren was spending time with him because George could help him get ready for his appearance as a guest host on *Talking Sports*, and for no other reason. And George allowing himself to feel anything for the former sports star just wasn't going to work. "Well, sort of, I guess." Darren rubbed the back of his neck with his hand. "I was sort of wondering if you'd like to work out together."

George checked the clock and saw that he still had almost an hour left to his shift and breathed a sigh of relief. "I can't."

"Go on, George," Josh said from behind him. "It's slow; I'll watch the desk."

Unable to refuse, he relented. "Thanks Josh." George smiled, allowing himself to let go of his trepidation. "I'll get my things and meet you outside the locker room." He retrieved his things from his drawer and walked back toward the locker room.

Inside he heard no one. He chose a locker in the first bay. Getting changed, he'd just dropped his pants when Darren strode in, carrying a small bag that he hadn't seen earlier. George wished he could hide, but it was too late now. Taking off his shirt, he hung it in the locker and heard Darren's sharp intake of breath. "What happened to you?"

George didn't look; he didn't have to. "When I was born, my hip wasn't formed properly and I had to have surgery so I could walk—a couple of times. The last one was ten years ago." George pulled out a pair of long sweatpants. "I know it's pretty ugly."

"No, it's not. It's just some scars." Darren began undressing. "I've got lots of them too." Darren took off his shirt and George did his best to try to turn his head away, but found he couldn't. Darren's body stunned him. He'd seen hints of what lay under the big man's clothes, but with his shirt off, George found he couldn't look away. Acres of honey skin pulled taut over thick muscles, with wide shoulders tapering to a narrow waist. George forced his eyes closed before turning around.

Peeking in the mirrors, he saw Darren drop his pants, a wide pink gash on his hip. "Is that what ended your playing?" George asked before he could stop himself.

"Yes. It seems we have a lot in common," Darren said without humor before pulling on a pair of shorts and a T-shirt. "Since neither of us can work our legs, I thought we'd do some upper body."

"With me?" George stared in wonder. "I can't lift what you can."

"You don't have to. We'll change the weights. Don't worry." Darren bumped his shoulder. "I won't let you get hurt."

George felt the look in Darren's eyes down to his toes. Was he flirting with him? George almost scoffed out loud, but kept it to himself. It must be his imagination; there was no other explanation. "Okay. I'll trust your judgment." George finished dressing about the same time Darren did, and followed him out onto the weight floor.

George followed Darren with a slight smile on his face. The tight shirt made Darren appear even bigger than usual, and George feasted his eyes on his wide back and seemingly tiny waist. At one of the flat weight benches, Darren began loading the bar to ninety-five pounds. "We'll start with light weights and build up. That way we can build slowly."

"Hey, guys." George recognized Dan's partner, Gene, as he approached. "How's it going?"

"Good," George answered before making introductions, "Gene, this is Darren."

"Yeah, I know." Gene smiled and extended his hand. "I've seen you play. You're amazing." Gene's eyes shone. "I'm sorry about the injury. How long will you be out?"

Darren's smile dimmed a little. "I think it's permanent. The doctors say if I play, I could reinjure it and then I probably wouldn't walk again. I was tempted to do it anyway, but it isn't worth the risk."

"So when's the competition?" George asked Gene, changing the subject as he saw the hurt and loss in Darren's eyes. "Gene's entered in the Mr. Universe competition," George explained to Darren.

"Mid-May. I came in second for the past few years and I'd like one more chance to win before I hang it up. I'm getting a little old, so regardless, this will be my last year." George tried to keep his eyes off Gene's massive chest, which was bursting from the string tank that barely covered it. He knew Gene caught him looking but said nothing. "I've got to finish my workout. I'll see you later." Gene turned, walking to the very back of the gym.

"Christ," Darren swore softly, "I've seen big guys before, but that's a big guy!"

"And he's all natural," George supplied, still watching Gene as he picked up the largest dumbbells from the rack. "He and Dan have been together almost two years. They're the best guys."

"You know them?" Darren asked, turning his attention back to him.

"From the gym, mainly. I've also met them at some of Lonnie's parties." George lay down on the bench, positioning himself beneath the bar. "I've done this weight before."

Darren stood behind him. "I'll be here anyway. I promised I wouldn't let you get hurt." Darren leaned over the bar. "And I meant it," he added waggling his eyebrows.

George pressed the bar up, getting it into position before lowering it to his chest, doing ten reps before clanging it back on the rack and sitting up. "Darren." He turned around, expecting to find Darren watching Gene. Darren's blue eyes were staring all right, but at him. "What's going on?" Darren simply continued looking at him, saying nothing. "Are you flirting with me?"

Darren's eyes darkened for just a second. "What if I am?" Darren looked away before starting to load the bar with additional weight, refusing to look at him.

That was not the answer George expected, and he found himself a little tongue-tied. "Why?" He whispered, getting up from the bench as flashes of what had happened in college had his stomach in instant knots.

Darren finished loading the bar, finally looking at him. "Why not, George? You're one of the nicest people I've ever met." As he watched, George saw what looked like a war going on behind Darren's eyes that continued as he lowered himself onto the bench, lifting the weight, pressing it up and down in rapid succession as though nearly two hundred pounds weighed nothing at all.

The weight clanked with a metallic ring into the rack and George hadn't moved or stopped watching Darren. "I don't understand, Darren. I thought you were my friend." He just couldn't understand why Darren would pick on him this way.

"You are my friend," Darren said softly, standing in front of him. "And I'm not like those guys in college. Not anymore." George saw Darren's eyes dart around the room. "You're a caring, nice guy. We've spent every evening for the past two weeks together." Darren huffed softly. "I don't do this well, George. But I'm not picking on you or trying to make you feel bad. I like you, George, and I'm sort of hoping you might like me too."

George couldn't believe they were having this conversation in the middle of the gym, but he wasn't about to let it go now. "Why me?" George looked around the gym with all its mirrors paying homage to the beautiful and hunky, his eyes falling on Gene. "You could have almost anyone you wanted." Letting his gaze shift back to Darren, George waited for some sort of answer.

"It's your turn," was all Darren said as he stripped the weights, and George didn't know what to think. Part of him wanted to believe what Darren had said, because as they'd spent time together, he'd found himself increasingly attracted to the handsome ex-football player. And it wasn't just physical either, although the man was hunkiness personified. He had a ready sense of humor and threw himself into his lessons like he was preparing for the game of his life. But Darren was just discovering who he really was. He'd only started to accept that he was gay, and George knew most guys were like tomcats once they made that realization, and he couldn't expect Darren to be any different. The doors had been thrown open and Darren was free, or would be as soon as he fully accepted who he was. Pulling himself out of his thoughts, George sat on the bench. Lifting the bar, he did his set, trying to concentrate on the weight he was lifting instead of the man standing just behind him. After the last rep, he racked the weight and saw Darren lean over the bar, his face just above his.

"One thing sports taught me, George, was to go after what I want with both hands. And if you hit a roadblock, either run around it, or work harder until it's nothing but dust. I like you, George, and I trust you. I'm hoping you like me too, but if you don't, just say so and I'll back off."

George gulped as he felt Darren's eyes burning into his. He knew he should lie for both their sakes and tell Darren he felt nothing, but he couldn't. Sliding down the bench, he sat on the edge, looking back at Darren, "I like you too, but—"

"No buts, George." Darren smiled and started loading more weight on the bar. "I like you," he said just above a whisper, "and I may not have been out, but that doesn't mean I've been some kind of saint."

"So what are you saying?" George asked warily as he sat up.

"I'm saying that we finish this workout and then I take you out for dinner."

George studied Darren to make sure he was serious; he sure looked it. "Okay." George couldn't stop a smile. Darren had just asked him out, sort of. Getting off the bench, he let Darren take his turn. The man pressed more than three hundred pounds, with George assisting him a little on the last rep, helping maneuver the bar into the rack with a clang that reverberated through the gym. George helped Darren change the weights and took his turn and his time admiring the view as he stared up at the bigger man.

"Are you gonna lift or look?" Darren asked, looking down at him.

"Look," George quipped. "Since you asked, I figured I got a free pass to undress you with my eyes all I want." George leered up at him before breaking into a smile as the huge man actually blushed like a schoolboy.

"As long as I can look too," Darren answered, and George scoffed lightly before lifting the bar. What there was for Darren to look at escaped him.

"Yeah, right," George grunted self-deprecatingly between reps as he worked his way through the set.

After finishing their chest work, they did a few sets of back before Darren led them to the mats on the floor. "Just a few sets of crunches for our abs and we're done." Darren flopped down and began pounding his way through the exercise, T-shirt riding up, giving George a glimpse of a strip of golden skin with lines that led beneath the waistband of Darren's shorts. George itched to touch, but lowered himself to the mat instead, mimicking Darren's movements.

Flopping back on the mat, George's stomach burned. Waiting for the sensation to pass, he watched Darren continue to bang out rep after rep of crunches, alternating with leg lifts and then scissors, where he lifted both his legs and shoulders, balancing on his butt. That was impressive and sexy as hell, because that tight shirt kept riding just a little higher. Finally, Darren stopped, sweaty all over. "Do one more set and then we're done," Darren encouraged, and George groaned but complied before getting to his feet.

In the locker room, George slipped out of his clothes, self-conscious that Darren would see him naked and withdraw his invitation to dinner. He knew that was probably a little irrational, but he couldn't stop the insecurity. However, as soon as Darren slipped off his shirt and slid his shorts down his legs, George forgot about himself, openly staring in the otherwise empty locker room. When Darren stood near him wearing nothing but a pair of white briefs, George thought he'd died and gone to heaven. Seeing Darren looking back at him, George colored and turned away, muttering apologies. "It's okay, George. I've been playing sports for years, and showering with other guys is a part of that. I stopped being self-conscious a long time ago. I've known some of the guys I've played with over the years were gay." Darren slipped off his underwear, giving George a glimpse of his perfect butt before a towel wrapped around Darren's waist. "I'll tell you a secret, though. In all that time, not one single person has looked at me like you did just now."

"Like how?" George was more than curious about what Darren had seen.

"I can't describe it, George. You're the one who's good with words, but it gave me goose bumps." Darren turned away and walked back toward the showers, with George watching him go, fascinated by every graceful move. How such a big man could move with such fluidity was something he couldn't understand. Slipping off the last of his clothes, George followed Darren into the showers.

Water already ran as George entered the showers. Slipping off his towel, he stepped into one of the stalls, starting the water and reaching for the soap. How it happened, he never knew, but as he washed his hair, his bad leg slipped out from under him. Before he could grab hold of anything, George found himself on the floor half in and half out of the shower, ears ringing, and his vision swimming.

"George." Darren knelt next to him, a hand stroking his cheek. "Are you okay?"

George couldn't answer. He shook his head slightly. All that mattered at that moment was Darren's hand on his face and the feel of his body touching his. "Darren?"

"Can you get up? Do you need help?" Darren asked softly, genuine concern evident in his trembling voice.

"I'm okay." Moving slowly, George carefully got his feet beneath him and somehow managed to get upright again. Looking down, he blushed as he remembered he was naked, and when Darren stood up, George colored even more as a massive wall of skin over muscle stood remarkably near. Close enough, in fact, that George could feel the heat from Darren's body against his skin. "I just sort of lost my balance," George stammered, torn between trying to hide and continuing to get an eyeful of Darren's hard body. Feeling that heat and feasting his eyes, as he got over the fall, George felt his body respond, and he stepped back, nearly tripping over the threshold of the shower as he hurried to get a curtain between himself and Darren. Yes, he'd told Darren he wasn't a virgin, and technically he wasn't, but in many ways, his inexperience embarrassed him.

"It's okay, George," Darren said from the other side of the curtain, but George turned on the water, cold as he could stand, wishing he could disappear into the tile. Seeing Darren walk away, George finished washing himself. He shut off the water and reached outside the curtain, searching for his towel. What he grabbed was significantly warmer and thicker. Peering around the curtain, George found his hand on Darren's shoulder, a set of deep blue eyes meeting his.

"It's really okay, George." Darren continued looking deep into him. "You didn't get hurt, did you?"

"No." Only his pride. Reaching for his towel, George took it, quickly wrapping it around his waist. "I just feel like a clumsy fool." George looked away and felt hands on his shoulder, and before he could breathe, he felt Darren's lips against his. At first he didn't react—he was too stunned—but it only took a few seconds for him to process what was happening and start kissing back.

The door to the shower area opened, startling him, and George jumped back, breathing hard as he stared at Darren. The last thing he wanted was to be caught kissing in the showers at work, even if he was off the clock. "Um, maybe we should get dressed," George mumbled softly. Darren grinned at him and began to laugh, loud and full. "What's so funny?" George demanded in a stage whisper, afraid that whoever had opened the door would come in at any moment.

"I got you shook up enough to say 'um'. You never say things like that." Darren's eyes glowed. "You must have really liked it."

"I did," George admitted, watching Darren watch him. "But this isn't really the place to talk about it." He could feel heat rising to his cheeks.

"Okay." Darren turned around and left the shower area, a small towel fastened around a small waist, swaying with each step the man took. George took a deep breath to clear his head as a pair of old men entered the shower area. Walking past them, he passed by the sauna and sink area before he opened the door, heading toward his locker.

The room was busy now, the after-dinner crowd changing for their workouts. George tried not to peek at Darren as he finished dressing, but gave up completely. There was too much to look at, and he found the man too attractive not to look.

Opening his locker, George peeked at Darren and found him looking back, the intense gaze heating his skin wherever it stopped. Dropping the towel, George pulled on a pair of briefs and his pants in rapid succession before he completely embarrassed himself.

"Would you stop that?" George whispered softly.

"What?" Darren asked, with what had to be mock innocence.

"Looking at me like…" George stammered, "like you're starving and I'm a steak." George pulled his shirt over his head, momentarily blocking out his view of Darren.

"What's wrong with looking at you? You're beautiful and I like it." Darren made a point of staring at him, ignoring the other men in the room.

"You're bad," George quipped as he sat down to pull on his socks and shoes. Darren leaned close to say something, but one of the other men walked into the bay of lockers and Darren backed away. "I just need to put my shoes on and we can go." Darren nodded and grabbed his bag, thankfully leaving the room. George needed to get his mind, and body for that matter, off Darren, even if for a few minutes, or he wasn't going to be able to walk very comfortably. Not that he was particularly comfortable now. Darren's touch and the kiss had his pulse racing, and as he thought about it, his cock throbbed in his pants. Thankfully, they were a little loose, so he wasn't giving everyone in the locker room a peek at his business.

Gathering his things, George walked slowly out of the locker area, seeing Darren seated in one of the chairs by the door. It was amazing to him to know that on the field or in the locker room after a game, Darren was a celebrity, or had been a celebrity, but here almost no one recognized him.

"Are you hungry?" Darren asked as he approached.

"Starved," he answered, and after saying good night to Josh, George followed Darren outside. "Where do you want to go for dinner?" A light snow had started to fall while they were inside, and a dusting covered the ground, the flakes glittering in the lights.

"Is downtown okay? I'd like to take you someplace nice," Darren answered as he clicked open the front-end trunk of his Porsche, pushed up the top, and dropped in his bag. "I'll drive, if you like."

"Let me put my bag in my trunk." George walked to his old car, opening the trunk with the key. Dropping in the bag, he closed it again and heard Darren start his engine, the sports car roaring to life.

Climbing inside, he buckled himself into the deep leather seat and waited, but Darren didn't back up. Instead, he leaned across the console, leather creaking, and kissed George ever so gently. "I get the idea that you still don't believe that I like you, that I think you're attractive." Darren's hand rested lightly on George's leg while the other stroked his cheek.

"It's just hard to believe that someone like you would find someone like me attractive."

Darren sat up, looking across the seat at him, a storm in his blue eyes. "Someone like me? You think that someone who is good-looking isn't smart enough to see what's really important? Yes, George, I know I'm good-looking. I've been told it all my life. I've also been told that I was stupid and good at only one thing. You looked past that and helped me. So is it so strange that I could see you for who you are and like you not because of how you look, but for how you treat me and for your good heart?"

George stared across the console, feeling ashamed. "I hadn't meant it that way."

Darren's expression softened before he leaned across the console again, and this time when Darren kissed him, George kissed him back.

Darren's lips stilled and then pulled away and George immediately missed their heat, following them for a split second before settling back in his seat. Darren put the car into gear and the engine revved as Darren backed out of the parking space. The wet roads flew beneath the tires, engine humming happily, seat cradling George as they rode through the largely quiet streets. It wasn't until they reached Second Street that traffic began to pick up. "Where can we park?" George asked, watching for an available place.

"That's not a problem," Darren answered, pulling up in front of the canopied entrance of Café Fresco. People shivered on the sidewalk, waiting to get into the popular eatery. Darren tooted his horn lightly and the doorman walked over. George's window slid down and Darren smiled at the man. "Do you have a place for us?"

The doorman looked at Darren, looked again, and smiled, "Of course, Mr. White." He stepped back and removed a pair of cones, motioning for him to park right in front. Darren pulled in, turning off the engine before getting out of the car. George opened his door and climbed out of the car, his leg nearly sliding out from under him again on a patch of ice.

"I've got you, George," Darren said, suddenly right next to him, one arm holding George's to steady him. As soon as George was on his feet, Darren released him and he shut the car door, following Darren past the clutches of people and right into the restaurant. He heard people muttering questions within their groups, but those voices were silenced and replaced by dozens of overlapping conversations as soon as the glass front door closed behind them.

"Would you like a table?" the hostess asked as they approached, and George figured they would be told they needed to rejoin the freezing masses outside.

"We'd like a quiet table," Darren specified, and handed her what George figured was money.

"Right this way." She turned without batting an eye and led them to the far wall of the restaurant, the noise immediately falling away, showing them to a small booth. "Is this satisfactory?" she asked formally without really waiting for an answer, as George slid into the booth, Darren taking his seat across from him.

"Yes," Darren answered, and George added, "Thank you." She turned and strode back to her post with her best look-at-me walk, which Darren completely ignored.

"What was that about? Why did we get right in?" George asked as he set his menu aside.

"One thing I found out is that it pays to let people know who you are, especially in places like this." Darren left his menu on the table, while George picked his up and studied it. "What are you having?" George asked, noticing the menu still on the table.

"One of the specials," Darren answered very quickly.

George shook his head. "No, Darren. Pick up the menu and read it. If you don't know something, ask me softly. I know you can do this."

Darren glared at him but picked up the menu. Their server approached the table, took their drink order, and told them the specials before leaving again. "See, I could just order the rockfish special."

"Yes, you could, and that would be easy, but sometimes it's more important to do things the hard way, especially when you're trying to learn something that's new," George explained, keeping his voice very soft. He had no intention of embarrassing Darren, but he wanted him to learn. "Just give it a try."

George studied his menu, watching Darren as he squinted, before eventually putting it down. The server returned and brought their drinks, turning to Darren for his order. "I'd like the filet, medium, and a salad."

She turned to George, and he placed his order, smiling at Darren's accomplishment, but waiting to speak until she was gone. "See, I told you."

"You did." Darren seemed pleased with himself as well. "There were things I couldn't make heads or tails of, though."

"That's because they were French names. Don't worry about it. The thing is that you were able to read the menu on your own and make the words order themselves." George sipped his drink, taking a second to look around the restaurant before returning his attention to Darren. "Would you excuse me for a second?" George asked before sliding out of the booth, walking toward the restrooms at the back of the restaurant.

George did what he needed to do, washing his hands before returning to the dining room. Looking toward the table, he saw another man sitting in his seat, leaning over the table toward Darren. Neither man noticed him as he approached. Nearly reaching the table, he opened his mouth to get Darren's attention, but snapped it shut again.

"Darren, you shouldn't be here with that gimpy-legged little fag. Everyone will think you're one too, man. You'll never get any team to play you if they think you're a fag. Come join our table."

George felt his heart thud in his chest. He should have known this was too good to be true. Things had gone way too well. And what did he expect Darren to do now, stand up and announce his sexuality to everyone in the room? No. George backed away from the table, heading out toward the front of the restaurant and the bar. "George!" He heard Darren's voice and felt a hand on his shoulder. "Where are you going?"

Turning around, he came face to face with those blue, imploring eyes. "Just giving you and your friend some time to talk." He had no intention of letting on about what he'd heard.

"That's no friend of mine." Darren spat between clenched teeth. "That's some wannabe from high school." Darren touched his back and George walked toward their table, sitting back down. "He just wanted me to join them so I could pick up their bar tab," Darren fumed as he sat down. "I get it all the time. I used to fall for it every time, thinking they really liked me, but they were only interested in what I could do for them." Darren lifted his drink, but then set it back down, pushing it away. "I can thank Lonnie for *that* revelation too."

George gulped his drink, swallowing hard. "I heard what he said."

"I sort of thought you did when I found you in the bar," Darren responded. "I told the ignorant bastard to go fuck himself."

George smiled into his drink. "You didn't?"

"I certainly did. I knew him in high school. He was one of the idiots I used to hang out with. Never did anything in his life but put other people down. He got me in more trouble and nearly got me kicked off the team." Darren glared across the dining room and George followed his gaze, seeing the guy talking to his buddies, their heads together, gossiping worse than a group of teenage girls. "I'll make you a deal," Darren said, his voice tearing George's attention away from the other table. "I'll stop thinking of myself as dumb if you'll stop thinking of yourself as anything but adorable."

George felt his eyes widen. "Adorable?"

"I call 'em as I see 'em," Darren responded with a sly smile and a wink.

"Then you need glasses," George said, returning Darren's smile, but secretly very pleased at Darren's assessment.

Their server brought their dinners, setting the plates in front of them and quietly leaving the table. They ate and talked through the rest of their meals. George could feel the other man's eyes on him from across the room, but ignored it as best he could, trying to enjoy his dinner with Darren. As the evening wore on, he found himself worrying less about the set of eyes behind him as he basked in the gleam of the blue eyes across from him.

"Would you like dessert?" the server asked as she cleared their plates.

"Yes," Darren answered, looking at George, "but I think we'll pass for tonight." He gave her a wink and she smiled, placing the check on the table. George reached for it and Darren snatched it out from under his fingers. "I said I was taking you to dinner, remember?" Darren dug out his wallet, handing the server his credit card when she returned, but George noticed that he barely looked at her, those big blue eyes staying focused on George.

When the server returned, Darren signed the bill before taking his card. Getting up from the booth, they threaded their way through the restaurant and outside to

Darren's car. A small group of guys stood nearby admiring it. Darren unlocked the doors and George slid into the cold seat, shivering until Darren started the car. Pulling out, they drove through the city streets and over the river toward George's car.

Darren dropped George at his car, but didn't open the doors. George waited and saw him fidgeting in the driver's seat. "Is there something wrong?"

"No. I just want to ask you something, but I'm not sure how to ask." Darren turned in his seat. "When I said in the restaurant that I wanted dessert, what I meant was that I wanted you."

George stared back, not sure he'd heard Darren right. But then an arm slid around his neck, lightly tugging him closer. Warm lips touched his, a tongue lightly teasing, and George found himself nodding slowly, pushing away that insecure voice that told him no, and going with the soft feel of those lips and the gentle touch of Darren's hands. "Okay, Darren."

Darren deepened the kiss, stealing George's breath. "I'll follow you home."

George nodded again, afraid to say anything. Getting out of Darren's car, he walked to his. Getting in, he started the car and pulled out of the parking lot, heading for home. George drove carefully, checking the rearview mirror constantly, afraid Darren would change his mind. Parking in front of his small house, he turned off the engine, walking up the snow-dusted walk to the front door. He heard Darren pull up and turn off his engine. Footsteps followed him, and seconds later a pair of arms snaked around his waist, a warm chest pressing against his back. "I half expected you to—"

Darren spun him around, kissing him hard, full, possessing his mouth. "Were you gonna say you expected me to ditch you?" Darren asked, voice husky, deep, resonating to George's feet—and other extremities. George nodded once. "Does this feel like I'm going to ditch you?" George swallowed, shaking his head. Pulling him close, Darren whispered into his ear, "Or does this feel like I'm going to make love to you?"

IV

DARREN felt George still, the body in his arms becoming rigid. "Did you mean that?" George asked quietly, the breeze blowing the fog from his breath away.

Darren had never meant anything so much in his life. It was too early to say the words, but it was how he felt. "Yes, George," Darren whispered, a finger brushing what he hoped was melted snow from George's cheek. "I never say what I don't mean." Darren captured those red, full lips with his, kissing hard, trying without words to show George that he was serious. Easing back again, Darren held George tight, feeling the man's heat through his coat and a slight shiver against his chest. "We should go inside."

George seemed reluctant to move away even as the temperature continued its drop and snow fell harder, now completely covering the grass. "Listen," George said softly and then became silent. "Everyone says that snow is silent, but it's not."

The world seemed to still, and as they listened, Darren swore he could hear the soft murmur of a million tiny flakes joining with their brethren as they reached the ground. Darren nodded to George's imploring eyes, neither of them wanting to break the silence. A car coming down the street finally broke the spell, and George moved away from him, toward the front door. Darren followed, and soon they were inside the small, toasty house, stripping off coats. Darren could see the doubt and insecurity in George's eyes, but he didn't give it a chance to take hold. Tugging George close, he kissed him again, running his fingers through short, dark hair as he kissed the breath out of the man. Darren wasn't the most experienced person on earth, but he knew what he wanted.

"Would you like something to drink?" George asked, as he began to fumble with the coats, hanging them up, his nervousness translating into motion.

"No thank you, George." Darren extended his hand and waited for George to take it before letting the smaller man lead him toward the back of the house.

The master bedroom was small, but comfortable, with a simple bed covered by a hand-sewn quilt. For a second, Darren wondered if George's mother had made it, but he didn't want to ask. Right now, the distraction wasn't what he wanted. Guiding George backward, he heard a small squeak when the back of George's legs reached the mattress. Easing him down with a light kiss, Darren continued, thrilled when George relaxed and really began kissing him back. "Is this what you want?" Darren asked, looking into George's dilated eyes in the light shining through the window off the pristine snow.

"Yes, Darren. I've wanted this almost since I met you." George's eyes drifted away and Darren stroked his cheek, feeling as well as seeing that gaze return. "But I was your teacher and I thought—"

Darren slid a finger across those soft lips. "I'm not a kid, and I hope you're more than just my teacher now." George nodded against the pillow. "A whole lot more," Darren added, before capturing those lips again, and almost instantly he felt the intensity and heat between them ramp up. George seemed to come alive, meeting him kiss for kiss and then some as the smaller man vibrated and throbbed with energy. Darren nearly jumped when he felt warm hands slide beneath his shirt, gripping his back as George arched beneath him. "George," Darren whispered softly, but his lips were taken in a bruising kiss and he gave up on talking as George pulled his shirt out from his pants, sliding it toward his neck. Breaking the kiss just long enough to get his shirt off, Darren groaned as lips latched onto one of his nipples, tongue swirling as lips sucked. "Damn, George," he moaned softly as fingers replaced George's mouth, tongue and lips moving their delicious torture.

Leaning back, Darren brought George upright with him, pulling off his shirt before running his hands down George's back as his tongue blazed trails across Darren's skin. Never had anyone driven him to the brink so fast, but every one of George's touches seemed to drive him higher and higher. Finally, George gave him a break, reclining back onto the pillow, tugging Darren down on top him.

Bodies squirmed and thrust, hands managed to open belts and buttons. Somehow, their pants ended up off the foot of the bed, thunking as they fell, along with their shoes. George sighed, his smaller body pressing tightly to Darren like he needed to touch him all at once. Darren knew exactly how he felt. He could not get enough of George's smooth, warm skin. Figuring he needed some time, Darren caught George's hand in one of his, holding them still before ducking his head, licking across George's chest, George's small whimpers egging him on.

"Darren," George groaned, and Darren shifted his eyes toward George's, his tongue sliding over a small, perky nipple, teasing it harder before flicking it with just the tip of his tongue. "I'm so close."

Darren stilled. "Not yet." Shifting on the bed, he pressed George into the mattress, but couldn't stop the small movements of George's hips, a chorus of delicate noises coming from the smaller man. Darren watched as his head fell back and his mouth opened, heat spilling between them.

"You okay?" Darren asked.

"Uh-huh," George answered with a grin, holding him tight. Darren had hoped to make it last, but seeing the delight on George's face wiped away those feelings. George's eyes shone as he kissed him and Darren felt his body take over, his mind shutting down as his own desire kicked in. The friction of George's searing skin quickly drove Darren over the edge, and he added his own release to George's as he clung to the man, his body shaking.

Coming back to himself, Darren petted George's skin, kissing him lightly, loving the glow from those brown eyes, which practically lit the room. "Is it always like that?" George asked, still grinning.

"George." Darren felt his eyes narrowing. "You said you weren't a virgin."

"I'm not," George said, and Darren felt a light swat on his butt. "But they were." George looked away. "Something I'm not very proud of, you know?"

"I think I do, George, and just so you know, it was pretty special for me too." Darren caressed George's cheek before shifting on the bed. He got out of the bed and soon Darren heard water running. Then footsteps and a warm cloth wiped over his skin, followed by a fluffy towel. George left the room again, returning to slip beneath the covers. Darren had expected him to curl next to him, but George lay on the far side of the bed. "What's wrong?"

"Don't you have to leave?"

"Do you want me to leave?" Darren asked quietly, heart pounding in his chest as he tried to figure out what he'd done wrong.

"No, but isn't that what people do?" George's voice was soft, sounded far away.

Darren rolled onto his side, head propped on his hand. "Is that what happened to you?" Darren asked, but George said nothing, the silence from the other side of the bed speaking volumes. Without answering, Darren pulled George to him, holding the man close until his body relaxed. Whoever had hurt George better not ever show his face, because Darren was ready to kill him.

Darren listened to the sound of George's breathing, his thoughts and worries about the upcoming appearance on *Talking Sports* running away with him. He knew George would be there for him; he only hoped that he didn't make a complete fool of himself and let everyone know just how dumb he was. Finally, after he forced his mind to turn off and forced the worries away, he drifted to sleep, holding onto George like a lifeline.

DARREN woke, knowing exactly where he was and knowing who he was hugging tightly and why. George still slept, his butt pressed back against Darren's belly. Peering at the alarm clock, he knew George must have to get up soon. Sliding his hand along George's side, he knew the minute he woke. "Morning, George. Do you have school today?"

He heard a low growl as George tried to bury his head in the pillow. "Tomorrow's the last day of school before Christmas vacation and the kids will be unholy terrors for the next two days." George snuggled up to him and Darren thought he might be trying to burrow under him. The alarm sounding brought a groan as George reached over Darren, slapping off the alarm. George threw back the covers, climbing out of the bed with a wide yawn. Darren leapt, catching him around the waist, pulling him back onto the mattress with a surprised squeak.

"You can wait a few minutes," Darren murmured as his lips nipped at one of George's ears. Darren felt George relax back against him, yawning a soft moan. "I won't make you late, I promise."

"What do you have today?"

"The television station wants me to come down for a rehearsal so I can get used to the cameras and the setup." Darren let his hand wander over George's stomach.

"Who's your guest for the show, anyway?"

"I'm not really sure. I'm hoping they'll tell me all that today. At least it'll give me some time to figure out what to ask." Now it was Darren's turn to yawn. Closing his mouth, Darren gave George a light kiss before letting him up. Slipping out from under the covers, Darren began retrieving his clothes before tugging them on. "Will I see you later?"

George picked up his own clothes, putting them in the hamper in the corner. "I hope so. I was going to go to the gym after school."

"Then I'll meet you there." Darren kissed George one last time, hating to see the bathroom door close between them. Pulling on the last of his clothes, he said goodbye to George and then walked through the house, retrieving his coat before opening the door, heading outside into a clean, white morning. The world seemed brighter, and, opening his car door, he looked at the house one more time, thinking of George before sliding into his seat.

The drive home was a nightmare, with everyone driving like idiots because of the snow. Parking in the garage, he walked into the house and went right to his room. "Dad, you still home?" he called on his way.

"Yeah, just gettin' ready to leave," was the reply that floated to his ears. "You need somethin'?" The voice got louder and Darren saw his dad standing in the doorway.

"Yeah." Darren felt his insides turn over and he thought he might be sick for a second. "I have to go to the television studio, but I was wondering if we could talk when you get home from work?"

"Sure." His dad looked at him like he wanted to ask what this was about, but Darren knew his father had to go or he would be late. "They're shutting the plant at noon for Christmas, so I'll be home this afternoon." His dad buttoned the last buttons on his blue work shirt before stomping toward the front of the house in his heavy work boots. Darren closed his bedroom door and got undressed. Walking to the bathroom, he heard the front door bang closed. He turned on the shower, waiting for it to warm before stepping beneath the spray.

Darren knew as soon as he'd left George's house that he had to tell his father. The way George had looked at him, touched him, Darren knew he couldn't relegate him to some dirty little secret. George deserved more than that. He and George had made love, a little clumsily and maybe a little fast—Darren smiled as he remembered the look on George's face—and spending the night holding George had felt right.

Reaching for the soap, Darren steadied his nerves as he washed himself, his hands retracing where George's had been.

Rinsing himself off, Darren turned off the water and stepped out of the shower. Standing on the mat, he looked at himself in the mirror attached to the back of the door, seeing himself as tall, broad, strong, and yet still governed by fear. He could stare down a line of men racing at him on the field, but telling his father who he really was scared him to death. He thought of backing out and not saying anything, but pushed that option away, far away. *No. Telling him is the right thing to do.* Darren almost added *for George*, but changed his mind. *For me.* Picking up his towel off the bar, he wrapped it around his waist after drying off. His decision made, the image in the mirror seemed to shift, the man staring back just a little taller, his eyes a little brighter, and he was smiling.

Leaving the bathroom, Darren put on dress clothes, making sure his shoes were shined and his tie was straight before finding his overcoat. Locking the door behind him, he headed for his car. Following the car's deep, male GPS voice, he arrived at the nondescript television studio. Darren had expected something flashier, newer, but the building looked worn, with huge satellite dishes standing next to it. Walking toward the door, Darren pulled it open, stepping into the small lobby. A woman was sitting behind a desk with a telephone headset in her ear.

"Mr. Williams is in conference." She began typing. "Yes, I'll give him the message." She looked up. "Good morning." Her eyes widened and a smile brightened her face. "Can I help you?" Darren thought she was going to start batting her eyes at him any minute.

"I'm going to be guest hosting *Talking Sports* and was asked to come in for rehearsal," Darren answered, trying to keep his nerves in check.

"Mr. White?" Darren nodded his answer. "Mr. Angeli is expecting you." She continued. "I'll call and tell him you're here." Darren shifted from foot to foot as he listened to her. "He's sending someone right down, if you'd like to have a seat." She motioned to a row of chairs that looked as though they came from another era, either that or Goodwill. Darren was quickly starting to wonder if all this was worth it.

Stepping away, he decided to forego a chair and pulled his phone out of his pocket. He wanted to call George. Checking the time, he realized George would be in class, so Darren dialed Lonnie's number instead.

"Big Pimpin'," Lonnie answered, a vocal smile coming through the phone. "How's it going?"

"Good," Darren answered. "I'm at the television studio for an initial walk-through." He looked at the receptionist. "The place is a dump," he said softly.

Lonnie laughed. "That's because everything goes in front of the camera."

The receptionist beckoned Darren over.

"I gotta go." Darren walked toward the desk.

"Okay. Call me later. Love ya." And Lonnie was gone.

Doors off to the side of the reception desk opened and a young man, skinny as a whip, walked up to him. "Mr. White. I'm Jerry, Dave's assistant." He didn't offer to shake hands, but held the door, and Darren walked through. "He's on the *Talking Sports* set, so we'll meet him there. Just follow me, and watch your step; there are cables everywhere right now."

Darren picked his way across the floor past various sets, including the one for the local newscast, to the far corner of the large room where he saw the familiar set for *Talking Sports* with its two large reclining chairs, coffee table, and painted gridiron background. "Darren." An older man with white hair and beard approached him, hand extended. "Dave Angeli, producer of *Talking Sports.* Glad you could come down." He turned toward the set as though it needed his approval. "We're all very excited that you could guest host for us." The man seemed to have trouble focusing on anything as his eyes wandered all over the room. "Have you ever been on television before?"

"A few times as a guest, and of course as a player."

"It's a cinch." *Easy for him to say*, Darren thought, as he watched Dave walk onto the set, sitting down in one of the chairs, motioning Darren to join him. "Sit, sit. That's the host chair, and the cameras will be right out there." He pointed toward the empty floor. A few days before the show, we'll have you back to work with our team to help load your questions and dialog into the teleprompter." Dave rubbed his hands together, leaning forward in the chair. "So, who do you have for us?"

Darren stared back at the man, wondering what in hell he was talking about. "What?"

"Who's your guest going to be?" Dave rephrased, looking expectantly excited.

"I was going to ask you the same thing," Darren replied, and saw Dave's face fall. "I understood that you had someone lined up." Jesus Christ. Darren felt his nervousness break out almost like a rash.

"Jerry!" Dave bellowed, and his assistant appeared almost by magic next to Dave's chair. "We don't have a guest for *Talking Sports*. We need to find someone," Dave said to Jerry, as he looked at Darren. "Maybe we can get…." Darren didn't hear much after that. He could feel the opportunity slipping away.

"Hold it," Darren said rather loudly, standing up, towering over both Dave and Jerry. "What's going on here?" Darren pulled himself up as tall and broad as he could, using his size to intimidate. He'd had enough of this nervous, mousy crap. He'd played professional football, for Christ's sake.

Dave swallowed, looking up at him. "The host arranges for the guests," Dave explained. "That's why we're giving you a chance." Dave motioned for him to sit back down, but Darren shook his head, glaring at the man. "Our host of *Talking Sports* left us for a gig in Chicago and we're looking to replace him. We heard that you were available and we thought with your connections…." Dave's words trailed off, but the meaning hung in the air. They wanted Darren at least in part for his connections, or perceived connections.

"It would have been nice if someone had told me," Darren said, trying to sound calm.

"Look," Dave started, his voice much calmer now. "It's okay. We'll get someone." The older man glared at his assistant, who looked like he wanted to melt into the floor.

"No," Darren found himself saying. "Give me a few days and I'll try to get someone." He could hardly believe he was saying this, but he wanted this job. He had no idea who in the hell he was going to get, but Dave's smile told him that was the right answer.

"That's the spirit," Dave said as he got to his feet, a hand patting Darren's arm. "Jerry will show you around and arrange for you to meet everyone." Darren watched as Dave began threading his way through the cables on the floor before turning to Jerry.

"That's our Dave," Jerry said by way of explanation. "You'd think he was in Hollywood instead of Harrisburg. Come on. Let's get you feeling comfortable in front of the camera." Jerry signaled one of the men and they wheeled a huge camera over, turning it on, and Darren saw himself projected onto one of the monitors. "Have a seat and relax. I'm going to bring in one of the makeup artists and prompters so you can get a feel for what it'll be like on production day."

Lights switched on, nearly blinding him for a minute, until he just looked in the direction of the camera and he could see. What looked like a large television was wheeled behind the guest chair into his line of sight. Darren saw text begin to scroll, and he froze. All the words and letters appeared jumbled, worse than he could ever remember. Closing his eyes, he made himself go through the exercises George had taught him, forcing his mind to take a second look, to reprocess the images. But everything still appeared jumbled.

"You okay?" Darren heard Jerry say from behind him. "Jesus Christ, guys, that's not funny! Run the real program." Darren turned, his heart still pounding in his chest. "They run that scramble tape on everyone," Jerry muttered to him. "You know that stopped being funny after the first eight million times," Jerry barked to the laughing men behind the monitor, and the screen went blank. Darren pulled on his collar, feeling warm under the lights and even more nervous. Different words began to appear, and Darren concentrated, remembering everything George had tried to teach him. Sweat breaking out on his brow, he did his best to read the text.

PULLING into the garage at home, Darren shut off the engine before collapsing onto the steering wheel. The morning had been a disaster. Yes, he'd read that stuff on the screen, although he'd felt as though he'd stumbled over every word and he knew that everyone in the studio had been watching him, waiting for him to fall flat on his face. He was sorely tempted to just back out altogether and say to hell with it. Opening the car door, he got out, shutting the door harder than was necessary before walking into the house.

"How'd it go?" He heard his dad's voice from the living room, the television already on.

"Fine," he lied, but he didn't want his dad to worry. "I did find out that they expect me to get my own guest for the show," he added as nonchalantly as possible.

"That shouldn't be a problem; you know all the guys on the team." He heard his dad lower his recliner, the thunk of the footrest hitting the chair. Then the television clicked off as Darren walked into the room, throwing his coat over the arm of the chair before sitting on the end of the sofa closest to his dad. "There was something you wanted to talk about?" Darren watched his father's head roll to face him, piercing eyes watching his every move.

The man had worked hard all his life to provide for Darren, especially after his mother was gone. Darren knew he had to have this conversation with his father, but he hated the thought of breaking his heart. "Yeah, I'm just not sure how to tell you."

His father stiffened in the chair, leaning forward, watching. "What is it that's so important you look like you're about ready to bolt at any minute?" his dad asked as he kept watching Darren.

"I spent all my life playing football." Darren didn't know where to start, but he knew he had to somewhere. "And I was good. So good that no one cared about anything else. Coaches and teammates helped me with tests, homework, everything. Dad, I'm twenty-four years old and can barely read."

"You what?" His dad leaned forward, disbelief on his face, voice barely above a whisper. "Is this true?"

"Yeah." Darren nodded his head slowly.

"Then how are you going to be able to make this television thing work?"

"See, that's the thing. Lonnie introduced me to a man who's been helping me. He got me tested and I have dyslexia, a learning disability that jumbles up all the words. George is a teacher and he's dyslexic too, so he's been helping me. A lot. See, with his help, I'll be able to read."

Darren's dad's blue eyes narrowed. "Is that what you wanted to tell me? 'Cause if it is, I don't know what you were so nervous about." His dad leaned back in his chair, obviously thinking the conversation was over.

"No, Dad. That was just the first part. See, Lonnie got me in touch with George and I've been working with him and I've come to realize some things about myself." Darren stopped, steeling his resolve. "You see, I figure you should know who your son really is, and I know what I'm going to tell you isn't going to make you happy."

"Don't beat around the bush, Son. Just say what's on your mind." His dad leaned forward again, his head, blond hair slowly turning to white, tilting forward.

"Dad, I'm gay." Darren said the words and almost closed his eyes as though he expected a bomb to go off at any minute. At the very least, he expected yelling and maybe a few threats. But instead, the room was quiet enough that Darren could hear the ticking of his mother's old clock hanging on the wall. "Aren't you going to say anything?" Each and every second seemed like an eternity.

"You expect me to be happy about this?" his dad started, and Darren felt his stomach drop to the floor.

"No, I don't. I know how you feel—you've made that clear enough over the years—but you deserve to know the truth no matter how much you may hate me for it."

Darren let his gaze travel upward, looking into his dad's eyes. He'd expected anger, even rage, but saw none of it. "Don't you know there's nothing you could ever do to make me hate you?" His dad slid forward in the chair, rising to his feet. "You're my son and you'll always be my son. I don't understand how you can be gay. You were always the toughest kid I knew. But that doesn't mean I don't love you."

"Thanks, Dad," Darren replied before standing up, his dad engulfing him in a hug.

"So I take it this George has something to do with this revelation," his dad added, after releasing him. He sat back in his chair.

"Yeah, he's really special, Dad. He teaches fourth grade and he's spent almost every evening for the past few weeks helping me learn to read while he grades his students' papers."

"Are you sure he's not just after your money?"

"Yeah, I am. If you knew him, you'd know that my money was the last thing on his mind. I mean, the man spends his own money to make sure his students have the extra things that there isn't money for in the school budget." He couldn't put these things into words, but Darren knew that anyone as generous with their time as George had been with him wouldn't be with him just for his money.

"Did you have lunch?" his dad asked, obviously changing the subject.

"No. I'm supposed to meet George at the gym in a few hours. Let me change and I'll take you out." He hurried to his room, changed out of his dress clothes and into jeans and a sweatshirt before meeting his dad in the living room. Putting on a heavy coat, he opened the door and they left together, getting into his dad's truck.

They talked through lunch, but not about Darren's earlier announcement. He figured his dad would ask when he was ready. Darren was just happy his dad seemed to accept him. After lunch, they drove back to the house and Darren packed his gym bag, saying goodbye to his dad.

"Will I see you later?" his father asked.

"Probably not tonight, but I'll be home in the morning." With a wave he hurried out to his car, speeding away toward the gym.

Darren felt as though he could breathe again, at least for a second. One problem solved—or at least the conversation hadn't completely blown up in his face. He'd actually told his dad, and his dad had said he loved him. That had to be about as good an outcome as anyone could hope for. Pulling into the gym parking lot, he popped the front-end trunk and got out of the car. Grabbing his bag, he closed the trunk and walked toward the gym, seeing George walking across the lot as well. At the door, George stopped and waited, holding the door open for him. Darren held the inner door, and after scanning their membership cards, they walked to the locker room.

"How did it go at the television station?" George asked as he pulled open his locker door.

Darren flopped his bag on the bench before sitting down, holding his head, grateful no one else was in the locker bay with them. "They had me read from the teleprompter thing and it was awful."

He felt George sit next to him. "You couldn't read the words?"

"I could." Darren lifted his eyes. "The words moved from top to bottom and that seemed to help me focus, but I came off really dumb."

George's eyes suddenly blazed. "Did they say anything?"

Darren smiled at the protectiveness in George's voice and his posture. "No." For a second Darren swore that if he'd have said yes, George would be driving them off to the station so he could give them a piece of his mind. "But I know it was terrible. They gave me a tape. Like I actually want to see how bad I was."

Darren felt George's hand on his shoulder. "Of course we'll have to watch it. You can't improve if you don't learn from what you did wrong. Besides, I doubt you did that badly." George patted his shoulder and went back to changing. "You may need to practice a little; that's all."

Darren stood up and began pulling off his shirt. "Maybe they'll let me borrow a teleprompter," he said sarcastically.

George glared back at him. "Did you give up that easily when you were down by two touchdowns? How many times did you dig deep to pull victory out of defeat? Plenty, or you wouldn't have made it as far as you did," George scolded as he pulled off his pants. "And a teleprompter is just a computer with rolling text. We can do that." George pulled on his shorts as Darren stepped out of his jeans. "Something else is bothering you," George observed, with keen accuracy.

"They don't have a guest for the show. I'm supposed to find my own guest. They dropped that little bomb on me today as well." Darren pulled on a T-shirt before pulling a pair of shorts out of his bag. "I think they figure I can get someone from the team, but they're in the playoffs, so no one will be available and the coaches will be way too busy." Darren sighed softly. "I'm not sure what to do, and they didn't give me much time." George had finished dressing, and was waiting for Darren to pull on his shoes.

"I can't help you there, because you're the only sports person I know. You could ask Lonnie, but I think most of his sports clients are on your team."

Darren nodded, trying not to take his frustration out on George, knowing that he was only trying to help. Darren wanted to put his fist through one of the locker doors, but he calmed himself. George was right about one thing: he probably couldn't help. This was something Darren would have to do on his own. Darren finished putting on his shoes and stood up, trying to put some of this worry out of his mind, and followed George out of the locker room.

They worked hard, with Darren taking George through his back workout. "I can barely lift my arms," George complained with a smile as he massaged his own biceps one after the other.

"We're not done yet. We've still got crunches to do. Last time you did three sets, so today we'll add leg lifts," Darren instructed as he flopped down onto the mat. "You've been quiet. Is something wrong?"

"No," George answered, lowering himself to the mat. "I've just been thinking. I don't know any sports people to be a guest on your show, but I was wondering, if you could have anyone as a guest, who would it be?"

Darren lay back on the mat, staring up at the lights. "Beckett Huntleigh."

"Who? I don't think I know that name," George said.

"He played for Pittsburgh a few years ago. He was a really good player too. I bet he'd make a great guest." Darren started doing his abdominal work, putting the muscles through their paces, peeking over at George as he did his sets. Darren only stopped when his stomach muscles screamed for mercy, burning and throbbing.

"So, can you call this Beckett Huntleigh? Is he someone you know?" George asked as he reclined on the mat.

"I don't know. Garrett played with him before coming to Philly. Maybe he knows how to get in touch with him."

George smiled. "See? You can do this. All you need to do is track him down." George began doing another set, and Darren watched him as he let his muscles rest. The man was so cute, especially when he looked pleased with himself. He just glowed with happiness. When George was done, he lay back on the mat, catching his breath.

"Why do you think this player will make a good guest on the show?"

"Well...." Darren thought for a minute. "He's good-looking, talks well—at least that's what I remember—and he hasn't given a lot of interviews and stuff, so talking to him could be kind of special. He has a following in this area being from Pittsburgh." Darren stopped, leaning closer to George. "And rumor has it, he's gay."

George hissed and sat up, glaring at him in a way that startled him.

"What?" Darren asked, wondering what he'd done wrong.

"You aren't thinking of outing him, are you? Because that's not right."

Darren shook his head. "No, I'd never do that."

George's expression softened. "Good."

"But speaking of outing," Darren lowered his voice, "I told my dad this afternoon, and he took it better than I thought he would. He even told me he loved me."

"That's good. My parents took it pretty well too. I think most of the time, our fear is worse than the reality. Not always, but most of the time." George took a huge breath and released it. "Let's finish up these crunches." George's voice lowered to a whisper. "So we can go and maybe get some different exercise." He waggled his eyebrows.

Darren rolled his eyes before chuckling and starting his set of leg lifts, which morphed into abdominal scissors. By the time he was done, his stomach ached. George stood on the edge of the mat watching him. "You're gorgeous when you do that."

"Hey, cockhopper," Lonnie said from behind George, making the smaller man jump. Darren stood up, glaring down at him. "You gonna work out with us?" Dan joined the group, standing next to Lonnie.

George smiled. "We're already done."

"Then join us for dinner," Lonnie said, but it sounded more like a command. Darren looked at George, who looked back at him. He'd go if George wanted to, but going out to dinner wasn't exactly what he had in mind.

"Lonnie," Dan said, sounding impatient.

"Come on. Come to dinner. It'll be fun."

"Lonnie," Dan reiterated.

"Don't be a pussy all your life." *Smack.* Lonnie rubbed the back of his head where Dan had hit him, and Darren put his hand over his mouth to keep from laughing. "What was that for?" Lonnie asked, turning to glare at Dan, who just smiled.

"For a smart guy, you can be really dumb," Dan said with a shake of his head, winking at them. "I think George and Darren have better things to do," Dan added in a whisper. "So let's get to work." Dan turned and walked away with Lonnie following him.

"Why'd you hit me?" Lonnie said as he walked away.

Darren saw Dan stop. "You know, Rosen, sometimes I think your brain is in that big fat ass of yours." Darren saw Dan give them a quick smile before dragging Lonnie off to their workout.

"Well, that's interesting," George said softly as they watched the men walk away.

"You think Dan's kidding, or...," Darren started, feeling nervous.

George grinned at him. "Oh, he knows. Dan has amazing intuition." George looked at him quizzically. "Dan won't say anything, and he'll probably tell Lonnie to keep his mouth shut too. I know I would—that slap sounded like it hurt." George looked up at him, brown eyes soft and warm. "Darren, you need to decide who you are. You took a big step today, and eventually other people are going to find out that you're gay." George swallowed hard, Darren watching his throat work, fingers itching to touch.

"I know. It just takes some getting used to." God, did it ever. What had been his biggest secret was probably going to become common knowledge if he let it. "I need to keep things private. I'm not going to lie about who I am, but I can't advertise it either, or I won't get this job, and while I don't need the money, I do need something to do. And I'm starting to think I could be a good television host. But will they hire a gay ex-football player?"

"All you can do is be yourself and try to make yourself happy," George said softly. "Why don't we get cleaned up? We can go back to my house if you'd like."

Darren moved closer. "Yeah."

They walked into the locker room and got undressed and cleaned up. Darren followed George back to his house. Shortly after arriving, Darren pulled George into his arms and went for a kiss, but George laughed and skittered away. "We need to eat, and then you have work to do." George moved closer again. "Then, as a reward if you're good…." George laughed, and when Darren lunged for him, George stepped back amid peals of laughter and tried to get away. Darren was having none of it, capturing the smaller man, kissing him hard. Soft lips tugged at his, meeting him kiss for kiss until they both needed desperately to come up for air.

"Do you need help with dinner?"

George chuckled lightly. "Very romantic." He squirmed away and walked toward the kitchen. "Why don't you have a seat and see if you can hunt up Beckett Huntleigh's phone number while I start dinner?" Darren picked up the phone, calling one of his former teammates. Lucky for him, Garrett was home, and he indeed had Huntleigh's number. After some sweet-talking, Garrett gave him the number. Darren hung up, waving the piece of notepaper in triumph.

"I got it."

"Excellent. Now sit down and we'll eat." George brought two plates to the table. "It's not fancy." He set down the plates and Darren dug in.

"What is this?" he asked between huge bites.

"Frozen ravioli. I make my own sauce though."

"It's delicious," Darren commented as his appetite really started kicking in. "So do you really think you can create a teleprompter?"

"Sure, but once we're done eating, we should watch the tape and see where your issues lie. That way we can work on the right things," George said. He got up and got two beers out of the refrigerator, handing one to Darren. "Then we'll design some practice exercises."

Darren reached out to George, caressing his cheek. "What would I do without you?"

George placed his hand on Darren's, holding it to his skin. "Let's not find out."

Darren heartily agreed, and they finished their dinners. Darren helped George clear away the dishes and then George led him to the living room, placing the disk in the player. "I know I was terrible," Darren explained, feeling as though he needed to soften the shock somehow. The television showed a picture of him sitting in the chair on the set. After some fudging around, he started to read, and after a few minutes, George stopped the player. "See, I told you I was terrible."

"You weren't," George countered with a slight snicker. "Yes, you stumbled over some words, but who wouldn't? They had you reading the copy from the news. It's not likely you'll have to remember that Mahmoud Ahmadinejad is the President of Iran, let alone pronounce it correctly. So give yourself a little credit. You've come a long way in a short time." George started the player again and they watched. Every mistake, every stumble, made Darren groan inwardly, but George just kept smiling. Finally, Darren switched it off.

"See, I told you it was bad," Darren added, cringing. He opened the player and removed the disk. He wanted to hurl it across the room.

"It's not that bad. You were actually reading strange things you'd never seen before. On your show, you'll be telling them what to say. You'll already know what's going to come up. So don't worry." George stood up and extended his hand. "Let's get the computer and we'll see what we can do." George led him back to the kitchen table. "If you could interview Beckett Huntleigh, what would you ask him?"

"Why he quit football," Darren answered quickly.

George booted up the computer. "This is a reading program we use. Give me a minute and I think I can get it to approximate a teleprompter." George typed for a few minutes. "Okay. Now let's input some questions." George typed for a while and Darren felt himself fidgeting until he turned the screen toward him. "Okay; look at this."

George pressed a button and text began to scroll up the screen. "So, Beckett," Darren read out loud. "Ever since your last game just over a year ago when you announced your retirement, I've wondered why? Why would you give up so promising a career while you were still in your prime?" Darren read the words with relative ease and looked at George smiling.

"See, I knew you could do it. The difference between now and this afternoon is that we wrote the questions together, so you know what to expect. Do you think those people on the evening news are reading what they're saying without rehearsal? They see most of it ahead of time."

"So what do we do?"

George grinned. "You get yourself a guest and then we can start writing the interview questions. I think the hardest part of the show is going to be the game commentary, but we can work on that too." George got up and moved closer. "I think that's enough for tonight."

Darren stood up, reaching out, taking George's hand. "Thank you for everything."

"You're welcome," George answered, and Darren bent slightly, kissing the man before lifting him into his arms and carrying him out of the room, toward the bed. "What's the big He-Man act for?" George asked as they reached the bedroom.

"I am a big He-Man,'" Darren answered, stepping closer to the bed.

"Are you my He-Man?" George asked, sounding a little scared.

"If you'll have me," Darren answered, setting George on the bed. "Because I love you, George. You're the kindest, caringest, most special person I know."

"Caringest isn't a word," George told him with a smile that turned to a sigh as Darren began tugging off his shirt.

"It's my word for you," Darren said, kissing George hard before he could argue. Climbing onto the bed, careful not to put his knee on George, Darren got his shirt off and began working on George's pants. "I want you so bad, George," Darren moaned, and George nodded, their lips coming back together.

"I'm all yours," George mumbled as his arms wound around Darren's neck, hanging on. "Because I love you too."

Darren saw the intense sincerity in George's eyes. Kissing his lover gently, Darren tasted and nibbled on supple lips. "Will you trust me?" Darren asked softly, and George nodded, eyes wide, head cradled in the pillow. Kneeling on the bed, Darren watched George, letting his eyes wander over his light skin, hands caressing, feeling the smooth softness slide beneath his hands.

Pulling off George's shoes, he let them hit the floor, socks following. George's belt came next. Darren watched George's eyes as he unfastened the belt, popping the button on George's pants and sliding down the zipper. "Lift your hips," Darren instructed, and George complied. Darren tugged off George's pants, leaving the man naked on the bed. Now, Darren let his eyes truly feast on his lover. As his hands roamed, Darren felt George's muscles quiver beneath his touch. "You really are beautiful, George."

"If you say so. I never thought I was anything to look at," George answered, his words trailing off into a moan as Darren slid his fingers along his length.

"You are beautiful, George. Even more so because you don't know it." Darren held George's cock firmly, bending to kiss him. "Everything you do is so honest and from the heart," Darren murmured against George's lips.

Darren felt George vibrate beneath him as his lips moved over his skin. Soft moans accompanied tongue swirls around pink nipples. He felt George's breath hitch as he swirled his tongue around his navel, stomach hitching before he kissed his way along George's downy treasure trail, lips ghosting over his length.

"Darren, please."

"What is it you want?" Darren asked, breath flowing over George's damp skin.

"You know what I want." George groaned, thrusting his hips forward.

"I do, huh?" Darren grinned before licking from base to tip of George's cock like a lollipop. "Is that it?"

"Yes, Darren. Just suck me, please." Darren ran his tongue just under the crown before sliding his lips down George's full length. The sound George made went right to Darren's dick, driving him on as he sucked his lover deep. George tasted sweet, spicy, and salty all at the same time, and Darren couldn't get enough of the man—and he hoped he never did.

George's whimpers and moans filled the room, driving Darren's own desire, but to Darren's surprise, George pulled away. "Wanna taste you too," George explained, and Darren reclined on the mattress, taking George deep again, moaning around George's cock as his own was taken deep. This was a dream and a fantasy come true. Darren felt George's hips thrust slightly, placing his hand on George's butt as he encouraged him, taking him as deep as he could.

Darren felt George's mouth slip away from him. "Not gonna...," George moaned as Darren continued stroking him. Darren sucked harder, encouraging his lover. With a soft cry, George climaxed deep in Darren's throat, and he took everything his lover had to give, relishing his unique flavor. This was his lover, his first true lover. The thought hit him hard, and as he felt George continue to stroke and taste, he, too, climaxed, clutching George's hips as he came.

Shifting on the bed, once he could remember his name, Darren held George close, caressing his skin. "You really love me?" George said softly, and Darren smiled as he tugged George closer. "Because I'll understand if it was just a heat-of-the-moment thing."

"No, George." Darren stroked George's soft skin and saw the man's expression darken. "I meant what I said. It wasn't a heat-of-the-moment thing," he added quickly, realizing George had misunderstood him. "I do love you," Darren said, settling under the covers, his eyes already closing. He had a big day tomorrow trying to get a guest, and so did George, at school. Darren would rather get ten guests for a television show than do what George was going to be doing tomorrow: spending a day alone in a room with almost thirty kids, the day before Christmas vacation.

V

DARREN paced across the living room floor. "I wish he'd call," Darren groaned softly as he continued his restless walking.

"I know you do," George answered, "but the pacing is driving me crazy." George set his book on the table and got to his feet, placing his hand on Darren's shoulder. "This isn't going to make him call."

"I know," Darren sighed, "but I have to let the station know first thing tomorrow morning if they need to get a guest or not, and Huntleigh sounded interested when I talked to him before Christmas."

George knew Darren was pinning his hopes on this one guy for his guest on *Talking Sports*. He really hadn't thought that was a good idea, but to his credit, George had stayed out of it, letting Darren handle things. He knew Darren had to sink or swim on his own. George had provided advice, but that was all. "It'll work out," George said softly, not knowing how, but it seemed like the right thing to say.

Darren stopped pacing. "How?" he asked, turning toward George.

"I don't know. It's a mystery," George quipped, and Darren glared at him for a second before smiling.

"We never should have watched that movie last night," Darren growled in mock frustration. "I'm an ex-football player and now I'm watching chick flicks."

"Fine. Tonight we can watch a movie where they blow things up. Will that make you happy and keep your fragile manhood intact?" George grinned and skittered back as Darren lunged for him. He wasn't fast enough, and George found himself surrounded by powerful arms, pulled close to Darren's big body. "I can think of something we could do to take your mind off things." George angled his face to Darren's, hoping for a kiss, which he got. The heat from the kiss and Darren's body mingled in George's mind as he held onto the larger man, already giving himself over to the anticipation of what was to come.

George groaned, and Darren tensed as a phone rang. Stepping away, George let Darren get it, listening to the apprehension in his lover's voice.

"Hey, Beck." George heard Darren answer as he walked out of the room to allow him some privacy. George wanted to follow and listen, his own excitement for his lover almost getting the better of him. He could hear snippets of the conversation from the other room. Picking up his book, he sat back down and tried to read. "Tried" being the operative word. Giving up quickly, George sat with the book on his lap and waited until Darren came back into the room.

"Well?" George asked expectantly, setting the book aside.

Darren burst into a grin, "He said he'll do the show. And," Darren's grin got bigger, "he wanted to talk about why he left football. This could be a really good interview if I can do it right."

"Did you schedule a pre-interview conversation with him?"

Darren nodded his head. "Tomorrow afternoon we'll talk by phone, and he'll come into town the day before the show." Darren seemed ready to jump out of his skin. "This is going to be great, and if this doesn't get me the job, I don't know what will." Darren had his phone back in his hand and was dialing a number. "Is Dave in?" He listened. "Then can you please give him a message? Please tell him that Darren White called and I have a guest for *Talking Sports*." Darren rattled off his phone number. "No, just ask him to call." Darren hung up, still grinning. "Before I forget," the smile faded slightly from Darren's face, "I got you something for Christmas. I wanted to give it to you before you left for Christmas with your family, but we sort of missed each other." Darren left the room, popping his head around the door. "I left it in the car; I'll be right back."

The door opened and closed and George peered beneath the tree, fishing out the gift he'd gotten for Darren. Fingering the package with its gold ribbon, he hoped he'd gotten something Darren would like. They hadn't known each other long and George hoped he hadn't gone too impersonal, but after walking around in the store for hours, he'd finally decided. George set the package on the table as the front door closed. A second later, Darren walked in carrying a big, wrapped box, setting it on his lap. "What's this?" George asked, looking at the top of the box with its silver paper and massive bow.

"Open it," Darren answered with a huge smile.

George pulled off the bow and tore into the paper before opening the large box. There were smaller boxes inside, thankfully unwrapped, and George reached in, looking at Darren as he opened the first one. "Stickers," George commented with a smile.

"Yes. I wasn't sure what to get for you, so I decided to get you things to make your job more fun," Darren said excitedly as George pulled the packages out of the box. "I got some for every holiday I could think of." George looked through the packages of stickers, almost unable to believe it: Christmas, Valentine's Day, St. Patrick's Day, plus dogs, cats, and animals of all kinds—everything.

"Thank you," George said as he looked into Darren's face, wondering what else could be in store. Lifting out the next box, he found packages of crayons, followed by a box of markers, then colored pencils, glitter, glue, glue sticks, highlighters—all the things George seemed to struggle to figure out how to get for his class. All of it, and more, was in the box from Darren. "I don't know what to say. Thank you." George swallowed and set the box on the floor, leaning forward to give Darren a kiss. "That was very thoughtful and perfect," George added against Darren's lips before reaching to the table and handing him the present.

Darren carefully opened the package, pulling open the ribbon and undoing each piece of tape. Finally the paper fell away and Darren opened the box. "I checked inside your shirts and found the label of your tailor. He made the shirt for you. I thought if you liked it, you could wear it when you're on television." George bit his lip slightly as Darren pulled the light blue shirt out of the box. "Do you like it? I thought it should be a solid color for television."

George found Darren kneeling in front of his chair, arms around his waist. Then Darren kissed him within an inch of his life. From the reaction, George had no doubt that Darren liked his gift, with George communicating his joy in equal measure. The physical expressions continued through the living room, down the hall, and into the bedroom.

PERCHED on the edge of the chair, unable to relax, George watched the television and checked the clock for the millionth time. The gym buzzed with activity, but George didn't care, his attention glued to the television. Darren's show was to start in about ten minutes. George had told Darren he'd go along with him, but they'd decided that it would make Darren more nervous. His phone rang and he saw Darren's number on the display. "Hi. You okay?" George asked eagerly.

"Yeah. I had a few minutes and thought I'd call." Darren sounded stressed beyond belief. "I wish I'd had you come with me. Everything's strange and they keep changing the teleprompter questions on me," Darren nearly whined.

"Tell them 'no' if you have to, and remember that you only have to use it if you get stuck. The best interviews seem like a conversation between friends, so think of it that way and do your best. That's all anyone can ask." George tried to keep his own excitement out of his voice so he could help calm Darren. "I love you and that won't change based upon a television show." George smiled into the phone. "So have fun, enjoy yourself, and that will come through to everyone."

"I'll try," Darren whispered into the phone.

"What is it you guys do before a game? Yell and scream to psyche yourselves up?" George asked.

"Yeah."

"Then it's crunch time, so get out there and kill, kill, kill!" George yelled into the phone, imitating what he thought a football coach might sound like, but all he heard from the other side of the line was laughter.

"Thanks, Babe. I'll call you after the show." Darren hung up, and George turned up the television, waiting for the show to begin. After an interminable number of commercials, the *Talking Sports* logo flashed on the screen. Darren was announced as the special guest host and the camera panned to the set. Darren ran onto the screen carrying a football, which he lobbed off camera before introducing himself and talking about the lineup for the show. George cringed when he heard Darren talking too fast, but his lover soon slowed down, and George could see him getting more comfortable. During one of the clips when he was giving a rundown on some of the local games, he highlighted a fumble that turned out to be the difference in a very close game. Darren described it perfectly before adding, "That's happened to all of us. Just go out and get them next week." George noticed a small note of encouragement added to the description of every game, and that brought a smile to his face because he knew those were all Darren—he'd heard some of those same phrases during their workouts at the gym.

After the highlights, the show went to commercial. When it returned, Darren was sitting in one of the huge chairs as he introduced his guest, Beckett Huntleigh. The two big men shook hands and hugged like brothers in arms before returning to their seats. Darren started with basic questions, making his guest feel comfortable as the two men talked about playing. Then he went for the heart of the interview. "Why did you retire at the height of your career?"

The camera moved closer, zeroing in on the former football player. George could see the war playing behind the man's eyes even as he framed the answer to the question. "A number of reasons," Beckett began his answer, and George found himself drawn in, forgetting he was supposed to be watching Darren, "but the biggest is that I reevaluated my life and priorities after I met someone who means more to me than football." The camera slowly moved back until both men appeared in screen. To his credit, Darren remained quiet, letting Beckett continue. "See...." Beckett squirmed slightly in the chair.

"Take your time," Darren encouraged, and George smiled as he watched the television. Someone jostled him on their way to the treadmill and George almost growled at her, stopping himself before returning his attention to the television. Beckett's voice came through the earbuds as George continued watching the show.

"I stopped playing football because I didn't want to lie anymore," Beckett said, and George felt his eyes widen, almost not believing what he was hearing. "Because the person I met was another man, and I wouldn't put him through all the lying and denial it would take to continue playing. Upton deserves better treatment than that."

"Upton," Darren prodded softly, and George knew in that second that Darren already knew what Beckett was going to say.

"My partner," Beckett said. "I'm gay." To Darren's credit, he kept his face neutral and serious, letting Beckett continue. "During my last season with Pittsburgh, I met Upton when I was at an away game in Philadelphia. It didn't take long for me to fall in love with him." Beckett smiled. "Upton is amazing, and he was willing to keep quiet and let me finish playing, but I realized he was more important than playing football. So I retired to a quiet life with the man I love."

"What do you do?" Darren prodded gently.

Beckett smiled again. "I coach community football. The thing that amazes me most is the number of people who accept me for who I am. The parents of the children I coach know I'm gay, and I have a waiting list of parents who want their sons on my teams."

George heard a woman on one of the treadmills say something as she watched the television, the closed captioning scrolling on the screen. "I'd never let my son near him," she said. George itched to say something, but he kept his mouth shut, returning his attention to the screen as Darren wrapped up the interview and signed off just before the credits began to roll.

"How did he do?" George jumped a little before turning to Lonnie, who was talking from behind him.

"Excellent," George answered with a smile on his face. "He's a natural."

"So, are you and he…?" Lonnie drifted off, making a rude gesture with his hands.

"That's none of your business." George lowered his voice. "Besides, he's a lot bigger than that." George quipped as he headed toward the stairs, grinning at the stunned look on Lonnie's face. Walking through the gym, he returned to work at the front desk.

GEORGE waited, expecting his phone to ring any time, but it remained silent in his pocket. Checking in members and handling questions as best he could with only half his attention on the job, George figured that the longer Darren stayed after the show, the better his chances were of getting the job permanently. Working on the computer, he did his best to take his mind off his worry.

A set of keys rattled against the counter and he automatically reached for the scan tag. "Darren," George said, as he looked up from the picture on the monitor, "I thought you were going to call."

"I decided to come right here," Darren answered, leaning on the counter.

"So what happened? I saw the show." George grinned. "It was really good. Did they offer you the job?" The question spilled out with no time for Darren to answer.

"Okay—one thing at a time. I think they were very pleased, but they didn't offer me the job, at least not yet. The producer was impressed, so I'll just have to wait and see what he decides." Darren leaned closer. "I think they were a little surprised at the tone and content of the interview. They were expecting a more straightforward sports interview."

George nodded. "I suppose, but it was great television. You looked nervous at first, but then you settled down and looked great for the rest of the show." He almost reached out to straighten Darren's tie, but kept his hands back. "You'll get the job." A member passed George his card and he scanned it. "They probably just need to make up their mind."

"I know." Darren smiled and looked as though he wanted to say something else, but he didn't. "How late do you work?"

George checked the clock. "I'm almost done."

"Then I'll wait for you here and I can take you to dinner."

George was about to protest that it was his turn, but members came in and he had other things to do, and by the time he was done, Darren had wandered out into the club, talking to some of the guys.

Finally, at the end of his shift, George gathered his things and signaled Darren, who walked over, and they left the club together. "A bunch of the guys saw the show," Darren told him as they walked across the parking lot. "They thought it was good." Darren stopped walking near his car. "One of them asked me if I was gay. He was only kidding." Darren scratched his head. "At least I think he was."

"What did you say?" George inquired softly, wondering if this was one of those moments where he and Darren became "just friends."

"I told him yes, I was gay, and that my boyfriend was the cutie behind the desk." Darren smiled. "They looked at me like they couldn't tell if I was serious and then burst into laughter. I don't think they believed me."

"That's the first time you've called me that."

"My boyfriend? That's what you are, isn't it?" Darren asked, and George felt his insides warm in the cold air.

"I had hoped I was," George said as people walked past them toward the club. Then George found his face cupped by two warm hands and Darren kissed him right there in the parking lot for everyone to see.

"You are my boyfriend and so much more. I owe you a lot."

George shook his head. "You owe me nothing."

"And that's why I owe you everything. You helped me, expecting nothing in return, and what I got was more precious than I could have imagined."

George wasn't sure if Darren was talking about him, or the worlds and opportunities that had opened up to him because he could read. George thought about asking, but realized it didn't matter—both were important. Instead, he returned the kiss, standing on his tiptoes, before walking toward his car. He followed Darren to a small restaurant, and while they were waiting for their meals, Darren's phone rang.

"Hi, Dad," Darren said with a smile as he answered. "You saw the show." George decided to go to the restroom to give him some privacy. When he returned, Darren had hung up and was waiting for him. "My dad asked to meet you."

"Okay?" George answered nervously.

"I thought we could go to lunch this Saturday."

George nodded, knowing this was a big step for Darren, smiling as the full realization of what this meant came to him. Darren was really serious. George didn't know why he'd doubted it. Darren had told him and shown him that he cared, but this seemed to bring it home. "That'd be nice. My folks will visit in the next month or so when the weather looks good. I'd like you to meet them too."

"I'd like that. Have you told them about me?"

George smiled across the table. "When I visited for the holidays, I talked about you all the time. They're very anxious to meet you." Their food arrived and the conversation slowed. They talked of everything and nothing, enjoying each other's company in the quiet restaurant. Afterward, Darren followed him home and up the snow-covered walk to the front door.

Inside, the warmth of the small house surrounded them, and George felt his coat being opened, slipped off his shoulders. He tried to reach for it, but Darren's lips met his and all other thoughts flew away. Even as Darren guided them through the house toward the bedroom, George went along, thinking of nothing but Darren's lips against his and the feel of his warm hands as they slipped beneath his shirt. When they reached the bedroom, George made no effort to turn on the lights—none were needed—and as they tumbled together onto the bed, he was caught in Darren's strong arms. Clothes melted away, Darren's warmth meeting George's own in the cool room. Clutching, tasting, caressing, everything seemed new as George felt the last of his concerns and worries slip away. Darren loved him. Every caress, every touch or kiss, communicated it more clearly than a thousand declarations. "I love you," George said softly, as Darren held him close, their bodies pressed tightly together.

Quick as lightning, they whirled on the bed, and George found himself looking down into Darren's eyes, the bigger man's legs locking around his waist. "Are you—" George began to ask, but found the rest of his words kissed urgently away.

"I love you, George," Darren murmured, and George felt hands slide down his back and over the curve of his butt.

"But I've never—" George started, and a finger slid over his lips.

"I want to give you this." Darren's voice rang in his ears, soft and deep.

As nervous as he was, the mere thought that Darren loved him enough and trusted him enough to give of himself this way sent a jolt of excitement through him. He felt Darren move under him, and then a small bottle pressed into his hand. George wanted to ask again, but Darren kept kissing and caressing. The bottle fell into the bedding, and George let his hands explore, sliding along Darren's side and along his thighs. "Is this okay?" he asked quietly.

"Yes, George," Darren answered softly and George slid his fingers along Darren's cleft, letting them skim over his opening, listening for any sign of doubt or discomfort, but all he heard was a soft sigh and then George was being kissed within an inch of his life.

Searching in the bedding, he found the bottle. Straddling Darren's hips, he opened it, slicking his fingers before closing the bottle. Capturing Darren's lips, he felt his lover's legs lock around him again, and gently, George teased his finger into Darren's body. A small hiss answered the intrusion and George stopped, hoping he wasn't hurting.

"Please, George," Darren whispered, and slowly, he sank a finger into the depths of Darren's body. George had no idea if Darren had done this before, and he suspected he hadn't. George had always figured that Darren would take the active role in their lovemaking and had never given much thought or consideration to the idea that Darren would want to share things equally. Carefully, once his lover was accustomed, George added a second finger, Darren's body squeezing him tightly.

Soft moans rewarded him as he scissored his fingers, stretching lightly before withdrawing. Reaching to the nightstand, he found a condom and opened the package. To his surprise, Darren's hand slid over his and the disk slipped from his fingers. Leaning back, George hissed as Darren's fingers rolled the latex down his shaft. "Shouldn't you roll over?" George asked, figuring that would be best, but Darren shifted on the bed, splaying his legs around George before placing his ankles on George's shoulders.

"Want to kiss you."

Smiling in the darkness, George slid his hand over Darren's skin before slowly pressing inside. The warmth from Darren's body called to him, driving him forward, and he had to stop himself from going too fast. "Darren," George whimpered as slick, smooth heat surrounded him. George had no idea being inside another person would feel like this—so right, so perfect.

"It's okay, Love. It feels good," Darren answered between steadying breaths. "Don't stop," he added breathily as George seated himself, fully surrounded by Darren's body.

"I couldn't if I tried," George moaned as his body screamed at him to move. Slowly, he withdrew before sliding back inside, a low groan echoing from Darren's throat. Those sounds reached deep down into him, and George pulled out again. Each time George repeated his thrusting, Darren made that sound, deep and rich. As George picked up the pace, the moans became higher and more frequent, urging him on.

Burying himself deep, George stopped, his body throbbing as he caressed Darren's chest, leaning forward to capture the bigger man's lips with his own. "God, I love you," George murmured as he licked Darren's lips.

"I love you too," Darren echoed as he slid a hand along the back of Darren's neck. "But I won't break, so fuck me, George—let me have everything. Give it all to me, whatever you're holding back."

Those words shot right through him, breaking the last bit of reserve that had been holding George back. Pulling out, he thrust deep and long before pulling back, thrusting again. Everything around him narrowed to the heat from Darren's body: his breathing, every sound he made, the touch of his skin under George's hand. The bed rocked and Darren rocked as well, meeting and encouraging George's movements, driving him into a frenzy of ecstasy and passion. George's heart pounded in his ears, his hips snapping, Darren reduced to whimpers that only fueled his desire.

"Don't stop, George!" Darren cried as he stroked himself frantically.

Pressure building deep inside, George felt his body shake, hips losing their rhythm as his mind clouded with desire and love. Barely able to remain in control of himself, George flew off ecstasy's precipice, soaring as he climaxed deep in his lover, filling the condom with his release.

Coming back to awareness, George heard Darren's excited breathing and saw his lover's blurred hand, then felt him clench as he cried out deep and loud, spilling onto his stomach.

George waited for Darren to still before slowly pulling out, both of them groaning low. Taking care of the condom and cleaning up a bit, George returned to the bed, slipping beneath the covers and curling around Darren, hugging the bigger man tightly. "I love you," George said softly.

"I love you too, George. You're the kindest, most wonderful person I've ever met."

"You know, you're right up there too."

Darren rolled over, tugging George to him, a big hand rubbing small circles on his stomach. "Today was crunch time and I would never have gotten through it without you."

George rolled over, facing his lover, "Yes, you would have, but I'm happy you didn't have to." He kissed Darren, settling his head on Darren's arm.

"So am I." Darren kissed his cheek. "So am I," he repeated, as he held George close, and they fell asleep.

EPILOGUE

"LADIES and gentlemen," Larry Schofield, George's principal, said into the microphone, standing on the stage at one end of the gym, "I'd like to introduce our special guest host for this evening's festivities. He's the host of *Talking Sports* and a former member of the Philadelphia Eagles: Darren White." Everyone applauded as Darren bounded up onto the stage from where he'd been sitting at the table next to George.

Taking the microphone, he said, "Thank you, Principal Schofield, and welcome to the first of what we all hope will become the annual Gala Night here at Wilson Elementary." George found himself smiling, and Darren winked at him before continuing. "Our schools and our children are important, as are our teachers." Darren's voice boomed around the room, adding to the excitement. "There isn't a single one of our teachers who doesn't spend part of his or her own money to make sure our children get the best educational experience possible. Tonight we're here to help them help our children. The money raised tonight will be used to buy additional supplies for every classroom, as well as playground equipment and anything else the school needs that isn't included in the regular district budget. So dig deep and help our kids." The applause started again as people looked around excitedly.

The gym had been converted for the evening into a banquet facility. The tables where children normally ate lunch had been transformed for the night with tablecloths, flower arrangements, and fine china, and banners and lights hung from the ceiling. George looked around at all the smiling faces, recognizing some of the parents he'd met during parent-teacher conferences. "A number of local merchants have donated some great items, so be sure to visit the silent auction table in the back. The live auction will begin shortly, but before we begin, I want to tell you a story."

George found his eyes widening. Darren hadn't said anything about telling stories, and he wondered what the man was up to. The principal sat at the table, looking over at George with a sly grin. "A few months ago, I was introduced to one of your teachers by a close friend," Darren continued, and George looked across the table at Lonnie, who surprisingly refrained from making one of his trademark rude gestures. "You see, I had this possible job, a really great job," audience members laughed lightly as Darren held them in the palm of his hand, "that I really wanted, but there was a problem. You see, I could barely read or write." The room became silent. "When they tested me, I tested out at the level of your fourth-grade children, but during that same testing, the wonderful teachers, who gave up their own time to help me, also found that I was dyslexic—something no one else ever took the time to figure out. So anyway, this particular teacher worked with me almost every night for a month, helping me get ready for my first appearance on *Talking Sports*. The man developed exercises, drills, and everything else you can think of to teach me how to read well enough that I could go on the show and not make a complete fool of myself."

George listened to the story, beaming with pride. In such a short time, Darren had worked unbelievably hard, and George was so immensely proud of him. He felt the principal's hand on his shoulder.

"As you can tell, since I'm here with you tonight, I didn't make a fool of myself, and I get the great honor of presenting the award for the Mechanicsburg School District Teacher of the Year to the very man who taught me how to read, your own George Higgins."

George couldn't move as he looked toward the stage at a smiling Darren. Everyone in the room was on their feet, clapping and cheering. Finally, George found his own feet and stood up, walking toward the stage and up the steps. The district superintendent stepped out from the side, carrying a plaque. He handed it to George and shook his hand, smiling.

"Ladies and gentlemen, your Teacher of the Year," Darren said into the microphone, and George looked out across the sea of applauding parents and colleagues all on their feet, looking at him. "Would you like to say something?" Darren asked from next to him, and George shook his head. The applause was enough.

Turning to Darren, George choked back his emotions and then felt the man pull him into a crushing hug. "Thank you, George," Darren whispered into his ear. George had an almost overwhelming need to kiss him, but now wasn't the time— that would come later. "I love you."

George found himself at a complete loss for words, not that he could really speak much around the grapefruit in his throat. But he finally managed to whisper "I love you too."

Positive Resistance

Andrew Grey

I

THE plane landed, taxiing to the terminal as Steven peered out the window at the concrete, grass, and terminal buildings that looked so familiar and yet so different. He'd never thought he'd be returning to the Harrisburg area to live, not after all these years, but fate must have had a sense of humor and the old bitch was certainly laughing now. Pulling up to the gate, the whine of the small plane's engines seemed to lower and then die away, replaced by the sound of air rushing through the ventilation systems. Steven stood up and pulled down his carry-on, waiting for the doors to open so he could exit. Taking his turn, he descended the stairs and walked across the tarmac and into the terminal. At least this was new and different, not like the old airport where he'd gotten on a plane after he'd graduated from high school and never looked back. And he'd been grateful, until now, fifteen years later, that he'd never been back, either.

Walking through the terminal toward the baggage claim, Steven stopped in the men's room. Passing by the mirrors at the sinks, he half expected to see the kid he'd been when he'd gotten on that first flight to take him away for his first semester of college, but "Blobby Bobby" was gone, never to return. He'd even stopped going by his first name altogether. Years ago, after he lost all that weight, he'd started using his middle name in an effort to truly change his life. Washing his hands, he looked at himself in the mirror again, wondering just why coming back here was so hard for him. He hadn't seen nor talked to his folks since he'd left for college. His father, the minister, preferred it that way, and after all this time, it didn't really matter. Taking a deep breath, Steven smiled, almost laughing. He was being completely silly. No one would recognize him, and he was making a big deal over nothing. A lot had changed in fifteen years, and it wasn't as though anyone would remember him.

Finishing in the bathroom, Steven strode out of the gate area and onto the escalators, riding down to baggage claim, where he picked up his suitcases. He walked to the Hertz counter to get the keys to his reserved rental car, and soon he was outside in the warm spring afternoon. Loading his bags into the trunk, Steven got in the car and started driving toward town, arriving at his hotel an hour later.

Checking in and unpacking didn't take long, and Steven found himself at loose ends on a Saturday afternoon. Picking up the phone book, he thumbed through the yellow pages, looking for a health club nearby. That was a great way to spend a few hours and maybe work away the blah feelings he kept having. Seeing that there was one nearby, Steven opened his suitcases and repacked his carry-on for the gym before heading out.

Walking through the doors felt comfortable. Even though he'd never been there before, the place sounded and felt like a gym, with the clang of weights and the sounds of music, talking, and the hum of treadmills.

"Can I help you?" the big-eyed blonde girl behind the desk asked cheerfully, her smile growing as he saw her look him over. Girls always seemed to, which was fine with him—not that he was interested, but it was always a nice compliment.

"I'm moving to the area and wanted to check out the club," Steven answered, looking around the building. This had to be one of the newest and cleanest health clubs he'd seen; everything from the floors to the desk seemed to shine.

"Let me get you with one of our salesmen. He can give you a tour and set you up with a guest pass." Picking up the phone, she made a call, and a large, well-built man walked to the desk.

"Are you Steven?" The man asked, offering his hand. Steven knew there was something familiar about him. "I'm Lane Parkinson. Come on over to the desk, and I can get you set up."

Steven nearly dropped his bag in surprise, but managed to hold on to it, smiling since Lane didn't recognize him. Not that Lane had ever paid much attention to him other than to pick on him all through high school. If he remembered correctly, it was Lane who'd originally coined the nickname "Blobby Bobby," along with a number of others that Steven didn't want to remember. Still smiling, he followed Lane to a desk and sat in one of the chairs. "I'm just interested in trying out the club for now," Steven explained.

Lane gave him a basic rundown on the prices of memberships and the specials they were running before taking him on a tour of the club. "Stop by my desk before you leave, and I'll set you up with a two-week pass," Lane told him before walking out of the locker room and leaving Steven to change. Checking the lockers, Steven found an empty one and began to change as people moved around him.

"Fruitbag," a voice zinged over the wall, and Steven looked around, wondering where that was coming from. "Are you and Gene going to dinner, or are you gonna be a prick all your life?"

Steven relaxed when he realized the comment wasn't directed at him.

"I'll ask him, but you really know how to issue a sweet invitation, Lonnie," the man changing next to him answered, and things got quiet until a naked man walked around the lockers and up to the man next to him. "I'll be nice to you and let you suck my love hammer." Steven could barely believe what he was hearing and jumped when he heard a smack and saw this Lonnie guy flinch, rubbing his butt. "Hey, what was that for?"

"You're being an ass," the man next to him said with a grin. "Besides, you liked it, you pervert," he added with a smile as the naked guy walked back around the lockers, and Steven continued to change, wondering what kind of place this was.

"Don't pay any attention to him," the guy next to him explained. "He's a complete pig who didn't get the gene that censors speech. I'm Dan, by the way, and the loudmouth is Lonnie. He's harmless except for his mouth." Steven slipped off his shirt before pulling on a T-shirt and changing into his workout shorts. "Are you new to the club?" Dan asked as he finished dressing.

"Yeah. I just got into town for a new job and thought I'd check out the place."

Lonnie poked his head around the corner. "Work out with us, then," he offered. Steven wasn't too sure about that, but Dan seemed nice, and Steven agreed before giving it too much thought. Working out was better with a partner, so he figured it couldn't hurt.

"If you're sure—" Steven started to say, but Lonnie interrupted.

"Of course." His head disappeared, and Steven heard shuffling from behind the wall of lockers. "You ready?" Lonnie's voice drifted over. Steven tied his shoes and grabbed his workout gloves before closing his locker, following Dan out of the locker room.

Lonnie had already scoped out one of the bench presses and had loaded a single plate on each end of the bar. Seeing them approach, he held out his hand to Steven. "I'm Lonnie."

"Steven," he said, shaking the offered hand.

"So, are you a butt pirate like Dan here?" Lonnie asked with a huge grin that lasted until Dan swatted at him. "What? I was just asking," Lonnie said with a laugh as he lay down on the bench before lifting the bar and pounding out a quick set. Dan looked a little uncomfortable, and Steven said nothing as Dan did his set. Then he took his turn, easily doing fifteen reps. "So are you?"

"What?" Steven retorted, rolling his eyes. "Are you afraid for your virtue?"

Dan hooted as he added a quarter to each end of the bar. "Lonnie doesn't have any virtue left to lose," Dan chided, and then it was his turn to jump back from a good-natured swipe. Amazingly, Steven felt himself relaxing. When it was his turn, he pounded out a set of ten before he and Dan stripped off the twenty-five-pound weights and added a second set of plates.

"How are you doing?" Steven saw Lane standing off to the side. "I see you've met Lonnie and Dan." Steven nodded, and another man joined them. Steven couldn't help staring a little. This guy was huge and sexy as hell. When he walked to Dan, slipping an arm around his waist, Steven felt a twinge of disappointment.

"Steven, this is my partner, Gene," Dan said, introducing him before turning to Gene. "This is Steven. He's trying out the club."

"It's nice to meet you," Gene told him, shaking his hand.

"So, what do you think of the club?" Lane asked from behind him.

"It's very nice," Steven answered, watching as Lonnie did his set and inwardly smiling at Lane as he saw Lane's eyes dart down his body. When it was his turn, Steven did his set, pushing out a set of ten, with Gene stepping behind to give him a spot, helping him slightly on the last rep as the others talked. Getting up, he saw Lane looking at him, arms folded across his chest, pushing the muscle forward, biceps straining his shirt. The man was handsome—hell, the man was freakin' hot. Normally, when he was being looked at like that, Steven would have said something, but he held back, reminding himself who this guy was, but he still couldn't stop himself from looking.

Adding more weight to the bar, they took turns once again. "Stop by my desk when you're done," Lane told him with a smile just before his turn came, and Steven watched him walk away.

"It's your turn," Dan told him, and Steven noticed that Gene had left the group to continue his workout. Performing his set, Dan spotted him, and after six reps, he clinked the weight back into the rack. Sitting up, Steven took a few deep breaths, his chest pulsing with blood from the exercise.

"It looks like someone is interested in you," Dan told him, keeping his voice low. "If you're not interested, that's cool, but I thought I saw you looking at him too."

Steven looked at Dan for a second, trying to size the guy up. "He's attractive," Steven told him cautiously, "but I knew him in high school. He obviously doesn't know who I am."

"Why wouldn't he? You gave him your name when you met with him. You'd think he'd remember."

Steven shook his head, wondering just how much to tell Dan, but it really didn't matter. "Steven's my middle name. As a teenager, I was really overweight, and the kids used to call me Blobby Bobby. Lane," Steven said as he looked toward the front desk area, "was the chief instigator."

"Well, it looks to me as though that kid is long gone," Dan told him. "None of us is who we were then." Dan looked to where Lane sat talking on the phone. "But I do know that Lane has a reputation as a bit of a player. I'm just saying, not judging," he clarified quickly.

"Lane's a good guy," Lonnie interjected. "For a fruitbag—no offense," Lonnie added with a grin. "You two ready to move on, or you gonna stand around exchanging recipes? You know, if you were real friends, you could jerk me off." Dan just shook his head at Lonnie as he ducked when Steven took a swipe at him.

"Now you've got the hang of it. Just don't hit him in the head. He's got enough brain damage as it is," Dan told him with a huge grin.

"If you ladies are ready," Lonnie chided, completely unfazed, before moving to the incline bench. When they finished their workout, the three of them headed toward the locker room. Steven couldn't remember the last time he'd had so much fun during a workout. "You guys saunaing?" Lonnie asked without stopping for an answer as they all went to their lockers. Changing into a bathing suit, Steven made his way to the sauna. As he opened the door, the heat surrounded him, and Steven took a seat on the bench. Dan and Lonnie followed right behind, and almost as soon as he sat down, Lonnie started talking, telling stories about his ex-wife and God knew what else. "So,

Stevie, ya pole smoker, you gonna join us tomorrow?" Lonnie asked without stopping to wait for an answer. "We meet at Panera at ten and then come to the gym."

He had no plans other than spending most of the day alone. "Sure, I guess."

"Don't be late or I'll bang you in the ass."

Steven turned to Dan. "Is he always like this?"

"God, yes. Lonnie's a complete pig and living proof that there is such a thing as Jewish pork." Dan bumped his shoulder against Lonnie's in a familiar, friendly way as the door opened and Gene walked in wearing a Speedo.

"Nice panties. I've seen larger bathing suits on a Smurf," Lonnie commented with a smirk.

"Lon, your mother called a few minutes ago, she wants her ass back," Gene retorted without missing a beat, settling on the bench next to Dan. Damn, they were a good-looking couple. Dan was definitely older than Gene, but Steven could tell they were happy just by the way they both seemed to brighten when they were together.

"So, Stevie, you're looking really buff—you juicing?" Lonnie quipped.

Steven looked down at his chest and stomach, suppressing a pleased smile before shaking his head. "No, never used the stuff. Have you?" Lonnie didn't answer since he was already talking to someone else about God knows what. The sauna door opened, and Steven looked up to see Lane stride in. The man looked good, strong arms, big chest, and wide shoulders with an intricate flowing tattoo covering one of them. Lane sat down next to him, the large man smiling at him, and Steven could almost feel Lane's eyes raking over him. He wasn't quite sure how he felt about the attention. It was nice and all, but Steven had no intention of getting played, and he really wasn't interested in an easy, good time. He'd done that plenty when he was younger, and while fun, it often left him feeling empty. Some guys loved as much sex as they could get with as many guys as possible, but that wasn't him, at least not anymore.

Lonnie kept talking and Steven got up, stepping toward the door. "There's a whirlpool out by the pool, isn't there?"

"I'll show you," Lane said, practically jumping off the bench. Steven looked to Dan and saw him smile as Steven left the sauna, following Lane out toward the whirlpool.

"Are you done for the day?" Steven asked Lane as he toed off his shower shoes before stepping into the hot swirling water.

"Yeah. I finished a little while ago," Lane told him as he sank into the water, settling a few jets over from him. "I didn't want to leave until I gave you your pass," Lane said, but Steven knew it was more than that. Relaxing against the side of the whirlpool, he let his head lean back and his eyes close. After a hard workout, there was nothing better than relaxing in the whirlpool. "I was wondering," Lane began, and Steven opened his eyes, looking at Lane, "would you like to get some dinner or something some time?"

"Are you asking me out on a date?" Steven asked, and Lane nodded, suddenly looking rather shy and vulnerable. "You really don't know who I am, do you?"

"No, should I?" Lane sat up straighter in the water, staring at him intently. "Where did you go to school?"

"Cumberland Valley," Steven answered before adding, "We were in the same class."

"No way!" Lane said, grinning. "I'd remember if we were."

"You might, but I doubt for the reasons you're thinking. Steven's my middle name. My first name is Robert, but in high school everyone called me Bobby." Steven watched Lane's face as he went through everyone he could think of, and he saw instantly when Lane remembered. The big guy's eyes widened and his mouth fell open.

"You can't be. You look so different. You're Bobby Phillips?"

Steven nodded. "Although you never called me by my last name." Steven stood up in the water, getting ready to leave, while at the same time giving Lane a good look at the man he'd become rather than the teenager he once was.

"God, I was such an ass in high school," Lane said softly. Steven stopped, turning quickly to face his high school tormenter. "I knew I liked guys, but couldn't face it, so I made everyone's life pure hell, including my own. But I think I treated you worse than anyone. Like I said, I was a complete ass, and all I can say is that I'm sorry." Lane's face remained serious, and then he smirked this sideways grin. "Would it make you feel better if I let you give me a swirly or stuff me in a locker?"

Steven shook his head before breaking into his own smile. "You're a nut, and I don't think you could fit in a locker anywhere on the planet." Lane stood up, and Steven got a good look at his muscled chest, water sliding down his smooth skin, whirlpool bubbles clinging to his chiseled stomach.

"So what brings you back to town?"

"Believe it or not, my job transferred me here, of all places." Steven smiled as best he could. "Who would have thought that after living in Chicago and San Francisco for the last ten years that I would be transferred back to the area where I grew up?"

"Did you request the transfer?" Lane asked, sitting on the side with his legs dangling in the water.

"Not particularly, no." In truth Steven had absolutely not requested the transfer at all. He'd been happy in Chicago, and he liked the bigger city. He would never have asked to come back to central Pennsylvania, not in a million years. There was nothing wrong with the area, per se, it was just that when he'd left, Steven had had no intention of ever coming back. There were way too many painful memories here, and they had nothing to do with high school, although those weren't the most pleasant either. "It just worked out that way," Steven added with a shrug before lowering himself back into the water.

"What is it you do?"

"Information technology work. I've spent the last five years or so managing large-scale software installations. My company has a huge project they're undertaking in this area, and they needed me here." Steven let his gaze wander over Lane's body as Lane leaned back, stretching a little, and Steven took in the sight of tan skin and rippling muscles. Sighing softly, he pulled his eyes away, instead looking across the pool and out of the windows to the bright spring sunshine that shone on the flowers outside the window. He didn't do that anymore; he couldn't. Sighing, he did his best to try to push away the stab of desire that shot through him. Regardless of their history, Lane was an attractive man. Steven would have to be blind not to see it. "I never thought I'd be back here," Steven said quietly, "and I certainly never thought I'd be talking to Lane Parkinson again."

"We're not the same people we were then. Neither of us is," Lane said. "You're not Blobby Bobby, and I'm certainly not Lane the Pain, either, or the myriad of things the kids called me." Steven snapped his head around. He'd forgotten the names he and his friends had used to describe their tormenter. "You didn't think I heard it?"

"I'd just forgotten, I guess."

"So," Lane said as he got up, walking toward the whirlpool steps, "what about that dinner? Are you interested?" Lane stopped, one leg on a step as he turned around, deep brown eyes shining with an unspoken invitation.

"Let me think about it, okay? I'm just getting into town."

"At least it's not a no. I can accept that." Lane climbed the rest of the way out of the water, his bathing suit clinging invitingly around his hips and a butt that could crack walnuts. Powerful leg muscles corded as Lane lifted himself the rest of the way out of the water. "Stop by the desk so I can give you the pass." Steven nodded, swallowing slightly, watching as Lane walked toward the locker room.

Steven sat in the water for a minute or so before getting out as well. Walking into the locker room, Steven heard the showers, and for a second his mind conjured up an image of what Lane would look like without the bathing suit. Resisting the urge to see if he could get a peek, he walked past and into the bathroom area, standing in front of the sinks. No one else was around, and Steven washed his hands for something to do before lifting his eyes to look in the mirror. For a brief second, he could almost see himself as he'd been all those years ago. Closing his eyes, Steven took a deep breath. Opening his eyes again, he let his gaze fall on the man he was today. Tall and strong, with tan skin, a flat stomach, strong arms, and chest. He hadn't thought about the person he'd been back then in years, and he wondered why everything was coming back now.

A swatting slap on his rear end brought him out of his thoughts. "A bunch of us are going to dinner. We're meeting at Sapporo East on Carlisle Pike at six thirty. Join us." Lonnie leaned over the sink and began spreading shaving cream on his chest.

"Thanks," Steven answered. He figured he could find the restaurant. "Do you do that often?" Steven asked as Lonnie began running a razor over his skin.

"About once a week," Lonnie answered, the razor moving quickly over his skin. "If I don't, I start to look like yeti."

"More like Chewbacca," Dan chided as he stuck his head in, "and no, I'm not shaving your back for you." Dan's attention shifted to him. "Steven, I'd make myself scarce before he tries to talk you into it."

"I'll see you at dinner," Steven said as he hastily walked back toward the showers.

"Six thirty, ya fruitcake," Lonnie called, his voice carrying through the area, and Steven heard a number of chuckles. Obviously, Lonnie's mannerisms and behavior were familiar territory for just about everyone at the club.

Finding an empty shower, Steven started the water, letting it warm before getting in the stall and pulling the curtain closed. Steven stripped off his suit and hung it over the bar before reaching around for the soap dispenser. Soaping himself up, he let his hands roam for a few minutes. He wasn't about to jerk off here, although he wanted to—his mind kept conjuring up images of Lane with his bathing suit plastered to his skin. Steven finished his shower and turned off the water before opening the curtain. He reached for his towel and began drying himself. Hearing another curtain open, he lifted his head just enough to see Lane standing in the shower across from him. Damn, he'd always thought his imagination was pretty good, but it paled in comparison to the real thing. Forcing himself to keep his mind on his task, Steven wrapped the towel around his waist and hurried to the locker room, where he finished drying himself and began getting dressed. Thankfully, Lane seemed to be in another bay, and Steven finished getting dressed undisturbed.

Leaving the locker room, he wandered to the front, where he saw Lane fishing around in a desk. "I have your pass," Lane said, and he handed it to Steven. "I'll see you tomorrow."

"Yup. I should be here in the morning."

"Cool. See you then," Lane told him with a wink before closing the drawer. Steven turned to leave the club, striding through the doors and out to his rental car. As he got in, he saw Lane walking across the parking lot.

Steven knew he was probably being ridiculous. Lane had only asked him to dinner, and he knew dinner wouldn't lead to anything he didn't want it to. Maybe that was the issue? He really wanted it to lead to something; he just couldn't bring himself to let anything like that happen. He couldn't. He had to face that that part of his life was over. Closing the car door, he watched Lane get into his car. Starting the engine, Steven pulled out of his parking space, driving out of the lot and onto the street going back to his hotel.

Everything about being back in the town where he'd grown up seemed to bother him. He hadn't thought about high school or Blobby Bobby in years, and here he felt like that fat kid again. He knew there was no reason for it, and he knew he had to get over it. He wasn't that person anymore, and it was time to put it out of his mind. He'd already met new people who seemed like a lot of fun.

Pulling into the hotel, he grabbed his bag out of the trunk before striding inside and up to his room. Steven still had a few hours before dinner, and he spent most of it lying on the bed mindlessly watching television. Turning it off, he picked up his phone, nearly dialing his parents' telephone number. The temptation was quite strong, and that surprised him. He hadn't had any desire to talk to them in almost ten years. For a while, he'd tried calling during the holidays, but they never answered and his messages went unreturned. Eventually, he stopped calling and went on with his life. This was just a place like any other, and after all these years, a lot had changed, and it was time for him to finally move beyond this.

As he set his phone on the nightstand, it began to ring, and he saw it was one of his friends from Chicago. Happy for the relief from his maudlin thoughts, Steven answered the phone, glad to push his ridiculous thoughts aside. He was an adult and he had his own life. His parents had thrown him out of their life a long time ago, and there was no going back. "Marky," Steven chirped brightly as he answered the call.

II

STEVEN woke late, but went through his morning routine like he always did, just as fast as he could. He'd stayed up late the night before, after going out to dinner with Lonnie and the guys. Leaving the hotel, he found his way to the bakery, parking his car in an empty space. As he got out, a red sports car pulled into the spot next to his, and Lonnie got out. Steven took a second look, admiring the obviously powerful automobile. "Nice car," he commented with a smile.

"It's a Porsche GT3. There are only twenty of them on the road in the country," Lonnie told him proudly, closing the door. "My fiancée, Cory, is driving the other one," Lonnie explained, as though everyone had two Porsches. Steven tried to keep the surprise off his face as he followed Lonnie inside. Standing in line to order, Dan and Gene joined them, as did another couple who Dan introduced as Max and Hugh. "It's a regular sausagefest," Lonnie quipped, and the other guys all laughed. Steven laughed as well, getting used to Lonnie's humor, realizing there was no malice intended.

"Careful, Lonnie," Max said from beside him, a grin on his young face, "you're outnumbered." Max turned to the others. "I figure it'll only take an hour for us to turn him to the dark side." Max waggled his eyebrows, and Lonnie got quiet before laughing with the others. Hugh leaned close to Max's ear, whispering something. Steven wasn't close enough to hear, but he saw Max turn beet red, his smile widening.

"Be good," Max admonished with no heat and a touch of embarrassment. Reaching the counter, everyone ordered, and Lonnie insisted on paying, refusing to hear anything to the contrary.

"Are you moving here permanently?" Hugh asked as they carried their orders to the table that Dan had scoped out.

"It looks like it. My stuff hasn't been packed yet, and I need to find a place here first." Steven began spreading his light cream cheese on a whole-grain bagel.

"Are you going to rent or buy?" Max asked from his chair next to Hugh as he cut a bagel in half, sharing it with Hugh.

"I was thinking of buying. In Chicago, I have a two-bedroom condo. If I sell it, I can probably buy a small house here with the money. I have an appointment with a Realtor next week to see what my options are."

"Let us know," Max said after swallowing. "There are some nice homes for sale in our neighborhood."

"I haven't really had much of a chance to think about what I want to do. They offered me the job early last week and told me to be at the office here on Monday. They'll talk about something for months, but once they make a decision, they want it done yesterday."

"What company do you work for?"

"Shoebox. They have an office near here."

Dan grinned. "Me too. I'm a programmer there. I'll look for you tomorrow."

"That would be great," Steven said, already feeling a little better about his impending first day in the new office. He knew people there already from past projects and conference calls, but he'd actually met very few of them, and it would be nice to already have a friend in the office. After eating, Lonnie told more stories and showed everyone interested pictures of the Babe Ruth baseball card he'd just purchased for more money than Steven made in a year. With their breakfasts settled, everyone left and headed over to the gym. Steven followed Lonnie in his car, surprised that the engine sounded more like a sewing machine than the throaty powerhouse he'd been expecting.

Inside the club, he showed his pass to the girl behind the desk and walked back toward the locker room with the other guys. Inside, he chose a locker and started to change as someone else took the locker next to his. Looking up, he saw Lane pulling off his shirt. "Aren't you working?" Steven asked, a bit surprised.

"Not today," Lane said with a wink. "I was hoping I could work out with you."

"If you'd like," Steven replied, feeling a slight flutter in his stomach. Pushing that aside, because he knew he had to, Steven finished changing before meeting the guys on the workout floor. Their group was too large to work out together, so they divided up, and of course Steven found himself with Lane. He had to give the man credit, he was persistent. "We did chest yesterday, so is back good for you?" Steven asked.

"Sure," Lane answered as he went to one of the racks, loading a bar for some bent-over rows. "Do you want me to start?"

"Go ahead," Steven told him, watching as Lane got into position, bending over the bar. As Lane lifted the weight, his pants tightened, shirt pulling taut. Steven became entranced as Lane's powerful back muscles rippled and moved beneath the fabric as he pulled the bar to his lower chest. *Damn if that isn't a beautiful sight.* One rep became two and eventually ten, and it was only the clang of the bar being set back on the rack that broke the attraction-induced trance. Stepping away, Lane made room for him. Breathing deeply, Steven lifted the bar and began his set, back muscles pulling tight with every repetition, exhaling with each pull of the bar. Placing it back on the rack, Steven turned around and saw Lane smiling. "Have you thought about having dinner with me?" Steven nodded once—he hadn't thought about much else, if he were honest with himself. "So, Steven, *will* you have dinner with me?"

"Okay," Steven answered, knowing he should have politely declined, but his animal attraction won out. "I'll have dinner with you, but I need to have a chance to settle in at the office. So is Saturday okay?"

"Sure," Lane answered, and for a second Steven could almost see him already figuring out where they were going to go.

Lane increased the weight before starting his set, and Steven watched once again as Lane's muscles flexed beneath his shirt. Halfway through, Steven's eyes traveled lower. Lane's butt strained inside his thin shorts, and Steven had to suppress the small sigh. Not wanting to be obvious, he looked around the weight area to see where the other guys were, and saw Dan looking back at him from across the weight floor. Steven swore he saw Dan wink at him, but before he could give it much thought, he heard the chink of the weight being dropped back on the rack. "Damn, that was heavy," Lane commented as he reached for a bottle of water, taking a swig as Steven got into position. "Keep your back straight," Lane told him, touching the center of his back. "You're arching and could hurt yourself."

Steven adjusted his back as he felt the heat from Lane's hand through the thin fabric of his shirt. He'd felt desire and a longing to be touched before, but never quite like this. Taking a deep breath to clear his mind, he lifted the bar and began powering his way through the set, determined to drive his thoughts from his head. *One... two... three....* With each rep, he told himself no, that whatever his errant body wanted... *four... five... six...* he could never act on it, anyway; that was closed to him now. *Seven... eight... nine....* His mind began to clear as his muscles screamed for mercy. *Ten!* Steven let out a groan and dropped the weight back onto the rack, huffing a small cry of frustration, letting the set he'd just finished act as cover.

"Good set?" Lane asked, and Steven nodded, still breathing hard, doing his best to look away from Lane's broad chest as it stretched his shirt taut, hard nipples pressing against the fabric.

"Damn," he half moaned before he could stop himself, and he could only hope the extreme set would cover for him. Stepping back, he let Lane increase the weight one more time as he swigged water from his bottle. During Steven's set, Lane had pulled off his T-shirt and was wearing just a string tank, showing off the plated muscle of his chest, dripping with sweat.

He and Lane took turns, doing three more sets before moving on to another exercise. A few times, he knew he saw Lane checking him out, but Steven ignored it and tried to keep his attention on the workout and away from the hard body he was working out with. He failed miserably. Every exercise seemed to make Lane appear larger, his muscles engorging with blood. And it wasn't just Lane's. Steven had never been so happy to be wearing a jock strap in his life.

"Hey, birdgazers," Lonnie said from behind him as Steven finished up his last set of lat pull-downs, his arms pulling the bar on its cable down behind his neck. Finishing the set, he stood up again, breathing hard, his back muscles straining. "You two cockhoppers lunching with us?"

"Sure," Lane said, "after this ass-kicking, I'm gonna need food." Lane turned to him, a hopeful look on his face, and Steven found himself agreeing as well.

Everyone seemed to be done at the same time, and all the guys headed toward the locker room, talking and laughing. Steven opened his locker, trying not to pay too much attention to Lane standing right next to him, but it was impossible, especially when Lane stripped down, standing naked next to him as he fished around for his bathing suit. Steven knew Lane was doing this on purpose and was about ready to smack him on the ass, but the man would probably think he was coming on to him, and Steven didn't want to encourage him. Slipping out of his own clothes, Steven put on his suit and found Lane openly checking him out. Thankfully, the other man said nothing, and Steven followed him to the sauna, where Lonnie was already deep into one of his stories. Immensely grateful, Steven took a seat on the edge of the bench near the wall, where he couldn't see Lane directly. The man was sex on wheels and had him so spun up that Steven had to check the front of his suit to make sure he wasn't embarrassing himself.

Once Lonnie finished his story, guys began to filter out, some to the showers and others to the whirlpool, and when Lane got up to leave, Steven lagged behind until it was just him and Lonnie. "What's up with you two?" Lonnie asked him. "Lane's a great guy, and he's smokin' hot. I'd fuck him if I was into that."

"I don't...," Steven started to say, but couldn't get his mouth around what he wanted to say. "It's complicated."

"Screw that," Lonnie chided. "He's interested, so take him home and let him suck some protein directly from the tap."

"Lonnie," Steven said with a sigh as he shook his head. "You don't understand. It's a lot more complicated than sex."

"What? Things not working? Because I can get you in touch with a good doctor who can help get things standing tall."

Steven laughed. "It's nothing like that." Standing up, he walked toward the sauna door. "I'll see you in a bit." Letting the door close behind him, Steven walked toward the showers. Finding one that was free, he showered quickly, drying himself before heading to the locker room to dress, listening to the guys around him jabber about this and that. He had to admit, they were a great group of guys, and it had been quite a while since he'd been a part of a group like this. He only hoped it lasted.

A hand settled on his shoulder. "I'll meet you out front," Lane said with a smile.

"I'm right behind you," Steven answered, putting his wet and dirty clothes into his bag before grabbing his jacket and following Lane out of the locker room. The rest of the guys were waiting up near the front of the gym, and everyone left together, trying to decide where to go for lunch. After they all finally settled on a restaurant, Steven got into his car, following the group there.

They had to wait a few minutes while the servers made up a table large enough for all of them. As they waited, Steven felt something tickle his hand lightly. Looking down, he saw Lane's fingers lightly brushing his hand, the man smiling at him like an excited kid. Being touched again felt nice, and he wound a finger around one of Lane's, letting himself enjoy the feeling.

"Your table's ready," the server said, and after grabbing menus, she led them to their table, where Lonnie saved the chair next to his.

"Hey, Chicken," he called in some weird voice as a beautiful woman seated herself next to him. Lonnie introduced her as Cory, his fiancée, as their server arrived and began taking drink orders. Everyone around the table began talking, with Lonnie telling more embarrassing stories. Fortunately they were mostly about himself and the stupid things he'd done, but he kept everyone laughing until the server brought their drinks.

Steven picked up the glass in front of him and the glass handle gave way. The body of the glass shattered on the table, and Steven looked down at his hand as blood ran down his palm, dripping onto the table. The others grabbed napkins, reaching to clean up the spill. "Don't," Steven said, "don't touch anything and drop the napkins." Lane reached for his hand, and Steven jerked it away. Grabbing for a napkin, he placed it over the cut, which didn't seem too bad, and carefully cleaned up the drops of blood on the table. A server came to the table, reaching over him. "Please, don't," he told her. "Bring a cloth from the kitchen that has been soaked in bleach water and don't touch the table."

"Why did you...." Lonnie started like he'd been kicked. "What was that for?" Lonnie asked, glaring at Dan, who nodded to Steven. "No, seriously, what's with that?"

Steven found everyone at the table looking at him, and he wanted to sink through the floor. The server brought the cloth and Steven cleaned up the table. "Please bring me a plastic bag," he told her, and the server left again, returning with a bag, and Steven put the cloth inside, not giving it back. The server left and the manager joined them at their table.

"Is there a problem?"

"No," Steven answered, "I cut myself on the glass and...." He swallowed. "My blood is a hazardous substance because I'm HIV-positive. I was probably overreacting, but I didn't want anyone hurt. I'll take the cloth with me and dispose of it properly." He had a hazardous material disposal bag back at his hotel. Leaving the table, Steven went out to his rental car, getting his first aid kit from his gym bag, and he checked his hand carefully, making sure everything was properly cleaned and that the bleeding had stopped.

Thankfully, the wound wasn't serious, and after checking it out, he bandaged it properly before putting his supplies away. Standing beside the car, he debated going back to his hotel. He'd already caused enough trouble, and he wasn't sure he wanted to go back inside to face either the looks he got from people who thought he was the devil incarnate, or the pitying looks he got from everyone else. Frankly, he really didn't need either one. Closing the car door, he huffed to himself before walking back into the restaurant.

The group had been moved to another table, and Steven looked to where they had been sitting, seeing someone from the restaurant with a sanitary kit, wearing gloves and cleaning the table with sanitizing spray. He'd seen this before and knew it was standard procedure, but it always made him seem like a pariah. "Are you okay?" Dan asked as he stood up, indicating the chair next to him. Steven nodded and sat down, noticing that he was seated between Dan and Gene, which he took as a sign of support, with Lane as far away from him as he could get. Steven guessed he should have expected that. Most everyone at the table seemed to be talking like they had been earlier.

"So as I was saying…." Lonnie raised his voice drawing everyone's attention to him. "It was New Year's Eve, and we were having this party. Jim, one of my friends," Lonnie said, turning to Dan, "You've met him. He's about three hundred pounds. He sits next to me and lets one rip so loud you could hear it over the television. I mean, I thought I was going to puke, and poor Cory ran out of the room, and I couldn't find her for ten minutes. That had to be the loudest fart in history."

Steven looked to Dan, figuring he must have missed something, but Dan just mouthed, "You don't want to know."

The server arrived at the table and took their orders. Steven gave his and watched the others around the table. Everyone seemed to be acting normal—everyone except Lane, who kept staring at him for a few seconds and then looking away. The look wasn't pity, but he knew those glances too. Steven had seen those looks before, and knew what those eyes that wouldn't meet his meant. He knew Lane was at this moment breathing a sigh of relief that nothing had happened between them, and that he was also trying to figure out just how quickly he could get the hell out of there. After all, Lane looked about two seconds from bolting to the door.

"Steven," Cory said quietly from next to where Lonnie sat, "are you all right? Some of my clients have HIV, and I understand what you've been through." She reached over and patted his uninjured hand, and he followed her steely gaze down the table to where Lane looked as though he were trying to hide. Steven knew she was issuing a silent challenge to him and everyone else at the table.

"So, how'd you get it? Take it up the ass one too many times?" Lonnie asked, but he didn't stop for an answer. "Not that I'm one to say anything." Lonnie leaned closer from their side of the table, as though he were sharing a secret. "Cory does this thing with her finger, makes me bust a nut faster than you can say love rocket."

Steven found himself laughing along with the other people at their end of the table, and he finally let himself relax a bit.

Their food arrived, and everyone began to eat, the conversation continuing around the table as though nothing had happened. Dan filled him in on some things about the office and arranged to meet him for lunch the following day. "Maybe I'll be assigned to your project," he told him excitedly. "I get so tired of maintaining the same systems all the time. It would be great to work on something new."

"I can ask," Steven said, glad he'd know someone at the office. He couldn't help looking down the table to where Lane sat quietly, his attention fully on his plate. Yeah, it was definitely like he'd feared. After his diagnosis, he'd spent some time at an HIV support group, and a lot of the guys had told stories of people they'd met and liked, but as soon as they learned they were HIV positive, they never heard anything from them again, and Steven had figured that would happen with Lane. Not that he should have been so surprised. Steven had already considered that part of his life over, anyway, but he'd liked the way Lane had touched him, and he liked having a friend. Well, that was over and he needed to accept it. Hell, they hadn't even gone out on a date or anything, so it was no use getting upset.

As they finished their lunches, the server took their plates away and brought the checks. Max and Hugh paid their bills and said their goodbyes, both of them shaking his hand. Steven saw Lane get up, looking at him, and hoped Lane would at least say something, but he simply said goodbye to everyone at once before grabbing his jacket and leaving the restaurant. "I'm sorry," Gene said from next to him, shaking his head. "I know you liked him, but if he can't handle it, it's best to find out now."

"I know, and it's not like anything could happen between us, but it still kind of stings, you know?"

Dan looked at him, puzzled. "What do you mean?"

"It's not important," Steven said as he pushed back from the table. "Thank you for lunch. It was great."

"See you at the gym tomorrow, about four thirty," Lonnie told him, surprising Steven when he was pulled into a hug. Steven felt an unexpected emotional tide wash over him, and he blinked a few times before Lonnie released him from the hug. "You know it doesn't matter—hell, you can still give me a hand job sometime if you want."

Steven began laughing as he saw Dan cuff Lonnie on the back of the head. "Why is it everything revolves around your dick?"

"Because it's where he keeps his brain," Cory told them as she took his hand, leading him out of the restaurant, waving with her other hand as she hauled the much larger man behind her.

"Gene and I have to be going, too, but I'll see you tomorrow," Dan told him as they walked out of the restaurant. Shaking hands, they said goodbye, and Steven got into his car, feeling a little relieved in some ways and just a little more alone in others.

III

SATURDAY, today was Saturday, Steven reminded himself as he got out of the hotel bed, padding to the bathroom. The first thing he did was clean up, and then he took his meds, just like he did every day. His first week at work had been good, and he was indeed pleased when Dan had been assigned to his team. It looked like they were going to work really well together. After work, he'd joined the guys at the gym, and to his surprise, no one had treated him differently or even said anything about his disease. They treated him the same as everyone else, and Lonnie had started calling him cockhopper or some other stupid thing, which Steven took as a sign of acceptance. The one person he hadn't seen was Lane. He hadn't been at the club at all, and he hadn't called. Even though they had talked about going to dinner, he hadn't heard anything, so he figured that Lane couldn't handle him being positive. Not that that came as a surprise after the restaurant incident last weekend, but Steven had kind of hoped Lane would come around.

Steven's phone buzzed on the dresser. "Hey, Lonnie," Steven answered, as he tried to decide what to wear after pulling aside the dirty clothes, reminding himself that he needed to do laundry.

"We're meeting in half an hour at Panera. You coming?"

"Sure, I'm just getting up, but I'll meet you there," Steven said before saying goodbye and hanging up. He hurried around the room, dressing and getting his dirty clothes together to go to the Laundromat. As he was leaving, Steven grabbed his gym bag and the dirty clothes, and had just closed his door when his phone rang again. Letting it go to voice mail, he hurried out to his car and drove to get breakfast.

He found the guys seated around a table, and to his surprise Lane was there, as well. Dan and Gene said their hellos before getting up to get in line. "Steven, can we get you anything?"

"A plain bagel with light cream cheese would be perfect. Thank you." Steven gave Dan money and found a seat. He looked across at Lane, wondering if the man even wanted to speak to him, but decided not to be petty. "I haven't seen you at the gym this week."

"I only work there on the weekends. During the week I'm a physical therapist," Lane explained, looking uncomfortable and ill at ease, and Steven didn't know what to say to make him comfortable. He was still HIV-positive, and that wasn't going to change.

"Sounds like you're a busy man. Why the extra job?" Steven asked as the other guys returned, trying to make small talk as he danced around the real questions he wanted to ask. He figured Lane was doing the same. Dan handed him his plate and everyone sat down as Lonnie immediately broke into a blow-by-blow of his evening the night before, including a detailed description of the things that Cory had done to him. Not that Steven was interested, but if half of what Lonnie described was true, then he was a lucky man.

After they'd eaten, everyone took care of their dishes and they left, driving the short distance to the gym. Steven got his things, and after scanning his new membership card, he walked back to the locker room. Changing quickly, Steven closed his locker and headed to the weight floor, where some of the guys were waiting for him. "Are you dick divers ready?" Lonnie asked, with what Steven had learned was his usual bravado. Gene had already moved off on his own, while Dan and Steven followed Lonnie. Lane joined them a few seconds later, and Steven found himself wondering just what he was up to. "With four of us, we need to split up, so Dan and I will work together. Steven, you and Lane work together," Lonnie instructed as he reached for a set of dumbbells.

Steven looked at Lane, wondering how he felt about that, but Lane got a pair of dumbbells and copped an incline bench, beginning his set without saying anything. Steven stood back and watched. It was only a workout, and if Lane didn't want to say anything, he could live with that. After finishing the set, Lane got up and Steven performed his, trying to turn off everything and concentrate on the exercise he was doing. When he was done, he put the weights back in the rack.

"How long ago did you find out you were...." Lane stumbled. "You know?"

"HIV-positive? About two years ago. I don't have any symptoms, and I take meds that have fought the virus to the point that tests can no longer detect it, but that doesn't mean it's gone," Steven answered. Lane got the dumbbells for his next set, saying nothing more. After he'd done ten reps, he stood up and put them back in the rack.

"How did you get it?" Lane asked, as Steven reached for his weights. Stopping, Steven turned to face him.

"I'd like to say it was something beyond my control, but it wasn't. I spent a lot of time playing the field. I used condoms most of the time, but I can think of a few times when I'd had too much to drink and caution went out the window. It was a stupid thing to do, and I was young and figured nothing could happen to me. I was wrong." Steven moved, standing with his hand on the back of the bench. "I wish I knew who I got the virus from, but I don't. I spent a lot of my time with one guy after the other. Looking back, I guess I deserve what I got."

"HIV isn't punishment for your behavior, and you don't deserve to be sick. No one does." Lane told him with a conviction that surprised him. After the way Lane had been acting, he'd been expecting less understanding and more hostility, or at least some uncomfortable silence.

"So what gives? Last week you treated me as though I had leprosy, and now you're Mr. Understanding. I don't get it." Steven stepped to the rack, picking up his weights before doing his set as a touch of anger had adrenaline coursing through his body. At the end of the set, he dropped the weights with a thud and then reclined back against the bench, his thoughts in a bit of a whirl.

"Steven, I don't understand it myself. When you told me, I guess I was stupid and scared. I like you and I was hoping to get to know you better," Lane said softly.

Steven stood up, turning around. "And you thought that getting to know me better would involve getting naked and horizontal," Steven supplied. "Well, now you know that that portion of my life is over, so you won't have to worry about it." Steven moved away from the bench, suddenly in no mood to work out at all. "I have no intention of ever putting you or anyone else in danger."

Lane lifted his weights, settling on the bench. Flicking his knees, he hoisted the weights in the air, pounding out a set before dropping the weights with a bang. "You know, Steven, you're kind of an ass," Lane told him, his head turning on the bench to face him.

Steven had no idea what to say to that, and he swallowed hard, tamping down the urge to simply walk away. "I'm an ass?"

"Yes, and a melodramatic one at that. Being HIV-positive does not mean your life is over, sexually or otherwise."

"How do you know?" Steven asked defensively, arms folded over his chest.

Lane got up from the bench, his expression soft, and Steven felt part of his indignation slip away. "I asked one of the doctors where I work, and he explained a number of things. Look, I'll admit the news that you have HIV was a bit shocking, and I'm also willing to admit that it scared me, okay?"

Steven nodded slightly. He of all people could understand the fear that came with his disease; he'd felt it often enough. "I'm not happy about how I acted at the restaurant," Lane added.

"Okay, fair enough," Steven said as he got into position on the weight bench. "Your conscience is clear and you can go on knowing everything's okay."

Steven did his set not knowing what to expect, nor really caring, for that matter. It wasn't his job to give Lane some sort of absolution for his behavior. Hell, Lane didn't even owe him an explanation in the first place. He knew how scared people could get, and the guy was trying, at least. Maybe he should cut him some slack, after all. Finishing his set, Steven dropped the weights before pushing them off to the side so Lane could use them again.

"You really are an ass," Lane told him as he got up.

"You already said that," Steven countered.

"Look, I wanted to tell you I was sorry for blowing you off and that I shouldn't have acted like that in the restaurant. No, that's not right, what I wanted to say was that I shouldn't have treated you differently once I knew." Steven almost jumped when he felt Lane's fingers brush against his hand. "I know you can't transmit HIV from touch or even kissing. I didn't then, but I do now."

"You really asked someone? Why?"

"We have a date for tonight, and I wanted to know what I could do."

"Look," Steven said, taking a step back. "You don't have to do that. You asked me before you knew, and for the record, I wouldn't have allowed anything to happen that would have put you in any danger."

Lane held up his hands in a kind of surrender. "I never said you would. That was one thing that never crossed my mind. I sort of know now why you were so reticent before, and I can't say I blame you, but I wanted to ask if you'd give me a chance. I really would like to have dinner with you."

"Lane, you don't have to do this to satisfy some sort of obligation." The last thing Steven wanted was a pity date. He'd had people do enough things for him out of pity; he'd hated it then and couldn't bear it now.

"I'm not," Lane told him with a slight smile and wink as he slid onto the bench before doing his set. Steven watched, the way he usually did, trying to keep himself from staring as Lane's chest expanded and contracted while he did the exercise. He knew he should be interested in other things besides the way Lane looked, but those muscles working had him completely enthralled. Lane had surprised him, and he found his resolve weakening. When the dumbbells thunked onto the floor, Steven picked up his weights, performing his set with Lane spotting him on the heavy weight, his hands on his elbows.

"So have you two made up?" Lonnie quipped as he wandered over to their bench. "Dan and I are done on the flat bench."

"We're done here," Lane told Lonnie, and they traded benches. Lane did his first set, and then Steven took his turn. They didn't talk much now, and Steven began to wonder just what Lane wanted. He'd been guarding his feelings for a long time, and it came naturally to do it now. Once they'd done four sets on the flat bench, he and Lane joined Lonnie and Dan for some work on the decline bench. Since there was only one, they took turns, doing their best to keep things moving. Steven noticed that Lane kept watching him, and hell, if he were honest, he kept watching Lane. There was something about him that really seemed to draw Steven's attention. He never thought he had a particular "type" of guy, but it seemed that Lane was it.

Steven had sweated through his clothes by the time they'd completed the workout. Grabbing his water bottle, he headed into the locker room, his thoughts still a little scattered. The thought of going out with someone on a date for the first time in a while was exciting, but he couldn't keep his nerves tamped down. Part of him was truly excited, but another part, the part that seemed to be weakening, kept saying it was best to keep that part of himself closed off and to not get his hopes up. Steven knew it would take a very special person to let someone with HIV into their life. "Stop it," he told himself quietly—it was only dinner and nothing more.

Changing into his bathing suit, he grabbed his towel, and after filling his water bottle, he walked to the sauna. He didn't stay long, though, before showering quickly and heading for the whirlpool. He needed to let his muscles relax, and the water helped. He was just lowering himself onto the seat below the water when he saw Lane stepping down into the pool before settling near him. "Have you always worked out?" Lane asked him over the sound of the water.

"I started working out when I decided it was time to lose the weight years ago, and after I was diagnosed, I kept it up, figuring the stronger and healthier I was, the less chance I'd have of the disease progressing. I don't know if that holds true scientifically, but it made me feel better."

"I take it you lost friends after you were diagnosed with HIV," Lane said, and Steven nodded slowly.

"There's still a lot of fear out there based upon outdated notions. It scares people, and it's often easier for them to simply write someone off as a friend than actually face their fears. Not that I can really blame them." Before he was diagnosed, he hadn't known anyone personally who was HIV-positive, so he'd learned about his disease firsthand. Thankfully, he'd had a great doctor who took plenty of time and answered all of Steven's questions.

"Bullpucky," Lane told him. "It's ignorance, pure and simple." Lane smiled before continuing, "Yes, I know I'm guilty of it, but I had most of the week to think, and I kind of realized that if I didn't take a chance that maybe I would end up the loser."

Steven shifted under the water so he could see Lane better. "I don't get it."

"I guess I'm saying that I think you're someone I'd like to know better, and if I write you off just because of one little thing, then maybe I'm not the person I'd like to think I am. I'm not the same person you knew in high school, but I acted like it last week, and I'd like the chance to make it up to you." Lane moved closer, and Steven felt Lane's hand touch his under the water. His skin was surprisingly soft, something he'd never noticed before, but he certainly did as Lane's fingers slid up his arm, sending a chill through his body regardless of the hot water.

"Lane, I think it's only fair to tell you that we can go to dinner, but we can't do anything more than that. It's just not safe."

Lane's hand stopped moving but didn't pull away. "Didn't they explain to you about safe sex?" Lane asked, looking surprised.

"Yes, but nothing is perfectly safe. Condoms break, and a small, unseen cut can make you vulnerable. I've been through a lot in the last few years, and I can't let someone else go through what I have because of me." Steven stood up, walking toward the steps to get out of the water. "I'm sorry, Lane, but that's the way it has to be. If you don't want to go to dinner, I'll understand." Steven climbed out, slipping on his shower shoes before padding his way back to the locker room. He knew what he'd said was the right thing, so why did he feel like he'd let himself down?

Finding an empty shower, he stepped in and stripped off his bathing suit before turning on the water and letting it warm. Washing quickly, he tried to keep his mind off Lane and on what he was doing, but it wasn't working. His imagination kept flashing images of Lane and what his hands would feel like on his skin. Dreaming of being touched again was all he'd done for the last two years, and he'd resigned himself to the fact that that was all he could ever do again. But Lane made him want more, and that was dangerous, or could be dangerous for Lane. Pushing his thoughts and imagination away, he rinsed and pushed the curtain back, reaching for his towel as Lane stepped out of the shower stall across from his as naked as the day he was born.

Whether Lane had done it on purpose or not, Steven wasn't sure and really didn't care. Stopping completely, he stared at him, his mouth hanging open. He'd gotten a glimpse of Lane earlier, but now he got the full-on effect. The man was perfect: defined chest, deeply grooved stomach, thick, strong legs, and…. Steven swallowed, then looked away. He did not need to be staring at Lane's dick, but damn if it wasn't perfect as well. Hurriedly reaching for his towel, Steven draped it in front of himself under the pretext of drying himself, trying to keep himself from getting excited standing in the showers where everyone could see. "Show-off," he said softly, because he had to say something. Peering momentarily over his towel, he saw a crooked-mouthed smirk and knew Lane had done it on purpose. *The fucker.*

Men moved around him and the sounds of water in the background abated until Steven realized they were the only two left. Steven wrapped his towel around his waist and was about to leave when he felt Lane's hand touch his arm.

"I'll see you tonight." Lane phrased it sort of as a question, but the tone said he wouldn't take no for an answer, and Steven nodded slowly.

"Okay." Gathering his things, he walked into the locker area, where he dressed quickly. He was just finishing when Lane joined him, and Steven explained where his hotel was.

"I'll pick you up at six," Lane said, and Steven saw that Lane had changed into his club uniform. "I have to work till then, but I'll be there." For a second, Steven thought that Lane might actually kiss him as their eyes locked, but he saw Lane swallow and the moment passed. Instead, Lane stroked his arm lightly before turning to leave the locker room. Steven wasn't proud of it, but he watched him the entire time and only turned back to his locker once Lane had left the room.

"It looks like everyone's on their own for lunch today," Dan said from across the bay, walking around the bench to where Steven was standing. "Gene's still finishing his workout, but I was wondering if you'd like to join me for lunch. There's a sandwich place a few blocks away."

"That'd be nice," Steven said with a smile, since he wasn't particularly relishing spending the rest of the day alone with his thoughts. He knew he'd invariably worry things to death.

"I'll meet you out front in a few minutes," Dan told him as he grabbed his things and left. Steven finished pulling on his shoes and socks before gathering his things as well. Out near the front doors, he met Dan, and they walked to their cars together. "You can follow me if you want. It isn't far," Dan said, and Steven nodded, hurrying to his car. Pulling out and waiting for Dan, he followed him to a restaurant Steven probably would have classified as a little old lady place. "Lonnie hates this place because he can't get enough food, but their sandwiches are to die for," Dan whispered to him as they stood in line. "I usually get the cranberry pecan chicken salad wrap," he added as they reached the front. Dan ordered his usual, and Steven followed suit, taking their number and cups before paying.

Steven got his drink and snagged an empty table. Dan joined him a few seconds later, and they waited for their food. "I have a confession to make—I sort of engineered this lunch."

Steven sipped his diet soda, looking at Dan warily, but he said nothing.

"I wanted to talk to you, and I knew I couldn't with Lonnie around. I love the man to death, but he's as gossipy as an old woman talking across the back fence." Dan gulped half his drink before setting his cup on the table. "Besides, it's hard to talk about something serious when he's around." A server brought their plates and took their order number from the table. "If I'm out of line, please tell me and I'll butt out. But some years ago, I had a dear friend, someone I'd known since college, who got HIV like you did, but at the time they didn't have the drugs therapies they have today. This was back when it was a death sentence. About six months after he was diagnosed, Jimmy met Paul. They were good together, for a while, but then Jimmy started pushing Paul away. At first Paul resisted, but eventually he did what Jimmy asked."

Steven picked up part of his sandwich and took a bite, but Dan ignored his and became quiet. "What happened?" Steven prompted after swallowing.

Dan swallowed hard and Steven realized how hard it was to tell this story. "Jimmy got sick and went into the hospital with pneumonia. When Paul found out, he went to visit, and again, Jimmy pushed him away. Jimmy got sicker and sicker, and Paul kept visiting. Then he started to care for Jimmy, making sure he was comfortable, sitting by his bed most nights. When I visited the hospital in those last weeks, Paul was always there." Dan picked up a napkin, wiping his eyes, and Steven looked away to give him some privacy, but he was enthralled by the story. "The last time I visited Jimmy, he couldn't lift his head he was so weak. I heard him ask Paul a question, 'Why did you stay now?' and Paul answered, 'Because you can't push me away anymore.'" Dan took another drink from his cup, and Steven did the same to try to wash down the lump that had formed in his throat. "Jimmy died in the middle of the night less than a week later, and Paul was the only one there." Dan stopped, and Steven took another gulp from his glass. "You have to be wondering why I told you that story."

"No, I think I get it. You're saying my life isn't over."

"That, and don't push away the possibility of love because you're scared. Jimmy and Paul could have had some good months together, but Jimmy wouldn't allow it. I can't tell you what Lane's thinking, but don't shut yourself off from the possibility of love."

"I'm not," Steven replied quickly, maybe too quickly, and he saw Dan give him a knowing look. "I don't want anyone else to go through what I went through."

Dan set down his sandwich, wiping his mouth with a napkin. "I know, and that's admirable, but let the rest of us decide what we're willing to risk. You know there are plenty of ways to be safe if you're careful." Dan chuckled a little, almost to himself. "I'm not saying you should go out and jump in bed with the guy, but Jimmy told me once that as soon as he was diagnosed, he figured the sexual part of his life was over, and I think that's why he pushed Paul away. Jimmy was wrong, and if that's what you're thinking, then maybe you're wrong too. Just think about it."

"It's not that easy," Steven said, wishing it were.

"Nothing worthwhile is ever easy," Dan replied before shaking his head. "Could I get any more cliché?"

"I doubt it," Steven teased as his hunger caught up with him, and he began to eat in earnest as what Dan had said rattled through his head. On one level he knew Dan was right, but what he couldn't get past was the thought that if he did get with Lane, or anyone, and they were intimate.... What if someone he cared about got HIV from him? Just thinking about it was unbearable and made his stomach clench every single time. "Lane and I are having dinner tonight," Steven said, but he felt almost like he was confessing.

"I know. He told me about it when you were doing one of your sets."

"Is he really a player?" Steven asked.

"He has a bit of a reputation, but we all did that at some point. I did, you did—we grow out of it, especially if we meet the right person. So don't let that worry you too much. Also, Lonnie says he's a good guy, and he can tell a poser a mile away." Dan leaned across the table. "I can tell you he was really excited about it. I don't know what happened between last weekend and now, but whatever it was, he seems to have gotten over whatever was bothering him."

"So you're saying I should relax and let things happen." Steven was starting to feel like he could do that, but reassurance was always appreciated.

"Exactly. You don't have to do anything you're not comfortable with, but don't cut yourself off, either. Just relax and have fun." Dan finished his drink. "We'd better go. Half the people in line are scoping out our table, and I need to see if Gene's done with his workout."

Steven got up as well, wondering what he should say to Dan, because he really did appreciate him taking the time to talk with him. Their conversation had made him feel better; now he just had pre-date butterflies. Looking around, he saw that they cleared the tables, so he headed for the door, bumping into someone when he turned back to see where Dan was. Excusing himself automatically, he turned and found himself staring into his mother's eyes.

She gasped softly and looked into his eyes for a split second. "Bobby?"

"Steven," Dan said from behind him, "are you ready to go?"

He saw her eyes blink a few times. "I'm sorry, I thought you were someone else," she said and moved on, but Steven saw her turn to look again as he and Dan left the restaurant.

Steven could barely feel the pavement beneath his feet as he made his way to the car. He hadn't seen his mother in over a decade. She still looked the same, but with more lines on her face and some gray in her black hair. Reaching his car, he opened the door and slid into the driver's seat, his legs tingling as he took deep measured breaths. Seeing her felt like being transported back to the day he'd packed the last of his things and left for college. They hadn't said anything, his father in his office and his mother nowhere to be found, the house he'd grown up in suddenly feeling empty and strange. Well, even stranger than it had for the previous three months, during which both his parents had basically half pretended that he didn't exist.

A knock on the window caught his attention, and Steven rolled it down. "What's wrong? You look white as a sheet. Are you feeling okay?" Dan asked.

Steven took another deep breath, filling his lungs with air, willing the numbness in his legs to go away, and it seemed to be working. "Yeah, I'm fine, thanks." Steven forced a smile as Dan stepped back. "I'll talk to you tomorrow morning."

Dan didn't look convinced, but let it go. "We'll text you about tomorrow morning," he said before walking toward his car. Leaving the window down, Steven started the car and pulled out of the lot, letting the fresh spring air wash over him as he drove.

Autopilot seemed to take over, and it wasn't until he made the final turn that he realized he was on the street where he'd grown up. Pulling down the block, he stopped in front of the familiar house. The yard had changed some, but the house itself looked exactly the same, a sprawling ranch house with white wood siding above red brick. Pulling off the road, he stayed in the car as he looked things over. Behind the house, he could see the large tree where he'd had a rope swing as a kid, and where there had once been a swing set. He had no idea what was there now, but it didn't matter. He could see it in his mind the way it had been as though it were yesterday, he and his friends playing baseball in the backyard with the trees as bases.

Closing his eyes, Steven could almost see inside the house to the kitchen where his mother had baked a nearly endless supply of cookies and treats for his friends. Growing up, the house had always felt warm. Steven felt a tear roll down his cheek before he could blink it away, and he turned his eyes away from the house, reaching for a napkin from the door pocket.

The warmth that had always surrounded him had been his downfall. He really hadn't thought his parents could stop loving him, but the day he told them he was gay, it seemed as though they had truly stopped loving him and frozen him out of their lives. He hadn't thought about all this in years. In fact, before returning to town, he'd rarely thought of his parents at all anymore, and this trip down memory lane wasn't doing him any good. Turning toward the house again, he took a final look before starting the engine and pulling away.

The maudlin feelings dissipated some as he put distance between him and the house, but he couldn't get the startled look on his mother's face out of his mind, or the flash of… was it disappointment he'd seen when she thought he was someone else? He'd felt that brief instantaneous look in his heart, but he didn't dare let it bloom into hope of any kind. It had been too long, and he'd come too far to let himself be disappointed and rejected all over again. Catching his breath as he drove, Steven arrived back at his hotel with his stomach still fluttering. After walking through the lobby and down the hall to his room, he pulled out his phone and dialed, thankful when his friend answered. "Marky."

"Steven? You sound terrible. What happened?" Mark, or Marky, as he'd been calling him for years, was his best friend. They'd met when they were both freshmen in college and ended up as roommates, lovers for a brief time, and then best friends. Theirs was a friendship that had survived tears and even living in different parts of the country after they'd graduated, and somehow they'd managed to stay as close as two friends could be.

"I saw my mother today," Steven told him, trying to keep his voice level. "I was out to lunch with a friend, and I literally bumped into her."

"Did she see you?"

"Yeah, and I think she recognized me, but Dan called me Steven and from the look on her face, she must have thought she had me confused with someone else. It was unsettling as hell."

"You need to see her, Steven," Marky told him, and Steven nearly dropped the phone in surprise, since this was coming from the man who referred to his relationship with his own mother as a hate/hate relationship. The two of them hadn't spoken in years. "I'm serious. You need to know how she feels. What if your parents have changed? I bet they both miss you."

Steven scoffed, "This, coming from you."

"Hey!" Marky started with mock indignation. "My mother may be the bitch from hell, but she's *my* bitch from hell, and don't you forget it. Get your own. Oh wait, you have one—kind of." Marky's queeny rant had them both laughing, and that seemed to be what Steven needed. "Seriously, don't do it alone, but call her or go see her. You deserve to find out. The worst she can do is say no."

"What about my dad?" His mother was bad enough, but the thought of facing his father nearly made him physically ill.

"Divide and conquer," Marky said, his voice ringing through the phone. "I know this will be hard, but in all the time I've known you, you've never really dealt with them and your feelings for them. And if I know you, being back there has opened a whole can of worms."

"You could say that." All the emotions he thought he'd locked safely away kept coming to the surface, and seeing his mother had only made things worse.

"If you want my advice, I'll give it to you, but I don't think you really need it. Decide what you want to do, and I'll be here if you want to talk. Now, there has to be something better to talk about."

"I have a date," Steven said. "I joined a gym and met this guy there."

"What's he like?" Steven could hear the piqued interest in Marky's voice.

"You won't believe this, but Lane was one of the guys who tormented me in high school."

"No way!" Marky squealed on the other end of the line. "That's too weird for words," he said, cackling. "So is that what you like, being bullied around in bed? Does being thrown into lockers turn you on?" Steven felt himself smiling at Marky's mirthful tirade. "Seriously, don't you find that a little strange?"

"I did, I guess, but he's so different now I really don't think about it much."

"Have you told him?" Marky asked, all mirth gone from his voice.

"Yeah. He had a hard time with it at first, and I'm not convinced he's really sorted through everything that dating someone with HIV entails, but he seems willing to try. He asked me out before he knew, but repeated the invitation afterwards, so that's a good sign I guess."

"You guess? I'd say you hit the jackpot."

"I don't know," Steven replied, chewing on his lower lip.

"I know that voice," Marky scolded lightly. "This isn't about him and you know it. You've shut yourself off ever since the diagnosis, and that's not healthy and you know it. Your support group said the same thing. Go out with Lane, have a good time, and don't worry about it. Take things slow, but it's time you rejoined the human race again and did something besides work." Marky halted, and Steven could almost hear him thinking on the other side of the line. "Just because you have HIV doesn't mean you aren't worthy of being loved."

Steven stared at the phone, wondering if that was really the heart of the issue. "Even my parents...."

"I know how you feel, because I felt the same way for a long time. Maybe that's why we've always been such good friends."

Steven felt the emotions that had been building in him ever since he'd seen his mother begin to boil over, and he needed to hang up the phone, but he couldn't, because if he did, he'd be alone again, so he held tighter to the small lifeline in his hand. "How can I expect anyone to love me when my own parents...." Steven broke down sobbing as he sat on the edge of the bed—something he could never remember doing before. He hadn't cried all those years ago when they'd first rejected him, or any time since, so why he was crying now seemed to be a mystery, but he couldn't stop it. "My own parents didn't love me, so how could anyone else?" he managed to croak into the phone, doing his best to get himself under control as he held on to the phone, listening to the sound of his friend's voice.

"It has nothing to do with you," Marky said softly, the words somehow slicing through his pain. "The way your parents feel or felt is their problem, not yours. You are worthy of being loved and always have been. I've loved you almost from the day we met, and you're my best friend." He heard Marky's voice break on the other end of the line. "And you know I could never love a loser, so you just need to get over yourself." Marky sniffled as Steven looked around the room, reaching for a tissue from the box next to the bed.

"I don't know why I'm so emotional all the time," Steven said after taking a deep breath and wiping his running nose.

"It's that place," Marky huffed in exasperation. "I told you to stay here where we love you, but nooooo," Marky crooned, and Steven couldn't help smiling at his friend's antics. The man was the biggest queen he knew, and Steven loved him for it. "There's a lot of hurt there that you haven't dealt with, and it's probably catching up with you," he added seriously. "But don't worry about it. Just have a good time with Lane." Steven loved how Marky could change topics on a dime. "By the way, you have to tell me all about him. Is he hot? You said you met him at the gym—have you seen him naked yet?"

"Yes and yes," Steven answered, his face breaking into a smile. "He's broad and tall with muscles to die for and a tattoo that covers his shoulder...." Steven told Marky what he knew about Lane, leaving out certain details that he wasn't about to divulge no matter how many times the big queen asked.

"I was thinking of coming out for a visit this summer," Marky told him. "I have vacation in June."

"That would be great," Steven said, already feeling his spirits perk up. "Hopefully I'll have a house by then. Tomorrow I have some appointments with the Realtor to see some places, and if I'm lucky, there'll be something I like." Steven went on to tell Marky everything that had happened since the last time they'd talked, and by the time he hung up, Steven was feeling much better and a lot less alone.

IV

STEVEN pulled off his shirt, looking in the closet to see if he had anything clean that he liked better. He'd already tried on almost every pair of pants and every clean shirt he had with him, and he still wasn't sure he looked okay. He wished he'd thought to ask Lane where they were going, but he hadn't, so he wanted to look dressy, but not too dressy. God, he was going to go crazy. Finally, he pulled on the shirt he'd just taken off and decided that was that. Picking up the rest of his clothes, he hung them back in the closet. This was it and he'd made a decision. Pulling out a leather jacket from the closet, he closed the door. He checked himself in the bathroom mirror before taking his keys and wallet from the table and leaving the room.

In the lobby, he looked around and didn't see Lane until the man stood up, moving away from one of the chairs near the fireplace. He looked stunning in black jeans and a black silk shirt that shimmered slightly in the light. "You look nice," Lane said softly, and Steven smiled, the look on Lane's face telling him Lane wasn't just saying that.

"So do you." Steven didn't move, looking into Lane's eyes, taking him in, and seeing Lane doing the same thing. "Where are we going for dinner?" he asked softly, not really wanting to break the spell, but he figured the people around them were going to start wondering what was going on pretty soon.

"I know this small, out-of-the-way Italian place, and I thought we could go there if that's okay." Lane nearly fidgeted, and Steven smiled, seeing that Lane was as nervous as he was.

"I love Italian," Steven said, and it was Lane's turn to smile. Pulling on his jacket, Steven followed Lane out of the lobby and to his car, figuring he'd let him drive since Lane knew where the restaurant was. He'd expected a flashy car, but Lane drove a basic sedan. After Lane unlocked the doors, Steven got inside and waited. Lane opened his door before climbing into the driver's seat, but he didn't start the car right away, and to Steven's surprise, Lane leaned across the seat, touching his cheek lightly as he kissed him.

Steven felt the light, almost sweet touch of Lane's kiss. He blinked twice, making sure this was real, but Lane was still kissing him, and Steven knew it wasn't a figment of his imagination. Lane's seat crinkled slightly, and the kiss lessened before fading away. Opening his eyes and blinking, Steven saw Lane's eyes shining back at him, and he swallowed hard, almost unable to breathe. "Why?" he murmured just above his breath. A kiss had been the last thing he'd expected, even after the way Lane had looked at him in the lobby.

"Why not, Steven?" Lane asked, still looking at him.

"I guess I expected you to be more reticent. Kissing is safe, but...." A finger touched his lips, and Steven leaned into the light touch before he could stop himself, hearing a small gasp from Lane. Tilting his head slightly, Steven let his confusion show in his expression.

"No one has touched you in a long time, have they?" Lane asked softly, and Steven lowered his eyes. "Not since you found out, right?"

Steven nodded his answer before shrugging. "That part of my life is over, remember?"

Lane shook his head. "No, it's not." Lane's hand lifted his uninjured one, fingers sliding along Steven's, warm skin making soft contact. "You deserve to be touched and kissed and held just as much as the next person." Lane's grasp tightened just a little to make his point. "I know I hurt you last week, and I'm sorry. I can only claim ignorance." Lane's fingers slipped away from Steven's, and then he felt the soft touch of skin on his arm, caressing gently before drifting away again. Slowly, Lane turned and started the car, but Steven could almost still feel Lane's warmth on his skin. Sitting back, he watched Lane as they rode toward the restaurant, talking about nothing, but making it feel important.

The drive to the restaurant took longer than Steven expected, since it involved a trip to the far east side of Harrisburg. They pulled into what looked like a shopping center with a small restaurant at the end. "It may not look like much, but they have the best Italian food in town. It's family-owned, with mom and grandma doing most of the cooking."

"Sounds good," Steven replied to Lane's explanation before opening his door and getting out of the car. They walked together across the parking lot, Lane holding the restaurant door for him, and they were seated right away at a table in one of the corners. The restaurant appeared clean and fresh, with pictures on the walls and none of the kitschy Italian touches that so often took over places like this. Their server brought menus and filled their water glasses before taking drink orders. "This is really nice," Steven complimented.

"The food is even better," Lane said with a smile before looking over his menu. Steven noticed that Lane set his aside pretty quickly. Steven took a few minutes before settling on the veal piccata and putting down his menu too. "Did you have a nice afternoon?"

"I guess," Steven answered. "I went to lunch with Dan and then hung around the hotel. I worked a little." *Very little.* His mind wouldn't let him settle, but he didn't really want to tell Lane all that. "I saw my mother at the restaurant. She recognized me. Well, I think she did anyway."

The server brought their drinks. "Did you talk to her?" Lane asked once the server had left.

"No. It's been too long." Steven didn't really want to get into this, but couldn't seem to find a graceful way to change the subject. "I spoke to my best friend, and he said I should go see her."

"You had told me it's been a long time."

"Yeah, and I'm not sure I want to open everything up again." Steven gulped his water, trying to think of something else to talk about.

"If you don't mind my saying, I think it may already be opened up. If just seeing her briefly is weighing on your mind, then it might be best to go for a visit and find out where things stand. You don't have anything to lose, and your parents just might surprise you. I bet they've missed you all these years but didn't know how to approach you, either."

Steven scoffed. "Somehow I doubt that."

"You won't find out until you try," Lane said, and Steven glowered at him for a second. He could almost see Lane mentally backing off, his eyes shifting from Steven's to the table. He hadn't meant to make Lane feel bad.

"Sorry," Steven said. "It's not your fault. It just seems that lately everyone has advice about what I should do, and I think I simply need some time to think."

"No, I shouldn't have pushed. It's one of the things that make me a good physical therapist, but it gets in the way sometimes." Lane didn't say anything more. "Let's change the subject. You told me you got in shape in college. Did you ever play any sports?"

Steven felt the tension lift like a stage curtain. "I played golf a few times, but it bored me to tears. I had some friends who decided to take up racquetball, and they convinced me to play with them." Steven smiled at the memory. "The first time I served, the ball hit the back wall and bounced right back, smacking me on the forehead." Steven saw Lane stifle a laugh and chuckled at the memory. "I realized right then that it wasn't my game."

"That really happened?"

"Swear to God. I had a bruise in the middle of my forehead for a week." Steven laughed. "I was always a bit of a klutz when it came to balls. The only balls I was ever good with are attached." Lane, who'd reached for his water, swallowed quickly, looking like he was about to spray the table, and Steven handed him a napkin, chuckling. Lane wiped his mouth, setting his glass on the table, still smiling. "Eventually I gave up and just lifted weights." He'd also found out very quickly that with slimming down and building his muscles came a lot of attention, especially once his skin cleared and he got over his shyness. A hedonistic buffet had opened to him, and he'd gorged himself.

"In college I played football for a couple years, but gave it up. I may have been a star in high school, but I learned pretty quickly that in college, the price was too high, the pressure to perform at the expense of everything else too great," Lane explained and then chuckled, and Steven waited to learn the source of his amusement. "It's sort of ironic—in college, you discovered the benefits of exercise, and I discovered I had a brain and learned how to use it. I dropped the rigorous sports regimen and really worked hard in my junior and senior years. I also managed to combine both experiences in physical therapy because I specialize in sports rehabilitation. I see more kids with over-use injuries because the coaches simply work these kids until their bodies can't take any more. Then they just move on."

"Did you have any permanent injuries? I know I hurt myself early on and spent time nursing sore shoulders." Steven's hand reflexively went to his left shoulder, rubbing slightly. "It still aches sometimes when I move just right." Their server returned, bringing bread and taking their orders, refilling their drinks.

"Where were we?" Lane asked once the server had left. "Oh yeah. By the time I was through with football, I had knee problems, neck problems, and my shoulders ached all the time. When I went to the doctors, they told me I'd quit just before I did permanent damage. They sent me to therapy, and I went for almost a year before the pain was largely gone." Lane's voice had slowly risen, and Steven could tell this was something he felt very strongly about. "That's why I teach my personal training clients proper form first and foremost."

"I hadn't really noticed that," Steven said, coloring slightly, and he saw Lane's eyebrows rise questioningly. Steven picked up his glass as cover, but Lane kept looking at him and wasn't going to let it go. "I'm usually too busy looking at you," Steven added, trying to keep himself from blushing like a schoolkid, especially since his mind flashed on the image of Lane naked as he got out of the shower. Thankfully, their server returned with their salads, and that gave Steven a chance to concentrate on something else, or so he thought.

"So you were looking at me," Lane commented mischievously between bites.

"You know I was, so you don't have to be all coy and stuff," Steven retorted before chomping on a bite of lettuce. "In fact, you were a downright show-off if you want to know the truth." He'd definitely been showing off in the shower, but Steven kept that to himself, and now it was Lane's turn to blush slightly under his richly colored skin.

After they finished their salads, the server took their plates, replacing them with their main courses. Steven felt surprisingly at ease, and for the first time he could remember in the past two years, he found he'd completely forgotten about what he'd come to think of as his condition. Since his diagnosis, it had never been far from his thoughts, but here with Lane, that worry and immediacy seemed to recede, and he could laugh and just be. It felt good.

The rest of dinner flew by in a blur of laughter and stories he hadn't told anyone in years. The food, the conversation, everything combined to make one of the best evenings he could remember. With their plates cleared, they lingered over a cup of coffee before Lane reached for the check. "I asked you to dinner," he scolded lightly when Steven balked, placing his credit card in the folder and handing it to the server before Steven could complain further.

With the check paid, they left the restaurant, heading back to Lane's car. Steven didn't know what Lane had planned next, but he was curious and didn't really want the evening to end, so when Lane drove them back to his hotel, disappointment bloomed in his chest. Lane parked in one of the spaces and turned off the car. Steven stared out the windshield, trying not to let his feelings show on his face. A gentle touch to his cheek made him turn, and Lane leaned closer, kissing him again. This time Lane unfastened his seatbelt, scooting closer, deepening the kiss as his hand stroked the skin of Steven's arm. Steven moaned softly, deep in his throat, and Lane backed away. Steven blinked, wondering if he'd done something wrong, but Lane smiled and opened his door. Getting out of the car, he walked around to Steven's side and opened the door, following behind him as he walked into his hotel.

"I have beer in my room if you'd like one," Steven offered, hoping Lane would stick around a little while.

"That'd be nice," Lane said as he followed him down the hallway, waiting until Steven opened his door. Once inside the room, the door closed and Lane pulled him close, kissing him again. At first Steven felt as though he should resist, but Lane felt too good holding him and kissing him. The room seemed to fill with all these soft sounds, and very quickly, Steven realized they were coming from him. Then Lane softened the kiss, their mouths separating, but his arms still holding him. "Have you had anyone touch you in the last two years?"

"You mean like doctors? Yeah, plenty."

"No, I mean like someone who cares for you." Steven shook his head. "I thought so. You act completely touch-starved, like you've craved someone's touch for months and months."

"It's not safe," Steven said softly, his resistance crumbling quickly.

"Touch is perfectly safe as long as you or I don't have any open wounds. I don't, do you?"

Steven shook his head. "Only my hand and it's nearly healed." Steven showed him, the skin red, but closed. Lane tightened his arms around him, and Steven rested his head against Lane's shoulders, holding him back. He found he desperately needed to be close to someone, and he wanted it to be Lane, but he still wasn't sure.

"Do you trust me, Steven?" Lane asked, and Steven found himself looking into those deep eyes.

Steven thought for a few moments. *Did he trust Lane?* With their history, he knew he probably shouldn't, but that was a long time ago, and surprisingly, Steven found that he did trust him. If Lane could overcome his initial fear enough to kiss him, then maybe a degree of trust was justified. "Yes," Steven answered softly, feeling Lane guide him toward the bed, and this time Steven balked, his body stiffening.

"Trust me, Steven. I will do nothing to hurt you or endanger either of us, but you need this. You need to feel cared for, and you need to feel truly alive again." Lane's words washed over him like a warm Caribbean wave, carrying him as Lane pressed him down onto the bed, continuing to kiss him. The bed dipped beneath him and his head sank into the pillow as Steven felt one of Lane's hands beneath his shirt, his warm hand against his skin, moving in slow, small circles.

"Lane, you know I can never...." Steven didn't know how to say what he wanted without breaking the spell Lane seemed to be weaving around them. Thankfully, Lane seemed to understand.

"There are many ways to show affection, and most of them do not involve fucking," Lane told him, his breath flowing warmly over Steven's lips. "Will you let me show you?"

"Yes." Steven was already too far gone to think of resisting anything. Lane's gentle touch had awakened a need in him he hadn't even known was missing. He'd written off intimacy from his life and hadn't realized just how much he'd missed it. Steven arched lightly into Lane's touch as that strong hand roamed further up his chest, fingers bumping lightly over his nipples.

"Just relax," Lane crooned, his voice soothing, wrapping him in a blanket of vocal warmth. "Close your eyes, let your cares go, and release all the tension from your muscles." Steven did as Lane asked, everything going dark as his eyelids seemed heavy all of a sudden. "That's it," Lane encouraged as Steven felt fingers working the buttons of his shirt. Cool air flowed over his skin, and he shivered, but not entirely from the chill, as his shirt parted. Heat spread over his skin as he heard and felt Lane place kisses along his stomach, and he did his best not to giggle and squirm as Lane's tongue tickled his flesh. "Ticklish, are you?" Thankfully, Lane moved on, fingers finding spots that made him moan and wriggle on the bed.

The sensation stopped, and Steven fought an urge to open his eyes and look around. Then hands, firm and sure, gripped his arm, fingers working deeply into his muscles until lifting it felt like a chore. The other got the same treatment before the magic hands pulled away again. This time, he waited, wondering what was next, but drawing pleasure from the unexpected.

A chink, pressure around his waist, and his pants opened. Steven wanted to caution Lane again, but didn't want to break the spell. He felt his pants lower and lifted his hips, letting Lane pull his pants off, and then warm hands massaged his legs, working deep into muscle. Starting at his feet, thumbs pressed against the bottoms, stroking from heel to toe, working the tension away, then his ankle and calf, the muscles letting go. Steven's mind began to float as Lane's hands worked the muscles on one of his thighs. A tremble went through him as Lane's fingers worked between his legs before retreating again. Steven didn't have to open his eyes to know his boxers were probably tented. "Do you know how stunning you look right now?" Lane asked, his hands not stopping or even breaking their long, slow rhythm. "Your eyes closed, skin flushed, body relaxed and excited at the same time." Lane's hands skipped to his other leg, working away the tension.

"When did you learn to do this?" Steven mumbled through his haze of relaxed desire.

"It's part of being a good therapist. One of the requirements is having magic fingers," Lane said, and Steven felt those fingers skim along the fabric of his boxers, making him gasp as he demonstrated just how magical those fingers could be. Steven bit his lower lip to keep from crying out.

When he was done, Lane gently rolled him over. His face buried in the pillow, Steven felt the bed shake as Lane stepped off, and he heard muffled sounds, then he felt what seemed to be a leg slide along his as Lane's weight settled just below his hips. "I found some lotion," Lane whispered softly, leaning forward, and Steven gasped as he felt Lane's chest press to his back, warm skin touching his. His first reaction was concern, and then Lane began to hum very softly, pressing them together, and Steven pressed back, needing to intensify the contact. He was lost and he knew it.

Lane's weight lifted, settling back, before cool, lotioned hands worked from his lower back all the way to his shoulders. With each long, firm stroke, Steven found himself moaning, willing Lane's hands not to stop. And they didn't. All sense of time fell away as Steven gave himself completely into Lane's hands. His boxers slipped away, and Steven barely comprehended it. Lane's massage extended to his butt and the very top of his lower legs. Skin he figured would never be touched by another person was languidly and lovingly worked until he felt his body had nearly turned to water.

"How do you feel now?" Lane asked him, and Steven sighed deeply, expelling every bit of air from his lungs before inhaling a deep, cleansing breath. "That's better. Keep doing that as you roll onto your back again. Keep your eyes closed and trust me." Steven managed a nod as his blissful state left him completely malleable. Lane's weight shifted, and Steven heard a soft tear. Gasping softly, he felt Lane's hand glide down his shaft, leaving tightness behind. "Trust me, remember," Lane soothed, and Steven realized Lane had rolled a condom onto him. "I want you to give yourself to me." Lane's lips touched his in a searing kiss that Steven felt deep inside as a slick hand slipped around his length, gripping hard, his cry swallowed by their kiss.

Steven could barely breathe as Lane's hands played his body like an instrument. After giving up on contact like this for so long, it was as though his very skin cried out for it, and the slight twisting motion Lane used with his hands made spots flash behind Steven's closed eyes. "What about you?" he asked softly, feeling rather selfish.

"I'll be fine," Lane answered, his hand moving faster, driving Steven wild, his hips bucking into Lane's hand. "You're so beautiful like this," Lane told him, "all laid out for me, trusting me. It's the sexiest thing I've ever seen in my life." Steven's mind soared at those words, his loose muscles contracting as his release built from deep in his being. Lane tightened his grip, stroking Steven harder, driving the release that he could no longer control. Crying out as his emotions broke along with his control, he came, tears leaking from behind his eyelids.

Steven gasped for breath as the lights behind his eyes dulled and what sounded like the roar of the ocean in his ears died away. Opening his eyes, he was greeted by Lane's eyes shining back in the light of the small desk lamp. "And you?" Steven asked, propping himself up on his elbows, seeing the wet spot on the front of Lane's briefs. "I guess I shouldn't worry."

"No." Lane climbed off the bed, standing nearby. "It's probably best if you clean yourself up."

Steven got off the bed, his legs feeling like limp noodles as he made his way to the bathroom. Stripping off the condom, he threw it away and cleaned himself up, carefully washing his skin before staring at himself in the mirror. His skin still tingled from Lane's touch, and he couldn't remember that happening before, but maybe he just wasn't remembering. Turning off the light, he stepped out, half expecting Lane to be pulling on his pants, getting ready to leave.

Instead, he saw him reclining on the bed, naked and beautiful, lying on his side, head resting on his hand with the covers pulled back. Lane patted the bed in front of him, and Steven stepped forward, letting Lane tug him into the bed, pulling the covers over both of them.

"I don't have to stay if you'd rather I leave," Lane said softly, but Steven didn't answer, burrowing closer to the warmth in his bed in the air-conditioned room.

"I was going to say something similar to you," Steven told him, glad that Lane was staying with him. He'd rarely had men he'd been intimate with stay the night. "You made me feel…." Steven's voice trailed off as he found it difficult to put what Lane had done to him into words.

"I think that says it well enough—I made you feel. You've shut yourself off for a long time, Steven. It's time you let yourself feel again, and maybe start to live again."

Steven nodded against Lane's chest, his hands skimming lightly over his bronzed skin. "I'm just so scared of passing this on to someone else. It's hard when the safest thing for everyone is for me to keep to myself and not put anyone at risk."

Lane stroked his belly. "You're not Typhoid Mary, and you don't need to be locked away from the rest of humanity. You don't have to lock your heart away, either." Lane huffed lightly. "I know my own track record in that area isn't the greatest, but I felt something tonight—not just when we were in bed, but at dinner, and whenever you smile at me." Lane's face moved closer to his, their kiss soft and sweet. "You, lying on this bed, all smooth skin with your eyes closed and your mouth open in wonder was the sexiest, hottest sight I could ever hope to see. You showed me tonight that there are few things more wonderful than being trusted like that."

Steven didn't know what to say, so he said nothing, taking the words and holding on to them. He wasn't sure he'd hear them again, and he wanted to remember them.

Settling next to Lane, he let himself enjoy being held, his skin caressed. Right now, if he were a cat, he'd be purring.

Lane slipped out of the bed, and Steven watched him through half-lidded eyes, taking in his skin and strength and the loveliest behind he'd ever seen. The light clicked off and Lane walked back to the bed, rejoining him, arms wrapping around him without saying a word. Steven closed his eyes, listening to Lane's soft breathing.

V

STEVEN hummed softly to himself as he finished the last of his work for the week. He'd actually found a house earlier in the week and made an offer. He and the sellers had gone back and forth a few times before agreeing on a price. The seller's expectations had been unrealistic, and it had taken some time for Steven to wear them down, but he had. He was humming now, because Lane had asked if he could see the house, and Steven had made arrangements with the sellers to take measurements that evening. It made him happy that Lane wanted to see what would be his new home. Turning off his computer, Steven grabbed his jacket and computer bag, saying good night to his team before leaving the office.

Normally, he'd drive to the gym to meet the guys, but tonight he hurried to his car so he could meet the Realtor and Lane at the house. Traffic held him up, but there was nothing he could do, and he arrived a few minutes late, recognizing Lane's and his Realtor's cars. Getting out, he greeted both of them, introducing Lane to Debbie.

"The owners are away for the weekend, making their moving plans, so you can take your time," she told them, and Steven felt a stab of excitement run through him.

"It looks nice, Steven," Lane told him as they approached the sidewalk in front. "I'm thinking there's even space for a few chairs on the front porch."

"Yes," Debbie said, "and the entire house was painted last year."

Steven saw Lane look up. "I'm not being mean, but it looks like half a house."

Steven laughed as Debbie explained, "It is, sort of. The house is half of a double house, but the other side was never constructed. The house was built in 1898, and the builder apparently had the plans for a full double house, but just built the one side. Come around to the backyard before we go inside—I want you to see the garden." Debbie started toward the side of the house. "I spent some time with the sellers' Realtor yesterday, and he told me that the previous owners had the brick tuck-pointed two years ago. At the same time they had the gutters and porch roof replaced." She approached the gate, pushing it open as she continued talking. "The owners did all the gardening themselves." Debbie turned to him, and Steven pulled his eyes away from the house to the small immaculate yard on three levels.

"This is amazing," Lane whispered softly.

Steven stood on the first level with its patio shaded by large trees around the edge, looking toward the second level with its small lawn bordered by beds filled with blooms, and then down to the third level with its colonial knot garden around a small fountain. The entire yard was made private by a manicured hedge. "It feels almost like a secret place," Steven murmured to himself before turning to Lane. "When I saw the house before, it was already dark, and we really couldn't see much back here."

"I probably would have bought the house just for this garden," Lane told him, bursting into a huge smile.

Leaving the garden reluctantly, Steven followed Debbie around to the front. The house wasn't huge, by any means, but it had felt cozy to Steven. And when he'd first walked through the front door, something deep inside told him he was home, and he got that same feeling now as he stepped into the nice-sized living room. "The sellers asked to take the draperies, so you'll want to think about what you'd like to do," Debbie told him, and Steven nodded almost absently as Lane squeezed his hand.

"I love that the woodwork was never painted," Lane said as he looked around the room, and Steven found himself following his gaze, sort of feeling the way he'd always thought he'd feel looking at a first house with a partner, but he pushed that aside. It was way too soon for thoughts like that.

"There's a big dining room and a nice-sized kitchen," Steven commented as he wandered through the first floor. Leaving Debbie in the living room, he and Lane wandered through the rest of the lower floor. "What do you think?"

"It's very nice," Lane said, opening the laundry room door off the kitchen. "Someone has taken good care of this house." Lane closed the door again. "You're really excited about this, aren't you?"

"Yeah. This is my first real house. In Chicago, all I could afford was a condo, but now I'll have my own yard and everything." Steven could hear the excitement in his own voice, and Lane leaned toward him, giving him a quick kiss. "Let's go upstairs."

Debbie waited in the living room as they both climbed the stairs, looking in each of the two bedrooms. "The one thing this house doesn't have that I wish it did is a fireplace," Steven commented as he walked into what would be the guest room before walking to the master bedroom. The room was large enough for a queen-size bed. "The wallpaper in both these rooms needs to go, but I can do that." Steven turned around and found himself wrapped in Lane's arms, his eyes closing as Lane leaned in for a deep kiss. Suddenly, he'd spent enough time exploring the house and was ready to leave, but not until Lane stopped kissing him, which didn't seem like anytime soon—and that was fine with him.

Eventually, though, they parted, and Steven led them back down the stairs and saw the quizzical look on Debbie's face. He must have had one of those just-kissed looks, because Debbie's mouth turned to a grin as she walked toward the front door, both of them following her out.

After confirming their upcoming appointments, Debbie left with a wave. "Would you like to get some dinner?" Steven asked, and Lane nodded. "I haven't had a chance to explore the area really well, but we can probably find something to eat."

"Why don't we drive back near your hotel? There are restaurants there, and afterwards we can go to your place." Lane's expression left no doubt about what he had in mind.

Pulling into the parking lot of the small sandwich shop near his hotel half an hour later, Steven saw Lane's car and parked next to it. He found Lane sitting at a table inside. Steven sat down, still excited from seeing his future home again. Their server came to the table. "Can I get you drinks awhile?" she asked in her best central Pennsylvania vernacular, cracking her gum.

"Would you give us a minute?" Lane asked, turning to Steven when she was gone. "Do you really want to eat here?"

Steven looked at the menu before shaking his head. "Not really."

"Then let's go," Lane threw a dollar on the table, and they walked to the exit. "Park your car at your hotel, and I'll meet you there in a few minutes." Lane got in his car and Steven did the same, pulling out and driving the short distance to the hotel. Getting out, he looked around, and a few minutes later, saw Lane's car pull to a stop near him.

"Where are we going?" Steven asked once he was buckled in, but Lane was already pulling out of the lot.

"Someplace really special," Lane answered with a wicked grin, speeding out onto the street before accelerating onto the freeway. Ten minutes later, they were traveling through a residential area, and Steven wondered what kind of restaurant they could be heading for when they pulled up in front of a suburban house.

"Lane?"

He turned in the seat. "This is my mom's. I called her, and she told me to come for dinner and invited you as well."

Steven swallowed hard. "Lane, you want me to meet your mother—now? I'm not dressed for that, and I don't have anything for her."

"You don't need anything, and you look fine."

"Lane, I am not going to meet your mother empty-handed." Steven put his arms over his chest. "You could have warned me, you know. At least you could have let me change my shirt at the hotel." He glared across the seat, seeing some of the light go out of Lane's expression, and he breathed out slowly, knowing Lane had meant well. "Is there a grocery store nearby?"

"Yes."

"Then let's go there. At least I can get some flowers or something." Steven let his face soften. He hadn't really been angry, just taken a bit by surprise. Reaching across the seat, Steven touched Lane's leg, squeezing lightly. Lane started the engine, driving him to the store. "Do you want to go in with me?"

"Sure," Lane told him as he found a place to park. "I really didn't mean to spring this on you. I was going to call for a reservation at a restaurant, then my mom called and wouldn't take no for an answer. I told her I was with someone, and she said, quote, 'Bring him along'. My mother knows me pretty well."

"Okay, but I'm still not arriving empty-handed." Steven opened his door and waited for Lane before going into the large store. He headed right for the flower area, picking out a bouquet of bright spring flowers. After paying for them, Steven walked toward the exit, turning to smile at Lane. "Now I'm ready to meet your mother, but I still wish I'd had a chance to change clothes."

Lane huffed exaggeratedly, but smiled back, saying, "You're not going to let me off the hook for that, are you?"

Steven opened his door, sliding into the seat, waiting for Lane to join him in the car. "You can make it up to me later." Steven could hardly believe he was being so forward. Yes, he and Lane had spent time together, but he couldn't let himself get too emotionally involved. Steven figured that Lane would wake up one day soon and realize that being with him was just too much trouble.

"I'll be sure to remember that," Lane told him as he drove back the way they had come, parking in front of the house. Steven got out of the car, following Lane up the walk to the front door. Lane opened it and walked inside while Steven hung back, not feeling completely comfortable.

"Come in, young man," the woman Steven assumed was Lane's mother said as she appeared in the doorway, wiping her hands on an apron.

"Hello, Mrs. Parkinson," Steven said, handing her the flowers. "I'm Steven and it's nice to meet you." Steven could see where Lane got his looks—in her day his mother had obviously been quite a looker, with high cheekbones and bright eyes.

"Please, call me Evelyn. Being called Mrs. Parkinson reminds me of my mother-in-law, and that woman is best left forgotten," she said, and Steven saw where Lane got his incredible smile. He shook her hand, and she ushered him into her living room, filled with the pictures and memories of a lifetime, including pictures of a man in uniform.

"That's my dad," Lane explained, picking up one of the photographs. "He was killed during the first Gulf war." Lane looked far away for a few seconds and then set the picture back on the table.

"You two must be hungry. Come on into the kitchen. I've got salads ready, and the steaks are ready for the broiler." She hurried around the kitchen, placing a huge bowl of salad on the table along with fresh rolls and bottles of salad dressing. A mountain of mashed potatoes appeared as well before Evelyn opened the oven door, the sound and smell of sizzling steaks filling the room. Steven felt his stomach rumble, but waited along with Lane for Evelyn to join them. "Go ahead and eat," she told them, "I'll be along in a minute." Steven watched as Lane began dishing up salad, passing him the bowl before passing the rolls as well. Neither of them ate until Evelyn joined them.

"So, Steven," Evelyn said once she sat down, her eyes sparkling with a bit of mischief as she set down her fork, "how did you meet my son?"

Steven gulped slightly, swallowing his bite of creamy mashed potatoes, wondering if that look was directed at him or not. "We knew each other in high school, sort of, but I really met him a few weeks ago at the gym. My job moved me back to town."

"You know my son is gay," she said matter-of-factly, and Steven could tell Lane's mother was a bit of a rascal.

"Yes." Steven tried not to look at Lane, but couldn't help himself. "At least, I hope so, after last night." He winked at Lane and saw him squirm on his chair, but the comment didn't seem to faze Evelyn in the least.

"Good. I worried about him for the longest time. I knew he was gay for years before he told me." She leaned closer, and Steven wondered which of Lane's secrets she was about to reveal now. "I kept hoping he'd say something, but he didn't. Instead he got meaner and more withdrawn."

"Mom, Steven doesn't need to hear about all this."

"Okay, okay," she responded before continuing to eat. Regardless of what she said, it was obvious by the looks she gave her son that Evelyn was very proud of Lane. "So, is Steven your boyfriend?"

"Yes, Mom," Lane answered right away, and Steven felt his eyes widen slightly before doing his best to keep the look of pleasant surprise off his face. He hadn't thought of Lane as his boyfriend, but it pleased him immensely that Lane thought of him that way. He'd been trying to keep his feelings for Lane under control, and regardless, he knew they'd grown, anyway. Steven was both relieved and pleased that he wasn't alone. "Steven is very special."

"I knew that," she added softly. "You've never brought your boyfriends home before." She turned her attention to the table, looking at Lane's and then Steven's plate. "Eat up, there's plenty more." She reached across the table, patting Steven's hand. "You're both way too skinny. Need some meat on your bones." Her hand slipped away, and Steven took a second helping of potatoes to make her happy, knowing he'd have to work extra hard at the gym tomorrow. "Are your parents still in town?" Evelyn asked, and Steven felt a sharp pang of loss.

"Steven's folks live in the area, but he hasn't really seen them in years. They don't accept him." Lane looked sad, and Steven felt Lane touch his knee under the table.

"I haven't seen them since I went away to college. I send a card at the holidays every year, but I haven't heard from them in over a decade."

"That's terrible," Evelyn said indignantly, looking at Lane, eyes blazing. Steven could tell she wanted to say more, but thankfully she went back to her food, attacking her slice of meat, fork scraping the plate.

"It's been a long time," Steven said, trying not to sigh. "Things are the way they are. So, Evelyn, what do you do?" he asked, changing the subject.

"Mom's a photographer," Lane answered proudly.

"I do portraits and weddings now. I used to do art shows and things like that right after Lane left for college, but not anymore," she answered, very excited. "I get all kinds of commissions." A wry smile formed on her face. "I even get people who want me to take boudoir pictures."

"Do you do those?"

"Of course," she answered brightly. "I had a man who wanted me to take pictures of him for his partner's fortieth birthday present. He was very handsome, and a few months later, both he and his partner had portraits taken. Can you image me alone with two gorgeous half-naked men? It was fabulous, and they were so nice and very loving to one another." Evelyn patted Lane's hand. "That's what I want for you."

Steven had finished eating and couldn't eat another bite. Getting up from the table, he helped carry the dishes into the kitchen over Evelyn's protests before settling on a chair in the living room, where she brought in coffee and a plate of homemade chocolate chip cookies. "You're trying to make me fat, aren't you?" Steven said to Evelyn with a grin as he took a cookie. "I can never resist these."

"Extra gym time tomorrow," Lane told him with a wink, waiting until Evelyn left the room before adding, "you'll need the energy later." Steven somehow kept from blushing as Evelyn came back into the room. They spent time just talking, with Evelyn telling him stories of what Lane was like as a child, and to his surprise, he could see much more of the Lane he knew now in those stories than the Lane he recalled from his high school memories. It was comforting.

"We should get going," Lane told his mother as he stood up, taking his and Steven's dishes to the kitchen before returning to take his mother's, as well. Evelyn hugged Lane goodbye, and to Steven's surprise, she hugged him too.

"Come back again soon," she told him before giving him another squeeze, then letting her arms slide away.

"I will. Thank you," Steven answered before following Lane out of the house and down the walk to the car. "Your mom is great," Steven told Lane once he had his seatbelt fastened.

"That she is," Lane agreed with a smile and started the car. "I couldn't have asked for anyone more supporting or caring."

Steven couldn't help wishing he'd had that kind of support from his own family. But he hadn't, and there was nothing he could do to change that. It was best not to dwell on it. "Where are we going?" Steven asked when he realized they weren't heading back to his hotel.

"My place," Lane answered, and Steven felt a surge of energetic desire shoot through him as he found himself nodding, not daring to actually say anything. A short, silent drive later, Lane pulled up in front of his place, leading Steven inside. He'd been here before, finding it clean and modern, but sort of empty. Steven couldn't place why, but it felt rather sterile and unlike Lane. Not that he had much time to think about it, because as soon as the door closed, Lane had him pressed back against it, hands under his shirt, drawing it up and over his head. As soon as the blue fabric slipped over his eyes, he felt Lane's lips on his. To say it was a kiss was an understatement—it felt almost like a possession, like Lane was staking his claim, and that if Steven didn't say something now, he was going to quickly lose his chance. Arms around Lane's waist, Steven held on, and Lane moved closer, his big body holding him tight, his scent filling Steven's senses as Steven's head began to reel.

"Lane," Steven gasped softly, his breath ragged, knees beginning to buckle.

"I know," he answered, hugging Steven tight as he moved them through the house and into the bedroom. The door closed behind them, and Steven tried to figure out where he was in the dark room, but between Lane nuzzling his neck and soft fingers tweaking his nipples, thoughts of everything except what Lane was doing to him flew from his mind.

"What are you doing to me?" Steven gasped, unable to ever remember feeling all floaty, as his legs gave out from beneath him. First, he felt as though he were falling, and then he was being caught, the bed stopping him, Lane kissing him. Something clicked inside him, he wasn't sure what, but he gave his pleasure over to Lane. The pillow cushioned his head as he felt Lane open his pants before pulling them down his legs. With a soft click, a dim light switched on, and Steven looked up into Lane's eyes, unable to decipher the warm look that greeted him. Steven knew what he hoped it was, but he couldn't quite let his heart believe.

"Steven, what is it?" Lane asked, barely above a whisper.

He rocked his head on the pillow and saw that expression intensify. "I can't...."

"Can't what?" Lane asked him, eyes on his, the hand that had been stroking lightly coming to a rest on Steven's belly.

Steven swallowed, trying to find the words. "I keep wondering when I'm going to wake up, or when you are."

"I don't understand," Lane told him, his expression turning to one of confusion.

Steven struggled to a seated position, tugging the bedspread around him. "I keep thinking this is a dream and I know it isn't, so then I keep wondering when you're going to wake up and realize you could have so much more than me."

"More than you?" Lane tried to meet his eyes, but Steven kept looking away. "Have you ever heard the saying, 'The heart wants what the heart wants'?" Steven nodded—he had, sort of. "What does your heart say?"

Steven looked toward the wall for a second. He knew what he felt, and it scared him. *What if Lane doesn't feel the same way?* Lane's hand slipped away from his skin, and the warmth went with it, drawing him back, and he realized this was one of those do-or-die, man-or-mouse moments. "It says that I love you," Steven told him before he lost his nerve. "But what if... Lane, what if I give you what I've got? What if...." Steven felt the fear build inside him. Blinking, he tried to keep his emotions under control.

"People have lived for years with partners who have HIV with no issues. You know that. It just means we have to be careful."

"It means more than that. It means I could die, and it means that one mistake and you could die." Steven clutched the blanket around himself like a shield.

"Steven," Lane cooed softly, "it also means I love you too."

Steven stopped, blinking a few times as he took in what Lane had told him. Slowly, his fingers released the bedspread, the fabric falling away as he reached for Lane, who moved back slightly, confusing Steven. "What?"

"You have to trust that I know what I want and what I'm doing, Steven. I haven't felt this way about anyone, and definitely never after just a few weeks." Lane moved closer, his touch returning. "You need to let go of the fear and trust that I know my own heart."

"It's not yours I'm worried about."

"I know." Lane pulled away the last of the bedspread that was covering Steven before easing him back down on the bed. "But you have to trust me with that, too, just like I have to trust you with mine."

Steven agreed as Lane kissed him again. "Someone's wearing way too many clothes," Steven said, and he watched as Lane got off the bed. Steven figured he'd strip quickly and join him, but Lane stepped back, slowly opening his shirt, a huge grin on his face. Steven reached for Lane, but he stepped just out of reach. "Just watch, baby. Don't touch me or yourself," Lane told him as he swayed his hips ever so slightly. Steven groaned softly as Lane pulled his shirt open, shrugging it off before dropping it on the floor. Smooth, tanned skin with the slightest sheen glistened in the light. Shoes came next, thunking onto the floor as Lane kicked them off. Lane's fingers unfastened his belt, pulling it off before it joined the rest.

"Lane," Steven pleaded softly, his fingers aching to touch the smooth, warm skin. Turning around, Lane opened his pants, sliding them down his legs while giving Steven a perfect view of his tight, firm butt. Damn, that was beautiful. Taking off his pants, Lane turned around, his briefs bulging.

Steven swallowed around the lump in his throat as Lane stepped closer. Aching to touch, Steven reached out to Lane with his hand, and this time Lane didn't back away as Steven's hand stroked along the silky skin on his chest and down his stomach. Curling his fingers beneath the elastic, Steven tugged down Lane's briefs. Lane stepped out of them and climbed onto the bed, pulling Steven into his arms. Skin to skin, lips to lips, Lane held him, letting their mutual warmth surround them, cocooning them in their own small world of newly professed love. Steven's heart soared as the last bands surrounding it fell away. Lane loved him back. "I do love you, Lane," Steven murmured just before he was kissed to within an inch of his life.

That floating feeling returned, and Steven held Lane tight, needing something to ground him as Lane's hands and mouth played his body like a fine instrument. Steven squirmed beneath Lane, his body begging for more.

Lane broke their kiss, and Steven groaned at the loss, only to have that groan morph into a cry of delight as Lane's tongue skimmed around a nipple before sucking and scraping his sensitive skin with his teeth. "Please be careful," Steven hissed between clenched teeth as Lane repeated the treatment on the other, moving back and forth, caressing his skin. Steven jumped, thrusting into Lane's hand when his fingers closed around him, gripping him in tight warmth. "Lane, we need…," Steven gasped as the hand around him tightened, stroking lightly, and Steven arched his back, trying desperately for more as Lane stilled his hips.

"You'll get what you want," Lane said as his hand slipped away, "but not quite yet." A hand rested on the center of his chest, right above his heart. "What do you want, Steven?" Lane asked, and Steven cocked his head. "If you could have anything right now, what would it be?"

"I want—" Steven started to say and then stopped himself. What he wanted wasn't something he should be able to expect.

"What is it? Tell me what you want."

"I want you, but we shouldn't do that." Steven lifted his head, looking into Lane's eyes.

"Lie down again," Lane told him, reaching to the bedside table.

"What are you doing?" Steven asked as he watched Lane pull open a drawer.

"Getting ready to make love to you." The drawer closed as Lane found what he was looking for. Packages opened, and Steven felt Lane roll a condom onto him. "Roll over," Lane said, tapping his hip gently. Steven wasn't sure about this, but Lane had asked for his trust, and he'd give it to him. After rolling over, he felt Lane's chest against his back, hands caressing the skin of his arms. "I love you, Steven. You're beautiful and kind," Lane whispered, placing kisses on his neck and down his back, hands trailing behind, making him shiver and shake. "Let me love you, Steven," Lane pleaded, fingers sliding over his butt, and Steven arched his back in anticipation. A finger skimmed his entrance, and Steven tensed. "It's fine, Steven, trust me." Forcing himself to relax, he peered over his shoulder, and Lane held up his hand, a small condom on his finger. His eyes shifting to Lane's face, Steven saw his lover grin before putting his head back on the pillow, giving himself over to Lane, letting his worries go.

The finger breached him slowly, and Steven sighed, a deep, cleansing sigh. He hadn't thought this could ever be part of his life again. Lane crooked his finger, and Steven saw stars. "Lane," Steven cried as he arched his back, willing his lover to do that again. And he did, making Steven forget his own name. "Fuck, Lane, please!"

"I know, baby, but it's been a while, and I need to get you ready, so just relax and...."

Whatever Lane did, Steven felt the air whoosh from his chest with a sharp cry, and he rocked on the bed as every nerve in his body short-circuited at the same time. Then the finger withdrew, the touch sliding away. The tear of another package had him on anticipatory edge, and then he felt Lane pressing for entrance. Slowly, steadily, Lane entered him. Steven's mouth hung open as his body experienced sensations he had long accepted he'd never feel again. He knew skin-on-skin contact wasn't an option, but the feeling of joining with Lane pushed all his last reservations aside. "Lane, God, so big," he gasped, willing his body to adjust, not wanting this to stop for any reason.

"You feel so good," Lane told him with a slight nip to his ear. Turning his head, they kissed sloppily as Lane moved in these small, tiny rhythms that massaged that spot deep inside. Unable to hold his head in that position, Steven buried his face in the pillow as Lane's fingers held his side, and Lane began moving inside him. Long and slow, each stroke drove him damned near to distraction. Steven tried meeting him, but every time he did, Lane slowed down.

"I won't break, Lane."

"Don't want to hurt you," Lane told him, and Steven growled, ramming his hips backward, and Lane got the message. Driving into him, the bed rocking, Steven heard Lane panting behind him as he writhed beneath his strong, forceful lover, adoring every second of it.

"Don't stop, Lane, so close, please...." Steven knew he was begging, but it didn't matter in the least. He'd beg, plead, and grovel to keep Lane driving deep inside him. Each stroke hit that spot, and Steven's body cried out for more.

His climax hit him without warning. One second he was screaming the start of his release at Lane and the next he was gasping for breath as his body reacted with more force than he could remember, driving him even higher. Lane fucked him through it, leaving him wrung out, and still he continued like a machine. Pulling out, Lane rolled Steven onto his back and reentered him with a hard thrust, Lane's cock, thick and long, filling him completely. Steven stared up at Lane, their eyes locking as they moved together, with Steven holding on the bed while Lane took him on a magical ride he never knew was possible. "That's it, sexy man," Lane crooned. "Take all of me and give me everything," Lane demanded, thrusting deep and stopping, pressing against his prostate and not moving. Steven felt his body reacting, the condom still around him stretching as he got hard again. "That's it, baby, show me how I make you feel."

"Lane," Steven breathed, stroking himself as Lane's hands skimmed over his skin, hips snapping against his lover's. With a final thrust that pushed Steven along the mattress, Steven came for the second time as he felt Lane throb inside him.

Steven tried to keep his eyes open, but they closed on their own, his spirit floating as he gasped for breath, every bit of energy drained from him. He felt Lane withdraw, and he felt the bed move, but he couldn't. Still gasping, Steven removed his condom, fumbling for the trash and thankfully finding it near the bed before closing his eyes again, listening, but hearing nothing. The next thing he remembered was Lane climbing into bed, covers being pulled over him, and arms holding him close as he drifted on warm, blissful clouds.

Waking some time later, he felt Lane's breath on his skin. Slowly, Steven rolled over to face Lane. Pleased his lover was still asleep, Steven took the chance to watch him as he snored softly. Stubbly cheeks made soft scraping sounds as Lane's face shifted, his mouth open just enough to be perfectly kissable, hair askew, falling into his face—in short, the man was perfect. And he loved him—Lane loved him. Looking toward the ceiling, Steven gave a silent word of thanks to whoever had been looking out for him. "Steven," Lane said softly, gathering him in his big arms. "Go to sleep."

"I can't," Steven answered, snuggling back into Lane's warmth. His mind raced a mile a minute as he tried to take in his good fortune. Lane loved him. Lane's mother had liked him. Steven stiffened and saw Lane's eyes drift open.

"What is it, baby? What's keeping you awake?" Lane's hand stroked his belly, an arm brushing against his side. "Close your eyes and go to sleep." Lane shifted his weight, pressing Steven onto his belly, and Lane slowly rubbed his back, long movements from his shoulders to his butt and upper legs before reversing. "That's it, relax and tell me about it." Lane's hands kept their slow stroking.

"I've been thinking about your mom," Steven confessed, and he felt Lane's hand stop moving.

"At a time like this, when I'm rubbing your butt, you think of my mother? That's disturbing." Steven lifted his head and saw Lane's smile, and they both chuckled.

"I was thinking about how your mother accepted you, ya sick nut," Steven teased, before putting his head back on the pillow. "You're very lucky."

"I know," Lane said as he continued rubbing Steven's back, big hands soothing away some of his worries.

"I wanted to ask you something," Steven said as he lifted his head off the pillow, looking toward Lane in the dark room. "If I went to see my parents, would you go with me?"

Lane's hand skimmed off the edge of his body, and then he was pulled to Lane and held tight. "Of course I will, but isn't this something you want to do on your own?"

Steven shook his head against Lane's skin. "If I had to go alone, I'd never actually go."

"Okay." He felt Lane kiss his hair. "We'll go whenever you say."

VI

IT TOOK more than a week for Steven to get up the courage to actually attempt to see his parents. Steven had to give Lane credit—he hadn't said anything and let him make up his own mind. "Lane." Steven drew the lat pull-down bar behind his head. "Can we stop by my parents' tonight?" Steven got the bar all the way down before letting it rise back into place and getting up from the machine.

"If that's what you'd like," Lane responded.

"And after that are you two having an all-you-can-eat sausage fest?" Lonnie chimed in as he finished his set from the machine next to them.

"God, I hope so," Steven retorted without thinking before adding, "and no, you can't join us, no matter how much you beg." Lonnie's eyes went wide for a second, and Lane hooted from next to him. "You know, for a straight man, you're way too interested in our bedroom activities." Steven reached over and caught Lonnie around the neck, and the big man squirmed away with a laugh. "Maybe you should give it a whirl, Lon," Steven teased. "There's that huge guy in the locker room who's always watching you. Heck, I bet he'll give you a fun time for your money."

Lane lost it next to him, doubling over with laughter as Lonnie stared at him openmouthed and speechless. "Come on, Steven, we should get cleaned up and leave Lonnie with a shred of his self-image intact," Lane commented through his laughter, slapping Lonnie on the shoulder as he walked toward the locker room.

Steven cleaned up quickly without using the sauna or whirlpool, and after dressing, walked out to the front, sitting in one of the huge chairs while he waited for Lane. Leg bouncing, his stomach fluttering, Steven wondered just what kind of reception he was going to receive. He had no illusions that his parents would welcome him with open arms, but he'd be happy if they would listen to him. Maybe they could come to an understanding. Hope rose within him, and Steven did his best to try to keep it in check, but damn, it wasn't working.

"Are you ready?" Lane asked as he approached. "I thought we'd take your car, if that's okay."

"Sure." Steven stood up, his nerves ramping up with each step.

"You okay?" Lane asked, watching Steven fumble with his keys as he unlocked the car door.

"Yeah," he answered, finally opening the doors and getting into the car. "I'm just a little nervous."

Lane pulled his door closed, leaning close to Steven, lips right near his ear. "If we were someplace private, I'd strip you down and fuck those nerves away."

"Great," Steven said with mock annoyance. "Now I'm nervous *and* have a hard-on. That's going to look great to my mother," Steven added before chuckling, some of the nerves dissipating.

"See, that's better. And know this, good or bad, I'll still take you back to my place and fuck you senseless."

"Giving me something to look forward to?" Steven asked as he started the car.

"You betcha, now let's go."

Steven noticed he didn't say, "Let's go get this over with," but that was what Steven was beginning to feel. Pulling out of the parking lot, he drove to the neighborhood he'd grown up in, wondering just what kind of reaction he would get.

Steven drove the streets he remembered so well, pulling to a stop in front of the house he'd shared with family and friends, the place he'd always felt safe even after the kids had picked on "Blobby Bobby" all day. A single car was parked in the driveway, so he knew someone was indeed home. Steven looked to the front of the house, shutting off the engine, but made no move to get out. "Do you want me to go with you?" Lane asked.

"No." Steven turned to Lane. "I'll be fine." Opening the door, Steven stepped out of the car, closing the door with a thunk without moving away. *What was he doing? He should just get back in the car and leave. Why rock the boat?* Looking through the glass, he saw Lane and smiled briefly to him before forcing his legs to move.

Approaching the door, Steven took a deep breath before knocking. Footsteps approached the door, and there was a rush of air as it opened and he saw his mother standing on the other side of the screen door. Steven said nothing, but waited a few seconds as her face went through a number of emotions. He saw her mouth the word "Bobby," but said nothing as she stared at him. She looked almost happy to see him.

"Who is it?" he heard from inside, his father's voice coming through the screen, and for a second, Steven felt himself smile at the familiar sound.

"It's Bobby," his mother said softly, before turning her head toward the living room. "Our son." Steven felt a lump form in his throat and half expected her to open the screen door and let him in.

"I wanted—" Steven started.

"We don't have a son," he heard his unseen father say forcefully from inside the house, and Steven stopped his thought right there. His mother turned back to him, and the two of them stood there for a second looking at one another before the door slowly closed, and Steven found himself staring at the outside of the white door with its diamond-shaped windows.

Blankly, Steven turned and walked back down the front walk to the driveway and out to the car. He'd barely reached the end of the driveway before he was engulfed in a deep hug. He hadn't even heard Lane get out of the car, but it didn't matter. "You okay?"

Steven nodded once, letting Lane hold him and then lead him toward the passenger side of the car. Getting inside, Steven handed Lane the keys without thinking, sitting blankly without looking toward the house. He heard Lane get in and start the car. As they pulled away, he couldn't help himself from taking a last look at the house. He wasn't sure, but he thought he saw the curtains move back into place. Not that it mattered. They'd made their decision; not that he should have been surprised, but it still hurt.

Lane drove them to his home. "What about your car? It's still at the gym," Steven asked, not really thinking.

"We'll get it later," Lane answered, pulling into his parking space.

Steven followed Lane inside, trying to put what had happened behind him. He knew he'd gone on a fool's errand, and he should have known that a door slammed in his face would be his reception. But he'd allowed himself to hope for something else, and it had carried him away. Flopping down on Lane's sofa, he let his lover hold him as he sat numbly. "I'll be okay, Lane," he said, wondering if it was for Lane or himself. "I shouldn't have expected anything different."

"It still hurts, though," Lane told him softly, a hand stroking his cheek.

"Yeah, I guess." Steven shrugged slightly before turning to look at Lane. "But what hurts worse is that I opened myself to it. They haven't made an effort in years, and I allowed them to hurt me again. Well, now I know and can move on." Steven rested his head against Lane's shoulder, letting his eyes drift closed in the still room as he listened to Lane's soft breathing. He'd made his own life, and he'd been doing it for years. He didn't need them and hadn't in a long time. Moping around and feeling sorry for himself wasn't doing him any good, especially not over people who'd written him off years ago.

"I'm sorry I pushed you," Lane said, and Steven kissed him.

"You didn't. You were right, I had to find out," Steven responded, before deepening the kiss, very happy, and Lane made him happier as he pressed him back on the sofa cushions, kissing him hard. Shifting around him, Steven felt Lane's weight press on him, the intensity of their kisses increasing fast.

Steven felt Lane pushing up his shirt, fingers plucking his nipples, making Steven arch into the touch. "I have a surprise for you," Lane said against his lips, as Steven felt Lane's hand on his belt, fingers deftly opening it before pushing down his zipper. Steven tried to get up, but Lane held him where he was. A hot palm stroked above the elastic of his underwear before delving inside, fishing his erection out of the fabric before pushing it down his hips. "Don't move," Lane warned before getting up and hurrying away. Steven felt a little weird lying on the sofa, clothes disheveled, until Lane returned, kneeling next to the sofa, hands moving over his skin.

Steven lifted his head when he felt Lane rolling a condom on him. "What's that for?"

"Mint-flavored," Lane replied with a grin before knocking all the air from Steven's lungs as he sucked him deep and hard.

"Lane," Steven cried, his hips bucking forward on their own. "Jesus, God!"

Steven tried to watch what Lane was doing, but gave up as the sensations overtook him, and he let the soft cushions cradle him as Lane sucked him into near total oblivion. That mouth, those hands... Steven felt the floaty feeling he always seemed to feel whenever Lane touched him. The man was like a drug, and Steven knew he was completely addicted. "Do you like that, Steven?" Lane murmured, his lips slipping away from him, and Steven thrust his hips forward again, searching for what had been taken away.

"Yes, of course I like it," he growled, trying desperately to get Lane to continue, his breath heaving in his chest. "Why did you stop?" Steven added just before Lane's hands rubbed their way up his stomach and chest, fingers latching onto his nipples, pinching and working them lightly. "Lane, please."

"Please what? What is it you want?"

"I want you to suck me," Steven answered, hoping those were the magic words. "I want the man I love to suck me." Lane smiled at him, and Steven felt his breath catch once again. A long, low sigh accompanied the return of Lane's mouth on him, taking him deep. Steven could barely control himself, and when Lane sucked him hard, tongue doing something magical he couldn't describe, he nearly lost it completely, babbling incoherently as Lane played him like a magic flute. "Lane, I'm gonna come," Steven managed to gasp as his balls tightened to his body, the last of his control slipping away. Lane didn't let up, sucking harder and meeting Steven's ragged movements until he exploded, screaming at the top of his lungs.

When he came back to his senses, Steven felt Lane's gentle strokes on his skin. Opening his eyes, he peered down at himself, wondering how he looked to Lane. Bulging arms encircled his waist, holding him tight, then they were gone, and he felt his pants being tugged off his legs and heard Lane curse softly when they caught on his shoes. Steven managed to kick off his shoes and his pants quickly followed before Lane manhandled him onto the floor, butt in the air. "Not gonna be gentle," Lane warned, his voice deep and gritty. A finger breached him, preparing him briefly before he smelled mint and waited impatiently while Lane got ready.

"Don't need gentle, just need you," Steven answered just before Lane sank into him with a deep, rumbling sigh.

"Damn, you look good around my cock," Lane told him, and Steven held on to the sofa cushions as Lane fucked him to heaven.

"Yeah!" Steven encouraged, driving back to meet Lane's thrusts.

"I promised I'd fuck you to oblivion, and I fully intend to keep that promise, so hold on, baby," Lane growled as he drove into him. Steven arched his back, his body pressing toward Lane, who grabbed his hips, driving their bodies together hard enough that their skin slapped together. Their cries filled the room, and in a moment of lucidity, he wondered if the people in the next condo could hear them. Then Lane hit his prostate and all thoughts other than Lane flew from his head with the speed of a bullet.

"Lane," Steven mewled softly.

"Am I hurting you?" Lane asked, stilling, that is until Steven shook his head, and Lane pulled him back, driving Steven against his body. Lane had never been like this with him before. Up to now, their lovemaking had been just that, not the primal coupling that this was turning into. Steven loved it. For the first time in a while, someone wasn't treating him like a china doll that would break.

"Don't you fucking dare stop!" Steven growled, and Lane didn't, thrusting home, and Steven heard him cry out and felt Lane empty himself before collapsing, his chest resting on Steven's back, while he in turn flopped forward onto the sofa cushions.

Lane's hands slid along his skin, palms resting against his stomach. Steven gasped for breath as he felt Lane slip from his body. "I didn't hurt you, did I?" Lane's breath tickled his ear.

"No," Steven answered, feeling Lane's weight lift away. Turning over, he hugged Lane tight and felt hands stroke his skin. "You were amazing."

"I don't usually lose control like that," Lane said, his eyes dark, but his voice quavery and unsure. "I loved it, but it scares me that I could have hurt you."

"You'd never hurt me."

"How do you know?" Lane asked, still shaking a little.

"I just do," Steven answered, resting his head on Lane's shoulder as a warm contentment permeated his spirit. "The same way I know I'd never intentionally hurt you." Steven shivered and Lane got up, walking naked from the room, returning a few minutes later with a trash can, a washcloth, and a blanket. After a quick cleanup from their activities, Lane settled next to him on the sofa. "Lots of people have hurt me, Lane. You did in high school." Steven touched Lane's lips with a finger to stop his explanation. "That isn't you anymore, I know that. My parents hurt me, and God knows how many others, but I know in my heart that the Lane I'm holding never will, and that's the man I'm in love with."

Steven saw Lane look him in the eyes, lean forward, and kiss him. "I love you too," Steven told him, hugging him so his head again rested on Lane's shoulder. "You know, we could move to the bedroom."

"Or we could turn on the television and order a pizza. We kind of skipped dinner." Lane chuckled and slipped out of the blanket. Steven heard him on the phone ordering food and then he was back beside him, warm and comforting. "What about the television?"

Lane lightly nuzzled his neck. "I think we can figure out something more special to occupy our time. Don't you?" Lane asked softly before kissing him once again as they waited for the pizza to be delivered, curled up together on the floor under a blanket. Steven couldn't remember the last time a half hour flew by so fast.

STEVEN finished his Saturday morning workout with the guys, the last rep feeling so wonderful. His arms and chest were tight with just enough soreness to let him know he'd worked them well, and he was done for the day. Standing up from the bench, Steven looked toward the front of the club, where Lane sat talking with a client. "You two seem to have really hit it off," Dan said from behind him, and Steven saw his friend and coworker following his gaze.

"We're doing very well," Steven said with a smile, not looking away as Lane stood up and walked to one of the filing cabinets.

"This has to be the gayest place in town," Lonnie added in his own special way. "It's a regular sausagefest in here." Lonnie looked around the room, and Steven saw Dan do the same thing. "You see the guy over there that looks like a Marine with the gray hair? That's Ivan, and the guy he's working out with is Maddoc. You've got Hugh over there with Max, and of course there's Dan here with that cockhopper Gene." Lonnie shook his head. "But you know the worst part? I introduced George and Darryl."

"Aw, Lon," Dan crooned, putting an arm around Lonnie's shoulder, "you're such a yenta." Dan dashed away as Lonnie took a swipe at him.

"We done?" Lonnie asked, already walking toward the locker room.

"Yes," Dan answered as he walked with them.

"Good. So," Lonnie said, stopping before turning back to them, "which of you two is gonna suck me off in the sauna?"

Both he and Dan rolled their eyes, and Dan reached over to Lonnie, smacking him on the back of the head. "You're a complete pig, and Steven and I gave up pork for Lent." Dan took off for the locker room with Lonnie right behind him. By the time Steven caught up with them near their lockers, both of them had towels in hand ready to snap them at the other. Steven ignored them and changed into his bathing suit, hearing the snaps of towels and ensuing cries, laughter, and increasingly outrageous threats. After grabbing his towel, Steven locked his locker and walked to the shower area, pulling open the door to the empty sauna. It didn't remain empty for long. Dan and Lonnie joined him a few minutes later, as did Gene, along with other men. Lonnie gabbed about something or other, and eventually Steven left to spend a few minutes in the whirlpool.

"Are you going to lunch?" Lane asked from near his head after he'd been in the whirlpool a few minutes. His eyes had drifted closed, and Steven hadn't even heard his lover approach. "I have a break in ten minutes and could join you."

Steven stood up, the water coming to his waist. "I'm almost done here. I can meet you out front." Steven walked to the steps, getting out of the water and following Lane's butt, encased in a pair of black pants, like he was the Pied Piper. In the shower area, Steven picked a shower at the opposite end from where Lonnie and Dan were throwing cold water on each other.

Steven cleaned up and dressed quickly, staying out of the line of fire. After saying goodbye to the guys, he hurried to the front of the club, where Lane was waiting for him. "Let's go to the sandwich shop down the street," Lane said as they walked across the parking lot. "I need something light, and their service is usually pretty quick."

"Sure," Steven said, following Lane to his car. "I know you don't have very long."

Getting in the car, Steven closed his door, and Lane gave him a sweet, if quick, kiss before starting the engine and driving to the restaurant. After waiting in line, Steven managed to snag the last empty table in the far corner as Lane got their drinks.

"Bobby," he heard whispered from near his shoulder. Looking up, Steven felt his breath catch in his throat as his mother stood near the table. "Bobby, I'm sorry," she whispered, reaching into her purse for a tissue, dabbing her eyes. "I know I don't deserve any of your time, but I've been coming here every day for lunch since I saw you a few weeks ago, hoping I'd see you again." Steven didn't know what to say. "There hasn't been a day that I haven't missed you."

Steven gasped as the anger rose inside him. "You missed me so much I haven't seen or heard from you in over a decade?"

"I know," she replied, her voice barely above a whisper. "I have no right to anything, but I wanted to see you and talk to you." She began to sniff as tears ran down her cheeks. "I wanted to see my boy again." Lane approached the table, setting down the drinks, and Steven saw him look from him to his mother and back again. His mother sniffed again. "I got to see you, and that's all I could hope for." She turned and walked away.

Steven turned back toward Lane, still feeling a little shocked. The server arrived and placed their food in front of them. "Are you just going to let her go?" Lane asked, but Steven couldn't answer. "Steven, you're the sweetest man I've ever met, and I love you so much it hurts," Lane added as he took Steven's hand. "But I have to ask you, do you want today to be the last time you ever see your mother again?" Lane fixed him in his gaze. "Go on."

Before he could second-guess himself, Steven jumped to his feet, hurrying between the tables and out the door to the parking lot, where he saw his mother getting into her car. "Mom," he heard himself call before he could stop himself. He saw her stop, looking around, and he ran to her.

"Bobby, I'm so sorry," she said as he approached, and then she was hugging him. "I missed you so much," she said through her tears. "You've changed so much since you graduated from college."

"High school, Mom, I haven't seen you since I graduated from high school."

"I know, but I've seen you."

Steven clamped his eyes closed as the tears threatened big-time. "Come back inside where we can talk." She nodded and fished another tissue out of her purse, wiping her eyes as they walked together back toward the door. "That man you're with—is he your boyfriend?"

"No, Mom. He's more than that—he's the man I love." They walked inside, and Steven saw Lane stand at the table waiting for them, a huge, happy smile on his face that got even wider as they approached. When he got close enough, Lane took his hand and squeezed it, and Steven wondered what he'd ever done to deserve him, if only so he could be sure he kept doing it. He had no idea what to expect from his mother, or even from Lane, but from where he stood now, things looked positive, and he could be happy with that.

Personal Training

Andrew Grey

I

"YES, Mom, just come to the neighbors'. You know, the ones with the cute dog," Holton explained as he juggled the phone while he cut vegetables.

"But why are we having the party there instead of your house?"

She was seventy-five, and Holton found he had to explain things to her multiple times. He tried to be patient, he really did, and he kept telling himself it wasn't her fault. She was getting old and forgetful—although he was beginning to suspect it was more than that. The doctors hadn't diagnosed Alzheimer's yet, but he figured that was coming anytime.

"They have a pool and a shaded deck, Mom. They volunteered to let me have the party in their backyard. It'll be nice for you and Dad to sit in the shade, and the kids can have fun in the pool. Are you and Dad about ready to leave?" Holton asked, trying to keep her on track. She could only do one thing at a time anymore, and if she got off track, it took her a while to get caught up again.

"Yes, I have my coat on, and your father is yelling at me to get a move on," she told him. "I'll be there in a minute, you old goat!" she yelled at her husband before returning her voice to a normal tone. "I'll hang up now and get in the car."

The line went quiet, and Holton waited to see if she'd hung up or was just being quiet, but the phone disconnected, so Holton set it on the counter, going back to work. He still had food to prepare and take over to the neighbors' for his father's seventieth birthday party.

The doorbell rang as he was finishing up the vegetable tray. "Come on in, it's open," he called, and he heard the front door open.

"Holton?"

"Hey, Brian, I'm in the kitchen," Holton said as he started what he hoped was his last task.

"Is there anything you'd like me to bring over? Heather has the tables out and set."

"You guys didn't have to do all that," Holton said, warmed by his friend's helpfulness. His Mechanicsburg, Pennsylvania neighbors were some of the nicest people he'd ever met.

"You know Heather—she loves playing hostess," Brian said, and Holton opened the refrigerator, setting some of the food on the counter. Brian picked up two bowls and began walking toward the door. "Leave the others on the counter, and I'll make another trip," Brian said, his voice carrying through the house.

Holton finished up the cold-cut tray he'd been making before picking up two bowls of his own to carry over to the party. Leaving the house, he walked through his yard and around to the neighbors' gate. Brian met him there, taking the bowls from him, and Holton returned to his house to get more. By the time he'd made three trips, he was sweating profusely, and once he'd taken over the last of the food, Holton went to his bedroom to change his sweat-soaked clothes.

Fifteen minutes later, feeling fresh and clean again, Holton walked next door, entering the fenced-in backyard. Tables with bright tablecloths decorated with flowers had been set up on the deck. "I took the dishes inside. I figured in this heat it would be easier to keep things cool if we served the food in the kitchen," Heather explained as she surveyed her handiwork for a second before giving Holton a hug.

"Thank you for doing this."

"Oh, you're welcome. You do so much for us all the time. We're just happy to help, and it's going to be so hot today that everyone is going to be happy we have the pool. Did you bring your suit?" Holton nodded, but doubted he'd go into the water until late in the afternoon or he'd burn in two seconds. The sound of a car horn out front drew their attention, and Brian stuck his head out the door.

"I think your parents are here," Brian told him before pushing the door open, and Holton followed him through the house, meeting his mom and dad on the sidewalk.

"There you are," his mother said when she saw him, looking thinner than she had the weekend before. "I couldn't remember where we were supposed to go."

"Susan, I told you it was this one," his father explained to her, pointing to Holton's house.

"We're good, Dad. Heather and Brian are hosting the party at their house." He led them inside and through the house as his mother talked the entire time.

"This is lovely. I didn't know your house looked like this. Oh, right, we're at the neighbors with the cute dog. Where is he? I don't see a dog." The litany went on and on and only stopped once Holton got her seated in the shade on the deck with a cool drink. She sipped it and put the glass on the table next to her before looking around. Holton knew she'd probably fall asleep soon. She always seemed to do that now.

"Dad, I'm going to help get things ready. I'll be right back. There are drinks in the coolers, and the other guests should start arriving soon. Okay?"

"Sure," he answered. "I'll keep an eye on your mother." Holton saw his dad head for the cooler, fishing out a diet soda before sitting in the chair next to his mother. So maybe they yelled at one another occasionally, but they also looked out for each other without even thinking about it. Holton made sure they were okay before joining Brian and Heather in the house.

"Holton, honey," Heather said when he got inside, "I've got this." The doorbell rang. "Why don't you make sure your guests make it to the backyard? We're almost done here, and then we can get this party started."

Holton spent the next little while directing aunts, uncles, cousins, friends, and assorted former colleagues of his father's to the backyard. Once he was sure all the guests had arrived, Holton joined the party himself.

"You look just like your father," Holton's Aunt Clare told him as soon as he emerged onto the deck, just before giving him a gentle hug. "Doesn't he look like his father?" she asked everyone gathered around, and Holton tried to keep himself from rolling his eyes. Gleeful squeals and yells floated up from the pool where the youngsters were already splashing away, having a very happy time. "This is so cool," one of the kids yelled, just before diving from the side of the pool.

Holton smiled, very pleased that everyone was having a good time. Stepping to the food table, Holton filled a plate with munchies before sitting in an empty chair to talk for a few minutes with some of the relatives, reminding himself to look for Heather and Brian if they didn't join the party soon. Holton didn't want them doing all the work, even though he knew Heather was in her element. They joined the party a few minutes later, and Holton relaxed, mouthing another thank-you to the couple, who smiled. Holton made introductions, explaining how all the myriad relatives were related to one another. Most everyone knew each another, anyway, and the level of conversation ratcheted up. Holton didn't mind at all. He sat on the deck, near the edge of most conversations, listening to snippets, but not generally taking part.

"My son just graduated from Dickinson Law with...."

"She mustn't have been very good at it. They caught her with the money, and she got twenty years...."

"He really looks like his father. But Holton is so quiet," one of his older relatives said. Holton couldn't determine quite who it was, but he knew they were talking about him. Holton heard parts of many conversations, especially his father, once he got going. George Hillman loved to tell jokes.

"Did you hear the one about the toothbrush salesman?" his father would ask someone he'd just met before launching into one of his classic jokes, complete with funny voices. He'd pull everyone around him into the story, spellbound, until the punch line. "This stuff tastes like crap—what is it? It *is* crap. Wanna buy a toothbrush!" Everyone laughed, and Holton found himself laughing along. He'd heard the joke so many times, but he still laughed, mainly because it made his dad happy.

"The food is ready!" Heather called from the doorway, and everyone lined up, circling the island in the big kitchen, filling plates while the conversation continued to flow along with the guests, outside, inside, and back outside. Holton helped his mother with her plate, getting her settled at one of the tables next to friends she'd known for years before filling a plate for himself. Taking an empty chair off to the side in the shade, he ate and watched the kids playing in the pool. They were having too much fun to even bother with food.

After cleaning his plate, Holton got a refill, resuming his place in the shade as he finished eating. Throwing away the trash, Holton made his way through the house and out the front door, hurrying to his house, where he pulled a professional-looking chocolate cake, his father's favorite, from the refrigerator, placing candles on the top before carrying it to the neighbors'. Holton climbed onto the deck, presenting his creation for everyone to admire. His baking was one of the things he was most proud of.

Heather lit the candles, and everyone gathered around, even the kids, taking a break from the pool, to sing happy birthday. Once the off-key but happy singing was done, Holton set the cake on the table near the plates and began to cut, handing out pieces to everyone, with a small slice to his diabetic father. Holton's dad loved cake, but he couldn't eat much without it wreaking havoc with his blood sugar, so Holton was very careful how much he got.

After the entire cake had been divided and devoured, people continued sitting and chatting until the sun began to go down. Then, one by one, couples said their good-byes with hugs and handshakes. Holton helped his parents to their car, watching as they pulled away, before returning to the house to help with the cleanup. It was just Brian, Heather, and himself when he returned. They sat on the deck talking softly for a while, relaxing. "Your dad is a real hoot," Heather told him as Brian refilled her wine glass. "He tells the best stories, and you really do look a lot like him."

"He always did tell a great story," Holton said softly. "When I was a kid, we used to belong to a camping club. Mom worked nights for a while, and I can remember Dad sitting around the fire, telling stories. One time Mom had to work, so Dad kissed her good-bye and told her he loved her. It was really sweet. He even waved to her as the car pulled out of the campground. Then he rubbed his hands together with unabashed glee and said, 'Now for the Sue stories.' Dad's storytelling subject was Mom. Every one of her foibles got broadcast to everyone." Holton took a gulp from his glass before reaching for the wine bottle. "I always wondered what stories he told about me when I wasn't around." Holton sat silently, trying to keep a lid on his resentment. He loved the man, but he'd hated being the butt of his jokes. Draining his glass again, Holton stood up and began throwing away the trash to have something to do. He'd let a little more of himself out than he'd intended, and he needed something to cover his discomfort.

Brian and Heather began to clean up as well, all of them working quietly. Holton gathered his things before helping with the rest of the cleanup. After thanking Brian and Heather once again, Holton carried his dishes home. Placing them in his kitchen sink, Holton decided to leave them until morning, and walked down the hallway to his bedroom.

After spending all day outside, Holton decided to shower before bed. Pulling off his clothes, he threw them in the hamper before going into the bathroom. Closing the bathroom door, he turned on the water, shutting the shower door again. He turned around and stopped dead in his tracks. In the mirror that had been behind the bathroom door since he'd bought the house, Holton got a good look at himself. Reaching into the shower, he turned off the water and stared. He *did* look like his father. Almost exactly like his father. Same face, eyes, and damned near the same body. He had nearly the same body as his seventy-year-old, diabetic father. Standing in his bathroom, Holton blinked as he stared at himself, wondering what had happened. He was over forty years old, alone, with no prospects. Hell, he hadn't been on a date in… God, he couldn't remember the last time he'd been out with anyone. Turning away from the mirror, he started the water again and got under the spray, washing quickly before getting out of the shower and drying himself off, making a point not to look in the mirror.

Pulling on light clothes, Holton wandered into the kitchen. He opened the refrigerator, scanning the contents before closing the door. Opening the freezer, he pulled out a half gallon of mint chocolate chip. Pulling up the top of the container, Holton grabbed a spoon from the drawer and scooped out a good-sized dollop of his favorite flavor.

The spoon stopped halfway to his mouth, and Holton held it there, wondering just what he was doing. All his life he'd turned to food whenever he was unhappy or upset, and today was no exception. Ice cream, cake, chocolate, you name it. Dropping the spoon into the sink, Holton closed the ice cream container and put it back into the freezer before walking back down the hall to his bedroom. Stripping down, Holton climbed into bed and went to sleep, trying not to think of the image that had stared back at him from his own mirror.

Holton woke the next morning, Sunday, thankful he had one more day before having to go to work… although he had no idea what he was going to do with it. Getting up, Holton wandered through the house, settling in the living room and turning on the television. After half watching whatever was on, Holton got up to get cleaned up. In the bathroom, he tried to avoid the offending mirror, but he couldn't turn away. He knew he was looking at himself, but he kept seeing his father. Brushing his teeth and shaving, Holton decided enough was enough. Leaving the room, he hurried into the kitchen, grabbing the phone book. Thumbing through the yellow pages, Holton found a listing that fit what he was looking for and dialed the number.

HOLTON parked his car outside the flashy, new-looking health club, wondering just what in the hell he was doing here. He'd called on impulse and made an appointment, so Holton got out of the car, wondering if he should carry in his small bag of clothes. He didn't really have anything to work out in, but he'd found a pair of shorts and an old T-shirt along with some of the other things he'd thought he'd need. Getting out of the car, Holton looked up at the façade of the building. It was a temple dedicated to the thin, healthy, beautiful, and young, and Holton knew he was none of those things and hadn't been in quite some time. Walking toward the building, ignoring the impulse to turn around and head for the nearest grocery-store freezer case, Holton pulled open the doors to the club and walked inside.

"Can I help you?" the young woman behind the desk inquired with a smile as the phone began to ring. She answered it, directing the call somewhere else before looking at Holton again.

"I called this morning and spoke with Marcus," Holton answered in a tone barely above a whisper, feeling more nervous all the time as people entered the club around him, scanning their cards before moving on. To Holton's eye, they all looked so thin and young. The women were goddesses and the men, Jesus, the men looked like the catalog models he'd lusted over since he was sixteen. He *so* didn't belong here.

"Are you Holton?" a deep voice asked from beside him. Turning, he saw a tall, tanned man with short black hair and the most striking deep blue eyes Holton had ever seen. When Holton nodded, the man held out his hand. "I'm Marcus. It's great to meet you," Marcus added with a lot of enthusiasm as he shook Holton's hand with a firm grip. "My desk is over here," he said, motioning toward a row of low workstations. "We'll talk a bit, and then I'll give you a tour of the club. I see you brought workout clothes. That's good. It's slow today, so once business is taken care of, I can show you how to use some of the equipment and help get you off to a good start."

"I'd appreciate that," Holton said with a little less trepidation before following Marcus to his area. Holton sat in one of the chairs while Marcus looked at his computer.

"The price of membership includes all club facilities, and gets you access to any of our clubs throughout the country with the exception of New York City and Venice Beach," Marcus began, and Holton nodded, barely paying attention to what the demi-god sitting just across the desk from him was saying. Dang, he had to get his act together, or he'd look like a complete idiot. "What are your goals?"

"Huh?" Holton hadn't been expecting those kinds of questions.

"What is it you're hoping to get out of your membership? What kind of changes do you want to make?"

"I want to lose weight," Holton answered quickly. "And I want to turn all this fat into muscle."

"Well, that we can't do," Marcus said plainly. "It's not possible to turn fat into muscle. What we can do is help you work off the excess fat and build new, lean muscle. Do you know how much you want to lose?" Holton shrugged. He hadn't been on a scale in years. "Okay, then, how about after we go through the business stuff and you decide what you'd like to do, we'll do a body mass calculation to tell you just how much excess body fat you have, and then we can start working it off."

"Okay," Holton agreed cautiously. If nothing else, he'd get to spend some time with this guy. Marcus really was handsome, and that voice, God, it reminded him of smooth, dark chocolate.

They talked for a while, and Holton was surprised just how little it cost to join. He'd been expecting a new place like this to be really expensive, but they were running a special, so Holton figured he didn't have much to lose, except inches, so fifteen minutes later, he found himself handing over his credit card and signing papers to join his very first gym.

The magnitude of what he'd done hit him once he got up and followed Marcus on the tour of the club. Then the intimidation factor kicked in big-time, and Holton wanted to find a place to hide. He wasn't particularly tall or broad, and some of these guys looked absolutely huge. *And* some of them were wearing next to nothing—flimsy little string tanks and shorts that left very little to the imagination. Not that Holton needed much help in that department. He'd been using his imagination all his life.

"That's the free weights area. The cardio equipment is upstairs, and the weight machines are in the center. We also have racquetball, basketball, volleyball, an aerobics studio, and a spinning classroom. You can use all of these with your membership," Marcus explained before leading him through to the locker room and finally the shower, sauna, whirlpool, and pool areas. "If you'd like to change, I'll meet you out front, and we'll get you started."

Holton nodded blankly, watching Marcus walk away before finding an empty locker in a corner and quickly changing his clothes before more people came in. Locking his locker, Holton walked out of the locker room and found Marcus chatting with another guy. Waiting off to the side, he watched Marcus finish his conversation, studying the man so he could resurrect his image later when he was alone.

"Are you ready?"

Holton nodded his response and followed Marcus to another desk in the back. "Let's weigh you," Marcus said, and Holton very reluctantly got on the scale. "Two ten," he commented before handing Holton a small device and getting it set up. "This will measure your body composition."

Holton did as Marcus asked and waited. He was surprised when Marcus told him that he was twenty-nine percent. "Does that mean one-quarter of me is fat?"

"Yes and no. What it does mean is that you're carrying a lot more fat than you need. But that's okay. You're here to change that, and we're here to help," Marcus said with a smile that made Holton feel like he could do anything. Or at least he'd want to in order to get Marcus to smile like that again. "Let's go upstairs and we'll get you started with some cardio. That's what you'll need to start with in order to burn the excess fat. Then you can start to lift and build new, lean muscle."

Like a rat following the Pied Piper, Holton followed Marcus upstairs. "What do you suggest?" Holton asked at the top of the stairs as he took in the array of different equipment.

"Let's start you on a treadmill. We'll just have you walk at a pace slightly faster than normal. That will get your heart moving and will start to signal to your body to burn fat." Marcus made it sound so easy, and for a second, Holton almost believed it could be that simple. Holton stepped on, and Marcus showed him how to use the machine, and he began to walk.

"How long should I go?"

"Since you're just starting out, try for twenty minutes. You can work up to more, but that should give you an idea of how you feel. Once you're done, come downstairs and we'll demonstrate some of the basic machines." Marcus gave him another smile before turning away and descending the stairs. Holton continued walking, looking at the floor below as he watched other people go through their workouts. He'd never seen so many beautiful people in one place before in his life. There were people who actually looked good in spandex and tank tops that showed off huge, sculpted chests, and for the first time in his life, Holton wondered if it was possible for him to look like that.

The timer on the treadmill beeped and the belt stopped. Holton stepped off the machine feeling winded but strangely invigorated. He didn't really know where that came from, but it didn't matter. Walking down the stairs, he made it to the bottom before the stiffness settled into his legs. Walking stiffly toward the locker room, Holton started to wonder what was wrong with him when he saw Marcus waiting for him. "Are you feeling it a little?"

"In my legs," Holton explained, wondering how he could make it stop and trying to figure out what he'd gotten himself in for. Crap, he'd even paid good money for this torture.

"Don't sit down and rest. It'll make it worse," Marcus explained, and Holton thought he was full of shit, but didn't say anything. "Come on, let me show you some of the other machines. You need to keep moving for a while, and the stiffness will dissipate on its own. Trust me." Holton took a deep breath and forced his legs to move as he followed Marcus across the gym, his legs screaming at him. "Let's stretch out the muscles," Marcus said, and he showed him how to do it. As soon as Holton did what Marcus showed him to stretch out the muscles in his legs, the pain began to slip away, and a warmth he'd never felt before blossomed in his legs. "Is that better?"

"Yeah," Holton responded, testing his leg before standing back up and following Marcus to the first machine. God, what a show that was. Marcus would demonstrate each exercise and Holton would watch him, trying to pay attention, but all he saw was the strong, tight body flexing and bending. Then it was his turn, and Marcus would stand in front of him to make sure he did the exercise correctly. Sometimes he got close enough that Holton would get a whiff of his skin. A few times Holton had to check to make sure he wasn't visibly excited.

The man was hot; there was no doubt about that. He was also nice and patient, which made Holton like him all the more. But Holton had no illusions that he was anything more than just another client. Guys like Marcus never looked twice at guys like Holton. Even if the man was gay, Holton would never catch the eye of guys like that. The best he could hope for was some eye candy, and he was getting plenty of that. "How does that feel?" Marcus asked him, that deep rich voice pulling him out of his thoughts.

"It feels okay," Holton answered as he finished the exercise.

"You don't want to start lifting heavy, or you'll really be sore, and you could hurt yourself. Take your time and ease into it. You'll be surprised how fast your body responds." Marcus held out his hand, and Holton shook it, trying not to look disappointed. For the last twenty minutes, he'd had Marcus's attention, and he hated to see it end because he doubted he'd ever get it again for any reason. Holton saw Marcus walk away, watching the man's pants as they clung to a butt that dreams were made of, and in, for that matter. Getting up from the machine, Holton walked toward the locker rooms, his legs still slightly stiff. He wished he'd thought to bring a bathing suit, but he'd have to remember one for next time.

Unlocking his locker, Holton pulled out his bag and began stripping down, conscious the entire time of everyone around him. Wrapping a towel around his waist, he padded to the shower area, getting into a stall and pulling the curtain closed before taking off his towel and hanging it on the hook outside. Then he started the water and began to wash. Holton took his time—after all, there were muscles aching that he never knew he had, but it wasn't painful, just… there. Letting the hot water course over him, he felt his body relax.

Once he was finished, Holton shut off the water and reached out for his towel. After drying himself, he wrapped the terrycloth around his waist and pushed the shower curtain aside just in time to see a very naked Marcus stepping into the shower across from his.

Holton froze, totally surprised and enthralled. There was nothing wrong with Holton's imagination, nothing at all, but all the things he'd imagined about Marcus earlier flew out the window in the face of the real deal: long legs, dusted with black hair that ended at the world's most perfectly dimpled butt. Holton let his eyes slide upward, taking in Marcus's narrow waist and the dark planes of his back that rippled as Marcus reached into the shower to turn on the water. Every inch of the man was tanned, toned, and completely tasty. Holton continued watching Marcus move for just a few seconds, but to Holton it seemed the world had suddenly switched into slow motion with only Marcus and him at the center.

Marcus stepped into the shower, and Holton lowered his eyes before hurrying out of the shower area and back to his locker. Mortified that he'd been staring and that Marcus might have caught him, Holton moved as fast as he could. He dressed quickly to get out of the locker area before Marcus finished his shower.

Holton pulled on his underwear and pants before tugging on his shirt and sitting down to put on his shoes and socks. He didn't really look around him or talk to anyone, even though lots of guys were talking around him. Making sure he had everything, Holton grabbed his bag and stepped out of the bay of lockers as the door to the shower area opened. Pretending he hadn't seen Marcus, Holton walked out of the locker room and into the club area, making his way toward the front door. Only then did he let himself slow down.

Leaving the club, Holton walked to his car, unlocking it along the way with the buttons on his key. After stowing his bag, Holton climbed inside and started his car, heading home. He was very pleased with himself. He'd actually joined a gym and completed his first workout. Part of himself said he deserved a treat, and his stomach wanted him to make a stop at McDonald's on the way home, but Holton ignored it and drove straight to his house.

Dropping his gym bag in the hallway, Holton went right into the kitchen, opening the refrigerator for something to eat. Digging through the food, he found an apple and an orange, but that was after shuffling around the tubs of sour cream, pudding cups, and God knew what else. Grabbing the fruit, he closed the door and leaned back against the counter. He had to stop this. Holton had just spent good money to join a gym, and he'd seen that maybe it was possible for him to look better and feel better. Cutting the apple with a knife, he ate a slice before setting the rest on the counter. It was time to make a change.

Rummaging under the sink for a garbage bag, Holton pulled open the refrigerator door and began pitching. The pudding went into the bag, along with leftover pizza and Chinese food, and cans of sugary soda. Closing the door, Holton opened the freezer, sending the ice cream, frozen pizza pockets, and God knew what other crap into the trash. Once he was done there, he opened the pantry cupboard, dumping in potato chips, cheese curls, bars of chocolate, and jars of caramel sauce, as well as more candy than any one person should ever eat. Shutting the pantry door, he closed the bag and carried it outside to the trash can, dropping it inside with a satisfying clang before slamming on the lid.

Returning to the kitchen, Holton washed his hands and picked up another apple slice, breathing heavily as his resolve continued to build. It was time to change his life. He'd joined a gym, he'd thrown out the junk food, and now he had to figure out how to learn to eat properly. Opening the door to his now nearly empty refrigerator, Holton realized that he needed to go grocery shopping. Taking his apple and orange with him, Holton sat at the kitchen table and began to make a grocery list.

THREE months. That's how long he'd been watching everything he'd eaten. Three whole months monitoring every bite, eating healthy and light, spending time at the gym six days a week. Gradually, his twenty minutes on the treadmill had turned to thirty, and then forty-five. After two weeks, Holton was spending an hour a day working out, bringing a book with him to help pass the time. The amazing thing was that the weight he'd carried around for years came off.

The first thing he noticed was that he had more stamina—things that used to tire him breezed by now. Then, about two weeks into his new program, he got dressed one morning and his pants felt loose, which was nice. But the really good part was when he pulled on his belt and the prong slipped into a hole that he'd never used before. That made Holton smile, really smile. Now, after three months, he'd dropped almost forty pounds. Last week he'd gone shopping for some new clothes, and when he bought new pants, he'd tried on a pair with a thirty-four waist and they were too big. He ended up buying pants with a thirty-two waist, walking out of the store grinning from ear to ear. He hadn't worn a thirty-two waist since he was in college, not since.... Holton had stopped mid-stride, shivering slightly at the memory he'd long tried to forget and never seemed to be able to for very long.

Holton rarely missed a day at the gym, and today was no exception. Pulling into the parking lot, he popped the trunk before getting out and retrieving his gym bag, which sat next to the bag for his computer. Holton had found out very early that if he went to the gym right after work, he was fine. If he went home first, he was more likely to skip the gym.

Walking inside the club, Holton scanned his card, saying hello to the girl behind the counter before striding toward the locker room. He changed his clothes and grabbed his book and water bottle before heading upstairs to the treadmills. Programming the machine, he started the belt and began to walk.

II

MARCUS watched the door of the club. He knew the guy he'd signed up months ago should be in just about now. He came in at the same time every weekday, and over the past few weeks, Marcus had found himself watching for him. He'd just barely remembered the man mainly because of how shy he'd been when Marcus had signed him up. What had really gotten Marcus's attention was the man's transformation. The change was so dramatic, and not just in the way the man looked, that Marcus had actually checked the club records to determine when Holton had joined the club. Holton had become more confident. He actually talked to people now, and Marcus admitted to himself as he looked toward the door once again, the man was damned cute and getting sexier by the day.

Marcus hated that he thought that way. He knew that he should have more depth—that a person's looks were only on the outside and what counted was who they were on the inside. He knew that, and though the man he'd signed up for a membership three months ago wouldn't have turned his head, the man who'd just pulled open the door to the club captured his attention like no one he'd ever met before. Marcus remembered how Holton had looked at him during the one workout session they'd shared the day Holton had joined. Marcus knew he was good-looking, but Holton had looked at him like he was the hottest man on earth, and Marcus hadn't given him a second thought, until a few weeks ago.

Catching Holton's eyes as he scanned his card, Marcus waved him over, pleased when Holton walked over to his desk. "I noticed that you've been doing a lot of cardio," Marcus began, hoping he wasn't overstepping. "Have you given any thought to lifting?"

"Yeah, but I don't know very much about it," Holton replied, and Marcus saw him fidget nervously as he looked toward the free-weight area with a touch of fear. "The guys over there seem so big."

"They're really nice guys. If you want to go change first, I'll introduce you to some of them, and I can show you some basic exercises so you don't get injured." Marcus flashed Holton a smile as he looked the smaller man over. "You've lost a lot of weight, and if you want to start building muscle now, you need to cut down on the cardio and start some strength training."

"You'll show me how?" Holton asked, and for a second, Marcus saw that look he'd seen a few months ago.

"Sure. Go get changed, and I'll meet you over there." Marcus flashed another smile, watching as Holton walked toward the locker room with what looked like a bit of excitement in his step. Standing up, Marcus wandered through the club, greeting members as he waited for Holton to come out of the locker room. When he saw him, Marcus felt a flutter in his stomach. Gone were the long pants and big shirts. Holton wore a simple pair of shorts that showed off his legs, and a white tank top. His legs weren't long, but they were thick and strong.

"Do I need anything special?"

Marcus shook his head. "Not for today, but you might want to get yourself a pair of lifting gloves. They'll protect you from the knurling on the bars. We won't go heavy today, so you'll be fine." Marcus began to walk toward the weight area. "The machines in this area use real weight and are built to handle hundreds of pounds. I thought we'd start with a chest exercise." Marcus pointed toward one of the Hammer Strength machines. "These will help you maintain good form while getting your muscles used to the work."

Marcus watched as Holton sat on the seat. Marcus loaded light weights on the bars, wanting to give Holton a feel for the exercise. Holton gripped the padded handles and pushed, contracting his chest muscles. There wasn't much there now, but Marcus could tell by his build and the way his muscles moved that Holton had plenty of potential. "Am I doing this right?"

"Perfect, try for ten," Marcus answered, watching the way Holton lit up at the praise. "You're doing it just right. Does it feel okay?" Holton nodded his answer as he continued the exercise. Once he'd done ten reps, he let the bars fall back against the stops.

"How many of these should I do?" Holton asked as he got up off the seat.

"Three sets for now. Use a weight that you're comfortable with, and only increase the weight a little at a time." Marcus saw the look of fear that flashed on Holton's face. "Don't worry. It's not hard. Just make sure you don't push it, to start. Now, why don't you do another set, and I'll be right back." Marcus waited until Holton had started before walking over to a group of guys working out in the corner. "Hey, Dan, Lonnie," Marcus called and saw both men turn around.

"Who's the fruitbasket you're working out with? Is he a client?" Lonnie quipped before ducking as Dan tried to smack him.

"His name's Holton and he joined a few months ago. The thing is, he seems to be afraid of most people in the club. He shies away from some of the bigger guys and really seems scared sometimes," Marcus explained as he turned toward Holton, who'd finished his set and was sitting at the machine, waiting for him. "When you guys get a chance, come on over so I can introduce you. Maybe he'll feel more comfortable," Marcus explained, and he noticed the knowing look Dan gave him.

"Sure," Dan answered. "Give us a few minutes." Dan got into position on the bench for his next set, and Marcus returned to Holton, who was sitting at the machine after his second set.

"Did I do okay?" Holton asked. "I added ten pounds to each side."

"Did you have any trouble doing the exercise?"

Holton shook his head. "I did ten without any difficulty."

Marcus smiled back at the shy man. "Then you did fine. Just don't push it. If you can do a set of ten and it feels easy, then add a little weight. But if you add weight too fast, even though you may be able to do the exercise, you could also hurt yourself. So take your time." Marcus glanced around the weight area, looking for a specific man, spotting him in the corner. "You see the man in the blue tank top and black shorts?" Holton nodded his answer after looking around. "You see he's using really light weights? Last year he had surgery to repair a torn shoulder, and it'll be months before he's able to use weights that you could do easily today, if he'll ever be able to."

"Okay, but how will I really know?" Holton looked confused, but the way he asked the question, with just a touch of excitement, told Marcus that he was really listening.

"Listen to your body. It'll tell you if you overdo it," Marcus answered, and Holton nodded again.

"So, Marcus, how's the new job working out?" Dan said as he approached.

"Really good," Marcus responded before adding, "Dan, this is Holton. And the guy over there walking toward us is Lonnie. Hey, Lon," Marcus called as Lonnie joined the group. "This is Holton. He joined the club a few months ago and is just starting some weight training."

"New job?" Holton asked from beside him.

"It's good to meet you, Holton," Dan said as he extended his hand. They shook hands, and Lonnie held out his hand so he and Holton could fist bump. "Marcus was promoted a month ago. He manages the entire club now," Dan answered before Marcus could get a chance. "By the way, I appreciate you having the sauna cleaned like you did. It was starting to get a little smelly."

"You bet," Marcus answered, and he saw Holton sort of backing away. "Dan and Lonnie are great guys. They're sort of the A-team around here. Dan's partner is a retired bodybuilder. He's won a ton of titles and only just gave up the professional show circuit last year. Is Gene around?" Marcus asked, looking around for the imposing man. "I haven't seen him much in a while."

"He's been in, but his work schedule's been a little weird. I haven't seen him much the last few weeks, either." Dan turned his attention to Holton. "If you have any questions, don't hesitate to ask. Everyone's pretty friendly around here. If you want, you could join us for a workout. Lonnie always needs someone new to tell his stories to."

"Come on, Dances with Dick," Lonnie quipped, and Marcus looked at Holton, who took a step backward, "we need to get back at it. Holton, it was great to meet you."

"Don't pay any attention to Lonnie," Dan explained to Holton. "He never got the gene that censors speech." Dan turned toward his workout partner. "Be nice, Chewbacca," he called as he swatted Lonnie on the ass, making the other man jump.

"Hey," Lonnie whined, rubbing his backside.

"Be nice," Dan admonished as they continued walking away.

"Dan's gay?" Holton asked sort of under his breath as he studied his feet.

"Yeah. There are lots of gay people here. The club is very accepting. Has anyone given you a hard time?" Marcus asked, suddenly concerned that someone might have said something to Holton and that was why he was so shy.

"No. I guess I'm just surprised." Holton looked up. "Umm, how did you know about me?"

Marcus smiled. "I guess I have good gaydar," he replied before moving a little closer. "My first clue was the way you looked at me." Holton blushed adorably but didn't say anything, and Marcus wondered if he'd gone too far and completely scared the shy man. Marcus had had lots of men and women look at him like he was a buffet, and he'd dated some of them, but Holton seemed different to him. Marcus thought it was probably his shyness and the feeling he got that Holton felt he didn't deserve Marcus's attention for some reason.

"I'm sorry," Holton replied. "Maybe I should go."

"Holton," Marcus said softly, trying not to make things worse. "I liked it." Holton's eyes widened like he didn't believe him, and Marcus nodded to emphasize that he was being serious. "Let's move to the next exercise so you don't cool off too much." Marcus stepped to the machine on the end of the line. "This machine will work your back." Marcus hoped that changing the subject would make Holton more comfortable, but it didn't seem to be working. Marcus could see Holton's arms shaking slightly as he reached out to grab the grips, and Marcus made sure the machine was properly adjusted for him before slipping on a little weight. Holton did a set and then got up. Marcus wanted to say something to make Holton more comfortable, but he didn't quite know what, so he remained quiet and let Holton concentrate on the workout. But that didn't seem to be working either, because Holton just seemed to be getting more and more nervous after each set. When they moved to the shoulder press machine, Holton's arms shook back and forth so badly that after doing a set, Marcus was afraid Holton might have hurt himself.

"What did I say?" Marcus asked. "I didn't mean to make you uncomfortable." Marcus looked at Holton as he still sat at the machine, fidgeting slightly. "Holton," Marcus said softly, "just talk to me. I don't want you to be afraid. I like the way you look at me."

"You do?" Holton asked.

Marcus grinned. "Of course I do. Why wouldn't I? I think everyone wants to be looked at by someone the way you look at me. It's sort of special."

"Oh." Holton didn't elaborate. Instead he put his hands on the grips of the machine and did another set. Marcus was quickly finding out that if he wanted to know something or get a response from Holton, he had to ask.

Marcus waited until Holton had put the arms of the machine back against their stops. "I was wondering if you'd like to have dinner with me."

"Who? Me?" Holton squeaked before looking around. Marcus figured Holton was making sure he was talking to him.

"Yes, you," Marcus confirmed. "Why don't we finish your workout and you can get cleaned up, then I'd like to take you to dinner." Marcus waited, and Holton finally lifted his eyes from his feet. Marcus let Holton's gaze meet his, and he looked into deep cerulean eyes and smiled. "I don't know why you're surprised that I'd want to have dinner with you. You're a very sweet man."

"Oh, okay. I'd like to have dinner with you." Holton smiled, and Marcus saw his face light up, those little crinkles around his mouth brightening his expression. Holton was obviously older than he was, but Marcus hardly cared about things like that. He liked to think that he cared about the person rather than their age or looks, although in some ways Holton had challenged that notion.

"You're handsome when you smile," Marcus said.

Holton shook his head. "I've never been handsome."

Marcus's eyes widened in surprise. "Then you haven't looked in a mirror lately. You're a very handsome man." Marcus didn't add that he thought Holton cute in a lot of ways. No man wanted to be told he was cute—that was the kiss of death. But Holton was cute. There was no doubt about that at all. "Let's finish the routine, and we can talk about this a little more over dinner if you like." Holton nodded his agreement and did his next set.

He and Holton spent the next half hour on Holton's workout. Between sets, Marcus introduced Holton to as many of the other members as he could, paying particular attention to the other gay members. Once they were done, Holton went into the locker room to clean up, and Marcus walked back to his desk to check on the status of everything before leaving for the day. By the time he was done, Marcus looked up and saw a rather nervous-looking Holton standing in front of his desk. "Are you ready to go?"

"Yes, but if you have things you need to do...." Holton's voice trailed off, and Marcus saw him biting his lower lip nervously as he shifted slightly from foot to foot.

"Nope. I'm done for the day. Let's go." Marcus grabbed his bag and walked toward the door, making sure Holton was still with him. "Tina," he said to the girl at the desk, "I'm gone for the day. If there's an emergency, I can be reached on my cell."

"See you later, Marcus," she said, and she waved as he and Holton walked through the front doors and out into the crisp autumn air.

"Would you like to ride with me?" Marcus asked Holton.

"I'll just follow you, okay?" Holton replied, and Marcus saw that same scared look he'd seen when Marcus had introduced him to the guys in the club—why, he didn't understand. Holton was no weakling, as he'd demonstrated during their workout, but there was definitely something gentle and almost fragile inside this man, and Marcus wanted him to feel comfortable.

"All right. I thought we could go for Indian food. There's a small place just up the road a few miles. The last time I was in there, I was the only non-Indian person in the place. The food was amazing."

"Okay," Holton answered nervously. "I've never had Indian food, but I'll try it."

Marcus led Holton to his car, dumping his bag in the trunk. "Where are you parked?" Marcus asked, so he could wait for Holton.

"That's my car just down the line." Holton pointed a few cars over.

Marcus watched as he opened the trunk on an older gray Volvo. Getting into his car, Marcus pulled out of his parking space, making sure Holton was behind him before carefully driving to the restaurant. The last thing he wanted to do was lose Holton at one of the many traffic signals. Marcus kept looking back to make sure Holton was still there. Pulling into the parking lot, he found a spot, leaving the one closest to the door for Holton. Getting out of his car, Marcus waited for Holton to park before joining him at the front door.

The host seated them right away and filled their water glasses. Marcus waited for Holton to sit before taking his own seat. His mother had taught him proper manners—drilled them into him, was more like it—and he'd never been more pleased about that than when Holton smiled at him from across the table.

"The food here is very authentic," Marcus told Holton as he opened his menu.

"I don't know anything about it," Holton commented, and Marcus watched as Holton glanced at the menu for a few seconds before looking all around the room as though he were looking for the nearest exit and the fastest means of escape.

"Is something wrong? You look like you want to make a run for it. If you'd rather go someplace else, we can. Or if I make you too nervous, you don't have to stay. I'll understand." That last part was a lie. He knew he wouldn't understand, not really, but Holton seemed to be getting more and more nervous the longer they spent together.

"It's not you," Holton told him. "You've been nothing but nice." Holton's eyes darted around the room. "Strange places make me a little nervous. I'll be fine." Holton lifted his glass and took a gulp of water, and Marcus saw Holton calm himself down.

"There's nothing to be nervous about. This is a nice place, and I won't let anything happen to you, I promise. Unless I'm what's making you nervous."

"Well, you are, sort of," Holton confessed, his eyes looking at Marcus over the water glass.

"Why? There's nothing to be nervous about."

Holton made a strange noise Marcus had never heard before, and he tried to cover it with another gulp of water. "Sorry. I haven't been on many dates before."

Holton's eyes widened and he gasped softly. "This is a date, isn't it? God, I'm such a lamebrain—this is just dinner. Why would a guy like you go out on a date with me?"

Before Marcus could answer, their server approached the table, explaining the specials and some of the basic things about the food before asking if they'd decided on their dinners in a very heavy accent that made his words almost indecipherable.

"I'll have the chicken biryani," Marcus told the server, and Holton nervously ordered the same. The server took their menus before leaving to put in their orders.

"Holton, why wouldn't I want to go out with you?" Marcus asked quietly, not willing to let him off the hook.

There was that sound again. This time it sounded like a cross between a cough and a snort. Holton looked up from the table in front of him. "You're beautiful, and I'm, well, I'm not. You could have anyone you wanted, and I can't figure out why you would want to spend time with me." Holton picked up his glass, draining the last of the water like it was a fortifying shot of whiskey.

"What if I wanted to get to know you?" Marcus asked, and he half expected Holton to make that sound again, but Holton simply stared at him like he was crazy. "You said I could have anyone. So I choose you."

"Why?" Holton asked in a whisper.

"Does there have to be a reason?"

"This isn't some joke, is it?" Holton twisted to look around the restaurant.

Marcus reached out and lightly touched Holton's hand. "No. This is not a joke. I would never do anything that cruel to anyone. I like you and you are beautiful. You're also handsome, and you have the deepest blue eyes of anyone I've ever met. I'd love to have blond hair that curls just like yours." Marcus smiled slightly. "You know, when I was young, in about the second grade, I asked my mother why I couldn't have blond hair like my friend Jimmy. He had hair just like yours and that was what I wanted. She told me that someday I'd be very happy I had black hair and darker skin."

"Your mother was right. I'm pale and you're gorgeous."

"Dang it. Holton, I'd love to be able to show you just how handsome you are." Marcus let a little of the fire he was feeling in his stomach show in his eyes, hoping Holton would understand that he really did feel something for him. But Holton's eyes filled with a touch of fear before looking away. "What is it?"

"Nothing," Holton answered very quickly.

"Okay. Then why don't we talk about something else? Do you have brothers and sisters? What's your family like?"

"It's just my mom, dad, and me. This summer my dad turned seventy. He retired a few years ago from Ford. Mom's a retired nurse. A few years ago, she started forgetting things, and I suspect she has Alzheimer's, but the doctors aren't ready to officially diagnose it yet. She gets confused sometimes and forgets things a lot, but she and my dad couldn't get along without each other."

"Sounds like you have a good family," Marcus supplied, pleased that some of Holton's nervousness was gone and he looked somewhat more at ease.

"They gave me the best they could. Dad worked in the parts department of a Ford dealership, and he had most weekends off. Mom and Dad always went camping. When I was a kid, they bought a pop-up camper, and we went all over in it. Dad hauled that thing from one end of the country to the other. When I was ten, we joined a camping club. There were a lot of other families that had kids my age, and we used to go camping all over most weekends in the summer and for vacation."

The server set their plates in front of them, but Holton didn't seem to notice, he was so into his story, which Marcus found incredibly endearing.

"One summer we went all the way to the Grand Canyon with some of the people from the camping club. That was one of the best times of my life." The last of Holton's reticence seemed to have slipped away. His blue eyes shone, and a bright smile lit his face. "What's your family like?" Holton asked.

"Right now it's just my dad and me," Marcus explained. "Mom died last year. Like your mom, she started experiencing memory loss and forgetfulness. At first she thought she was just getting older. But in her mid-fifties, she was diagnosed with early-onset Alzheimer's. By the time she was sixty, she couldn't remember me or my dad at all, and she died at sixty-two."

Holton nodded his head, and Marcus knew he understood. "I think that's coming for my mom."

"Sorry," Marcus said, picking up his fork and tasting his meal. "I didn't mean for our conversation to go down this particular road."

"No. I suppose not," Holton told him quietly. "You must have done fun things with your mom and dad."

"Dad and I used to go to the car shows together. Dad loves cars, and we used to spend most of our weekends working on whatever project he had at the time. He'd find some car that needed a lot of work, and we'd do it together. I was the only kid in my school whose first car was a '66 Corvette," Marcus said, and Holton whistled. "I didn't drive it for long, though."

"Did something happen to it?"

Marcus shook his head. "Someone offered me enough money for it that I could go to college, but it was the first car I worked on by myself, so I turned him down, and we put the car up in Dad's garage."

"Where is it now?" Holton asked, swallowing a bite of his dinner.

"In my garage," Marcus answered, and he took delight in the look on Holton's face. "It's not all original, but I've kept it as close as I can."

"Did you work on other cars too?" Holton asked him, and Marcus nodded as he continued eating, pleased they'd found something to talk about that didn't seem to make Holton nervous. The man was definitely jumpy about something, but Marcus figured Holton didn't want to talk about it.

"Yeah. Mostly we worked on the cars and then sold them. It was a way to make extra money. My dad still does it in his spare time. Do you like cars?"

"I never worked on them, but yeah, I do. I work as an engineer doing CAD drawings, so I like most mechanical things. I spend most of my days designing and drawing parts for industrial machines."

"That's pretty cool," Marcus said. He'd figured Holton was pretty smart. "Did you ever design the parts for cars?"

Holton shook his head. "Mostly parts for filling and bottling machines. I get the specifications from the client and do the drawings and layouts." Holton looked back down at his plate. "It's not very glamorous, but I like it."

"I bet you're good at it," Marcus told Holton, wondering what had put the shy look on his face again, but thankfully it only lasted for a few seconds. They talked through the rest of the meal, changing subjects easily and often. Marcus hadn't known quite what to expect when he'd asked Holton to dinner, but he hadn't expected someone who knew so much and could carry on a knowledgeable conversation on just about any subject Marcus could think of. When their plates were empty, they continued talking over coffee before the server brought their bill. Marcus handed him his credit card, expecting Holton to balk, which he did. But Marcus explained that he'd invited Holton to dinner. "You can pay next time."

"Next time? You want there to be a next time?" Holton asked, turning shy once again.

"Yes, I would, but I'd like to invite you back to the house." Marcus knew in an instant that he'd probably pushed things too far. Holton's eyes went wide, and Marcus thought he might have even backed away from him. Marcus had already concluded that Holton was shy, but now he realized his behavior went beyond shy. He'd seen what he thought were glimpses of fear a few times today, and now he was sure of it. "I thought you'd like to see the car. I have a two-stall garage, and I keep the Corvette in one of the stalls. I haven't taken it out in a while, and since you seemed interested, I figured we could take it for a ride." Marcus kept his voice light and saw the ghost of a smile around the edge of Holton's mouth. "I live just a few miles away."

Holton swallowed hard, and Marcus watched him, wondering just what kind of war was being fought behind those incredible eyes. Marcus had no doubt Holton was fighting with himself, and Marcus hoped the side that would give him the benefit of the doubt came out the winner. Because if it didn't, Marcus knew somehow in his heart that he would truly be the loser.

"Okay," Holton answered after quite a while. "I'll follow you to your house."

Holton stood up from the table, and Marcus did the same, leading the way out of the restaurant and into the parking lot. Marcus waited until Holton was in his car before pulling out and turning onto the busy street. For a second, he thought he'd lost Holton, but saw him a few cars back and slowed down to let others pass until Holton caught up to him, and then Marcus wound his way to his duplex. Parking on the street, Marcus waited for Holton to park and then met him on the front walk.

"I bought this about five years ago, and I rent out the downstairs apartment and live upstairs. My dad lives just down the street, so it's easy for me to help him out when he needs it," Marcus explained as he led Holton around the side of the house and through the backyard to the garage. "I'll need to go around. I'll be right back," Marcus told Holton as he hurried around to the overhead garage doors. Unlocking one and pushing it up, Marcus turned on the lights before pulling the car cover off the Corvette and placing it in the trunk. Then he ushered Holton inside.

"Wow," Holton crooned softly as he walked over to the car, caressing the body with his hand. "I've seen a few of these but never up close."

Marcus smiled before opening the door. "Go ahead, try it out," he offered, and Holton grinned at him before sliding into the driver's seat. "Would you like to drive?" Marcus dangled the keys in front of Holton, and you would have thought he'd just won the lottery.

"You're going to let me drive?"

"You can handle a clutch, right?" Marcus asked, and Holton rolled his eyes. "Okay. Let me put the top down, and you can take us for a spin." Marcus unlatched the locks and manually lowered the top before getting in the passenger seat. "Go ahead, it's all yours."

Holton started the car and slowly backed out of the garage, driving like he'd just graduated from driver's education, he was being so careful. Cautiously, he negotiated the alley before turning onto the street. "God, I can't believe I'm driving one of these."

"Isn't it awesome?" Marcus commented, and Holton nodded his head. "Go ahead and take it on the freeway for a few miles." Holton looked at him for a second to make sure he was serious before pulling onto the on-ramp and accelerating, merging into freeway traffic.

"Everyone's looking at the car," Holton said over the noise of the freeway, the air, and the engine.

"No, they're not. They're looking at you," Marcus told Holton, patting his leg lightly to reassure him.

"They are not—they're looking at you. No one would ever look at me," Holton told him.

"Take the next exit," Marcus instructed, and Holton got off. "Pull off to the side," Marcus added, and Holton did as he was instructed. "Holton, you look perfect driving this car, with your hair furled by the wind and the biggest smile on your face. You were made to drive this car, so don't tell me that everyone who passed us wasn't looking at you, because they were. Just like I'm looking at you now," Marcus said very softly as he touched the skin on Holton's arm. "You're a handsome man, Holton, and you need to realize that."

"No, I'm not… I'm broken," Holton said before turning to look out the other way as cars passed by them on the road. Marcus caught the unusual words, wondering just what Holton was saying, but from the set of his mouth, there was no way Holton was going to tell him.

"Holton, you aren't broken, and you are handsome, very handsome." Marcus waited until Holton looked toward him again before leaning over the seat and lightly touching his lips to Holton's. "You're very handsome, Holton, but you're also smart, funny when you want to be, and incredibly attractive."

Holton stared at him as though he were looking to see if Marcus was serious, and Marcus stared right back into the incredible blue eyes. At least this time Holton didn't shake his head or try to deny it, and Marcus took that as a small victory. "Let's continue our ride."

Holton put the car back into gear, and they started back toward the house, pulling the car back into the garage ten minutes later. Holton got out, and Marcus put the top back up before re-covering the car. "Thank you for letting me drive the car," Holton said, his voice rushed, "but I should be going home."

"Holton," Marcus said softly as he finished up with the car, closing the garage door behind them. "I didn't mean to make you uncomfortable, but I wanted you to know that I like you, and I'd like to get to know you, if you'll let me. You're a sweet man, and it's been a very long time since I've met someone like you."

Marcus saw Holton swallow hard, like he did whenever he seemed to be unsure of something. Slowly, Marcus stepped a little closer, cupping Holton's cheek in his hand before kissing him lightly. Holton's lips tasted slightly of the spices from dinner, and beneath that, a slight sweetness that had to be Holton himself. Not wanting to push more than he had already, Marcus backed away and waited.

Holton touched his lips with his fingers and looked at Marcus with an expression he couldn't read. "I should be going," Holton said softly, and Marcus watched as Holton walked through the yard to his car.

Marcus knew he should be upset, but he'd seen Holton almost continuously touch his lips as he walked across the lawn. Marcus watched, waving once as Holton's car pulled away, and he thought Holton might have waved in return.

III

HOLTON sat in his quiet, out-of-the-way cubicle, staring at his computer screen, wireless mouse in hand, but it wasn't moving, and his eyes weren't really focused, either. Thankfully, it was still early, and very few people were in the office. Not that it really mattered, anyway. No one stopped by his desk very often, and as long as he got his work done on time, no one would. And in the last five years, he'd never missed a deadline, not even those impossible, last-minute ones that occasionally seemed to pop out of thin air. He just couldn't seem to concentrate this morning, though, on anything except the fact that Marcus had kissed him, twice.

Holton tried to remember the last time he'd been kissed by anyone who wasn't a relative, and he really couldn't. Forty-two and he'd never been kissed. "God, I'm pathetic," Holton mumbled under this breath. "A real loser."

"What?" A voice floated over the soft wall that divided his cubicle. "Did you say something?"

Shoot, he hadn't realized Marie had come in, and now she'd heard him talking to himself. He really was pathetic. "It's nothing," he answered softly, forcing his attention back to the task at hand. Or at least he tried to, but his mind wasn't exactly cooperating, any more than it had last night when he'd tried to put Marcus's kisses out of his mind and instead ended up jerking himself off twice to the memory of Marcus's lips on his, and the way he'd looked the few times he'd seen him naked in the showers at the gym.

What Holton couldn't seem to get past was that the man was so big and strong, and yet he'd kissed him so gently and with such care. In his fantasy, Marcus had always pulled him tight and kissed him hard, taking what he wanted, because that's what Holton expected other guys would be like. But Marcus had surprised him, and after the way Holton had nearly run away after Marcus's last kiss, Holton figured that was that and there wouldn't be any more. Getting up from his desk, he locked his terminal and walked to the break area, hoping a cup of tea would help clear his mind so he could get to work.

Waiting for the water to heat, Holton leaned against the small counter, letting his mind drift. "Morning, Holton," he heard Sherry say as she lifted the coffeepot off its heater, pouring two cups. "You're looking really good," she told him, and Holton saw her looking him over. "Are you working out?" she asked, setting the mugs on the counter.

"Uh-huh," he answered, busying himself getting out a teabag and placing it in his mug.

"Some of us go out to Mister J's on Fridays after work for a drink. You should come with us sometime," she told him with a smile, and Holton saw her eyes drift over him once again. Finally the light went on, and he realized she was flirting with him. Holton had no idea what to do and abruptly turned away to pour his hot water.

"Umm, thanks, I appreciate that." Holton managed a smile he hoped didn't display the discomfort he felt before walking back to his cubicle, setting his mug on his desk.

"Was Sherry flirting with you?" he heard Marie ask over the cubicle, the click of her computer keys pausing. "I heard her say that she was going to invite you out." Holton sat at his seat, hoping if he said nothing that the whole thing would go away. But a few seconds later, he felt someone watching him and looked up as Marie peered over the wall. "Since you went on the diet, all the single women are trying to get your attention. Haven't you noticed?"

Holton shook his head, hoping his mouth wasn't hanging open. That was the last thing he needed, people talking about him behind his back. "Tell them to stop, please."

"You really aren't interested, are you?" Marie asked. Holton would probably consider her the closest thing to a friend he had at work. She was nice and safe. He knew because of the picture of her girlfriend she kept on her desk and because she was approaching fifty and gave off this warm, motherly vibe that Holton found made her easy to talk with, not that they talked all that much. "It's okay, Holton. I understand, I really do." Holton looked up and nodded. "You know you have nothing to worry about or be ashamed of."

Holton didn't really want to talk about this at work, or anywhere for that matter, but he nodded slowly a few times. "Thank you."

Marie's head disappeared below the wall, and Holton unlocked his computer, going back to work on the drawing. "I understand that this isn't the place to talk about it," Marie said as she walked into his cubicle, sitting in his visitor's chair that rarely saw any visitors. "I know you're shy and pretty quiet, but if you want to talk to someone, I'll listen."

"Thanks, but...." He wasn't sure how to talk about things like this. He never really had, other than a single conversation he'd had with his parents after... the incident. He'd kept that part of himself closed off for so long he wasn't sure he could ever really open himself up to anyone. Standing up, he peered over the nearly empty work area and then sat back down.

"I sort of met someone," he said with a smile, "but I may have messed it up."

"Because you were shy?" Marie asked, and Holton nodded. To his surprise, Marie chuckled softly. "Honey, shy is one of the things guaranteed to spark someone's interest. Most people put everything out there and what you see is what you get, there's nothing more. No, if he's interested, he'll be back because you've sparked his curiosity. It is a he, isn't it?" Holton nodded and smiled. "I just wanted to be sure we were on the same page." She patted his leg lightly. "Don't you worry, honey." Marie gave him another smile before returning to her work area, and soon the sound of computer keys drifted over to the wall. Holton sipped his tea before opening his work files and getting busy. He had a lot of work to get done.

The rest of the day was very ordinary. Additional requests for drawings came in. Many of them he'd already done a version of previously, so he just needed to make changes to things he already had and send them on. At the end of the day, he wished Marie a nice weekend as he shut down his computer and made sure his workstation was just so.

"Is this guy you're seeing from the gym?" Marie asked, sticking her head over the wall as he was leaving. Holton nodded, but didn't answer. "Well, then, go get him," Marie said with a wink and a smile, and Holton walked down the aisle and out of the office.

The gym was only a few miles away, and as usual, he drove right there, parking in his normal space. Opening the trunk, Holton grabbed his bag and headed for the front doors, but stopped before going inside. He knew Marcus would be working, and he wondered what kind of reception he'd get, if any at all. What if he had blown it completely? Holton looked up at the front of the building like he was hoping some inspiration would come. Getting nothing, he walked to the front doors and entered the club.

Scanning his card at the front desk, he hurried back toward the locker rooms without looking toward Marcus's desk. He couldn't bear the thought of being ignored, or worse, rejected outright. Selecting a locker, Holton changed and grabbed his book, deciding that today was a good day for cardio. After locking up his things, Holton headed toward the workout floor, going straight upstairs and jumping onto a treadmill, where he started the machine and opened his book, quickly getting into the story.

"You didn't even stop to say hello."

Holton stumbled and nearly fell off the machine, and his book dropped onto the belt, zooming around his feet before shooting off the back of the machine. Holton regained his footing before turning off the machine and retrieving his book. He had no idea what to say to Marcus, so he did everything else he could think of.

"You know," Marcus started to say, and Holton raised his gaze from where he was picking up his book. Marcus leaned against the machine next to his, looking surprisingly amused. "You should be more careful."

"Well, you shouldn't sneak up on people," Holton snapped as he closed his book before stepping back on the treadmill.

"Do you want to tell me why you didn't say hello?"

Holton shrugged and began pushing the buttons to restart the machine. "I guess I figured I'd blown it and didn't need you to tell me."

"You didn't blow anything. But I think you might owe me a teensy explanation for yesterday. I know you're a little shy, but you didn't need to run away after I'd kissed you. A 'no thanks, I'm not interested' would have done just as well."

Holton stood on the belt, listening to Marcus, but not really comprehending what he was saying right away.

"Huh?" God, now he sounded totally dumb. Closing his mouth, he let his brain process what Marcus was telling him. *He thought Holton wasn't interested in him.* Holton blinked a few times and then looked down at his feet.

"Holton, just say something," Marcus whispered.

"I thought you'd be mad at me."

"For what? Being shy? I don't think so. I thought I'd pushed you too hard," Marcus said, and Holton felt some of his nerves drop away when he realized that Marie had been right.

"So you decided to scare me and try to get me killed on one of the treadmills," Holton said before he could stop himself, and then Marcus surprised him—he laughed.

"That wasn't in the plan, but it did get your attention." Marcus's eyes twinkled a little. "It also got you to talk to me, although the part about you nearly getting hurt wasn't intended, I promise. And at the risk of scaring you off again, I have something I'd like to tell you." Holton nodded, and Marcus leaned close enough that he could feel his breath against his ear. "You're a really nice kisser."

Holton felt himself blush, and he took a step back to see if Marcus was still teasing him, but he wasn't. His eyes looked totally serious, and Holton felt his cheeks color even more.

"I am?" Holton asked, and he stared at Marcus, wondering just what he should do. He'd loved the way Marcus had kissed him. He'd still been able to feel that touch hours later. But all this was so new. The part of him that was comfortable and quiet told him to turn the machine back on and open his book, to keep himself the way he'd always been. No one could hurt him then. He had a good life, quiet and peaceful. But was that what he really wanted? He was forty-two, for God's sake, and yesterday was the first time he'd ever been kissed, really kissed—the first time anyone had touched him tenderly, and Holton wanted more. Was he scared? *God, yes.* He just hoped his knees weren't shaking so much that everyone in the gym could see how scared he was. Swallowing around the lump in his throat, he saw Marcus smile.

"Yes, you are, a really good kisser," Marcus told him, stepping back slightly, and Holton felt some of the nervousness abate. "Like I said, I understand that you're shy and a little uncertain." Holton couldn't hold back a soft snort. "What?"

"I think that's the understatement of the century. Shy? I'm not shy. Most of the time, I'm scared to death." There, he'd actually said it out loud to someone. Why he'd actually said it to Marcus was beyond him, and Holton turned away, not able to look at the stronger, more confident man. He felt like such a failure. Holton turned on the machine before smacking the stop button. He wasn't in the mood to exercise. What he really wanted was a chocolate bar, or three, and maybe half a gallon of ice cream!

"Would you like to talk about it?" Marcus asked, and Holton shook his head as emotions he'd tried to keep buried flowed to the surface. He used to drown them in food. That had never worked, so he tried running from it with exercise, and that hadn't worked, either. "Do you want me to go?" Marcus asked him, and Holton hesitated before shaking his head again. Holton had no idea what he wanted, and he found himself doing what he usually did—pulling inward where it was safe and quiet, and where he couldn't be hurt.

Marcus lightly touched his arm. The warm touch felt so good, but it wasn't enough to pull him out of himself. Then the hand slipped away, and Holton watched as Marcus walked toward the stairs, turning to look at Holton one last time before disappearing from view.

Holton stared at where Marcus's head had disappeared, wondering just what he was doing. This beautiful man had been nice to him, and Holton had ignored him and run from him. Stepping off the machine, Holton grabbed his book before hurrying down the stairs. He practically ran into Marcus at the bottom of the stairs. Holton looked at him and held his breath, and somewhere deep inside, he figured out that maybe he'd done too much hiding. "Could we talk?"

Marcus nodded. "I'm working till seven."

"I can meet you here," Holton said. His nerves and the urge to run, literally and figuratively, returned big-time, but he'd made his decision, and he wouldn't go back on it. If Marcus decided he wasn't worth it, then Holton would just have to deal with it.

Marcus moved back toward a little-used desk in an area that was originally designed for the personal trainers but rarely got used now because most business was conducted up front. "You don't have to tell me anything you aren't ready for," Marcus said softly. Holton was about to explain when his phone buzzed in the pocket of his shorts. Fishing it out, he saw his parents' phone number on the screen.

"Hi, Mom," Holton said, since she was the one who usually called him.

"Holton, it's me." His dad didn't sound right.

"Dad? Is something wrong?"

"Yes. Your mother took a nap, and when she woke up, she didn't know where she was and she thought I was a stranger out to hurt her. She ran away from me and fell in the hallway. I called an ambulance, and they're taking her to the hospital."

"I'll meet you there," Holton told him right away, and the call disconnected. Still holding his phone in his hand, he looked at Marcus. "They're taking my mom to the hospital. She didn't know where she was and fell."

Marcus nodded his head slowly. "Here," he said, reaching for Holton's phone. A few seconds later, Holton heard another phone ring and then Marcus handed his back.

"I called my number so you have it. Please let me know how she is. I know how hard it is to see someone you love slip away from you."

"Thanks," Holton answered before hurrying to the locker room. Thankfully, he hadn't done enough exercise to get sweaty, so he just changed his clothes and threw his things into his bag before hurrying through the club to the exit and out to his car.

The drive to the hospital took awhile with traffic, but he finally made it. After parking his car, Holton hurried into the emergency room and gave the lady behind the desk his name and told her who he was there to see. "The doctor is examining her, and your father is back with her now. I'll let them know you're here."

Holton sat down in one of the chairs, absently thumbing through a magazine. After a while, his dad came out and sat next to him.

"How is she, Dad?"

He shook his head. "She's remembering things better right now, but they want to keep her and do some tests. They think she has Alzheimer's."

"We already figured that," Holton said, and his dad nodded.

"But they're saying she may have dementia as well. They called her regular doctor, and they're bringing in a neurologist, but I suspect they'll want to put her in a home."

Holton felt as though he'd been punched in the gut. He knew his mother forgot things, but he hadn't known how bad it really was. "How long has she been like this?"

His dad sighed. "Off and on for a while. We didn't want to worry you. The doctor told me there really wasn't much they could do when I took her for her last appointment."

"You should have told me, Dad," Holton insisted, and he saw his father nod slowly and look away. Holton knew this wasn't the time to discuss this and let the subject drop, but he still felt hurt and a little angry that they'd both kept this from him.

"They said we can see her once they move her to a room."

"Okay," Holton answered and settled back for a wait. His thoughts swam all over the place. One minute he was worried about his mom and the next he was thinking about Marcus and how he'd made a complete mess of everything with him. After sitting for a while longer, a nurse came to talk to them.

"We're working to find a bed for your wife," she said to Holton's dad. "It's taking a little time."

"Can we see her?" his dad asked, already getting out of his chair.

"If you'd like, but right now the doctor has given her something to help her sleep. We've stitched her head, and she doesn't appear to have a concussion. Right now, it's best to let her rest." Holton's dad nodded and sat back down. "We should have a room for her soon, and I'll come get you."

"I'd like to see her," Holton's father said, and the nurse nodded. Holton stayed where he was, knowing they'd only let one of them back with her at a time. Once his father was gone, Holton fidgeted, looking through various magazines and watching the door for his dad. He thought of going to find something to eat, but didn't want to be gone in case his dad came back, so he simply sat and waited. With nothing else to do, he watched the front door as people came and went.

Holton checked his watch for what seemed like the millionth time in the past hour. Hopefully, his mother would be taken up to a room very soon. Resting his head against the back of the chair, Holton tried to still the worries that kept surfacing. "Holton." He jumped when he heard his name, and looked up to see Marcus standing next to his chair.

"What are you doing here?" he asked, never so happy to see anyone in his life.

"I didn't hear from you and was worried," Marcus said, sitting in the chair next to Holton's. "I also know what you and your dad are going through." Holton watched and waited for Marcus to continue. "I wanted to make sure you were okay," he clarified rather reluctantly.

"Thank you. That was very nice," Holton said softly.

"I'm a nice guy, Holton," Marcus told him, and Holton nodded slowly. He was realizing that Marcus really was a nice guy. He'd worked out with him, let him drive his car, and he'd even come down to the hospital to sit with him. What more proof did he need?

"They're trying to get a room for my mom, and once she's settled, I can go. There isn't anything more I can do tonight other than make sure my dad's okay." As if on cue, his dad walked into the waiting area to tell him they were moving Holton's mom to a room.

"She's asleep, and I doubt she'll even know she's being moved," he explained before looking at Marcus.

"Dad, this is Marcus. He's a good friend from the gym." Holton had no idea how he should introduce Marcus, and he hoped what he'd said was correct. His dad and Marcus shook hands.

"Let me go see my mom before I leave. I'll be right back," he told Marcus, who nodded and sat back down. Holton followed his dad through the doors and to the small room where his mother lay sleeping, a bandage on her forehead. Walking to the side of the bed, Holton took her hand and held it for a few minutes. She looked so frail like this. She'd always been small and thin, but with a huge personality. Now she seemed much older than she had just a few days earlier.

"We're going to take her to her room now," the nurse said from behind him. "She probably won't even wake up during the trip."

"Go on home, son. I'll make sure she's comfortable and then go home too," Holton's dad told him, patting him lightly on the back.

"Are you sure?"

"Yes. There's nothing either of us can do," he answered, and Holton released his mother's hand, placing it under the blankets before leaving the room so others could get in to move her. Holton watched as they got her ready, and then they slowly wheeled her out of the room and down the hallway. Holton waited until they'd turned the corner before slowly walking back toward the waiting area.

Marcus stood up as soon as he saw him. "They took my mom to a room," Holton said as he approached.

"If you want to see her, I'll wait for you."

Holton thought that was one of the nicest offers possible. "No. She's asleep, and there's nothing we can do tonight. I'm just going to go home."

"I'll follow you," Marcus told him, and Holton didn't have the strength to argue with him. Leaving the hospital, Holton walked to his car. Marcus pulled up a few minutes later, and Holton turned out of the parking lot, driving toward home. He wasn't sure about Marcus coming home with him, but it was too late to say anything now. Pulling up in front of his house, Holton parked and waited for Marcus before unlocking the house and going inside.

"This is really nice," Marcus commented after Holton turned on the lights.

"I found the house a few years ago," Holton explained as he hung up his jacket. He'd have hung up Marcus's, as well, but he didn't have one. "The place was a mess. I had to level and re-support parts of the back of the house, and then I renovated everything. It took months, and I did every bit of the work myself," Holton added proudly.

"The woodwork and floors are amazing," Marcus told him as he looked around.

"The floors were hidden under old carpet. That's the one thing that saved them, I suppose. When I pulled up the ugly green stuff, I found these underneath," Holton pointed to the rich floors with intricate borders around the edges. "Everything else in the house had been completely tackified with hideous wallpaper and the ugliest colors of paint you've ever seen in your life. Dad helped with the woodwork and stuff, while Mom is amazing with a paintbrush… I mean, used to be," he corrected. "We saved what we could and replaced what we couldn't with like materials." Holton ran his hand over the woodwork he'd so lovingly restored.

"Holton," Marcus murmured, and Holton turned to face Marcus, who stepped close, placed his warm hands against Holton's cheeks, and drew him into a kiss.

Just like the day before, Holton felt his lips tingle, and for a second he thought of pulling away, wondering why Marcus would kiss him. Then their lips moved and the tingles spread throughout his body. Holton placed his hands on Marcus's shoulders to steady himself, and Marcus drew him closer, strong arms twining around his waist while deepening the kiss.

Holton didn't know what to do. He didn't even know if what he was doing was right, but then he heard Marcus make this sound deep in his throat that raised goose bumps along his back. If he could make Marcus sound like that, he must be doing something right. Holton felt the pressure against his lips lessen, and Marcus pulled back. Holton took a deep breath and noticed that Marcus still held him, and he rested his head against the taller man's shoulder. "Holton," he heard Marcus say into his ear.

"Am I really a good kisser?" Holton asked, looking into Marcus's eyes.

"Hasn't anyone ever told you that?"

Holton shrugged. "Never kissed anyone before to find out." God, he was so embarrassed he wanted to sink into the floor. He was a complete freak. Forty-two and never been kissed. He expected Marcus to start running for the door at any moment once he realized the kind of weirdo he held in his arms.

"You've never kissed anybody?" Marcus asked, and Holton shook his head. "Then you haven't...." Marcus's eyebrows lifted in surprise, and Holton squirmed out of his arms and walked into the living room.

"I know I'm freaky, but you don't need to make fun of me." Holton turned away, staring at one of the pictures on the wall. He jumped slightly when hands slid along his shoulders, and initially he tensed up, but then relaxed as he felt Marcus's fingers lightly stroking.

"You're not a freak. You're a sweet man, and it's really special that you're a virgin."

Holton whirled around. "I never said I was a virgin." Holton glared at Marcus and felt his blood start to boil as the anger and resentment that he'd kept bottled up for so long shot to the surface. "I was forced! My innocence was ripped away from me over and over again! Hours, days, I don't know!" Holton took a step back. "I told you I was broken, so you may as well go and leave me alone." Holton dropped onto the sofa, covering his face with his hands as he listened for the footsteps he knew would signal Marcus realizing he really was a freak and leaving him alone in his shame.

"You aren't broken," he heard Marcus say and then felt his weight next to him on the sofa. Before he knew what was happening, Holton had been pulled into a hug. Not knowing quite what to do, he hugged back and felt his emotional tide burst like a wave on the beach, and he cried silently on Marcus's shoulder. "You're beautiful and you aren't broken or damaged. You're simply you," Marcus said softly, over and over again.

Once he got his emotions under control, Holton lifted his head and immediately flushed when he realized what he'd done. "I'm sorry."

"Nothing to be sorry for," Marcus told him, not releasing the hug before giving him a very light kiss. "You must have been holding that in for a very long time." Holton nodded his agreement, not wanting to trust his voice. "Do you want to talk about it?"

"Not now," Holton answered, and thankfully Marcus didn't push. Instead, he held him against his hard, warm body, and Holton felt his body react to Marcus's nearness, almost to his shame.

"You have nothing to be ashamed of." Marcus placed his fingers under Holton's chin, tilting his head up so Marcus could kiss him. Holton started to give Marcus the arguments he'd always given himself, but they died on his lips as Marcus kissed him again while he shifted them on the sofa.

Marcus leaned back, his head against the arm of the sofa, and Holton rested against his side, cradled in Marcus's arms. They didn't talk much. Marcus seemed to find so many other fun things to do with their mouths. Holton's phone rang at one point, and he fished it out of his pocket, trying to sit up, but Marcus held him close, and Holton listened as his dad gave him an update on his mother before telling him he was home and that he would be going back to the hospital in the morning. After saying good night to his dad, Holton closed his phone and set it on the coffee table. "Don't you have to go to work in the morning?" Holton asked, wondering just how long he would be held in Marcus's arms.

"Not until noon," Marcus answered, squeezing him a little tighter. Feeling bolder, Holton ran his hands along Marcus's arm, feeling his muscles and soft, smooth skin. For a second, he wondered why Marcus felt so smooth, but the thought flew from Holton's head as Marcus kissed him again.

IV

MARCUS woke with a start as someone slapped at his chest. Jumping slightly, he opened his eyes in a darkened room, feeling someone curled around him. Things came back to him fast. Holton.... Marcus almost smiled when he was smacked again, this time hard. Looking at Holton, he saw his eyes were still closed, and he was thrashing and whimpering in his sleep. No, that wasn't right—he seemed to be fighting in his sleep. "It's okay," he said softly, stroking Holton's back to try to soothe him. It seemed to be working, because Holton settled down, still holding him tightly as he slept.

After Holton's emotional outburst, Marcus had held Holton on the sofa, and the day seemed to catch up with both of them. They'd kissed for a while and talked softly, but eventually Marcus had drifted off. Holton must have as well because he'd suddenly jumped, jerking them both awake. At the time, Marcus had expected to leave, but Holton didn't seem to want to let him go, and Marcus would hold the man as long as he wanted. Marcus had slipped off his shoes and socks, lying on the bed next to Holton, fully expecting to leave once Holton fell asleep. Instead, he'd drifted off as well.

Holton was now quiet and appeared to be sleeping peacefully again. But Marcus's mind kept running over Holton's revelation. He'd thought Holton was just shy and a little nervous. But to find out that he'd never been kissed and had been alone all these years because of what someone else had done to him—Marcus felt his fists clench and unclench as he thought about it.

The things that raced through Marcus's mind made his blood boil. Holton hadn't just been attacked; he'd been violated and had had his peace of mind ripped away from him. *How did anyone ever get over that?* Marcus silently asked himself, and he realized that Holton probably never had. Holton had never been kissed or loved, and he had probably never let anyone close. God, so many things made sense to him now: Holton's fear of the bigger guys at the gym, the way he always looked around him and watched everyone, the way he jumped whenever anyone touched him. Marcus couldn't imagine going through life knowing he'd been hurt and then worrying that someone was going to do it again.

Holton wriggled against him, the room a little chilly, and Marcus thought of getting up to find another blanket, but he didn't want to wake Holton. He seemed to be sleeping, and if the thrashing and small cries were any indication, Holton probably didn't usually sleep very well. Holton shifted once again, and Marcus realized that while Holton was asleep, part of him was quite substantial and very much awake and rubbing against his hip. Marcus tried to ignore it, but his body would have none of that thought.

Marcus saw Holton's eyes slide open and look at him for a second. In the early morning light, he saw Holton color before moving away rather quickly. "You have nothing to be ashamed of, you know." That was true in so many ways. Marcus moved closer to Holton, drawing him into a kiss before scooting closer. Hoping it would help, Marcus drew Holton on top of him, letting the smaller man have control as they continued kissing. "You taste so good," Marcus crooned softly when Holton lifted his head away, breaking the kiss for a second before Marcus drew him into another. He did his best not to push or press Holton, but he could feel the other man's arousal sliding against his own through their pants. It was heady, erotic, and exciting, and Marcus wanted Holton so badly he could barely think straight. He felt one of Holton's hands slide under his shirt, caressing the skin of his chest. Holton's touch felt amazing and made his skin come alive. He wanted more. He wanted to tear the clothes off both of them and make love to Holton right then and there. But he thought that would just scare him, and that was the last thing he wanted. No, it was better to try to go at Holton's speed. But when Holton began lifting up his shirt, Marcus felt as though he were coming to the end of his control.

Pulling the T-shirt over his head, Marcus settled back on the bed, and Holton's hands caressed trails over his skin. When Holton's fingers found Marcus's nipples, Marcus moaned softly and began to tentatively tug off Holton's shirt as well. Holton let him, and soon their chests were skin to skin. Holton's skin felt incredible against his—hot and smooth. To Marcus's surprise, Holton started making these deep, throaty moans and kissed him hard. Marcus could tell Holton was beginning to lose himself, but Marcus reminded himself that he had to remain in control to ensure things didn't go too far or too fast. This was Holton's first time, after all.

Taking Holton's cheeks in his hands, Marcus tenderly lifted Holton's lips away from his, breaking the kiss so he could look into Holton's now midnight-blue eyes as he lightly nipped at Holton's lips. "Lie back on the bed," Marcus whispered as he coaxed Holton onto his back on the mattress. "We're going to take this slow and easy."

Holton looked at him, quite confused, but rolled slowly onto the mattress, his eyes following every move Marcus made. Caressing Holton's chest, Marcus rolled onto his stomach, sliding down the mattress as he kissed the skin of Holton's chest. Opening Holton's pants, Marcus slid down the zipper as his eyes locked onto Holton's. He was prepared to stop at the first sign of nervousness, but what he saw was wide-eyed wonder. Parting the fabric, Marcus nuzzled the bulge he found inside, inhaling Holton's rich, musky scent. Marcus silently asked Holton's permission with his eyes, and when he saw the other man nod, Marcus drew Holton's cock out of the white cotton. "So beautiful," Marcus said softly as he caressed the silken hardness. Holton gasped softly when Marcus whipped his tongue along Holton's thick length. Then all he heard was quiet. Looking up, he thought he saw the first hints of nervousness. Marcus knew he could stop or go for broke and try to drive the nerves away. Going for the second approach, Marcus opened his mouth and sucked Holton deep.

The gasp and shallow breaths told him he'd chosen correctly. Sucking hard, Marcus took all of Holton he could before sliding his lips back along Holton's big dick, then sucking him deep once again. Holton went wild, groaning softly as he thrust his hips forward. Marcus liked to think he was talented when it came to sucking cock, but Holton stretched him to the limits of his talents. Still, he wasn't about to stop now. Holton tasted heavenly, and Marcus bobbed his head, sucking Holton hard.

Getting comfortable on the bed, Marcus rested on his stomach, his hips grinding into the mattress as he gave Holton the blowjob of both their lives. Marcus knew Holton felt it, too, if the sounds he was making were any indication. And in Marcus's experience, they always were. He wanted to tell Holton to make all the noise he wanted, but that would mean stopping, and he had no intention of doing that. Holton tasted too good and felt too hot to do that. "Marcus," Holton gasped between heaving breaths, and Marcus answered by sucking harder, his own body getting lost in the taste, feel, and sounds Holton was making.

Holton cried out softly, and Marcus felt Holton's climax. Taking him deep, Marcus swallowed hard as his own orgasm barreled into him, shuddering as he came as well.

Holton's gasping breaths joined Marcus's as he let Holton's cock slip from his lips. Sliding up the bed, Marcus captured Holton's lips, letting him catch a taste of himself.

Climbing off the bed, Marcus stripped out of his sticky clothes, wiping himself quickly before helping Holton slip off his pants. Then Marcus climbed back into the bed, pulling Holton close. He could tell there were probably a million questions Holton wanted to ask, but Marcus pulled up the blankets before rubbing Holton's stomach. "Go to sleep. We can talk in the morning." He felt rather than saw Holton nod, and then Marcus closed his eyes, listening as Holton's breathing evened out, and Marcus followed him back into sleep.

MARCUS woke a few hours later to sunlight shining in his eyes, his body plastered to Holton's. Carefully releasing the other man from his arms, Marcus slipped off the bed and tiptoed to Holton's bathroom. After making use of the facilities, he returned to the bedroom to see Holton propped up in bed, looking at him. "Did we really...? I didn't dream that, did I?" Holton asked as he rubbed his eyes.

"No, you didn't dream it," Marcus answered as he approached the bed and saw Holton's eyes widen. Marcus had worked hard on his body, and he wasn't ashamed to let Holton look his fill. Standing by the side of the bed, Marcus watched as Holton tried to slip from under the covers, trying to find his clothes. "Please don't pull away," Marcus said, and Holton stopped, already beginning to slip on his shirt. "Last night you were beautiful, and you still are. You don't have any reason to hide or feel ashamed."

"I don't? I used you like…." Holton let his words trail off, and Marcus climbed onto the bed, desperately needing to close the distance between them.

"You didn't use anyone. What we did was mutually agreeable and very pleasurable. There was no 'using' involved." Marcus extended his hand to Holton, waiting and hoping he'd take it, unsure whether Holton would just continue to get dressed. He saw the indecision on Holton's face, but he finally joined Marcus, letting himself be guided back onto the bed.

Marcus lay on the mattress, tugging Holton on top of him as he guided his lover into a deep, penetrating kiss that he hoped showed Holton just what he was feeling. He wasn't sure Holton was ready or willing to believe words right now, so he let his feelings show in his touch and in his kiss.

Gentling the kiss, Marcus nipped lightly and sucked on Holton's bottom lip before letting him catch his breath. "You really are a great kisser," Marcus told Holton with a smile.

"If you say so."

"I do. I really do," Marcus replied.

Holton turned his head to gaze at the clock by the bed, and Marcus followed his gaze, groaning when he saw how late it was getting. "As much as I'd love to stay here in bed with you, I have to be at work in a few hours."

"I should call my dad," Holton told him as he sat on the edge of the bed.

"Hey," Marcus said as he shifted to sit next to him, "you were wonderful and you have nothing to worry about." Marcus stood up, searching for his clothes. "Are you going to work out this morning?"

"Yes," Holton answered without moving or looking up.

"I have to work till about eight tonight. Would you like to meet me for dinner?" Marcus asked, wondering what was wrong. Holton shrugged, but didn't answer him. "Hey, sweetheart, you need to tell me if something is bothering you."

Holton turned to look at him. "What if I can't give you what you gave me? Like last night." Marcus could almost hear a comment about Holton being broken, even though he hadn't actually said it.

"Come on," Marcus said, tugging Holton to his feet. "You never, ever have to do anything that you're not comfortable with. Ever! Whatever you want to give is enough, just because it comes from you. That makes it more than enough." Marcus stepped close to Holton, kissing him softly. "Now, why don't you get dressed and grab your gym things. We can meet at Panera near the gym in half an hour. I need to stop by my place and get some fresh clothes, but I'll meet you there, and we can have breakfast and maybe work out together before I have to start work."

"Are you sure?"

What would he need to do to make Holton understand that he really did want to spend time with him? "Of course I'm sure."

"Okay," Holton answered with a smile that, for the first time, looked bright and relatively carefree. "I think I'd better get dressed first, though."

"Why?" Marcus said, leaning close to Holton. "I like you like this." Marcus kissed him quickly before backing away and then kissing him again, this time harder and definitely more intense. "I'll see you in about half an hour." Marcus kissed him one more time before searching for his clothes and pulling them on. After saying good-bye, Marcus hurried out of the house to his car. He hated to leave, but he needed to get ready for work, and he knew he'd see Holton in a few minutes. Why he couldn't get enough of Holton sort of boggled his mind, but everything about Holton enthralled him. Getting into his car, Marcus sped away, hurrying through traffic as fast as he could.

Arriving at home, Marcus rushed inside, where he stripped off his clothes, cleaned up quickly, and dressed again. After making sure his gym clothes were packed, Marcus grabbed his bag and locked the house before hurrying to his car again. Pulling into the parking lot of the restaurant, he checked his watch, smiling when he realized he'd made it with two minutes to spare.

Walking inside, Marcus found Holton waiting for him, looking excited. Then Marcus saw a group of the guys from the gym at one of the big tables, and Lonnie motioned them over. "Hey, guys," Marcus said as he pulled up two more chairs so he and Holton could join them. "You all know Holton," Marcus said, knowing he'd made introductions.

"Glad you could join us," Dan said as he reached over the table to shake Holton's hand. The others did the same, reintroducing themselves, and Holton shook everyone's hand before settling in his chair.

"Would you like anything?" Marcus asked Holton.

"No thanks, I'm good," Holton answered, and Marcus got in line to place an order. While waiting, he kept looking at Holton, who seemed to have struck up a conversation with Dan. Once he got his order, he returned to the table and found Holton in a technical conversation with Dan about some new computer software. The conversation around the table continued as Marcus finished his bagel and coffee. Dan and Holton seemed to have exhausted their conversation, and now Holton sat and just appeared to listen, every so often looking at him with a half-smile.

"Would you excuse me?" Holton told him before standing up and heading to the back of the restaurant.

Marcus watched Holton for a second as he wove between the tables. When he turned his head back to the table, he saw a few of the couples exchange knowing looks with one another. "So, are you guys dating?" Max asked with a big smile.

"I don't know what we are," Marcus said, answering the question. "It's too new to put a label on it right now, but yeah, we've been out a few times. Holton's quiet, but still waters run deep, and I think that's very true in his case."

"So, is he kinky or something?" Max asked with a lift to his eyebrows, and his boyfriend Hugh nudged him lightly. "What? I'm just asking." Hugh leaned to Max's ear and said something that made the smaller man blush big-time, and the other guys around the table snickered at Max, and the topic dropped.

"I never would have expected you to go for someone like him," Lonnie said, cutting through the other conversation, and Marcus shifted his attention. "I mean, he seems nice enough, but you're a really hot guy. You could have someone younger who looks like Gene or Ivan."

The sound of a smack reverberated through the restaurant, and the people at the nearby tables all turned their heads to look where Dan had just smacked Lonnie on the back of the head.

"Sometimes you can be a complete ass," Dan said without his usual humor as he glared at Lonnie.

"What?" Lonnie asked as he rubbed the back of his head. "I'm just saying that I'm surprised. I didn't mean that there was anything wrong with the guy. It's just surprising."

"Not all gay men are as shallow as you, and thank God you're straight, because you'd give us all a bad name," Dan told him.

"You mean I'm not good enough?" Lonnie pouted for a second before shifting his expression to a randy grin.

"You're damned right, and if this conversation is about to change into a discussion of your bird, I'm going to smack you again. We've all heard about your dick, and we've all seen it more than once. Been there, done that." Dan rolled his eyes as his smile returned.

Marcus realized that Holton had been gone a while. Looking around, he didn't see him, but everyone seemed to have finished their breakfast, and the conversation shifted to their workouts as the guys stood up and began shrugging on jackets. Marcus walked back toward the restrooms and saw Holton come out. Meeting him by the back door, Marcus walked with him until he reached his car. "I'll meet you at the gym."

"Okay," Holton answered and walked toward his car.

Marcus drove to the club, parking in the area designated for employees and watching for Holton's car. When he saw him park and get out, Marcus waited for him, and they walked into the club together before heading right to the locker room. Marcus changed in a hurry and waited for Holton to join him on the weight floor. "Last time we worked upper body, so this time I thought we'd do lower body," Marcus explained once Holton joined him. "We'll start with the heavier exercises and work down to the ones that work the smaller muscle groups, but first we should stretch." Marcus walked to the mat, watching as Holton joined him. "You know, you have great legs." He wanted to reach out and stroke them, but that wasn't proper behavior in the gym. Maybe after dinner tonight, he could give Holton a massage.

"They're short and fat," Holton said without looking at him.

"No, they're not. You have strong legs," Marcus explained before reaching over to where Holton sat on the mat. "Your upper legs are thick, but that's from muscle." Marcus motioned for Holton to turn a leg over. "You also have thick calves, see?" Marcus touched the back of Holton's lower leg. "Guys work for years to try to build their calves. It's the one place that's hardest to build, and you have great ones naturally."

"Yeah, people are going to like me for my calves," Holton groused.

"People are going to like you for your personality, at least the people who matter." Marcus wondered where this was coming from, but he didn't like it. "What's bothering you?"

"I heard what Lonnie said, and he's right. You could have someone who's so much more than me."

Marcus had had it. "You know, Lonnie was right about one thing. I've had men and women after my attention for a long time." Marcus kept his voice low, but intense. "I've dated a lot of guys, and most of them were after one thing—a crack at my body and nothing more. So, yes, I probably could date a guy who looks like Gene or Ivan. Those guys are one of a kind. Did you know that Dan is significantly older than Gene? Do you think that matters to either of them? Max is a lot smaller than Hugh, and he's never going to be big and buff, but do you think that matters to Hugh? It doesn't, because he loves Max for who he is." Marcus was on a roll, lowering his voice when he realized he was talking too loudly. "And is it so hard for you to believe that someone could like you for who you are? Or is it that you only like me for the way I look?" Marcus stared at Holton, but Holton just looked away and didn't say anything. "Well, I guess that answers that question," Marcus said before getting to his feet. "You know, for the record, I liked you because I thought you were bright and honest, someone who didn't play games and would be fun to spend time with and get to know better. I thought you were someone I could care for and someone who might return those feelings." Marcus felt the squeeze around his heart as he realized Holton was just like all the others.

"I'm not sure I can do that with anyone," Holton replied softly.

Marcus was hurt, and he wasn't buying it. "You've been hiding behind whatever happened to you for so long, you don't know how to stop. But maybe it's time you stopped hiding and started living." Keeping his temper and frustration under control as best he could, Marcus turned and walked away.

V

HOLTON sat on the mat watching Marcus's retreating back. He thought about getting up and trying to talk to him, trying to explain, but he couldn't. Marcus had been right, at least partially. Holton had been hiding behind what had happened to him, and he'd been using it as an excuse for years. Marcus deserved someone better than that. He had been wrong about Holton only liking him for his looks, but what did it matter? Marcus was better off without a bundle of neuroses in his life. Marcus was a good, kind man who deserved better than what Holton thought he could ever be.

"You okay?" Holton looked up and saw Max standing near the mat. "I came by to apologize to Marcus for something I said earlier and saw you sitting here."

"Don't know," Holton said, honestly feeling sort of surprised and numb at the same time. "I think I hurt Marcus, and I didn't mean to."

"Have you been dating long?"

"Just a few days I guess, but it seems like longer." Holton shifted on the mat, getting ready to get up. "I heard what Lonnie said at breakfast," Holton confessed.

"And you listened to that loudmouth? No one *ever* listens to what Lonnie says," Max told him. "He talks all the time and makes a ton of money, but the only reason he has a girlfriend is because Corey is a complete and total saint. Most of the time he talks to get attention."

"Well, this time what he said was true. Marcus could date guys a lot younger and hotter than me," Holton said honestly.

"Maybe, but was someone forcing him to date you?"

Holton looked at Max like he had two heads. "Of course not," he answered indignantly.

"Then it sounds to me like he was dating you because he liked you," Max told him as Holton got to his feet. Without saying more, Max smiled and waved, walking over to where some of the other guys were working out. Holton watched them and decided he really owed Marcus an apology.

Holton walked through the machine area to where the salesmen sat, and saw Marcus sitting at his desk, with a man and a woman occupying the chairs across from him. Feeling better that he'd decided what to do, Holton decided to begin his workout and wait until Marcus was alone so he could speak to him. Walking back toward the weights, he saw Max motion him over. "You can work out with us if you want," Max offered, and Holton pushed away the nervousness that threatened to creep in like it always did.

"Thanks, I'd like that."

"We're doing legs," Max informed him as he got into position on the leg press, pushing more weight than Holton would have ever though the small, thin man could manage.

"You should go after Max," Hugh told him, and Holton suspected it was because he'd need a lot more weight. "Have you ever used this machine before?"

"No." Holton looked to where Marcus sat talking with his clients. "Marcus was showing me how to use the various machines, and we hadn't gotten to this one yet."

Max finished his set, and Holton got into position. "Put your feet here and extend your legs. Now release the stops by pushing down on the lever next to you." Holton did as Hugh instructed and slowly lowered the weight before pressing it back up. "Very good. How does that feel? Is it too heavy?"

"It's okay," Holton grunted as he performed the exercise, concentrating on completing his reps. When he was done, he threw the stops and rested. "That's hard."

"Your legs are big muscles, so they need heavier weight in order to work them properly. If it's too heavy, don't be afraid to lighten it. We all started where you are now." Hugh added additional weight to the machine and began his set, with Max encouraging him while Holton saw the couple get up from Marcus's desk. Holton began to walk over, but then he saw someone else sit down. Damn, he was really hoping to talk to Marcus, and as time went by, Holton felt himself getting more and more anxious.

When it was his turn, he did another set at the same weight, with both Max and Hugh cheering him on. After that, he joined in the cheerleading, but couldn't stop himself from looking over at Marcus's desk after every set. He knew Marcus was working, but Holton also knew he had hurt him, and that was the last thing he'd wanted to do. Marcus had been kind and thoughtful—that was why Holton liked him. Yes, he liked the way Marcus looked, he was stunning, after all, but he liked the way Marcus treated him even more, and he needed to tell him that.

By the time, he, Hugh, and Max had done their last set, Marcus still hadn't had any free time, and Holton was starting to feel antsy. After checking one last time, Holton went into the locker room to get cleaned up and changed.

Fifteen minutes later, Holton walked out of the locker room and up toward the front of the club. Marcus was with yet another client, and for a second, Holton thought about trying to get his attention, but decided not to and walked outside. He and Marcus had made plans for dinner, but he didn't know if they were still on or not. He suspected not. Walking to his car, Holton decided to go home where he could be alone.

Alone, the way he'd spent most of his life. Looking back inside the club, he saw Marcus through the windows sitting at his desk talking with another prospective member. For a second, Holton thought he saw Marcus glance his way, but he wasn't sure. "Damn it!" He'd really blown it. Well, then, he had to fix it. He wasn't sure how, but he'd changed his life in the last few months. He'd gotten healthy and lost weight. He could do whatever he wanted, and he wanted Marcus.

Holton wasn't quite sure what to do. He'd never done anything like this before, but at least some of his nervousness abated once he'd decided he was going to do something. He and Marcus had made plans for dinner. Holton wasn't sure if the plans were still on, but they hadn't officially cancelled them, and Holton hoped that Marcus would at least see if Holton would show up. That was the hope he was clinging to right now, well, that and the fact that he knew where Marcus would be until eight in the evening.

Holton got in his car, closing the door and rolling down the window before fishing his phone out of his pocket and dialing his father's telephone number. To his surprise, his mother answered. "Mom, are you feeling better?"

"Yes, but I get confused," she said. At least she realized there was something wrong, for now. If what Marcus had told him about his mother was right, Holton wasn't too sure how long that would last.

"Mom, I sort of need your advice," Holton said, not really sure how wise it was to ask her opinion right now, but she was still his mother. "I met someone."

"That's very good," she said, sounding distant and very tentative.

"I know we haven't talked much, but you do remember that I'm gay, right?" God, this was so hard.

"Yes, dear, I remember." Now she sounded sad. "I won't ever have grandchildren. But that's okay as long as you have someone who makes you happy." Then she was quiet for a few seconds. "Who is this?" The phone shifted and he heard his father's voice.

"Hi, Holton."

"Hi, Dad. How is she doing?"

"Well, as you heard, she remembers things sometimes and then it drifts away. Right now she's looking at me like she's trying to figure out who I am. The doctor says that sometimes the disease progresses really slowly and sometimes faster. They're hopeful that some new medication can help stabilize things. Are you going to come to the hospital today?"

"Yeah. I went to the gym this morning, and I was going to come up to the hospital once I get something to eat. Is there anything you want me to bring you?"

"No. I'm good."

"Okay, I'll see you soon." Holton disconnected before starting the car and driving toward the hospital. On his way, Holton pulled into a fast-food place and got a salad. Eating quickly, he continued toward the hospital. After stopping at the desk to get his mother's room number, Holton hurried to the elevators.

Walking into his mother's room, he found his father sitting in the chair next to the bed, his mother asleep. His father got up slowly, and they walked into the hallway, talking softly. "She just fell asleep."

"Have you had anything to eat?" Holton asked, and his dad shook his head. "Then let's go down to the cafeteria. We won't be gone long, and she can rest." His dad agreed, and Holton walked with him toward the elevator. They didn't talk much on the ride down, and Holton knew that was his fault. He just didn't feel like talking about anything.

"Your mother is going to be okay," his dad said, trying to reassure him. "Things will be different, but the doctor's pretty confident that, with medication, she'll improve for a while. He did tell me that she'll probably have to go into a home eventually, but he's hopeful now that she'll be able to come back to the house for a while." Holton could hear the hope welling in his father's voice. The elevator doors opened, and they walked down the hall toward the cafeteria.

His dad got in line while Holton snagged a table and sat down to wait for him. The line seemed to move rather quickly, and his dad joined him after a few minutes. "What's on your mind, son?"

"Nothing important," Holton answered. His mother was what counted, not his loneliness.

"Just tell me what's got you so tied in knots."

"I sort of met someone, Dad, and I messed it up."

His father took a spoonful of his potato soup. "Did I ever tell you how I almost lost your mother?" Holton shook his head. "I'd only known Sue for about a week, and we'd made a date for Friday night. I got to working on a project and lost track of time—you know me. I showed up an hour late, and your grandmother told me she'd gone out with friends and that someone who couldn't be on time wasn't good enough for her daughter, right before she slammed the door in my face." Holton nodded. He knew his grandmother hadn't liked his father at first. "Initially, I thought I should just go and lick my wounds. After all, I'd just met her. But I liked her, and she made my heart skip a beat when she smiled at me." Holton saw his dad smile as he took another bite of his lunch. "I figured the only way to make things right was to show her what she meant to me."

"What did you do?"

"I tracked her down with flowers and chocolates in hand. I know it's not very original, but it was enough for her to give me a second chance. She told me later that it wasn't the flowers or the chocolates that impressed her. It was the fact that I pursued her. She liked that I thought enough of her to go after her and to try to win her back. It's nice to be wanted and to have someone demonstrate their feelings for you. Isn't that what Marcus did for you when he came to the hospital to be with you?" His dad raised his eyebrows. "I'm not as old as you seem to think I am." Holton saw his father smile mischievously before returning to his lunch. "Do you like this young man?"

"Yeah, I do, Dad." On the one hand it felt weird to be talking to his dad about Marcus, but in some ways, it also felt very natural. "He's incredibly kind and giving."

"Have you talked to him about what happened?" his dad asked, voice sounding really tentative, which was unusual for his father.

"Outside of you and Mom, I've never talked about it with anyone after the trial."

"Maybe that was our fault. Maybe you should have talked to someone about it." Holton's dad pushed his tray away, looking at him with what Holton thought might have been tears in his eyes. "At the time, we thought it best that you try to put it behind you, so we never brought it up because we thought it would be painful for you. But over the years I've worried that we were wrong. That we should have encouraged you to talk about it, or at least let you know that you could talk about it with us at any time." Holton watched his dad lift his cup of coffee. "I know it was very traumatic for you, for all of us, but I've come to realize that your mother and I were wrong. Not that she'd ever admit it, but we were."

"No, you weren't, Dad. You were supportive and loving through everything." Holton could feel his throat tighten in response to his dad's hurt as well as his own.

"Holton, it happened almost twenty years ago, and in that time you've never seen anyone romantically. I can't tell you how happy I was yesterday when I saw you look at Marcus. You really care for him, and that's a wonderful thing. I'm just sorry it took you so long to allow yourself to find someone. No, let me rephrase that, to open yourself up to someone. So, have you been seeing each other long?"

"Not really. He signed me up at the gym, and we saw each other there, but he first asked me out a few days ago." Holton couldn't keep his face from flushing when he spoke about Marcus.

"Then see where it leads and don't be afraid. Finding someone you care about and could love is the greatest feeling in the world. Not something to be feared."

"But what if I get hurt?" That was what he'd tried to avoid for years.

"Then you get hurt," his dad told him. "But I can tell you from experience, it feels better to go down fighting than it does to roll over and just let things happen to you. If you care for this Marcus, then fight for him. Win or lose, you'll feel good about yourself, and you'll know you tried."

Holton knew his dad was right. Once he'd figured out what he wanted to do, he'd already felt better. "We should go back up and see if Mom's awake," Holton said before picking up his dad's tray, throwing away the trash, and placing it on the counter for the dishroom. He and his dad rode the elevator back to his mom's floor with a feeling of companionship that lately Holton had rarely felt with his dad.

Holton's mother was awake and waiting for them when they returned, and she seemed alert and focused. Holton found that he talked about nothing of any importance, not wanting to disturb or frustrate her. While he was there, a nurse came in to give her some medication, explaining that the doctors were trying something new. Holton stayed for a while until his mother began to tire again. Then he said good-bye, kissing his mother on the cheek and telling her he'd be back tomorrow. After saying good-bye to his dad and receiving a bear hug, Holton left the room and walked back down to the elevator.

CHECKING the clock once again and realizing it was only two minutes later than the last time, Holton got out of his chair and made sure he had everything one more time. Figuring it wouldn't hurt if he arrived early, Holton hurried to his bedroom where he changed clothes. He then loaded the car and drove to the gym.

He did indeed arrive early, and spent the next twenty minutes watching the front of the club. He could see Marcus working at his desk, occasionally disappearing from view, but always returning to where Holton could see him. "I feel like a stalker," Holton said to himself before checking the clock once again and getting out of the car. It was almost eight, time for Marcus to get off work. Walking toward the door, Holton knew he looked really out of place, but he wanted to make an impression, and one didn't do that in sweats and a T-shirt.

Going inside the now relatively quiet club, Holton looked around and saw Marcus walking through the club, inspecting and making his rounds before he left. Taking a seat in one of the large chairs by the door, he smiled at the girl behind the desk and waited. Eventually he saw Marcus walking toward the front of the club, and he knew the minute Marcus saw him. For a second, he saw a smile, but it was quickly replaced by a look of confusion. At first, Holton thought Marcus was going to ignore him. Instead, Marcus motioned that he'd be a minute and walked to his desk to retrieve his bag.

"I wasn't expecting to see you," Marcus said to him once he was ready to leave.

"I know, but I wanted to talk to you," Holton said as he followed Marcus outside. "I owe you an apology, Marcus, or at least an explanation." *God, this was so hard.* "I shouldn't have let you think I only liked you for your looks, because I don't. I mean I like your looks, but I like you for other reasons too." *Jesus, he was babbling like an incoherent idiot.* But at least Marcus stopped walking away from him. "But you owe me an apology, too, because you didn't give me a chance to explain earlier." Holton stared into Marcus's eyes, determined to meet his gaze and not back down. "I was feeling bad because I heard what Lonnie said around the table, and I thought he was right."

"Well, he's not," Marcus told him.

"I think I get that now," Holton replied before walking to his car and reaching into the backseat. "I brought you something." Holton pulled out a bouquet of red roses.

"Those are for me?" Marcus asked.

"Yes. I hope they're not too girly, but I wanted to bring something to show you what you mean to me. That I care for you." Holton handed Marcus the flowers, but found his usually open face unreadable. Marcus didn't say anything, and Holton turned toward his car.

"I shouldn't have presumed to know how you feel," Marcus told Holton quietly.

"No, you shouldn't, and I shouldn't have projected my insecurities onto you. I guess this means that if we want to explore a relationship, we should learn to talk to one another," Holton said, sticking his neck out, but someone had to say it.

"Is that what you want?" Marcus asked, stepping closer, still holding the flowers in one hand and his gym bag in the other.

"Yes. I'd like to try," Holton answered, swallowing hard. "And I think the talking thing needs to start with me."

"Is that why you got all dressed up?" Marcus stepped even closer, his bag hitting the ground near Holton's car.

"No. I wanted you to know I was serious," Holton said before looking down at himself and beginning to feel a little foolish in his best clothes.

"You look very nice," Marcus told him softly.

"You always look nice," Holton countered. "I sort of made something for dinner."

"Pretty sure of yourself, weren't you?"

"Hopeful."

"I shouldn't have walked off without listening to you. I'm sorry," Marcus whispered, his lips so close Holton could feel their warmth.

"As much as I want to kiss you, we probably shouldn't do this here."

"No. I could meet you at your house," Marcus said, and Holton nodded, not wanting to let Marcus out of his sight.

"Or you could ride with me," Holton said.

"I have to be here to open the club tomorrow," Marcus explained. "If you don't mind an early start, we could probably work out together." Holton unlocked the doors to his car, and Marcus picked up his bag, throwing it onto the backseat before getting in himself, still holding the flowers. "No one's ever given me flowers before," Marcus said as he leaned toward the driver's seat, giving Holton a kiss. "They're just beautiful." Marcus beamed at him. Holton returned the smile, started the engine, and began the drive home.

"How's your mom?" Marcus asked.

"She remembered me when I saw her today, but she gets confused. They're trying some new medication. I know my dad is hoping she'll be able to come home, and the doctors say it's a possibility. I hope she's able to, because I think he'd be lost without her."

"I hope so, too, although you know it's just a matter of time," Marcus told him, his voice caring and understanding.

"I know. I keep hoping I'll have her for a little while yet, but things have happened so fast. I always thought it would progress slower, and we'd have more time." Holton stopped at a light and took a moment to look at Marcus for some sort of reassurance.

"That's the bad part of this disease. It progresses differently for each person. My mother declined by inches over a decade, with bits of her life disappearing." It was obvious from Marcus's expression that the loss Marcus felt was still quite acute.

"I know it sounds bad, but I sort of hope that if she's going to go, she goes fast rather than lingering on. I think that would be a blessing for both her and my father," Holton said as the light changed, and he drove the remaining distance toward his house.

"If it's any help, I agree with you. No one should have to go through what my mother and father did. Dying by inches is not the way anyone should go. I don't think you should feel bad," Marcus told him as they pulled up in front of his house. He should have known Marcus would understand what he was going through. As he turned off the engine, Holton sat looking out the windshield. With the exception of the argument earlier today, Holton realized that Marcus seemed to understand so many things about him.

"Marcus," Holton said without turning to look at him. "I have something I think I need to tell you, but I don't know if I can." He continued staring straight out the window, and he heard Marcus shift in his seat. Holton sighed as all the fears and insecurity he'd buried for years bubbled up close to the surface. Finally, Holton opened his door and got out of the car, waiting for Marcus before walking up to the house.

"You don't have to tell me anything you aren't ready for," Marcus said gently, and Holton felt himself being pulled into a hug.

"Thanks," Holton replied, resting his head against Marcus's shoulder, watching the sunset, and letting go of his nerves as he decided he could trust Marcus. "But I need you to know why I've been so tentative, and I need you to know it's not about you," Holton told Marcus, and he felt Marcus hug him even tighter. Neither of them moved for a while until it became completely dark, and Holton unlocked the door so they could go inside.

Holton had made a nice dinner. Turning on the oven right away, he placed the food inside before returning to where Marcus sat waiting in the living room. At first, Holton didn't know where to sit, but Marcus answered that question for him, tugging him gently onto the sofa. "Why don't you tell me what you want to, and I promise to listen without interrupting. Okay?"

Holton nodded, not quite sure exactly where to begin. "I was twenty-two and set to graduate from college in a few weeks. Some friends had decided to go to a gay club, and I went along with them. It was Saturday night, and we figured on one last hurrah before finals and graduation. The club was a ways from campus in an area I wasn't familiar with, but the other guys said they'd been there before, so I went along." Holton tried to keep his voice steady, but found it hard.

"When we got there, the club was a lot rougher than I had expected, but everyone seemed like they were having a good time. After a while, it started to get really warm, so I stepped outside to cool off for a few minutes. There wasn't a lot of light outside, and I walked to the car and then back toward the club, not feeling very comfortable out there alone." Holton began talking faster, like he needed to get this out as quickly as possible. "I felt someone grab me, plastering my arms to my side. At first I thought it was one of the guys playing a joke, but he didn't let go and squeezed tighter, lifting my feet off the ground. Almost before I could figure out what was happening, I found myself hurled onto the hood of a car. My hands were bound in duct tape. But it wasn't until the tape closed over my mouth that the magnitude of what was happening hit me." Holton could almost feel the sticky tape on his lips and the closed-off feeling as he tried to breathe through his nose. "Once he'd done that, he threw me in the backseat of the car and bound my legs and feet so I couldn't move. 'You so much as make a sound, and I'll put a bullet in your head,' he said to me, waving a pistol in front of my face. Then he got in the car and began to drive. I lost track of how far we went, but it was pitch-black when we stopped, and he dragged me out of the backseat and hauled me to the front of the car." Holton felt tears well in his eyes, and he made no effort to stop them.

"He bent me over the hood and flashed a knife in front of my face. I thought he was going to cut me, and I felt the cold metal against my skin and down my backside. My pants fell away and I knew he hadn't cut me, but...." Holton swallowed hard as he shut his eyes. He felt Marcus reach out to him, but Holton pulled away. Standing up, he began pacing around the room. "The next thing I knew, he was forcing himself inside me, and there was nothing I could do to stop him." Holton somehow stopped himself from reliving that part of the experience. "When he was done, he cut away the rest of my clothes and told me not to move. I must have leaned against the hood of that car for God knows how long, afraid to make a sound. I thought he might have left, but then I heard footsteps, and I was lifted again and shoved to my knees. He forced himself on me again and then shoved me away."

Holton swallowed the bile in his throat and thought he might have to make a run for the bathroom, but then got himself under control. "I heard footsteps, and then the car engine started. I was afraid for a second that he was going to run me over, though I also figured that might be a blessing, but instead I saw headlights and then heard the car pull away, leaving me alone."

Holton felt his voice trail off and saw Marcus almost bounce off the sofa as he rushed to him. Then Holton found himself encased in a strong hug. "Damn, I'm so sorry," Marcus said almost breathlessly.

Holton didn't try to get away and simply let Marcus hold him. "It took me a while to work the tape off my hands. Then I was able to get the tape off my feet and mouth. What was left of my clothes were still on the ground, and I tied what I could around my waist and started walking. I had no idea where I was, and the road was completely dark. After hours of walking, I finally saw a light and walked toward it. When I knocked on the door, a woman answered, and I heard her gasp in shock before I fell on her porch in exhaustion. The next thing I remember was being taken to the hospital. After that, everything was a blur."

Holton stopped talking for a while before explaining the rest. The hospitals, the doctors, the police, everything that happened afterward was almost as bad as the attack itself. And questions and more questions that he couldn't answer. The police actually insinuated that he had willingly gone with the man and was only complaining when things went wrong.

"What did you do?" Marcus prompted gently.

"I told the police I wanted a lawyer and clammed up. Then was the hardest part of all—I had to call my parents and tell them. What a way to find out your son's gay, right? Mom and Dad helped as best they could and got a good lawyer who gave the police a great deal of shit and threatened to take them to court for harassing a victim. She was a firebrand, and I remember because she pushed the prosecutor no end, he managed to work in the way I was treated by the police, and I remember the judge ordering an investigation or something. The thing that swayed everyone was when the medical reports came back definitively proving I'd been forced."

"Did you have to testify in court?"

Holton nodded against Marcus's chest. "They caught the guy, and I had to take the witness stand. That was the hardest thing I've ever done. I'd lived through it, and then had to tell the story again and again and again. The slightest deviation was questioned over and over. Then, after all those horrible months, it was over, and my parents never spoke about it again, and I didn't, either. I realize now I was just withdrawing from the world and life. Dad told me today that he and Mom thought I didn't want to talk about it and hadn't wanted to pressure me. I just thought they were as ashamed of me as I was of myself, and withdrew further. I wish I'd have known."

Holton didn't look up from where his head rested against Marcus. He could hear Marcus's heart beating and feel the energy coursing through him.

"I can't begin to know what you went through or judge how you handled it. But I will tell you, I want to kill the guy who hurt you." Holton heard a hitch in Marcus's voice, and he lifted his head so he could look into Marcus's eyes. "I'm so touched that you felt you could tell me this. Because I bet you haven't told anyone in a very long time."

"I haven't, not anyone. I just kept it to myself," Holton confirmed before closing his eyes and letting Marcus's warmth and his masculine scent surround him. "I realize now that I let that one incident dictate my life for nearly twenty years. I stayed away from people if I could and refused to trust anyone."

Holton angled his face upward and waited to see how Marcus would react.

Tender lips touched his in a soft kiss that deepened slightly but remained gentle and reassuring. It wasn't until Holton put his arms around Marcus's neck, deepening the kiss, that he felt the intensity ramp up. He'd bared his deepest, darkest pain, and Marcus had shown he cared. In his mind, Holton had been so ashamed of what had happened to him that he'd honestly expected to be rejected.

A ding from the kitchen brought him out of the kiss, and Holton slowly backed away. "I need to take care of dinner."

Marcus tugged him close once again. "I'll help you, and then maybe we can go upstairs and I can make you forget about everything except you and me." Holton's body wanted what Marcus was offering, and he heard Marcus's desire in his voice—and he could feel it against his hip. Desire wasn't the issue at all. Marcus kissed him hard. Holton wasn't quite sure what he'd expected from Marcus when he'd told him what happened. Part of him figured he'd run, but never had he dreamed that Marcus would truly desire him.

"Marcus," Holton moaned as he pulled his lips away.

"I know this is hard, but I'm not the man who hurt you, and you know you have nothing to fear from me. I only want to love you the way you should be loved. That man, years ago, what he did was about power, control, and pain. What I want to give you is nothing but happiness and love. Will you trust me?"

Holton knew Marcus was right. He simply wasn't sure he was capable of giving Marcus what he deserved, but if Marcus was willing to... wait.... Holton's thoughts stopped. Marcus had used the word love. Marcus wanted to love him. Holton stared into Marcus's eyes, afraid to ask if he meant what he thought he meant. Marcus had asked Holton to trust him, and he hugged the larger man tightly, making up his mind in Marcus's strong arms. "Yes, I trust you." So much went unspoken.

Marcus kissed him again. Then, arms still around him, Marcus led him to the kitchen. Holton pulled their dinner from the oven before pointing out where the plates and glasses were to Marcus. It only took a few minutes for them to have the food on the table. "It's vegetarian lasagna. I try to keep it as light as I can," Holton explained as he cut portions from the pan, placing one on each plate before pouring glasses of ice water.

"Where did you learn to cook?" Marcus asked after he'd taken a bite. Holton had seen his eyes close in pleasure as he tasted dinner.

"Three or four months ago, I took a long look at myself. That was when I joined the gym. After that, I realized my problems stemmed from what I ate and why. So I bought some cookbooks for low-fat and healthy food and started to teach myself. I can tell you there were some nights I could barely eat what I made," Holton said with a smile, remembering the eggplant dish that came out with the consistency of concrete. "I also realized I ate to feel better and did that a lot." Holton took his first bite.

"It takes a strong person to make a real change in his life, and you did that," Marcus told him with a huge smile.

"I never felt strong."

Marcus set down his fork before taking Holton's hand. "Yes, you were. You survived what he did to you, and you made something of your life. Furthermore, once you recognized something wasn't right in your life, you changed it. That's a strong person." Marcus's eyes met his, and Holton knew what Marcus was saying came from the heart. Holton had never considered himself strong, certainly not after all the years of being afraid and hiding. Taking another taste, Holton watched as Marcus picked up his fork again, taking a small bite of dinner as he squeezed Holton's hand.

They ate the rest of their dinner in near silence, Marcus's hand on Holton's. Every few minutes, Holton noticed the way Marcus would look at him, heat simmering in his eyes. Whenever Holton saw that look, he wondered just what Marcus was planning. A few times, he squirmed in his chair under that very heated gaze, the anticipation beginning to get to him. *But anticipation of what?* Thoughts raced through Holton's mind, remembrances of the way Marcus had touched him interwoven with the way he'd been hurt all those years ago. Then Marcus would look at him, and once again the memories of last night would exert their influence, pushing back what was unpleasant.

Once their plates were empty, Holton took care of the food before picking up their dishes, carrying them toward the sink. Turning on the water, Holton had begun rinsing the dishes when a pair of strong arms wrapped around his waist. Holton stopped moving, standing still for a second as his heart skipped a single beat. Then he caught hold of his nerves and relaxed back against Marcus, letting Marcus's heady scent fill his nostrils.

"I didn't mean to startle you," Marcus murmured before kissing Holton's neck. Holton's head lolled to the side, and Marcus took advantage, licking and kissing his neck while Holton felt Marcus's hands lift his shirt before sliding beneath. Warm hands moved slowly along Holton's skin, and he let go of the dishes, turning off the water. "Just stand still," Marcus told him gently as warm hands and lips caressed his skin. Holton moved back slightly, pressing close to Marcus, and felt his sizable erection against his backside.

For a split second, he almost pulled away, but Marcus kept touching him softly, petting him almost like a skittish dog that needed to be soothed. Holton's nerves melted away along with the last of his resistance.

Marcus's hands slid further up his chest, and Holton lifted his arms in an act of emotional surrender. Marcus tugged off Holton's shirt, and Holton wondered what to expect, but Marcus kissed his shoulder and back while his hands slid over his pecs, fingers tweaking each nipple lightly until Holton could barely keep his legs beneath him. Marcus didn't let up and continued to caress and kiss Holton's skin. When he could barely stand, Holton leaned back against Marcus with all his weight, and Marcus held him up, supporting him, and once his knees buckled under Marcus's exquisite torture, he felt Marcus lift him off the floor, carrying him out of the kitchen, Marcus's lips taking his in a searing kiss that left Holton breathless.

Marcus set him on the bed, the bedspread sliding against his back. Holton watched Marcus's eyes as he stepped away from the bed, stripping out of his clothes. Marcus said nothing, but looked at him the entire time, never taking his attention from Holton. At first, Holton tried to figure out a way to cover himself, but as Marcus's shirt and then his pants fell to the floor, Holton's attention shifted from himself to the extraordinary man standing in front of him. Wide shoulders, powerful arms, and a defined chest gave way to a stomach crisscrossed with deep grooves, above narrow hips. Once the last of Marcus's clothes was gone, Holton gasped at Marcus's thick, strong thighs and his thick cock, standing straight and tall. Holton could hardly believe he could make Marcus that excited, but there was no denying that he had.

Marcus prowled toward the bed, strong legs moving slowly, cock swaying slightly with each step. Holton didn't know what to expect, and Marcus was saying nothing, except with his eyes and body.

Marcus's hands opened Holton's belt and pants, sensuously slipping them down his legs. Shoes hit the floor before Marcus tugged his pants off, leaving Holton naked as well. "Beautiful," Marcus whispered as he joined Holton on the bed. "You are so beautiful," Marcus told him, and then Holton felt himself embraced and kissed hard, possessively. They rolled on the bed, and just like last night, Holton found himself on top. Marcus pulled him into a kiss while Holton felt hands caress the skin of his back before setting to hold each of his cheeks. Holton might have objected, but he was too far gone, his skin sliding against Marcus—the taste of Marcus, and Marcus's touch, all of it combined into a deeply heady experience that left Holton almost unable to think.

"Will you lay back for me?" Marcus asked between kisses, and he brushed the hair off Holton's forehead.

Holton nodded and rolled onto his back, waiting to see what Marcus had in store. "Oh God!" Holton cried as Marcus took him into his mouth, surrounding him in heat that made his head throb in the best way possible. Marcus worked him deeply, sliding his lips up and down his length while Holton simply tried to breathe. "Marcus," Holton moaned softly as he finally felt himself let go of everything he'd been holding on to. The pain and fear were replaced by sheer passion and love. Yes, love. Marcus had used that word earlier, and Holton had wondered, but right now, that wonder and doubt were gone. Marcus was giving him pleasure only love could bring—he knew that now.

Marcus shifted on the bed, his lips slipping away, and Holton opened his eyes, wondering what was going on. "Just stay there for me," Marcus told him, and Holton nodded. "Do you have any supplies?"

Holton shook his head disappointedly, and Marcus jumped off the bed and began fumbling through his pants before hurrying out of the room. He returned a few seconds later carrying his gym bag. After rummaging briefly, the bag hit the floor, and Marcus was with him once again, kissing Holton hard. "I want to show you how special two people joining together can be."

"I don't think I...," Holton started, and Marcus touched his lips gently with a finger.

"I want to feel you inside me," Marcus told him, and Holton's eyes widened in surprise.

"You want me to...?" Holton swallowed, not sure he could do that. But damn if his body didn't jump at the idea. "What should I do?" Holton whispered. "I want to see you."

Marcus seemed to be opening a packet and reaching around behind himself. "I know," Marcus answered, lying on his back, guiding Holton between his legs.

Holton gasped when Marcus sat up and rolled the condom down his length, strong hands stroking him through the latex. "I don't want to hurt you," Holton said, suddenly concerned.

"You could never hurt me," Marcus told him before guiding Holton into position. "Just go slow."

Holton felt the head of his cock against Marcus's body. Locking his eyes onto his lover's, Holton pressed forward as slowly as he could. At first, Marcus's body resisted, but then Holton felt him open, and he slowly slid inside. Holton was immediately surrounded by the most magnificently sensual heat he could ever have imagined. Trying his best not to go too fast, he watched Marcus's face, nearly pulling back when he saw Marcus scrunch his eyes in what looked like pain. "Just give me a minute," Marcus told him as he placed a hand on Holton's leg.

Holton held still and waited while his body went into sensory overload, the urge to drive forward so overwhelming he nearly tried to overpower Marcus. The only thing stopping him was the knowledge he could hurt Marcus. Holton felt Marcus tap the back of his leg, and he moved forward, letting Marcus's body take him all in.

"Oh God, Marcus," Holton panted, buried deep in Marcus's body.

"Yeah, I know," Marcus said. "Now start to move slowly."

Holton pulled back, and he heard Marcus moan softly. Holton joined him, the feeling nearly overwhelming. When he sank back into Marcus's body, the tone of his lover's moan shifted. Each sound drove Holton's passion higher. "Are you okay?" Holton asked, to be sure.

"Jesus, yes!" Marcus answered, grabbing the back of Holton's leg, pulling him forward. Holton began moving faster and harder, with Marcus encouraging him the entire time. It wasn't long before Holton was driving deep and hard into Marcus, propelled by the ever-louder sounds Marcus made. Holton wondered if he should be helping Marcus, but then he saw Marcus begin to stroke himself, the moans getting even louder as Holton snapped his hips with more and more force.

His mind went in a million different directions, but all of them centered on Marcus and the pleasure Marcus was giving him, and the amazing things he seemed to be giving to Marcus, if those sounds were any indication. Looking down at his lover, Holton felt everything start to hit him all at once. His breath hitched, and his movements became ragged as pressure built from deep inside him. "I'm gonna...!" Holton gasped loudly as he started to lose it. Skin tingling, a zip running down his spine, Holton thrust deep and stilled, gasping once again as he came with time-stopping intensity feeling Marcus's body clamp tightly around him.

Catching his breath, Holton slid his eyes open and looked down at Marcus. Still buried in his lover's body, Holton thought Marcus looked totally decadent, eyes half closed, covered in his own release, with a small smile on his face. Holton suppressed a chuckle as he leaned forward, kissing Marcus hard as their bodies separated.

Marcus held him tightly for a long time. Eventually, Holton got up, and after a quick cleanup, he joined Marcus under the covers, falling asleep in his lover's arms, dreaming only happy dreams until morning.

VI

IT WAS still dark when Marcus woke him. At first, Holton rolled over with a grumble, sliding toward Marcus's warmth. He didn't want to get up at all, but he'd promised Marcus. So, still sleepy, he got out of bed, padding to the bathroom, scratching his butt as he closed the door. After relieving himself, Holton had begun to clean up when the bathroom door opened and Marcus slipped inside, standing behind him. Holton smiled at Marcus's naked reflection, and then Marcus held him, pressing his body to his lover's. Holton's body reacted in a second, and if the hard length sliding against his butt was any indication, Marcus's had as well. Holton stilled, setting down his razor as Marcus's hands began to wander.

"I wish I could stay here all day with you. Making love and"—Marcus licked the base of his neck—"making you shiver just like that."

"I know you have to go to work," Holton told him, keeping the disappointment out of his voice. "But will I see you afterward?"

Marcus snickered and moved his hips slightly, his cock sliding against Holton's butt. "You betcha, sweetheart." Marcus kissed the skin of his shoulder. "You get cleaned up, and I'm going to get dressed. We can work out together. If you want, I can come back here after work." Holton nodded; there was nothing he wanted more. After another kiss, Marcus stepped back and walked to the door, with Holton watching his luscious body move in the mirror. Once he was gone, Holton was able to think about what he should have been doing again, and went back to his shaving. When he was finished, Holton pulled on some jeans, packed his gym bag, and went in search of Marcus. Holton found him in the living room, waiting for him. "Do you need something to eat?" Holton asked, but Marcus motioned him to come closer.

"Just need a kiss," Marcus cooed before Holton gave him more than one. Then they left the house, and Holton drove to the club.

They arrived before the eight o'clock opening, and Marcus unlocked the club, walking inside. Holton heard a beeping, and Marcus turned off the alarm, flipping on the lights. He let in another employee, and Holton wandered back toward the locker rooms. Getting changed in the normally busy room, Holton enjoyed the quiet. He was nearly done changing when other guys wandered in to change.

Holton met Marcus on his way to the locker room. "I forgot that I have a personal training session this morning with Max, but I can work out with both of you if that's okay?"

Holton mock pouted. "You mean I have to share you?"

Marcus smiled and leaned close. "Only during the workout. Tonight you're all mine." Holton shivered and had to look away or his desire was going to show through his gym shorts.

"Hey, Marcus," Max said as he hurriedly approached. "I'll be right out. Are you working out with us?" Max asked, and when Holton nodded, Max flashed him a pleased smile. "Cool." Max hurried away, and Holton waited while Marcus changed as well.

Max and Marcus joined him a few minutes later, and they got started, with Marcus pushing both of them hard. "You know, I thought Hugh was a slave driver," Max commented when Marcus made him do two extra reps on the bench press. Marcus laughed and pushed Holton equally hard when it was his turn.

"You two do another set each," Marcus instructed. "I have to see what's got Cindy in a tizzy." Marcus hurried away, and Max took his turn while Holton spotted him.

"It looks like things are working out for you and Marcus," Max said with a smile as he got up from the bench.

"Yeah. We talked and worked things out. I think." Holton bit his lower lip nervously. "I just hope…." Holton trailed off, not wanting to whine.

"Whatever it is, I wouldn't worry about it too much. He cares for you," Max commented as Holton sat on the bench, getting ready for his set.

"How do you know?" Holton asked, lifting the weight off the bench and starting his set. Max spotted him, helping with the last rep until he clanged the weight back against the stops.

"By the way he looks at you," Max told him, answering his question. "Whatever's bothering you is probably your imagination. Just listen to your gut and trust how you feel."

"How'd you get so smart?" Holton asked the younger man with a smile as Max got ready for his set.

"You almost ready to move on?" Marcus asked as he joined them.

"Just one more set," Holton answered before getting into position to spot Max. They finished up their sets before moving on. Marcus took them through an entire routine, and by the time they were done, Holton was more than ready for the whirlpool.

"I know you're busy now, but I'll see you tonight," Holton said softly to Marcus, who nodded and gave him a smirk that let Holton know exactly what Marcus was thinking.

Max stepped to Holton as Marcus walked back toward his desk. "Life's too short to be ruled by fear," Max said, sort of out of the blue, and Holton stared at the younger man, wondering how he knew. "It's in your eyes," Max explained. "I recognized the same look I used to see in the mirror almost every morning when I was still living at home. My dad was, or is, an alcoholic, and when he got drunk, which was almost all the time, he sometimes got mean. I never knew what I was going to come home to. Hugh helped me realize that I was worth more than that, and that I deserved to be happy and have a life that didn't include living in constant fear. I don't know what's got you afraid, but I know the look, and if you can let it go, you'll be so much happier." Max gave him a smile and a reassuring pat on the arm before walking into the locker room, leaving Holton alone with his thoughts.

So much had happened over the last few days with his mother, Marcus, and his life. In just a few short days, he'd opened himself up and shared his deepest secret with someone, and Marcus had accepted him and shown he cared for him, and might even love him. He knew it was too soon for either of them to declare their feelings, but Holton could feel the warmth taking root in his heart, and he could do nothing to stop it. He was in love for the first time in his life. Following Max into the locker room, Holton found his locker and changed out of his gym clothes, pulling on his bathing suit. After grabbing his towel, Holton headed to the showers before walking to the whirlpool. It was otherwise empty, and Holton slipped into the hot bubbling water, his muscles relaxing while his mind wandered.

"Max is right," Holton muttered to himself. It was time he let go of the fear that had ruled his life for so damned long. Yes, his attacker had put him through hell, both physically and emotionally. But he'd come through it and survived. Whatever happened with Marcus, he'd already experienced the worst. He could certainly handle anything life threw his way. "I wish I'd have figured this out years ago," he added under his breath.

"Figured out what?" he heard Max ask as he joined him in the whirlpool.

"That you were right," Holton answered, settling back into the water, and he knew exactly what he wanted to do. "I'm just sad it took me so long to figure it out."

Max shook his head. "It didn't. You figured it out when you were ready to. Until then, nothing or no one would have helped. The real question is what are you going to do about it?"

"What did you do about your dad?" Holton asked, hoping he wasn't overstepping.

"I was lucky. When I was ready to stand up to my father, I had Hugh there to back me up. But I still had to be the one to stand up to him," Max explained. Holton nodded his head before resting it on the edge of the whirlpool, letting his mind float once again.

After a while, Holton said good-bye to Max and left the whirlpool, spending a few minutes in the sauna before moving to the shower area to clean up.

Turning on the water, Holton stepped under the spray and closed the curtain before stripping off his bathing suit. His mind immediately returned to the way he'd felt when Marcus had come into the bathroom that morning—Marcus's touch, the way his chest felt against his back, Marcus's insistent hardness sliding along his rear end. Holton's body reacted quickly, and he had to resist taking care of himself in the shower. He wanted to so badly. He could imagine his hand was Marcus's. Closing his eyes, Holton slid his soapy hands over his skin, wishing they were Marcus's hands touching him, caressing him. Holton's legs began to shake, and he knew he'd come as soon as he touched himself. Opening his eyes, Holton brought himself back to reality as the sounds of other guys showering and talking invaded his fantasy. Returning to the business of showering, Holton washed his hair while he waited for his body to cool down, which didn't seem to be working too well, especially when he heard Marcus's voice drift into the shower area. Turning the water to cold, Holton shivered for a few seconds before turning off the water and reaching for his towel.

Holton dried himself in the shower stall before wrapping the towel around his waist and heading to the locker area. Lonnie and a bunch of the guys were there, laughing and snapping each other with towels. "You're such a child, Lon," Dan scolded just before making Lonnie jump as he snapped him with a towel.

"We missed you at Panera," Dan said to Holton as he dodged a towel snap.

"I came in with Marcus," Holton explained with a smile he couldn't stop.

"Join us for lunch," Lonnie told him before adding a real sweetener. "Don't be a pussy all your life."

"You really know how to sweet-talk a guy, don't you?" Holton retorted as he opened his locker and pulled out his bag. "Where should I meet you?"

Lonnie explained the time and place before going on about his exploits the night before. Holton half listened as he got dressed. It felt nice to be included. By the time he was ready to go, the guys had already left the locker room, so Holton grabbed his bag and left. The guys waved as he walked toward the exit, and as he approached the front of the club, he saw Marcus's smiling face. He had someone at his desk, so Holton raised his hand in greeting before leaving the club.

Holton spent the rest of the morning running errands before joining the guys for a raucous lunch that had him laughing his butt off. He met even more people, and all of them seemed to be so nice. Holton was really beginning to see what he'd been missing all these years. After they'd finished eating, and Lonnie had regaled them with plenty of his X-rated tales, everyone left the restaurant, and Holton drove home, parking in his usual spot in front of the house.

"Holton," Heather called from their porch as he got out of the car. "We're cooking out with friends this evening and wanted to know if you'd like to join us."

"Sure," he called, readily accepting with a smile. "What time?"

"We're eating about seven. It's supposed to be a lovely evening, and we won't get many more of those, so we thought we'd enjoy it," Heather explained as Holton walked closer.

"Ummm," Holton started, wondering how he should ask. "I have a friend who's joining me this evening, though."

"Holton," she squealed, "of course you can bring your guest. Is it the guy you came home with last night?" Heather asked, and Holton felt himself color for a second. "Don't be mad. I was just checking to make sure you were okay. I wasn't spying, I promise!" She held her hand up like a Boy Scout. "I'm just so happy for you," she added with another excited squeal.

"Yes. That's him. His name's Marcus," Holton said proudly.

"Then we'll see you and Marcus about seven," Heather told him, her excitement growing. Holton waved as he walked back toward his car, getting his bag out of the trunk before closing the trunk lid and unlocking the door to the house, smiling to himself, because he was pretty danged excited too.

HOLTON spent most of the afternoon doing chores around the house to keep himself busy. When Marcus arrived a little after six, Holton explained about the invitation, and they went over to the neighbors' together, where they had a great time. Marcus charmed everyone, and Heather stared googly-eyed at him for most of the night. After saying good night, they'd strolled back to Holton's in the dark, with Marcus holding his hand as they went. As they approached the front walk, Holton felt Marcus tug his hand lightly, and they continued walking down the quiet sidewalk in the near dark, the only light coming from passing cars and the occasional street lamp, Marcus's hand in his. Holton said nothing, his attention shifting to the soft touch where Marcus's hand met his. When they arrived back at the house, Holton didn't want to let go to unlock the door.

Once inside, Holton reached for the switch. "Don't turn on the lights," Marcus told him, and Holton shut the front door, locking it. When he turned around, he felt himself pressed to the door as Marcus kissed him hard, possessively. Something about Marcus always seemed to make him go weak in the knees and tight in the pants, and this time was no exception. "I want to take you to bed and make love to you until you can't move, okay?"

Holton nodded, his head rolling against the wood of the door. "Yes." He expected the usual fear and nerves to assert themselves, but they didn't. This was his Marcus—he could feel him, hear him, smell him. Marcus surrounded him, and he was safe. Marcus stepped back and took his hand once again, leading him through the house and into his bedroom.

Holton moved toward the bed, but Marcus stopped him with a kiss. He felt Marcus peel off his own shirt, discarding it onto the floor. Then he heard Marcus's pants hit the floor and felt his legs move as he stepped out of them. This entire time, Marcus had never stopped kissing him. Holton's hands itched to explore Marcus's sensually smooth skin, but Marcus tugged at his shirt, pulling it over his head. Holton toed off his shoes before opening his pants and letting them fall to the floor. As soon as he stepped out of them, Marcus pulled him close, chest to chest, hip to hip, moving him slowly backward until his legs hit the bed. Then Holton was falling for Marcus, literally and figuratively.

His legs dangling off the side of the bed, Marcus straddled him, kissing his lips while stroking his skin. Holton tried to touch Marcus in return, but found his arms caressed and moved, splaying them on the bed.

When Marcus's lips slipped away from his, Holton groaned softly, wondering what had happened. When Marcus's lips clamped onto one of his nipples, sucking hot and hard, the groan turned to a deep moan, and Holton writhed under Marcus's torturously delicious attentions. "Marcus," Holton gasped as he tried to shift on the bed. Holton felt Marcus's hands on his legs, and the two men moved together up the bed, Marcus licking and kissing trails on his skin.

"You taste like sunshine," Marcus told him, and then he licked a long trail from Holton's hip up his side, and over to first one nipple and then the other.

"What about you?" Holton asked, still slightly nervous, but his excitement seemed to win out. He felt Marcus shift on the bed, his lips moving as well. Holton gasped loudly when Marcus engulfed him in his mouth before straddling his body. Before he could think or become nervous, Holton guided Marcus's cock to his lips. Marcus's unique flavor burst onto his tongue, like the flavor of his skin, but more, better. Slowly, he moved his head, taking when he could as Marcus did the same to him. Holton felt like a porn star. He'd seen guys do this in movies, but this was no movie. This was Marcus, his Marcus, and Holton, lust and passion taking over, guided Marcus deeper onto his mouth, hands exploring the perfect backside right above him. Holton heard a soft grunt when he skimmed his fingers lightly over Marcus's opening. But before he could explore further, he felt Marcus lift his legs, and Marcus's lips slipped away from his length. A few seconds later, Holton cried out, his head flopping back onto the pillow when Marcus skimmed his tongue over his opening. "Oh God!" Holton gasped.

"You like that?" Marcus cooed before doing it again.

Holton thought his entire body had burst into flames. Never in his life had he thought he could feel like this. Whenever Marcus touched him, he felt as though Marcus were touching his soul. "Please, Marcus," Holton whined, as he felt Marcus wrap his arms under his waist, lifting his lower body as he thrust his tongue deep. All Holton could do was hold Marcus's legs as he cried out his desire.

"Is this what you want?" Marcus asked coaxingly.

"No, I want you," Holton responded before he could even think. All worries and nervousness had left him long ago. All he wanted, all he could think about, was Marcus. A slick finger breached him, swirling, touching something deep inside that had spots flashing behind his eyes. Holton could no longer think; all he could do was hold on to Marcus and react to whatever amazing sensation barreled through his body.

Marcus lowered his legs back to the bed, but continued to play his body like a fine violin. Gasping for breath, Holton almost didn't realize that Marcus had shifted on the bed before additional fingers filled his body, stretching him further. "Is this what you want? Will you give yourself to me?"

"Yes," Holton answered, barely aware of the word as it left his mouth. The fingers slipped from his body, and Holton waited, shaking as his body thrummed with anticipatory excitement, waiting for Marcus to get ready. Then he felt Marcus press against his entrance, slowly pushing, and his body opened to him. No pain, no force— just love, pure, beautiful love. Holton could feel it bursting into bloom as Marcus pressed deeper, filling him more and more.

Breathing ragged, Holton sighed when Marcus stopped moving, his hips against Holton's butt, cock throbbing and jumping deep within his body. Marcus didn't move, not for a long time. He simply stayed still, and Holton savored the feeling of their bodies locked together, connected down deep. Then Marcus leaned forward, kissing Holton so hard he felt it all the way to his toes. Once they broke the kiss, Marcus locked eyes with him, and then, and only then, did he begin to move.

Slowly at first, Marcus began withdrawing at a pace that stole Holton's breath. He nearly pulled out completely, and Holton whined at the potential loss of contact. Holton gasped, crying out when Marcus drove deep into his body and stopped again, throbbing, pulsing deep inside him again. "Marcus, oh God, Marcus," Holton rasped through his passion.

All the begging and pleading in the world had no effect on Marcus. Their eyes locked, and Marcus moved slowly, deliberately, every snap of his hips, each withdrawal, meant to slowly lead them both to the top of the mountain of passion. Holton felt each and every step of the climb, his body shaking, hands clutching the bedding, body covered in a sheen of sweat. The scent of their lovemaking filled Holton's nose, adding to the sensory stimulation that threatened to overwhelm him. "Marcus, please!"

"I promised to make love to you until you can't move, and I intend to keep that promise." Marcus drove into him and stilled. "I want you to remember forever the first time someone made love to you, and I want you to remember that it was me. I want this memory etched on your brain forever. I love you, Holton, and I want you to know that deep in your soul." Marcus began moving quicker, his hand now stroking down Holton's length.

"I love you too," Holton gasped. "So close… please, Marcus."

"Not yet," Marcus said as his hand stilled, squeezing Holton firmly. Holton tried to thrust his hips, but didn't have the energy; Marcus had drained him completely. "That's it, Holton, come for me. I know you can."

"Marcus."

"That's it. I want you to come now, show me that you love me. Show me what I do to you." Marcus drove into him, and Holton rolled his head back and forth on the pillow, his release building from his feet and up his throbbing legs. "Yes, that's it!"

Holton could hold back no longer—he didn't have the strength as his orgasm slammed into him with the force of a rocket. He came, crying out hoarsely, eyes clamped closed for fear they'd pop from his head. Then Marcus's cries joined his own, and Holton knew Marcus had joined him in the throes of passion.

How long the waves of pleasure lasted, Holton didn't know. All he knew was that once he came back to himself, Marcus rested next to him, a hand stroking his brow. "It's all right. Come back to me," Holton heard Marcus saying to him. Once he began to stir, Holton felt himself being held tightly.

"Did you really say you loved me?" Holton asked once his brain was working. "I didn't dream that, did I?" God, he sure hoped not—because he was pretty sure he'd confessed his love through his haze of desire.

"No, you didn't dream it. I do love you." Marcus held him tighter, kissing Holton lightly on the neck.

"That's good," Holton gasped softly, "because I love you too." Curling closer, Holton was held and loved. He'd tried to hold the ghosts of his past at bay for years, but nothing had worked until he'd found Marcus and fallen in love. Holton closed his eyes, and instead of seeing the memories he wanted to forget and couldn't, what he saw now was Marcus. And instead of pain and fear, all he felt now was love.

ANDREW GREY grew up in western Michigan with a father who loved to tell stories and a mother who loved to read them. Since then he has lived throughout the country and traveled throughout the world. He has a master's degree from the University of Wisconsin-Milwaukee and works in information systems for a large corporation. Andrew's hobbies include collecting antiques, gardening, and leaving his dirty dishes anywhere but in the sink (particularly when writing). He considers himself blessed with an accepting family, fantastic friends, and the world's most supportive and loving partner. Andrew currently lives in beautiful historic Carlisle, Pennsylvania.

Visit Andrew's web site at http://www.andrewgreybooks.com and blog at http://andrewgreybooks.livejournal.com/.

E-mail him at andrewgrey@comcast.net.

Also by ANDREW GREY

http://www.dreamspinnerpress.com

Contemporary Romance by ANDREW GREY

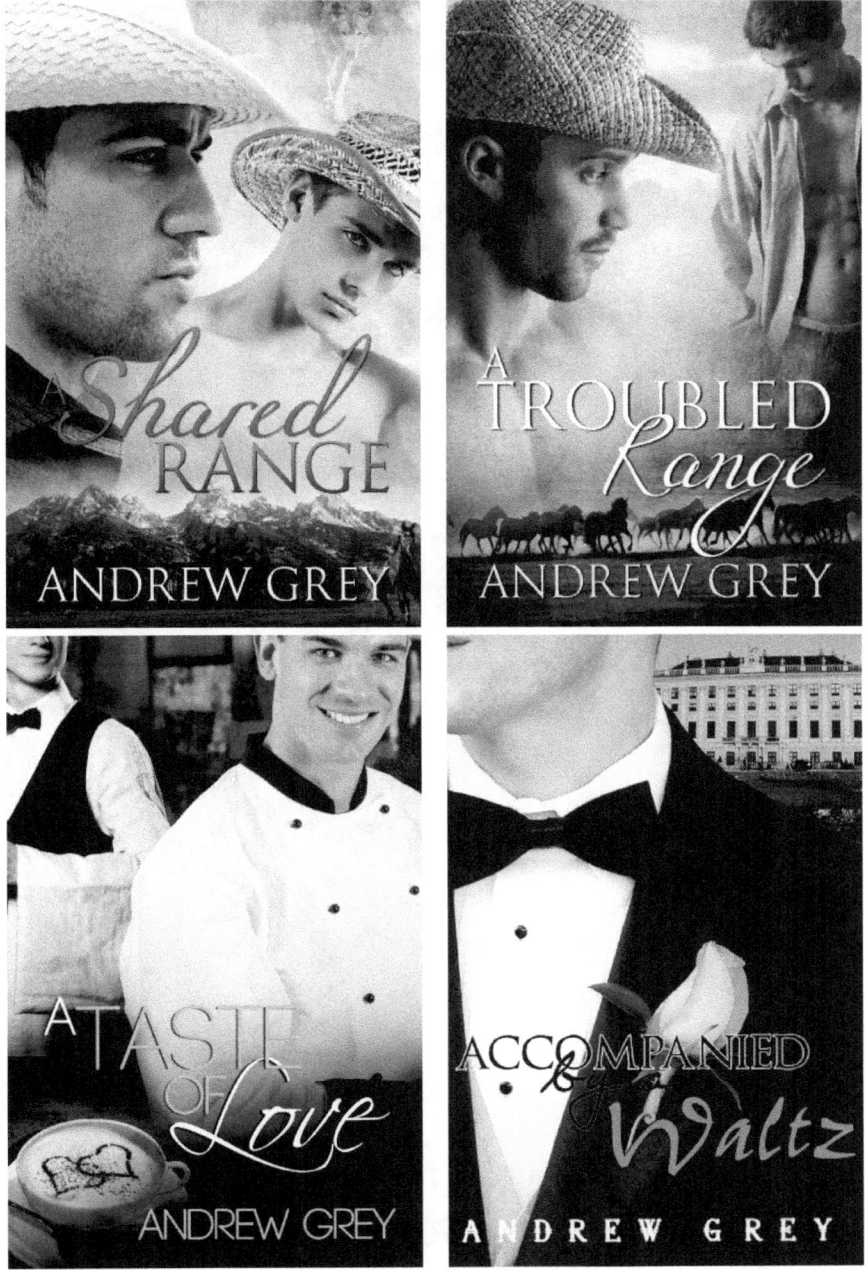

Contemporary Romance by ANDREW GREY

Bottled Up · ANDREW GREY

Uncorked · ANDREW GREY

ANDREW GREY · DUTCH Treat

ANDREW GREY · 7 SEVEN DAYS

http://www.dreamspinnerpress.com